'Another fat book offering plenty

'*The Lost Art* is fast-paced, readab
sparky enough to suggest that,
Morden is a man with a future' *SFX Magazine*

'Simon Morden is what sci-fi and fantasy fans alike have been
waiting for . . . Totally satisfying and highly recommended'
www.thetruthaboutbooks.blogspot.com

'Morden combines science fiction and fantasy in a novel with a
cracking pace that pitches savagery and bigotry against reason'
TES

'Highly recommended as a summer read for all s-f fans'
www.thebookbag.co.uk

'There is no doubt that this novel is compelling. The various
mysteries in the story combine to keep the reader turning
the page, and the world in which it is set is fascinating'
www.writeaway.org

'A potent vision of the future that cracks along at a fair pace'
www.dwscifi.com

'This is science fiction, a whodunnit, an adventure and even
a bit of a love story all rolled into one. Oh, and by the way,
the author is a genuine rocket scientist, so he knows his stuff.
Brilliant! *****' *www.flipside.org.uk*

'Morden is clearly a writer to watch' *www.sfrevu.com*

'If you like Iain M Banks Culture novels then this is an absolute
must . . . A brilliant adventure for Sci-fi lovers of all ages'
www.waterstones.com

SIMON MORDEN
THE LOST ART

CORGI BOOKS

David Fickling Books edition published 2007
Corgi edition published 2008

1 3 5 7 9 10 8 6 4 2

Copyright © Simon Morden, 2007
Cover design by www.henrysteadman.com

The right of Simon Morden to be identified as the author of this work has
been asserted in accordance with the Copyright, Designs and Patents Act 1988.

The Random House Group Limited supports the Forest Stewardship Council (FSC),
the leading international forest certification organization. All our titles that
are printed on Greenpeace-approved FSC-certified paper carry the FSC logo.
Our paper procurement policy can be found at www.rbooks.co.uk/environment.

Set in Garamond

Corgi Books are published by Random House Children's Books,
61–63 Uxbridge Road, London W5 5SA

www.kidsatrandomhouse.co.uk
www.rbooks.co.uk

Addresses for companies within The Random House Group Limited can be found at:
www.randomhouse.co.uk/offices.htm

THE RANDOM HOUSE GROUP Limited Reg. No. 954009

A CIP catalogue record for this book is available from the British Library.

Printed in the UK by CPI Bookmarque, Croydon, CR0 4TD

For Sarah,
For ever

PART 1

CHAPTER 1

The smell of smoke woke him up, and Va realized he should never have been asleep in the first place. He got back onto his knees in the forest clearing, wiped the cold fragments of pine needles from his face and blew out a breath that condensed into a white cloud. Above him, snow-laden branches creaked and swayed against a pale southern sky.

He shut his eyes and tried to empty his mind of the concerns of the world. His fingers tightened around the cross in his hands. He ignored the coarseness of his habit, the steady drip of ice water from the firs that patted his bowed head. His lips might be blue, but they could still move in the trembling mouthing of rote prayers.

The drift of the wind brought the smoke back to him. As it entered his nose, it touched that part of his memory which he had thought locked away for ever.

Va stood. He turned slowly, letting his senses tell him which way to go. Then, with a feeling bordering on sickness, he started to run. The tears that streamed down his face never dared to blind him.

3

The closer he got, the stronger the stench of fire and oil and meat became. He knew what it meant even though he couldn't see through the forest. He hesitated only once, when he burst through the tree line and found that his world was on fire. Then he plunged through the swinging, smouldering gates of the monastery of Saint Samuil of Arkady. There were so many dead that Va couldn't find anyone who could tell him what had happened.

The five-domed basilica glowed brightly from the inside. It didn't stop him from going in, again and again, calling out, listening above the roar of the flames and the cracking of timbers for any kind of answer. He only retreated when overwhelmed by the smoke and the heat. He reeled out, his black habit steaming, his lungs choked with soot and harsh vapours. He rolled in the last of the spring snows to extinguish any embers that might have fallen on him, coughed until he vomited, then raised himself up for another attempt.

The doors to the church had been barred from the inside, burst by force from outside. Most of his brothers had died there, by sword and spear and club, even as they knelt in prayer. The floor was thick with boiling blood. Va pressed himself to the wall, trying to get round to the north aisle.

'Brothers! Father! Can anyone hear me?'

The roof trusses started to snap, one by one, failing like falling dominoes. Va jumped for a window recess. Tiles rattled down in a shower, and the smoke whistled up through the hole. The sudden rush of air turned the blazing church into an inferno. The glass shattered, and he was alight. He fell backwards, outwards, through the window and into the mud.

Blessed mud: he twisted and turned, wallowing like a pig until all the flames were out. Then he crawled away on his hands and knees as the great central copper dome creaked and groaned, and plummeted into the nave. He was far enough away that the explosion of red-hot masonry only pattered the ground around him with smoking missiles.

He kept crawling until he was safe. Every building was burning. The dormitory, the workshops, the storehouses; even the trees in the orchard were smoking, their new green leaves brown and curled.

A pair of brown leather boots walked across his line of sight. They stopped, and when he moved his hand, they moved closer.

'Va?'

He tried to turn over. He was starting to feel the pain, and not just the pain but the loss. His world had just been torn in two.

'Elenya?'

She bent down and looked at him. 'Are you going to die?'

His hands were blistered and cut. His face felt stiff and wet, and he couldn't tell whether he was caked in dried mud or melted flesh. His throat was burning and his chest felt crushed. If it hurt this much, it must mean he was going to live.

'Die? Not today.'

'Oh.' She walked away again but not so far that she couldn't watch him gasp and twitch like a stranded fish. After a while she sat down on a low wall.

Va lay there, listening to the life he knew consumed by fire. He had been almost happy here. The rituals, the order, the brotherhood, the closeness of his community; they all served to quieten the voices inside. Now it was all gone. If he concentrated, he could hear their whispering beginning.

He levered himself to his knees and shuffled like a penitent over to where Elenya sat.

'You look like shit,' she said. 'Are you sure you're not going to die?'

'Shut up, woman. No, don't. Tell me what happened.'

'There were – I don't know – thirty or so men, maybe more. I was gathering firewood when I heard them coming, and I was certain I didn't want to meet them. So I hid.'

'Then what?'

'I waited until they'd all gone past. Every one of them was on horseback; it didn't take long. They just stormed in, killing as they found them. Some of the monks barricaded themselves in the church but that didn't hold much hope, really.' She shrugged. 'It was over very quickly. They came, slaughtered everyone and left. Not quite. There were two big thunderclaps. I don't know what they were. They didn't come from the sky.'

Va got to his feet, staggered, almost put out his hand to steady himself on Elenya's shoulder, but at the last moment managed to grab a gatepost instead. 'The scriptorium.'

'I don't think there'll be anything left of that.'

'No, you don't understand. The books.'

'Va, they'll be ash by now.'

'No they won't.' He started walking painfully towards the burning annexe to the dormitory. 'Don't think that we haven't tried.'

'What are you talking about?'

But he wouldn't answer. He kept on with his stiff gait until he stood under the wall of the scriptorium. All the books, all the inks and quills and gold leaf and leather and string and glue, all gone. The psalters and the gospels and books of the law, the prayers and the rules and the records of centuries, almost as back as far as the Reversal: destroyed. Yet all of this incidental to the reason for their destruction.

'You can't go in,' said Elenya. 'It might be days before you can go in.'

'God will provide a way,' said Va.

'And what do you expect to find when you do?'

'Nothing. Precisely nothing.'

'So why look?'

'So that I can tell the patriarch what I've seen.'

'Seen nothing? I can see him taking that seriously.'

'That's because you don't realize what it is that's not there.' He banged his blistered fist on the stonework. It was hot and hard against his hand. 'Enough!'

The scriptorium roof caved in. All the first-floor windows blew outwards, spilling shards of glass and twisted ribbons of lead across the ground, where they lay like diamonds and worms. Tongues of flame twisted out then pulled back.

Va picked his way back to the low wall. There had been pigs in the pen, a sow and six piglets, but they were dead too. Perhaps only the pigeons had escaped.

'Who were they, these men?'

'I was hiding,' said Elenya. With night falling and moving away from the fire, it was getting colder.

'Who were they?' he repeated. 'Were they Rus?'

'No. They didn't look like us. Northerners.'

'Yellowmen?'

'No. I've met Yakut, and the yellowmen look a bit like them. Further north still. Turks?'

'You were there.' Va realized that he needed to eat and drink. The raiders couldn't burn down the well, or steal all the snow, but the stores were up in flames. He took out his knife and swung his legs over the wall of the sty.

'They had darker skin than me, so they might have been

8

Turkmen. They had a leader. I only saw him for a moment. He was dressed all in black.'

'Like me.'

'No. It wasn't a habit, more a shroud: black cloth wound around him, over his head. I didn't see his face, or anything of him.' She watched him slice the sow's belly into strips. 'I couldn't stop what happened, Va. Even you couldn't have.'

'Even me.' His voice was self-mocking. He concentrated on his bloody work.

'You're the one who surrendered himself to God. Made all those vows. Poverty, chastity, obedience.'

'And I will keep them till the day I die.'

'Which, as you've already said, won't be today.' She turned away. 'Perhaps the Turkmen came for you, only to find that you weren't here. Imagine, all that way. It might even be that if they'd found you, they would have spared everyone else.'

Va stopped cutting for a moment. His hand tightened around the blood-slick bone handle of his knife, to get a better grip on it. 'You might deceive yourself as to my importance. I don't. I'm nothing. A nobody. A man of no consequence at all.'

'You're the man I love.'

'That counts for nothing.' Elenya did this periodically. She would provoke him, and he would have to be resilient, surrounding himself with the armour of God until she grew tired. 'It never did.'

'Never? It's a sin to lie, Va.'

'I renounced the deeds of the flesh, and if I could, I would renounce the flesh itself. Be quiet and leave me alone.'

'I'll be quiet,' she said. 'I'll never leave you alone.'

He had to pray. The physical necessity of prostrating himself in humility before God was overwhelming. He finished his work and gathered up the belly strips. 'Quiet will do for the moment.'

There was a place where the east wall had fallen completely outwards. Stone and brick were piled with burning wood. He laid out the pork on a slab of masonry and pushed it into the heart of the fire. Then, facing east, he lay down, arms crucifix-wide, face in the mud, and began to recommend the souls of his brothers to the care of Heaven.

He was the only one left, and he should have died with them. Now he had to wrestle with the idea that his survival wasn't a quirk of random fate but served a higher purpose. He had been chosen to bear witness to this atrocity for certain. But what else? Did God want more from him?

'I am unworthy,' he groaned. 'Send another. Send anyone else but me, Lord God. I am a worm, a dog, a maggot. I am unclean. I am untrustworthy. I am weak and I will fail. Don't spare me. Take me. The least of my brothers was better than me. Give life to one of them, please. Give them new life and destroy me.'

He was not struck down. After a while he got up, pulled back the stone with the charred meat on and ate slowly, resenting every mouthful.

'I'm surprised you can eat, with your brothers' bones cracking in the fire.'

'If I don't eat, I can't bury them.'

'Oh.' Elenya sat down next to him, put part of a rye loaf on the stone and exchanged it for a piece of meat. 'Isn't this just like old times, Va?'

'No. I wasn't a monk, and you weren't mad.'

'But here we are all the same, under the stars, firelight—'

'If you're going to eat, eat. I have work to do.'

'You can't do anything now. Everything is gone. Only we remain.'

'There's plenty I can do. Like pray for rain.'

'Rain?' She looked up into the clear night sky. The stars were brittle-bright, twinkling at them from above. 'There won't be rain for days.'

'Which is why I'm going to have to pray until I sweat blood.' Va pulled back his hood and ran a fat-smeared hand over his shaved head. 'God will hear me. He heard me before.'

'So you say.'

'He sent his angels.'

'And He saved you.'

'It is true.'

11

'And you have the nerve to call me mad. At least my madness is my own fault.'

'And mine is divine madness, one that I gratefully accept.' He took the hard black bread and bit into it. 'I wake up and my first thought is to thank God.'

'Mine is to curse Him for making me want you.'

'Each to their own. I won't fight with you.'

'You won't fight with anyone. Not any more.' She took another strip of meat and stood up. For a moment he looked up at her, her face lit by the same flames that consumed the bodies of his beloved brothers. She was still beautiful, and it made his rejection of her all the more pure. He had chosen the steepest road, simply because he had the furthest to climb.

'Goodnight, Elenya.'

'Goodnight, Va.'

When she had gone, but not too far, he went to the well. He drew up water and doused himself over and over again until he shivered with the cold. He stripped off his habit and washed it in the trough, abusing his blistered hands until he thought he would faint with dizziness. His body was scarred – more scarred than any man alive had a right to be. He'd picked up some more today, but he was proud of those, not like all the others: the burns to his forearms and thighs were gained trying to save life, not end it.

Finally his face. He had protected it instinctively by

covering it with his cloaked arms. It was unmarked because his reactions were still that fast. If his features had been turned to bubbling ruin, would Elenya still adore him? He knew the answer was yes, and it was futile wishing otherwise. He would have disfigured himself long ago if it could have given her release.

He pulled on his sodden habit, which stole more heat from him. Now he was mortally cold. His lips were blue and his limbs spasming. His teeth chattered with a life of their own. To pray like this was not only his duty but his right. There was nothing to rely on, no earthly power, no inner strength. He had nothing. He had no status, no wealth to bribe the Almighty or position to lever influence. His name – even his name was not his own.

Va went back to where the east door had stood and looked down the ruined nave to the twisted remains of the great green dome that was once raised over the basilica, now thrown down and smashed. Elenya was right. It would burn all tomorrow and into the night. It would stay hot until the Sabbath and precious time would be lost.

The books were gone. He knew it in his heart. The raiders hadn't picked at random. They hadn't come to steal the plate or the crosses, the grain stores or the livestock. This place, in all of Mother Russia, hidden away in the far south where there was nothing but trees and wolves, was the one place they'd come. If he waited until the fires died down of their own accord, they'd be back in the heathen north and nothing could be done.

But something *was* being done. Gritting his teeth, Va prostrated himself again in the direction of the rising sun.

'God, this is a test. I know it. A test of my faith. I won't fail. I need rain. I need such a quantity of rain that I might drown here in the dirt. I want a deluge, a flood. I want the vaults of Heaven opened and a cataract to pour down. I need to get into the scriptorium, to check on the books. I know they're not there, but the patriarch will ask me if I have checked and I cannot tell a lie to him. I have to look him in the eye and tell him that I have seen the place where they were and that the books are not there. If we're going to get them back, we have to start as soon as possible. So, please: I need rain, and I need it now.'

CHAPTER 2

Elenya found him at first light, still stretched out before the ruined church. She was already soaked to the skin.

'I suppose you think this is a sign,' she said.

Va said nothing in reply. Instead he got up wearily and started over to the remains of one of the workshops. There would be a spade, or a pick – probably without a handle, but he was used to working with impossibilities.

He kicked at the smoking timbers, and moved aside the remains of a fallen wall. Underneath was an iron-shod shovel, scorched but intact. It would do. His gaze strayed to the scriptorium, sweating and creaking as the rain lashed down. Later. There would be time later. He had a solemn duty to fulfil.

Under the unwavering watch of Elenya, he marked out a patch of bare earth as close to the high altar as he could get, and began to dig into the frozen ground. The metal blade scratched and scraped against stones and ice, jarring his hands, bringing out blisters that soon rubbed raw and bled. They joined the fresh burns and stained the handle. Still he dug.

When he had gone as far as he could, though not as deep

as he ought, he started to scour the monastery grounds for remains. The first few weren't so bad, hacked and bludgeoned to death as they'd run or knelt. It was those trapped in the buildings that wore him down, the endless sifting and lifting: a skull here, a ribcage there, a thigh bone or a foot. Disarticulated or whole, they were glazed with the remnants of their skin and contorted with the heat of the fire.

He finally wept as he carried another charred bundle of bones over to the grave. He'd been backwards and forwards all morning, and he was sick of it.

Va couldn't recognize them any more. He thought that he could: a rosary of a certain style, a scrap of cloth. But they were just guesses. These men had been his brothers. They deserved better than this. They deserved full ritual: three days in an open coffin on the chancel steps, the air rich with incense and prayer.

Instead he was tipping bits and pieces of them in a hollow-sounding shower into a hole he'd carved from the ground.

'My friends. My family. Gone.' He had never felt so wretched, never less able to contend with the urge inside him to go out and take terrible revenge.

'I know,' said Elenya. 'I am genuinely sorry. They were good men; rough, but good. They treated me better than you did.' She watched him as he brushed a fragment of bone into the pit. 'Is that the last?'

'It's the last I can find.' He wiped his eyes with his filthy sleeve. 'They're all dead.'

'Except you.' She took the spade and started shovelling dirt back into the ground. 'Say your words, Brother Va. Commend the souls of the lost to the God who didn't care enough about them in the first place to stop this from happening. Then we can go.'

He stared at her for a long time, watching her as she attacked the mound of freshly dug earth with quiet violence.

'You don't have to do this,' he said.

'I honour them. Not you,' she grunted. The blade of the spade bit down hard.

He dropped the hem of his habit down from where he had tucked it into his waist cord, and raised his hand upwards, feeling the pat of raindrops on his palms. As he stood, he started to chant, using the ancient language of the Church that had not changed for two thousand years. Old Russian, heavy with meaning and mystery. The learned words rolled off his tongue and he was in another place.

No longer beside an open grave filled with the bodies of his brothers, no longer outside in the rain and the cold, no longer a wretched man smeared in mud and decay. He approached the holy throne of God Almighty, and he was oblivious to anything else. No pain, no hunger, no thirst, no loss, no rejection. He could smell Heaven, it was so close.

When he opened his eyes again, Elenya was dragging a

burned crossbeam upright. She forced it into the ground and hammered it home with the flat of the spade. On the last blow, the handle finally broke with a crack.

She threw both halves away. 'That's that.'

He looked at the grave site. It was pitifully small for all that it contained. 'Now for the other thing.'

'Give it up, Va. There are no books left.' She caught his defiant expression and tried another tack. 'Aren't you tired? Don't you want to rest?'

'Rest, like they do? Or rest like the northerners who killed them?' There was mud in his mouth and he spat it out. He lowered his head and watched a dribble of rainwater run down the bridge of his nose, tremble for a moment, then fall. 'There'll be no rest from now on.'

They cleared the rubble on the floor of the scriptorium.

'We haven't seen so much as a whole page yet.'

'Dig, woman. The noise of work is the only thing I want to hear.'

'But of course. Brother Va prays for rain and look, it comes. Then he searches for books in the heart of a fire and expects them to be there. He takes the miraculous in his stride these days. Once you would have been terrified.' She heaved back a blackened timber with an iron bar still warm from the fire.

Va looked up at the remaining walls and judged his position. 'It should be here. Go straight down.'

'It would help if you told me what we're not looking for.'

'There's a stone slab on the floor. Huge – too big for a dozen men to lift.'

'And we're going to lift it? How? Another miracle?'

'Dig.'

Va did everything by hand, picking up, turning, throwing, and all the time the rain came down, turning the soot into black slurry. He worked not as if his life depended on it, but as if everyone else's did. He never broke off to ease his screaming back or wipe the sweat mixed with rain from his eyes.

'Va? Va. Stop.'

'Not until we're done.'

'You're lower than floor level. This,' she said, banging the heel of her boot down, 'is the floor.'

'What?' He peered around him. She was right. He was in a hole, which he tried immediately to widen, searching out the edges.

Elenya was content to watch him. She wiped a raindrop from the end of her nose and left a black smudge.

'Look,' he finally said. 'This is the slab I was talking about. It's cracked in two, at least.' He dug under the remaining piece, opening up a gap between the debris and the stonework. Then he lay on his belly and started to slither into the void he'd made.

He pulled himself forward, down the face of the rubble slope. The air inside was rank, thick with the stench of smoke. He tried not to breathe deeply, but took fast, shallow sips. As his eyes grew accustomed to the dark, he started to make out the corners of the hidden vault.

There should have been a chest, lined with lead inside, covered with lead without, sealed by heating it up and beating the join until it disappeared. A chest that he would have comfortably fitted in twice over.

It was gone, and now he could tell the patriarch that he'd seen the truth of it.

He turned himself round and dragged his aching body out again, out into the rain and the fresh air. He struggled onto his back and lay there, mouth wide open, drinking and breathing in great gasps.

'Are they there?'

'No. I have to go to Moskva now.'

'To tell the patriarch.'

'Yes.'

'And what makes you think he'll listen to a single word you say?'

'He'll listen,' said Va. He sat up, his feet still in the hole made by two parts of the shattered capstone. He had to get ready. The journey was going to be long, difficult, painful. 'He'll listen to me even if I have to write him a letter in my own blood.'

'That sounds like fun. If you dictate, I'll gladly be the scribe.'

'I need a horse. You still have a horse, don't you?'

Elenya threw down the iron bar. It clattered off the stonework and came to rest by Va's side. He looked at it, sensing its weight, judging its length, feeling the motion of it as it spun and twisted in his hands. What an excellent weapon.

'No,' he hissed, louder than he intended.

Elenya heard. 'No, what?'

'I won't. I won't . . .' He dropped his voice, muttering to himself under his breath. 'Not in my hands.' He got up and climbed out of the pit.

'I won't give you my horse,' she said.

He couldn't just take the animal. If he'd been a different man, he would have done. If he'd been a man who fought. So he had to persuade her instead. 'This is a matter of the utmost importance. The books must not leave Mother Russia.'

'All the books are gone, Va. Even the ones that were buried beneath the floor of the scriptorium. The heat would have destroyed them.'

'They took the books before they set the fire. You said there were two great noises? Black powder, I'd swear on it. And in any event, these books would survive an iron forge.'

She tilted her head just so. 'Yes, of course they would.' She started to pick her way out from the ruins.

He called after her. 'We tried. We tried everything to get rid of them. We burned them. We turned them red-hot and

21

pounded them on an anvil. We scratched at them with diamonds. Nothing. Not a mark. Rather than taking them to sea where there was always the chance of them washing ashore somewhere, they were kept here. Safe. Safe for seven centuries. Now they've gone.' He shouted at her back: 'Disaster waits for us all.'

She stopped and looked over her shoulder. 'Va, what the hell are you talking about?'

He clambered over the rubble, his feet slipping on the wet stones in his haste. 'I can't tell you. It's a secret. But we have to get those books back.'

'We?' She arched an eyebrow.

'Stop it. I mean us, the Church, and anyone who'll help us. Clearly that doesn't include you because all you do is hang around and wait for me to die. So either give me your horse or leave me alone.' He sat down on what remained of the scriptorium wall and pressed his palms hard against his temples. 'Why now? Why not in fifty years' time when this wouldn't be my problem?'

'Because all the people you ever killed are crying out from beyond the grave, and God wants to dispense justice by giving you a really shitty time.'

He sighed. 'There may be something in that.'

'And while you're speaking to the Almighty, you can tell Him we've had enough rain. A light shower would have done, but this is beyond a joke.' Elenya picked up the hem

22

of her coat and wrung it out on the ground in front of Va. The water formed a puddle, where more rain added to it.

'The Lord is nothing if not bountiful.'

'Shut up, you sanctimonious shit.' Her shoulders sagged. 'I'll get the horse.'

He raised his head, and the rain dripped off his nose. 'Thank you.'

She wagged her finger at him. 'You misunderstand me. You're going to Moskva. I'm going to Moskva. You can argue all you like, but you know as well as I do that you're desperate to get there quickly. You'll have to travel with me.'

'No. *You*'ll be travelling with *me*.'

'And whose horse is it?'

'Yours,' he admitted.

'So I'll be letting you come along. Remember that.' She walked away, through the ruined courtyard and out into the woods beyond.

Va went over to the well to douse himself in bucket after bucket of freezing water, scraping his skin with stones to remove some of the dirt. More water after that. A memory: his baptism in a river, still frozen at the edges, surrounded by awed villagers, held under for longer than necessary by the priest, who needed to know that the sacrament would genuinely take.

'You look like a rat. A wet rat.'

'I no longer care what I look like – that's not how my worth is judged.'

She was leading a horse, a shaggy-haired beast, snorting and stamping. 'I take it you remember how to ride.'

'I cannot ride with you.'

'And you can't take my horse.' She wiped her hands on her hips. 'You're not leaving my sight, and you've run out of options. You have to ride with me, or not at all.'

'Then,' said Va, 'I choose not to ride at all. I can't share a saddle with you, Elenya. It would be too cruel to you. If you did not love me so, then I would say yes, let us ride, no matter how unseemly it looked, a monk and a woman so close together. But you do. Five years, and you've sat outside these walls, with the wolves and the bears and howling wind and biting cold, the snow in winter and the flies in summer.'

'Don't flatter yourself.'

'I don't. But neither of us is stupid. You stayed, and you still say you love me. I say you're in the grip of some intractable madness. Whichever: I can't share a saddle with you because it would send you out of your mind with longing. I haven't touched you for all this time, praying that your passion for me would die. My prayers are unanswered. I don't know why.'

'Perhaps because I'm praying that you'll throw off your habit and take me, even now. My prayers also remain un-answered. Isn't God cruel?' She bit at her lip. 'So how are you going to get to Moskva? Walk?'

'No. It would take too long. Those who stole the books

would be gone, and the traces of their passing gone as well. It's a week's walk. The ice is melting, and boats can't navigate the rivers.'

'So?'

'I'll run.' He adjusted his waist cord.

'All the way?' She was incredulous. 'Just because you won't ride with me?'

'All the way. It's kinder for you if I do.' He turned round and judged the weather, the wind.

'I'll be right behind you. On the horse. When you get tired of running, I can give you a lift.'

'My mind's made up. Wish me Godspeed.' He shook his arms out, rolled his neck this way and that. Then he set off, taking an easy pace, hands loose by his side. His bare feet scarcely touched the ground.

'Men. Stupid, stubborn men. They get one idea in their heads and it's the only thing they can think of.' She shouted after him: 'You haven't even got any shoes!'

He was gone, out of the gate. There was a track of sorts that led into the forest of close-packed pines. It headed north, towards the city of Moskva. If there had been no track, Va would have made one.

Five years of isolation was over. He was back in the world.

CHAPTER 3

There was a body floating in the sea. It was caught at the surf line: as the waves broke and rushed in, spilling foam up the white beach, the body turned and dragged itself towards the shore. But as the water sank through the sand and the sea retreated, the pale, bloated corpse slipped away again.

Benzamir watched from the strand line. He held a selection of objects he'd combed from the beach – a shell, a translucent stone of sea-worn glass, a red crab carapace, a worm-bored piece of driftwood – and occasionally glanced down at his treasures, feeling the smoothness of the pebble, the roughness of the wood. He was barefoot, and scrunched the soft, dry sand between his brown toes.

Everything was amazing to Benzamir. The sky was huge, stretching from horizon to horizon, the sea filled his vision, the warmth of the sand and the heat of the sun: he couldn't stop grinning. He even relished the bead of sweat that was working its way down his spine, the sand flies circumnavigating his ankles, the blinding glitter of sun on sea.

Not so far away, to the north of where he stood, his ancestors had lived in little mud-brick houses and kept goats. Then they had gone away on the greatest adventure imaginable: Benzamir had heard all the stories as a young boy and been thrilled by them. They had changed his life, directed his choices, inspired his very soul. Now he was here, finally home, and it felt fantastic yet slightly unreal. All that way for a dream.

He carefully put down what he was carrying and waded out into the sea. The hem of his robe caught against the water, pushing up waves of its own. As he strode out, he listened intently to the swoosh of his legs, the feel of the cool, shallow sea against his skin.

The beach dipped gently away. He was up to his knees when he reached the body, still bobbing up and down, pulled towards the coast and thrust away with each cycle of waves. The water was clear enough to see the problem. The man's hands were shackled together with a length of heavy iron chain that acted like an anchor. Little brilliantly coloured fish darted in and out of the body's shadow, scared of Benzamir but interested in scavenging.

Benzamir dipped his arm into the sea, took up the chain and started to haul the body behind him back towards the beach. It was easy while there was enough draught to float the man, much more difficult once he'd grounded. Benzamir was young and strong, and the dead man thin and pale, like a ghost. The limp feet dragged in the sand, making two parallel furrows. They were bound, like the hands, but on a much shorter length of chain.

The body hadn't been in the water long. Long enough to drown, for certain, but not long enough for the little sea creatures to make much of a mess. Benzamir rolled him over. The blue eyes were wide and staring, the mouth open in a great fish gulp. The man's pale skin had gone blue-white, making the thinness of his chest all the more obvious. He could count his ribs, and see his pelvic bones stand out like axe blades over the top of the thin loincloth he still wore.

Benzamir closed the dead man's eyelids with his thumbs, and examined the shackles to see how they'd been closed. While he was running his fingers over the crude hinge and single hot rivet, two more men came up behind him.

Both were in white desert robes and riding horses. Benzamir had heard of this practice, of how you could use a bit and bridle to control a horse, use a saddle and girth strap to provide a seat, a pair of stirrups to give a better ride. He'd never seen it before, let alone seen it so casually done. The air was suddenly filled with the sharp perfume of hot beast.

One man threw himself off his saddle with practised nonchalance, despite the height. His horse, rather than running off, shook its mane and made a staccato sound in its throat. Its bridle jingled. The man pushed past Benzamir to kick the corpse rudely in the kidneys and give a rough grunt of frustration.

'*Salam alaykum,*' said Benzamir. He rather hoped it was the right thing to say. He had nothing else to go on but what he'd been told.

The man turned sharply, his head cloth falling away from his face to reveal a mouth more used to being twisted in a sneer than raised in a smile. He had dark, pin-bright eyes, and he looked Benzamir up and down.

When he spoke, it was difficult for Benzamir to tell what he was saying. His ancestors had left this part of the world many, many years before, and the language had changed: vowels shifted, tenses reordered, pronouns subtly different. He realized he must look a complete idiot, standing there in a soaking wet jellaba, no sandals, and smiling all the time, squinting into the sun and nodding. The horseman was jabbing his finger at the body by their feet and speaking increasingly quickly.

From what Benzamir could glean, the dead man was a slave from a ship. He'd jumped overboard and drowned. The horseman was complaining that his investment had been rendered worthless.

'Yes, I see.' If Benzamir had had any money, he would have recompensed the man for his dead slave. If the poor soul hadn't been free in life, at least he could be in death. As it was, he had no currency, local or exotic, with which to redeem anyone.

The horseman was still gesturing, and Benzamir started to get the feeling that he was being blamed for the man's troubles. He was starting to catch more of what was being said.

'Who will take his place at the oar? Who will move my family's cargo? Are we to be ruined for the want of one pathetic slave? Are my wives to be thrown out into the street, my children to beg for scraps? You could not wish this on any man!'

Benzamir might have been a stranger, but he was no fool. He chose his words carefully.

'If it were my family, I would consider it both my duty and my honour to row myself.'

The second man stifled a laugh behind his white head cloth, but the first was furious. His hand went to his belt, where he had a great curved sword sheathed. Benzamir had thought it for show, or that it held some ceremonial function. He could see when it was brandished that he had misjudged. The length of the blade was notched, and the way it was held told him that it was balanced for fighting. That was all right, because Benzamir knew about fighting.

The sword being shaken in his face was both functional and highly decorated. There were patterns cut into the flat, and the hilt was made of rich red leather, topped with a faceted jewel. He thought it quite beautiful, and he wanted to examine it closely: perhaps later, when it wasn't trying to cut him in two.

'You are not from around here, are you?'

'No,' said Benzamir, taking a step back but still smiling. 'You could say that.'

'You lack the protection of your family and clan?'

'So it seems.'

'Good. Then I will take you as a slave, or I will kill you. Which do you prefer?' The man completed a series of finely executed practice swings. The sun flashed off the blade, which sung as it moved.

Benzamir was enormously impressed. 'You're very good with that,' he said, and he meant it.

The second man had sized up the two opponents and was already fetching rope from his saddlebags. Clearly he fancied slight, lithe Benzamir's chances not at all.

'Kneel,' said the man.

'I am Benzamir Michael Mahmood, and I kneel only to God.'

For his pains, he was slashed at. He danced out of the way. It had been a long time since he'd fought anyone quite like this. His body relaxed into the moves he had learned: he barely had to think at all.

He turned, once, twice, slipped effortlessly round the singing-edged blade and grounded his right foot at the point where the man's ribs met his belly. He didn't wait for him to fall, but was suddenly behind him, chopping with an open hand at the base of the stiff neck.

Never forgetting that he had two enemies, he stepped lightly across the sand, barely disturbing it as he loped. When he was in range, he leaped and spun, catching the second man across the throat with his fist. He cleared the horse completely, landed on the ground shoulder first, rolled, stood and waited.

The angry sword-wielding horseman was still upright, but motionless. Then he fell face first onto the beach like a felled tree. His rope-holding colleague was clawing at his chest in a vain attempt to stimulate breathing. After a few moments he too was unconscious, face down in the soft sand.

'That was fantastic,' said a grinning Benzamir to the bemused horses. 'I'm really home.' He did a little jig, because he was so absurdly happy.

He used the men's own rope to bind their hands, and took the opportunity to search them for weapons. Both had steel knives, and then there was the sword. Benzamir made a few practice lunges and sweeps with it himself. It was a little too heavy for him, and he imagined he'd get tired quickly using it.

'Unhand the sword of my fathers, infidel.'

'You're awake.'

'Untie me, or you will suffer unimaginable torments.'

'Of course I will,' said Benzamir. He sat cross-legged with the sword across his knees, close enough to his captives that he didn't have to shout. 'What do they call you?'

'I am Ibn Alam; my father is Sheikh Alam, who owns the land from the sea to the mountains. When he discovers the insult you have served on our family, he will strike off your head and mount it on a spear.'

'I believe the insult is yours and yours alone. Who's your friend?'

'Said, the useless mongrel. My father pays him to protect his bloodline.'

'And that's worth preserving, is it?' asked Benzamir in all innocence.

Ibn Alam spat at Benzamir. The gob of spittle arced through the air but fell short of its target. 'The world is not large enough for you to hide in, even if you started running now.'

'No. It's more than big enough, I think. However, since Said is incompetent at keeping your precious balls intact, I'd better take you back to your father myself.'

Ibn Alam's olive skin turned purple. 'You would not shame me so. I am the sheikh's son.'

'I'm not at all concerned about your shame.'

'I demand you release me.'

Said was coughing himself awake. Benzamir got to his

feet and retrieved a supple skin bulging with water from the saddle of one of the horses. He took the opportunity to press his hand against the flank of the creature, feeling its sides heave with each breath.

He let Said hold the water skin and drink his fill, then offered it to Ibn Alam. He received more spit at his feet. So he tilted the bottom of the skin to the sky and drank his own fill. The water was warm, slightly brackish, with a hint of whatever the skin was made from. Benzamir thought it so very different to what he was used to.

He dried his mouth on the sleeve of his jellaba.

'How do we get you two back? Without you trying to kill me, that is.'

Said finally cleared his throat. 'If we swore on our honour not to attack you, would that be sufficient?'

'You I trust,' said Benzamir, 'though I've doubts as to whether Ibn Alam's honour will extend quite so far.' He gave the matter some thought, then came up with a perfect solution. 'Said, hold the horse's reins.'

He poked Ibn Alam to his feet with the point of the sword and marched him across to his horse. With Said at its head, he told Ibn Alam to mount up.

Both men looked at each other, barely suppressed delight on their faces, until Benzamir told them: 'Face backwards.'

With a growl, Ibn Alam did as he was told. Benzamir lashed his hands to the projection at the back of the saddle.

'You too,' said Benzamir to Said, and once he'd fastened him on, he tied the reins of Ibn Alam's horse to the saddle of Said's.

'You will pay for this humiliation,' called Ibn Alam.

'Pay? What a fascinating concept. We'll have to discuss this later.' Benzamir lifted his face to the desert sun and tugged at the lead rope. Said's horse obediently trotted on and, with a jerk, so did the other. 'This is the right way, isn't it?'

Said twisted in his saddle. 'East. There is a harbour, and above the harbour a town.'

'Shut up, you traitorous worm.'

'Do you want to be killed out here with your own sword? Are you that stupid? This man has the power of life and death over us and you choose to stamp your feet like a child. Grow up.'

'How dare you speak to me like that!'

'Do shut up, I beg you. Do you value anything but your precious honour? East, I say. Let Allah decide our fate.'

'Thank you, Said.' Benzamir turned full circle, trying to get his bearings. East used to be in that direction, parallel to the coast; it was not just the language that had changed. Said meant the other way, the way that used to be west but was now east.

Said watched him dither. 'Who are you? Where do you come from? You look like us, but you are not, are you? Your skin is paler than it should be: have you come from the far south where the sun does not shine?'

'I can honestly say I've come even further than that.' He picked up his sandals from the strand line and dropped them one at a time in front of him. He walked into them without breaking step. He looked behind him. A body, stretched out on the sand, hands and feet chained together. Birds, no more than dark smudges, circling overhead and waiting for them to leave. Two horses, one glossy black, one a rich brown; their riders both facing away from the direction of travel. Ibn Alam's shoulders slumped in defeat, Said's a less hunched hopefulness. Bright white sand underneath, fierce white sun overhead.

Nothing could be better than this, surely.

CHAPTER 4

Two arcs of broken rubble stretched out into the sea like arms, protecting the little wooden boats from the worst of the weather. Benzamir was excited by weather: he wanted a storm, a real storm with fat drops of rain, the echoing roll of thunder, the wind so strong it howled. He couldn't wait.

The boats in the harbour, a dozen in all, were bobbing on the choppy sea, their masts dancing to and fro. Further out beyond the wall was a single larger vessel. It was long and low in the water. On the gracefully curving bow there was a painted eye.

'That's beautiful,' said Benzamir, stopping to admire it. 'The sheikh must be very proud to own such a magnificent ship.'

Ibn Alam didn't answer. Said looked out to sea and nodded. 'It is the source of his great wealth. He can trade with anywhere along this coast, as far as the Outer Ocean.'

'That's to the' – he thought about it for a moment – 'east of here. Has he ever gone across the sea to the south?'

'Why would he do that? There is nothing there but trees, no one there but savages. They make nothing of worth. They are all mad, and no trade is possible with such people. They would sooner grind our bones to bake bread with.'

'I have heard,' said Benzamir, 'that they were once rich and powerful.'

'I have heard those stories too, but I do not believe them. They are too weak, too stupid and too untrustworthy to have ever been great.'

'Animals!' spat Ibn Alam. 'Good only for the simplest of tasks.'

'Like rowing.'

'Yes. You – you are worthy of death. They are not fit even for that courtesy.'

'I'm glad you think so highly of me.' Benzamir closed his eyes for a moment, gently moving his head from side to side. Then he opened them again, and led the horses towards the cluster of buildings that sat away from the coast. There were fields, and a complex series of water channels for moving the precious liquid from the river to the crops. It was the height of the day, and there was no one to be seen.

'Man. You, Benzamir Mahmood. Untie me now. This is your last chance. My father will not take this lightly.'

'Your father, Ibn Alam, is not just wealthy, but wise as well. I expect he'll treat me as I deserve.'

He found the road into town, even though it was nothing more than a dusty track. As they came closer, an avenue of tall trees beckoned; each one was crowned with a head of great green branches. They looked familiar. Date palms, they called them, and Benzamir knew that seven dates made one meal. He was anxious to try just a single fruit. Would they be sweet or sour, hard or soft, big or small? He would get hold of one as soon as he could.

It was suddenly cool under the shade of the trees. There was a young boy sitting beside the road. He had no good reason for being there, no toy or book or task; just sat with his back against one of the hairy trunks, stirring the dust with a stick.

When he saw them coming, he leaped to his feet. Perhaps he recognized the horses first, and thought it would be politic to stand aside for someone as important as Ibn Alam.

Benzamir smiled as he walked by. '*Salam alaykum,*' he said.

Then the boy saw the truth of the matter. The sheikh's first-born son and his man were being led into town tied to their own mounts and backwards. He dared not reply. He hid instead, averting his eyes from his master's shame. But Benzamir knew that as soon as they were past, he would run into the town by a different route and tell all his friends that he'd seen Ibn Alam's face set like stone in a grimace of fury and embarrassment.

It was just how he wanted it.

As they entered the town with its huddled buildings and narrow streets, he felt himself being watched. Faces would appear at windows for the briefest of moments, confirm the scandalous rumour, then dart back. The bolder ones, all dark-eyed boys with their faces obscured in their father's second-best head cloth, peered down from the roofs. They nudged each other and whispered.

It was different as they penetrated further in. The horses' hooves clattered on the packed stone surface, and craftsmen looked up from their labours at the strange procession. They fell silent as Benzamir approached, and either scuttled back into the darkness of their workshops or studied their laps so closely as to be oblivious to anything else.

In the very centre of the town was a paved square. On one side was the mosque. On the other was the fortified palace of the sheikh. The minaret's shadow fell across the ground like a sundial's gnomon, marking the passage of the high-thrown sun. Three old men sat on the steps of the mosque, smoking from a shared pipe. Almost as if they had booked seats for the performance.

Benzamir led his captives into the middle of the open space, to the place where there was a raised stone slab, worn and crumbling with age. He ran his hand over it, thinking that some of the depressions in its dry and chalky surface could have been writing. He hopped on top of the slab and called up to the sandstone walls of the palace.

'*Salam alaykum*, noble Sheikh. I bring you greetings and gifts.'

There was a long silence. Eventually one of the shuttered windows was thrown open and a voice called out: 'Who disturbs my lord's rest?'

'My name is Benzamir Michael Mahmood. My humble apologies for intruding on your lord's righteous slumber, but I believe I have certain items in my possession that rightly belong to him. If he would deal with me direct, I can return them to him without further delay. The sun is damaging them as we speak.'

Said hissed a warning. 'You have a brass neck. Do not stretch it out so far that you find it cut.'

'I know what I'm doing, despite appearances to the contrary.' Benzamir looked up at the window, wondering if the sheikh would make an appearance. 'But thank you for your concern, Said.'

The entrance to the palace was barred by a pair of heavy wooden doors, studded with iron. They creaked, split and swung apart. Four white men each carried the corner of a sheet on a pole. The sheikh walked in its shade, slowly and deliberately, as if he were processing. In the time it took for them to cross to Benzamir, he was able to judge his welcome. These were no men-at-arms, only slaves. However, there were at least two men on the toothed battlements of the palace, and they both had bows.

Benzamir wondered if they could hit him from their vantage points. He presumed that they thought they could, otherwise why would they be there?

'*Salam alaykum*, my lord.' He jumped from the plinth and landed lightly in front of the sheikh.

'*Salam*, Mahmood. You return my son to me.' When he spoke, he growled.

'The Prophet, peace be upon him, instructs that the release of captives is an act of compassion. I've no wish to own a fellow man, so I release him to your care. Said, you're also free to go.'

'Most generous for one so obvious in his poverty,' said the sheikh. His gaze fell on the sword at Benzamir's side.

'However, custom demands that for the wrong done to me by your son, I ought to keep both horses and this rather fine sword. I hope it doesn't have any significance to you or your family.'

Sheikh Alam reached up to stroke his grey and black beard. Lines of age deepened around his eyes. 'I might offer some exchange for that poor piece of workmanship. It has sentimental value. Nothing more.'

'Your favour would be enough, but a man cannot eat favour.' Benzamir was trying so hard to be serious, but the corners of his mouth kept on turning up. 'I can't deny such a bargain might tempt me.'

The sheikh's beard-stroking reached a steady rhythm –

first two fingers and thumb of the right hand from the cheeks down to the point of the chin. 'Perhaps we can talk in more comfortable surroundings. You would be my guest, of course. Come, we will walk back together.'

Benzamir stepped under the flapping sheet and held his arm out. The sheikh rested a nut-brown hand on his forearm. As they turned, so did the slaves, all starting the slow walk to the palace.

It suddenly occurred to Benzamir that the sheikh was moving so slowly because he was so very old. Not just of great age, but actually old – creaking limbs, shrinking spine, failing hearing and eyesight, forgetfulness and a tendency to reminisce about events from childhood.

He was leaning on Benzamir's arm, using it for support. The walk from his rooms to the square had tired him out, and now he needed help on the return journey. Benzamir felt terrible: he'd thought of Ibn Alam's father as someone vigorous and vital, not as a sick man he would drag out of bed.

'Again, many apologies for disturbing you, great one. Had I known, I would've waited until evening before calling.'

'Never mind,' said the sheikh. 'It is well worth being woken from my slumbers to see my first-born son humili-ated in such a fashion. The vulture.'

Benzamir was smiling again. 'I'm delighted I could bring you even a small pleasure.'

'You have done much more than that, but we must not show it. My son's wrath is legendary, and he will bear a grudge longer than any other man I know. Most likely he is already plotting to kill you as soon as you leave my protection.'

'I thank you for such wisdom.'

'My son may have underestimated you. Do not think that I will make the same mistake. I see more than he does, perhaps more than he ever will. But at the moment I see the dust of many days on your feet. My servants will refresh you, and then you will join me in my rooms. We can get business out of the way, and then talk. I wish to hear of the outside world. My body has become my prison, and only in my mind am I free.' The sheikh curled his bony fingers around Benzamir's wrist and gave a half-hearted squeeze. 'See? Once I wielded a sword in battle, and fought like a lion. Now I am but a little cat, with little claws.'

Behind them, more of the sheikh's men were trying to help Ibn Alam and Said dismount the horses. Said was content to let himself be cut loose, and climb down on his own; Ibn Alam kicked every servant who came in range.

Benzamir and the sheikh walked through the main gateway into the courtyard beyond. Within the high walls were more date palms and a well. A woman – at least, Benzamir assumed the veiled figure at the winding mechanism was a woman – drew up a bucket and emptied it at the foot of one of the palms.

'My servants will attend to you now. When you are ready, they will bring you to me.'

A man – a local, not a slave – touched his hand to his forehead, his lips, his heart. 'Follow me.'

Benzamir had his feet washed, which he felt uncomfortable about, but recognized that it was an act of hospitality, not ablution. A clean jellaba and a finely woven kaftan were laid out for him, and he accepted them eagerly. Hand-made, hand-stitched, the raw materials grown in a field or cut from the back of a sheep. They felt odd to the touch; imperfections in the weave marked each piece as unique.

He washed his face in the well water, and dried himself with the towel provided. Then he picked up the curved sword and asked to be taken to the sheikh.

Despite the burning sun outside, the reception room Benzamir was ushered into was cool, with a gentle breeze fluttering the thin sheets of coloured cloth draped across the walls. He would have to ask how that was done.

'Peace be on this house, Sheikh Alam. You've shown a traveller much kindness already.' He approached the sheikh, who reclined on a low seat, buoyed up by plump cushions. 'I make a gift of this sword.' He presented it hilt first, and the sheikh took it, clasping it tightly.

'My youth returns all too briefly, Benzamir Mahmood. Sit.' He tossed two small bags at Benzamir's feet. The bags chinked as they landed on the patterned red carpet. 'For your troubles.'

Without looking inside them, Benzamir bowed low, and then sat on a tasselled floor cushion. 'Your generosity does you great honour.'

'Enough of the small talk. We could do this for hours, dancing around each other, never saying what we mean.' The sheikh clapped his hands, and servants brought brass plates and dishes to set between the two men. Each plate held a different type of food, and Benzamir goggled at the variety. He didn't know where to start.

The sheikh waved to dismiss the waiters, and carried on: 'My son was foolish enough to attack you. I expect you beat him without raising a sweat.'

'I was sweating already.'

'You carry nothing, yet you do not behave as if you are poor. You act as if touched by the sun, but beneath that skull of yours there is something going on that I am not at all comfortable with. You are a son of the desert, though your skin is wan as if you had spent too many winters with the Ewer people. None of this tallies. So I ask you plainly: Who are you, and what do you want with me?'

Benzamir's hand was hovering over the dishes, working out which delight to try first.

'You know my name, and I want nothing from you. That,' he said, 'is the truth. My people are nomads. They left this very place centuries earlier, and I've come back to see what has become of our friends.'

'Ah, a traveller then. But you came with nothing. No satchel, no camel, no coat, nothing. Do you always rely on the kindness of strangers?'

Benzamir took a piece of flat bread flecked with herbs. He sniffed it, breathing in its pungent aroma, then took a bite, savouring its taste.

'Yes. There are no strangers, only friends not yet recognized. This is excellent, by the way.'

'So you have found friends. What of your enemies? . . . These you must try. They are grown here in the courtyard.' The sheikh allowed himself a wrinkled black fruit. Benzamir realized that these had to be the fabled dates.

'I have enemies. They'll hide as best they can, but I'll find them too. I'm very determined.'

The sheikh spat the date stone out onto an empty brass plate. It sounded like a gong. 'If I were them, then I would quake to know Benzamir Mahmood is looking for me.'

'You're very kind.' Benzamir's face split into a brilliant smile. 'Your people are fortunate to have you rule over them.'

'Their good fortune is running out.' The sheikh took another date. 'Hassan Ibn Alam wonders how much longer he has to wait before he takes my place.'

'Many years, I hope.'

'Now it is you who is being kind. I am an old man, soon off to meet his maker. My people love me all the more because they fear my passing. This has its benefits, but I have other sons I can leave my land to. Hassan believes that because he is first-born, it is his right – and so it is – but I must look beyond narrow tradition. I must choose wisely. Bloodshed is, well, regrettable.'

Benzamir reached out for a date, felt its texture, judged its weight. 'There's one favour I must ask you.' The sheikh nodded his assent. 'I need to talk to someone who knows the stars.'

'A mystic? You wish to know what the future holds for you?'

'After a fashion. There are signs in the night sky. I need help to interpret them.'

'There is a man, the imam. He keeps a careful watch on the heavens, the better to instruct men as to when to plant their crops and when to harvest them, when to expect the rains and when scorching winds drive from the north. I will send you to him after you have eaten your fill.'

'That might take some time. Your generosity exceeds my appetite, but only because you're extremely generous.'

CHAPTER 5

His name was Bin Haji, and he wore a circular cloth hat that had been his father's, and his grandfather's before him.

'He came from the far west, from the mountains. At that time there was lots of fighting and he had had enough of it.'

Apart from that, Bin Haji wore the jellaba and looked like everyone else.

'Fighting?' asked Benzamir. 'Who was attacking your grandfather's people?'

'He told my father everybody. But I think it was the Rus. Their land lies to the south and it is poor. Where are you from? You sound like you learned your Arabic from the Holy Qur'an.'

'Near enough. My people speak a different dialect now, and it's all but incomprehensible to anyone but us.'

'But you keep the teachings of the Prophet, peace be upon him. This is good.'

It was later. The sun was starting to slide down towards the east, and a cooling breeze was beginning to drift in from

49

the sea. They stood on the steps of the mosque and watched the men of El Alam stroll around the square, talking in twos and threes.

'The sheikh said you know the stars,' said Benzamir.

'Yes, though I am puzzled as to why you want to talk to me. Are you after learning, or do you seek your fortune? I tell you now, I do not deal with that. Allah, the Most Merciful, gives me all the direction I need.'

'Learning only.'

'Then that is good.' Bin Haji looked at the shadows in the square. 'There is an hour or so before prayers at sunset. Come with me.'

Benzamir padded barefoot through the silent mosque to reach the imam's rooms at the back. In the first room were divans and cushions, like the sheikh's, only less rich and padded. There was also a trunk, its lid hanging back on a chain. It was full of books.

'A library,' breathed Benzamir. 'May I?'

'Of course. It is good to meet another man who can read.'

Benzamir knelt by the edge of the trunk and touched the cover of the topmost book. It was bound in red leather, hand stitched, with brass corners. He picked it up and slowly, almost reverentially, weighed it in his hands. It was heavy, and smelled of age.

It was closed by a metal clasp, and he had to study it for a moment. Then he worked it loose and creaked back the wooden cover. The Arabic script inside was upside down: of course – he had the book back to front.

Bin Haji was watching him. He said nothing about the mistake.

Benzamir looked down and leafed through the first few pages. Lines of dense type, black ink on a worn cream background, together with diagrams and notation.

'Geometry,' said Bin Haji. 'Do you know geometry?'

'Yes, yes I do. Tell me, is this an original work or a translation?' He kept on turning the pages to see if there was something he didn't recognize. It started very simply, with regular shapes and solids; how to bisect lines, how to calculate angles. It moved on to the properties of a sphere: these pages looked well-thumbed.

'I believe it is a translation of a much older work. You know how it is with these things.'

Benzamir didn't, but nodded slowly as if he understood. 'Fascinating.' He looked at all the hand-drawn conic sections. He put the book on a low table and went back to the trunk for another.

'You wanted to ask me about the stars. What is it you want to know?'

'Hmm? Oh, yes. I'm sorry. We don't have such magnificent books where I come from. These are really very special. The pages . . . ?' He angled the book to the light to see them edge on.

'Vellum, mostly. Some are cloth treated with fine clay.'

'Where do books like this get made? There must be a king's ransom in this box.'

Bin Haji smiled nervously. 'I . . . yes. They are very precious. Most are out of the scriptoriums of Misr.'

'I'll have to go there.' Benzamir slipped onto one of the divans, still holding the second book. 'The stars. More specifically, stars that move.'

'The stars are fixed: they do not change. If there were something new in the sky, it would not be a star. Perhaps you mean one of the planets.' Bin Haji frowned. 'You do have some knowledge of the heavens?'

'Yes,' said Benzamir enthusiastically, 'I do. I need to know if you or any of your congregation have seen a bright light, or maybe more than one, falling from the sky to touch the ground. Have you?'

'No. Nothing out of the ordinary. There are the usual lights in their seasons, the so-called shooting stars, but nothing like you describe. Are you searching for a thunder-stone?'

Benzamir had to think. 'A meteor. It would look like one, wouldn't it? If one had fallen, where would I go to find out about it? Who would gather news of that sort?'

'If you dare, the emperor of Kenya's court. His spies are everywhere.'

'Are they? Why?'

'Because,' said Bin Haji, 'he has the vanity to want to know all things. You really are from far away not to have heard of Kenyan spies.'

Benzamir opened the book on his lap. It was an atlas. He gasped with delight. The pictures were just what he'd expected. 'This is pre . . . pre . . . what do you say here?'

'Before the world turned.'

The pages were thick and crisp, faded with age. Benzamir could see errors wherever he looked: bays lost, headlands flattened, mountains moved, rivers erased. But the gross features were all intact, and even some of the old names persisted. North was still north, though much of the writing was upside-down. He moved his finger along the coast from where he was to Misr El Mahrosa. Except that the city was far inland and there was El Iskandariya on the edge of the blue sea.

He turned more pages. Each one was a painstakingly copied work of art. The maps the transcribers had recent knowledge of were annotated heavily. Those of lost lands were sparse, and often wrong.

'You're a rich man. I thought the sheikh was blessed, but you . . . you've the wealth of knowledge here, and it'll keep you and your children's children in high regard.'

'You would like to think so. I have no wife yet.'

'Then you have to find one. These are too precious to pass into the hands of someone who doesn't appreciate them. Or worse,' said Benzamir, 'Ibn Alam.'

'We do not speak ill of the heir of Alam in this house,' chided Bin Haji. But he seemed neither outraged nor scared by Benzamir's criticism. 'There is time enough for marriage later. I am not so old. If you like my maps, perhaps you will also enjoy this.'

He bent down and reached under a divan. As he lifted the cover, he revealed a row of boxes, all different shapes and colours. He picked one, and slid it out. He beckoned Benzamir over and gave the brass key a half-turn.

Benzamir knelt on the floor and watched as the lid of the box was lifted clear. What was inside was delicate in the way carved ice was delicate. There was a ring of metal, engraved with script and pierced with tiny holes. Then, balanced on fine wire above five concentric rings, small coloured balls. Around the third ball there was an additional ring, with its own tiny ivory sphere.

'It's an orrery.'

He touched the polished brass orb that represented the sun, and watched the way his fingerprint evaporated in the heat.

'It used to be clockwork. My father had it converted to a hand crank. The dust causes havoc with the mechanism.'

'Is it accurate? I mean, it has to be more than a toy.'

Bin Haji reached inside the box and retrieved the little handle. There was a hole in the side which fitted the square end perfectly. 'The Earth goes around the Sun once, and the

Moon goes around the Earth thirteen times. The Moon keeps its face to us, while we turn and turn, once a day. The other planets do not spin, but make their circles about the centre. Watch.'

He worked the orrery, and the planets danced for Benzamir. Each individual ring was inscribed with its Arabic name: Zuhra, Ard, Quamar, Merrikh, Mushtarie, Zuhal.

'The planets fall out of alignment after four or five years, and need to be reset by making your own observations. It is a toy, though a very beautiful one.'

'Don't you use it to teach with?' asked Benzamir. 'Such a thing is worth any amount of explanation.'

'The people here – well, they are not scholars. They fish. They grow crops. They keep sheep and goats and camels and cows. To know when Venus rises, or when Saturn and Jupiter are in conjunction? It might be interesting, but it is not necessary.' Bin Haji stopped winding, and sat back on his haunches. 'They are not ignorant, but their priorities direct their learning.'

'Yes, of course. My people value learning highly. We're always looking for the opportunity to learn something new.' Benzamir peered into the heart of the machine. He could see the toothed cogs and wheels. Each one would have to have been cut with great accuracy by hand. 'Where was this made?'

'In the west. Misr El Mahrosa perhaps, or in lost Iskandariya. Long before I was born.'

'Could it be made now? I mean, are there craftsmen who could replicate this? There's so much engineering and astronomy that's gone into this: differential gearing, the understanding of elliptical orbits, even the rings are angled slightly from the ecliptic.'

'I do not know. You would have to go and ask,' said the imam quietly.

Benzamir looked up, troubled by Bin Haji's sudden change of tone. 'Have I said something out of turn?'

'You use words that I do not understand, yet you use them with complete familiarity. Again I ask you, where are you from?'

'From here, originally. My ancestors lived in the Atlas mountains.'

'How many generations ago did your people leave? There are no clans up there you could belong to. You are too different.'

'We left seven hundred years ago, before the world turned. We left in ships that landed on strange shores, beyond . . . beyond wherever you think of as far away. Now it's my privilege to return. Of all my people, I'm the first to make the long journey back.' Benzamir smiled in what he hoped was a friendly fashion. 'It's changed less than I thought.'

Bin Haji looked sceptically at him. 'Aside from north being south and south being north.'

'I'm a son of the desert, as the sheikh says. The stories of my forebears live in me. I'm not so different after all.'

'You would do well to guard your tongue. Talk of "differential gearing" is likely to lose you friends and risk you being mistaken for a sorcerer.'

'That would be bad, I take it.'

'You would be stoned. Or drowned.'

'Ah. Thanks for the warning.' Benzamir stood. 'I don't want to outstay my welcome. You have evening prayers to attend to.'

'You are a confusing man, Benzamir Mahmood. I would have you down as a Kenyan spy were it not clear that you had never heard of them before.' The imam started to close up the orrery, and Benzamir put the books carefully back in the trunk.

'*Salam alaykum*, Imam.'

They exchanged kisses on their cheeks. 'Why do you search for stars that fall from the sky?' asked the imam.

'Because it's a sign that my enemies are near. If you hear of such things, send word at once.'

'Where should I tell the messenger to go?'

'Everywhere. Sooner or later, he'll find me. After all, that's how I'm having to search.'

Benzamir took his leave and walked back through the

mosque. The first few worshippers had arrived, and the low murmur of voices filled the hall. He was almost out into the light when someone tugged the hem of his jellaba.

He looked down and saw the boy he'd noticed at the side of the road.

'*Salam*, little one.'

The boy said nothing, just looked around and stepped behind a pillar. It was hardly inconspicuous, but the boy thought it would do.

Benzamir followed him, and sat on his haunches in the dust and shadow.

'What's your name?'

'Wahir,' said the boy.

'Is this about Hassan Ibn Alam?'

'Yes. I heard him by the stables. He wishes you dead.'

'Wahir, my friend, this isn't news. He seems to be a man of great passions. It'd be better for everyone if he had more self-control, but who am I to change him?'

Wahir looked around again. 'He means to follow you and kill you in an ambush,' he whispered. 'He cannot kill you while you are under his father's roof, but the moment you leave, he will give chase.'

'I'm not afraid of Ibn Alam. I beat him once, and I'm sure I can do it again. But thank you all the same. I'll keep a careful eye behind me.' Benzamir was about to stand when he had a thought. 'You know your way around, don't you?'

'Yes, sir.'

'I need you to tell me some things. Things better said outside, perhaps – we will disturb the men praying.'

They stepped out of the mosque. The sky was turning a bold blue as the sun set, with a streak of orange on the horizon. They sat on the steps, a little to one side, and spoke between the muezzin's cries.

'I need to get to Misr El Mahrosa. How best would I do that?'

Wahir thought about matters for a while. 'By boat,' he concluded. 'It is the fastest, and safest. There are pirates, but fewer of them than the robbers who attack the camel trains.'

'But the only boat capable of making the journey is the sheikh's, yes?'

'So you need to travel to a port. El Asnam is not far.'

'When you say not far, you haven't actually ever been yourself, have you?'

Wahir shrugged. 'I am told it is not far. Some of our slaves come from the market there.'

'A three-, four-day walk?'

'Walk?' The boy was surprised. 'Are you not rich? Only poor people walk.'

'I'd share my wealth with you if I had any. No, hold on. The sheikh ransomed his ancestor's sword. So I do have money.'

'Then buy a horse.'

'I don't think I'm quite up to that. These camels – can I

get one of those?' Benzamir had in his mind the picture of a camel, but had yet to encounter the reality.

'Of course,' said Wahir.

'Then meet me here after morning prayers. You can help me choose one.' He spotted his sandals in amongst the neat rows of footwear at the mosque's door. 'Don't be late.'

CHAPTER 6

In the evening of the third day Va came to a breathless standstill at the gates of Moskva.

For half a day the dark, smoky haze that hid the great city from view had been visible on the horizon as a growing cloud. For the past hour he had run along a wide, flagged road raised up above the level of the fields that lay dormant, waiting for summer sun. As he finally approached, he could see the endless wall of wooden stakes that ringed the city. Each was cut from a single pine, bound to its neighbour with iron, and sharpened. There were towers – some of stone, some of wood, some of great antiquity and others newly built – that marked the perimeter. At the base of the wall there were bundles of sticks, points outwards, nailed into place. Beyond that, a steep-sided ditch filled with icy water. Further out, a killing ground for archers, where all cover was ruthlessly cut back and back until it was bare earth.

This was Moskva the never-conquered, the ancient still-beating heart of his adopted country, whose gates had been closed against him.

Va had been in the city before, many years ago. They said that all human life was on show in Moskva, and he had seen and heard enough to convince him of that. But on the outside, as he stared up at the massive, tar-painted gates studded with nails, the city showed its other side: not the welcoming embrace of Mother Russia, but the stern, distant father who turned his back on his needy children.

'Let me in.' He banged his fist on the rough wood. He couldn't have been the only man ever to do this, even if he was going to be the first man to be successful. 'I need to see His Holiness the patriarch, and I need to see him now.'

Of course, he was going to be ignored. The sun was setting in the east and the four gates had been barred for the night; the guards safe behind the walls had no reason at all to open up for some indigent monk. He was going to have to find them a reason, and to do that, he had to get them talking.

He carried on hammering at the gates with his hands, then prised up a stone from the road and used that instead.

'Hey, stop that,' growled a voice. 'We're trying to get drunk in here, and your infernal noise is distracting us.'

'Then let me in. I've got an urgent message for the patriarch.'

'Of course you do. Which angel gave it to you? Gabriel?'

'You can go to hell with your blasphemy. I've a message for the patriarch from the monastery of Saint Samuil of Arkady.'

'Tell you what,' said the guard. 'You give me the message, and I'll make sure I pass it on. You can't say fairer than that.'

'You'll go to hell with your lying too.' Va was certain he had their attention now. 'You have to let me in so I can give him the message in person.'

'Well, there's a problem, you see. I'm not allowed to. No exceptions. Now you just hurry along – there's a camp of sorts at the south gate; a bit rough, but someone will have a fire if you can fight your way to it. We'll let you in come the morning.'

'Right. Nothing else for it then. I'll have to break in.'

'Very droll. You and whose army?' There was laughter, muffled by the thickness of planking. 'Go away.'

Va rubbed the palms of his hands on the gates. Certainly no purchase there, and there was no way over the top, either. The timber wall, however, had stumps where branches had been lopped. They protruded only a finger width, but that was more than sufficient for someone like him.

The first of the sharp stake bundles was a distance from the gateway. He walked along the foot of the wall until he reached it, and simply started climbing.

The light was failing fast. He realized he should have chosen the east gate to make his entrance, but there hadn't been time. He had to feel for each handhold, remember where it was when he needed it for his foot. It was clear that the guards didn't expect anyone to be able to do what he was doing now, and equally clear that was because they lacked the imagination to do so. His hands were as rough and hard as stone. His feet were strips of leather. It was as if he stuck to the wood, and it was an effort to peel his limbs away from its surface.

He was now halfway up. The distance below was more than enough to kill him if he fell; uncontrolled, he would hit the spikes or plummet into the ditch. He knew of ways of breaking his fall, but he was out of practice.

Better not to fall at all then. He kept on climbing, fingers reaching out for the next grip. His legs, having run so far for so long, started to fail. He felt the first stab of cramp in his thighs.

Then, from behind him, the sound of hooves plodding wearily on.

He didn't look round. 'Not now, woman. Please, not now.' He was nearly three-quarters there. Twice his height left to reach the top of the palisade. If someone spotted him – a guard not down below drinking shots of vodka – he was easy prey. A swift stab with a spear, a swipe with a sword, and it would be all over.

'Va? Is that you, Va?' she called up. 'What do you think you're doing?'

'Quiet,' he hissed, as loudly as he dared.

'You can't do that.'

His left foot slipped from the minuscule knot it was balanced on. He was ready for it, and was able to transfer the extra weight onto his other foot.

Elenya's voice carried into the darkening night. 'There are laws against that sort of thing.'

He screwed his eyes up against the pain and swallowed hard. He had to make a dash for the top. One last effort. Hand over hand, trailing his spasming leg behind him. He wedged his fist in the V-shaped gap between two trunks just as his other leg betrayed him.

His wrist jerked hard as he dropped, and he gasped. So did Elenya, down below. His hold stayed firm, and using his free hand he grabbed at the top of the wall. No matter that as he groped and grasped, he filled his palm with splinters; he pulled hard and got his body into a position from which he could swing his right leg up and over.

He landed with a graceless thud on the parapet. He started to stand, somehow missed the ground and slid back down. A moment later there was a curse and a cry, and the sound of feet banging down on wooden boards. The leaf blade of a spear point was pressed against his throat.

'Give me a reason why I shouldn't kill you.'

'I have a message for the patriarch,' panted Va, his voice twisted in agony. He tried to straighten his leg, but it wouldn't work. 'I told you that before.'

'I heard you talking to my captain,' said the guard. He

searched the battlements for a grappling hook and rope, or a scaling ladder. 'How did you get up here?'

'I climbed. God lent me the strength.'

'No, really. How did you get up here?'

'Are you deaf, man? I told you. I climbed. Now, take me to see this captain of yours. I have to see the patriarch tonight, and you're delaying me.'

The guard's leather armour creaked as he bent down. 'You're in no position to make demands of me. Only thieves and bandits come over the wall. Good people use the door. You're my prisoner and don't you forget it.' He reinforced the point with a sharp jab of his spear.

Va ignored the poke and finally managed to stretch out his leg. He pulled hard on his foot to put his hamstring under tension. 'Then I surrender to you. What's the first thing you do to prisoners?'

'Apart from rough them up a bit? Take them to see the captain.'

'Then, by all that's holy, get on with it, before we both die of old age.' The pain in his leg was starting to ebb, to be replaced by aches that told of all the other injuries he'd inflicted on himself. His hands were bleeding freely. His wrist, the one he'd used as a piton to stop himself from falling, was cut deeply on each side. Now he'd stopped, exhaustion threatened to overwhelm him there and then.

He had to stay awake, just a little longer. Enough to

smart-talk the captain of the guard into escorting him to the patriarch, at least. He got to his feet and leaned against the palisade, taking the opportunity to see if Elenya was still there.

She was. When she saw his head bob up, she started calling to him again.

'Va? Va! Tell them to let me in. Get them to open the gates. You're not escaping from me, you hear?'

'Who's the woman?' asked the guard.

'No one of importance.'

'She knows you. Va? What sort of name is that? Short for Vasily?'

'No. I'm a Finn.'

'A stinking Finn? Barbarous Wotan-worshippers all. How dare you set foot on Christian soil.' The spear glittered in the dark, poised for a blow. 'Who's the woman? The truth this time.'

'I told you the truth. It's a sin to lie.' Va staggered upright and stood his ground.

'Gah. Captain Mikhaelov will beat a confession from you. Get moving.'

They walked the narrow parapet back to the gatehouse, through an open door and down a staircase. Halfway, wood gave way to masonry, and the sounds and smells of a meal wafted up. It served to remind Va that he hadn't eaten all day.

As they reached the door of the guardroom, he felt a boot

in his back. Too late and too tired to ride the blow, Va sprawled face-first onto the mouldy straw on the floor.

Everything was silent for a moment, before someone started laughing and the rest joined in.

'What's this? The cat's caught a mouse? How many times have we told you, Boris? Don't play with your food.'

Va picked himself up, and the laughter drained away again. He blinked his eyes in the hot, smoky air. Five men were sitting around a table. There was bread and soup, and drink. A fire in a brick hearth. A sword was drawn, ringing, from its scabbard, and he focused on the man at the head of the table.

'Captain Mikhaelov? I have a message for the patriarch.'

'Not you again? I'll give you this: you're persistent.' The captain had a round belly that hung over his sword belt, and a huge beard streaked with grey, which he brushed away from his face. He looked like he was peering out from the undergrowth.

'There's a woman with him,' said the guard whom Va had allowed to capture him. 'She's outside the walls.'

'A woman, eh? You dress in a monk's habit, yet you get to keep your bed warm at night. Good work, I say. That makes much more sense than sticking to some cock-and-bull story about needing to see His Holiness.' Mikhaelov stood and his chair fell over behind him. 'Get her in here, and make damn sure there's no one else skulking around in the night before you open the gate.'

The four other men left, muttering at having their meal interrupted.

'That your blood, or someone else's?' said Mikhaelov, pointing at Va's hands.

'Mine. You wouldn't let me in. I climbed the wall. I have to see the patriarch.'

'He's a Finnish spy,' said the guard called Boris. 'Don't listen to him.'

'A Finn, eh? Taken a break from sacrificing virgins to your odious heathen gods to bother us God-fearing Rus?' The captain swaggered across the floor, swinging his sword as he walked. 'I've the right to put your head on a spike and feed your body to the dogs. Don't suppose for a moment that I won't. Recite the Troparion of Saint Xenia.'

'What?' said Va, nonplussed for a moment. The sword came up, and he managed a little more: 'Xenia the Righteous or the Fool for Christ of Saint Petersburg?'

'The Righteous.'

'You lived the life of a stranger in the world and were a stranger to every sin. You abandoned comfort and status and wedded yourself to your Immortal Bridegroom. Glorious Xenia, call on Christ our God to grant us His great mercy.'

'Very good,' said Mikhaelov. He lowered the sword and sat on the edge of the table. 'How does Divine Service finish?'

'The choir sings, *Preserve, o Lord, Our Great Master and*

Father Yeremai, His Holiness patriarch of Moscow and of all Russia, and our Master His Grace Metropolitan Pavel, the brethren of this holy house, and all the Orthodox Christians, for many years.'

'Not that I'd know the real thing, but you clearly do. What's your name, monk?' The captain sheathed his sword with a hiss. 'Boris, go and find out what's happening with those sluggards. I'll be all right with the brother.'

'Va.'

'You've got balls, Brother Va, but breaking into Moskva is still a capital crime. What's so hellishly important that you'd risk your life for it?' Mikhaelov poured a slug of vodka from the flask on the table and, as an afterthought, offered Va a tot from one of the cups.

'I have a message for the patriarch. For him alone.' Va took the cup, drained it in one and passed it back.

'Something's happened to your abbot?' Mikhaelov handed Va a loaf of bread.

'My entire monastery was slaughtered by raiders four days ago. I survived only because I wasn't there.'

The captain narrowed his eyes. 'My sincere condolences, Brother. Where was this?'

'Arkady.' Va hesitated, his mouth poised over the bread. Then he tore into it, swallowing mouthful after mouthful.

Mikhaelov grabbed Va's wrist. 'There's no way you could have got here in four days. You're an impostor.'

'I know Systema,' said Va quietly. 'I could take you any time I want, sword or no sword.' He watched the captain's face go through a series of contortions, but eventually the man released his grip. 'I didn't get here in four days. I did it in three, as the woman Elenya will testify. Now, are you going to take me to the patriarch, or am I going to have to kick the crap out of you, your men and anyone else who gets in the way?'

There was a commotion in the corridor outside the guardroom, and after a good deal of yelling and fighting, Elenya was thrust through the door with the same sort of ceremony as Va had been.

Mikhaelov backed away from the pair. 'I suppose you're an expert in Systema too?' he asked.

Elenya brushed the loose straw off her robe. 'No. Just him.' There was blood on her lips, and one of the guards was cradling his hand to his chest.

'Where did you come from?'

'Arkady.'

'How long ago?'

'This is the night of the third day.'

'You're both bloody liars, but I'm going to get you off my hands as quick as I can. Kostya, get hold of a runner and tell him to go to the Danilov. Find someone who'll come and collect this lunatic before he infects us all with his madness.' Mikhaelov looked at his sword hilt, fingers twitching, but then thought better of it. 'Boris, you arrested him, you can get him out of here. Lock them both in the storeroom – anything – I don't care.'

'But the Systema. We should all go to guard them.' Boris was as shaken as his officer.

'He doesn't do that any more,' said Elenya. 'He won't fight you or anyone else.'

Mikhaelov realized he'd been made to look a fool. He spat on the ground at Va's naked feet. 'If I ever see these two again, it'll be too soon. Get them out of my sight.'

Boris motioned to the door with his spear, the point of which was noticeably trembling. Va tore the loaf he was holding in two and gave half to Elenya. 'I told you I'd get to see the patriarch. You should have more faith. Or at least *some* faith.'

'I've got every faith in you, Va. It's God I have grave doubts about.'

'Out!' bellowed Mikhaelov.

They left, eating.

CHAPTER 7

After the great mechanical clock of the Kremlin had slammed its hammer twelve times into the bell of Tsar Ivan and the echo of its final ringing had drifted away into the night air, the door to the storeroom was unlocked.

Va, asleep on a tabletop, woke instantly and dropped to the floor. Elenya had the ruder awakening. She had slid down against the door, and the door opened inwards.

'They've barred the door,' someone said from the other side, their voice rising with panic.

'Don't be so stupid,' she growled. 'Just let me get up and you can come in.'

They were still pushing as she rolled to one side, and the heavy door banged back against the wall. It made the gaggle of black-robed priests jump, and they had to reposition their tall hats before anyone noticed that they were awry.

The guards were staying well back. Va saw the truth of it: in the telling of Mikhaelov's story, he had grown fiercer and Elenya more wild, until they had become two untamed and untameable beasts of the imagination. They had walked out of the taiga, yet it was the city dwellers who behaved like ignorant peasants.

The greyest of the priests stepped forward, unsure of what to expect. He had listened to the message; he had heard the guards' talk. He was now confronted with a filthy, lice-ridden monk, more dirt than man, and a woman who looked nothing like Baba Yaga.

'You're the one they call Va?' he said. 'From Arkady?'

'Brother Va of Saint Samuil, Arkady. Father, I have an urgent message for His Holiness the patriarch.' Va thought his journey was almost over. In that moment of weakness he fell to the ground, his legs suddenly numb, his ears buzzing, his vision dark.

'Get a proper light in here,' he heard the priest call, and when he opened his eyes again, he saw the man's bright blue eyes staring down at him. 'Are you ill? Infected?'

'No,' said Va. 'I've run a long way. It must be catching up with me.'

'What's this? Woman, I was told you came on a horse.'

'Not him,' said Elenya. 'He didn't want to lead me into temptation. And you can stop calling me woman, priest. I have a name and I was born a lady.'

'The message, Brother? What's the message?'

'For the patriarch.' Va was starting to lose his grip on the world.

'Gospodova? Do you know what this message is?'

Elenya replied: 'I can guess at most of it, though it'll be as much of a riddle for you as it is for me. But it's not my story to tell; it's Va's. Save him if you can. If he dies, then I'll tell you what I know.'

'This is intolerable. Why have you come here?'

Va tried to sit up, tried to stand. Even with the priest's help, his knees kept on buckling.

'What's wrong with the man?' It was all too strange for the priest, who turned on the guards himself. 'Have you beaten him? Poisoned him? By Saint George, if this man doesn't live to see the patriarch, I'll have you all flogged and banished.'

Mikhaelov's voice could be heard over the heads of his men. 'We don't serve the patriarch. We're the tsar's men. Take it up with him.'

'And I will, you pigs. Brothers, lend a hand. We have to get him out of here.'

Va was surrounded by priests, who hauled him none too gently to his feet. His arms were looped around a pair of necks, and he was dragged from the room.

'Sasha, he stinks like a latrine, and there's more life outside him than inside.'

'Then give your place to someone who doesn't have such cares. Father Filip, get a cart ready.'

'Father Aleksandr, where am I going to get a cart at this time of night?'

'Use your God-given imagination, man. I don't need a horse – a barrow will do.'

By the time they reached the gatehouse door, a handcart had been commandeered from the front of a nearby shop; whether or not the owner had given permission was a question not asked.

Va was hoisted onto the bare wooden boards and left there while there was an argument as to who was going to pull.

'Get out of the way,' said Elenya. She elbowed to the front and took the shafts under each arm. 'Where am I supposed to be going?'

'The Danilov,' stuttered someone.

'I've never been to Moskva, you idiot.'

'That way,' said Father Aleksandr. He took one of the shafts from her. 'Are you younger ones shamed yet? Look, an old man and a woman – a lady, no less – doing your work for you.'

He started the cart rolling, and after a few steps both he and Elenya had been replaced. They walked behind, watching Va's limp and almost lifeless body bounce around on the boards like he had the Vitus disease. Va, for his part, lay on his back, pummelled by the vibrations as the priests hurried him through the midnight streets of Moskva, and looking up at the slit of sky between the roofs of the houses.

He heard the senior priest Aleksandr and Elenya talking:

'Did he really run all that way?'

'Sunrise to sunset, without a rest. If there was a river to cross, he used ice when it was there, swam when it wasn't. He slept where he fell, and he got up when it was light enough to see.'

'And where do you fit in, Gospodova?'

'I'm his shadow, an echo of a future that might have been had your God not got to him first.'

'You sound bitter.'

'That's because I am, Father.'

And he submerged beneath a thick black blanket, and was almost smothered by it.

He felt that it was a betrayal of his vows. He was lying *in* a bed, not just on one. Linen sheets were cool against his skin, and such skin as he hadn't seen in years. It was clean, scraped and scrubbed and pink. Around him was the smell of incense, and behind that, tints of stale sweat and long-dried bodily fluids.

The infirmary at the Danilov monastery then. In the cot to his left was an ancient man, so thin he was more skeleton than flesh. On his right was a younger novice, his arm a freshly bandaged stump. Further down the infirmary there were other occupied beds, and a monk at a table, reading intently by candlelight and ignoring the soft moans and fevered gasps around him.

He knew it had to be bad for him to be there. The old

man looked dead; the young man would most likely be dead in three days. But when he tried to get up, nothing would work. He was either drugged or paralysed, and neither boded well.

He found his voice, and it was softer than he intended. 'Brother? Brother! The patriarch needs to be warned.'

The monk on duty must have been charged with keeping an eye on Va. The moment he called, the man looked up sharply and carried his candle over to Va's bed.

'You're awake,' he said.

'The patriarch—' started Va, but he was silenced by the reply.

'I'll get him.' The monk hurried from the room.

It was incredible. Unheard of. The patriarch himself, His Holiness Yeremai, was going to step into this house of sickness and grant Va an audience, simply because Va couldn't get up. As much as he struggled with his arms, he could barely make them twitch. Naked beneath the sheet, unable to bow or abase himself, even prevented from kissing His Holiness as duty demanded.

'I have to get dressed,' he fretted. 'I have to show the proper respect.'

The heavy smell of incense overwhelmed all other senses. A priest with a censer, chain creaking with each swing, stood at the end of his bed. Clouds of blue-tinged smoke billowed out, filling the air.

Two more priests came in, carrying the sort of moveable screens the surgeons used for amputations. They set these up on either side of Va, blocking him off from the rest of the infirmary. Little black blood scabs dotted the unwashed cloth like flies.

Then two more appeared, carrying a great wooden chair with a small red cushion. Without a word, they positioned it at the head of the bed, then retreated. Finally the censer was taken away, and Va was alone.

When he looked again, there was a man, all in black save a white koukoulion that framed his serious face and mighty beard.

'My lord?'

'I believe,' said the patriarch, 'you have a message for me. Quite insistent, so I understand.'

'Forgive me, my lord.'

The patriarch stood next to Va, looked him up and down, then sat on the chair with a sigh. 'It's a long time since I've seen this hour of the night. My day is full of carefully controlled noise: petitions, meetings, services, trials. But here, at night, is when quiet chaos reigns. How is old Denis? Old? Listen to me. I have two decades on him.'

'He's dead, my lord,' said Va.

'That's always the problem of living so long, my son. All the good men around you are taken up to Heaven, and you are left behind.'

'My lord, the monastery of Saint Samuil, Arkady, is gone. Everyone is dead. Except me.'

The patriarch's hand went involuntarily to his mouth. 'The books?'

'Taken.'

'Who? When?'

'Four days ago. Many raiders, from the north. A witness said they might have been Turkmen.'

'Witness?' Patriarch Yeremai's voice was barely above a whisper.

'The woman Elenya who came with me. She witnessed the whole attack.'

'This – this is terrible. Do you know what was in those books?'

'Yes, my lord.'

'We have to get them back. Before they're read. Before they're copied. Before, God forbid, they're used.'

'I will go,' said Va, 'but—'

'There are no buts, Brother Va. You see, I know of you, Va Angemaite, Va of the Iron Hand. Look at you.' The patriarch gripped the sheet and pulled it away, exposing Va to the chill air.

Va looked. His white skin was crisscrossed with scars, lines of puckered flesh from swords and knives, pockmarks from arrows and bolts, patches where fine hair no longer grew and the surface was molten-shiny.

'You used to be a soldier, Va. Do you remember?'

'I remember nothing of it. I gave it all up. I could not kill again. I will not. I wasn't a soldier. I was a killer. A hired murderer who took coin and slaughtered innocents.' Va gasped at the memories, began to weep and turned his face away.

The patriarch's voice was slow and deep. 'Don't you feel forgiven, my son?'

'It's with me every day. Every time I wake up. Every time I lie down. Forgiveness for such sin is a lifetime's work.'

'And perhaps saving the world from destruction will bring you the forgiveness you long for. You could be at peace.'

'I will go. I've already said I'll go. To the ends of the Earth if I have to. But don't ask me to fight.'

'Is it true you know the Systema?' asked the patriarch.

'Yes, my lord.'

'You may have guessed, but you are indeed drugged. My advisers insisted on it. They told me that you were raving, and that a mad man who can kill with his bare hands, feet, knees or elbows should not be trusted. It's poppy juice, nothing more, and it'll wear off by morning. Tell me, my son: your monastery is attacked, your brothers killed, the books stolen, and yet you're still alive. How could that be?'

Va hid his face again, pressing it into his mattress as far as he could.

'Brother Va, you have to answer.'

'I wasn't there.'

'And why weren't you there?'

'Because I'd been sent away! Archimandrite Denis told me to spend a day and a night in solitary prayer because I'd got into an argument with one of my brothers. I've only taken the lesser vows and he won't let me take the greater ones, and after five years I thought I was ready.' Va's voice cracked.

'Ah,' said the patriarch, curling the tip of his beard between his fingers, 'here now is the truth of it. Guilt. It will break your spirit and corrupt your faith. But what would you have done? Would you have used the Systema to defend Father Denis? Or would you have died next to him?'

'I don't know. How can I know what I would have done? How can I know if it would've made any difference?'

'I need to be certain of the men I'm sending. It won't be just you. It'll be everyone who'll go. North, south, east and west. Mainly north, of course. I'll tell them what I'm going to tell you now. I need devout men who'll use every skill they possess, and I include skill at arms in this. The books must be brought back, and if you have to fight for them, I need to know that you'll fight for them. If a man holds one of the books behind him and denies it to you, will you struggle with him to get it back? If he stands in your way with a sword, will you pick up one of your own and strike him down?'

'No.'

'Not even if your patriarch demands it of you?'

'No.'

'Not even if the fate of everyone in the world depends on your one thrust? You'd deny them the chance to save their souls before they died?'

Va was screaming. 'You can't do this to me. I won't break the vow I made to God.'

The patriarch stood up. He looked down at Va and crossed himself. 'I had to try. I had to test you; to see how strong your resolve was. You cannot go, Va. Others will go in your place, but you must stay and pray for them. Your zeal is commendable, my son.' His words were kindness, but his face showed his bitter disappointment.

As he turned to leave, Va tried to lunge after him, grab his robes and demand his blessing. He strained and strained, just managing to lift his hand and claw his fingers. Even that little effort exhausted him, and it was far too late. The patriarch had gone, and he watched helplessly as the screens around his bed were carried away.

He was left staring at the heavy chair with its red cushion, a reminder of the patriarch's decision. Finally the two priests came to collect it.

'Tell His Holiness that I'm sorry,' whispered Va. They nodded, not looking at him, and hurried off with their burden. But he never told them what he was sorry for.

CHAPTER 8

Va slept. Not for a long time, and then only fitfully. He was awake as the Kremlin bell sounded five.

He found he could move again, although it was like wading through deep mud. His mind felt sluggish too, and that was worse. He needed to be alert. The amputee in the next bed was dozing in between fevered dreams. On the other side, the old man lay perfectly still. His chest had stopped even the slight rise and fall of earlier.

The monk who was watching over them had his head on the open pages of his manuscript, contaminating them with his greasy skin and drool. The lantern that should have illuminated his reading had burned low, and there was no light save for a tiny yellow guttering flame.

Va slipped slowly and carefully out from under the sheet that covered his nakedness. He found the floor with his foot, then his hand, then lowered himself down until he could feel the rough boards prickle his skin. He turned, rolled as quietly as he could, and reached up to touch the old man. He was cold like stone.

Untucking the bed sheet from top to bottom, Va delved inside until he'd found the hem of the old man's habit. He tugged it up, and up, and over the course of a half-hour he relieved the dead man of his clothing. He only had to kneel once, to force the rigored arms into a position where the habit would keep moving. He knew where to press, which ligaments to pop, to accomplish his task. He rearranged the sheet over the body and sank back down.

When he got the garment back to floor level, he discovered it was in a ruinous state. It stank of post-mortem bowel movements and a decade's worth of foetid toil. But it only had to be worn for a minute, just long enough, and it would have to do.

He put it on, then crawled on his belly under the beds until he'd made it to the door. This was the moment of greatest risk. Not all the patients were asleep, and many of those who were slept lightly. It would only take one of them to cry out, ask for water or prayer, and he'd be found.

There was a metal ring latch, inherently noisy, but Va raised the bar with the tip of his finger and dug at the frame with his other hand. When the door opened a fraction, he let the latch back down on its stop. He knew how wide the gap had to be for him to slip out. He did it quickly and calmly, knowing that a fast-moving hinge was less likely to creak like a ship at sea than a slow one.

He checked outside, and slipped unseen into the cloisters.

He pulled the door back to almost closed and drew his hood over his head.

The Danilov was a maze of buildings, a collection of architecture that stretched all the way back to before the Reversal. It worked to Va's advantage in that no one would challenge him if he moved purposefully, but against him because he would have to quickly find a way out, and not spend the remaining time until dawn blundering around getting lost.

He chose to circumnavigate the enclosed cloisters and examine the structures all around. On one side was a church, its five domes gazing up in pregnant contemplation. There must be a door leading into it, and Va picked the most likely one.

The flavour of incense flooded his lungs, and the pinprick light of candles showed him the way. His bare feet made no sound as they crossed the tiled floor, and his shadow was unseen behind the row of pillars that led first to the north, then the east end of the basilica. He ran his hand over an iron-bound chest of vestments, but he had no beard to speak of; he'd never pass as a priest.

When he turned and looked down the length of the nave, he saw that there was a man at the altar, prostrate before the icon, hands outstretched on the floor. For a moment he struggled with the urge to join him, throw himself down and acknowledge his betrayal, his stark disobedience of the patriarch. There was a higher calling, though. God Himself. Va's guts went through turmoil as he clenched his fists and broke into a cold sweat.

It passed, and he left the lone penitent to his vigil. He opened a small door set into the great east porch, and was outside.

Because he had not been conscious when he arrived, he didn't know which way to turn. The Danilov probably had more than one gate, and even though inside Moskva's walls, those gates were going to be guarded. He had to be careful.

He orientated himself using the night sky and the beginnings of the dawn's air-glow in the far north-west. The paths were mostly deserted, and there was plenty of shadow to hide in when someone passed by. At one corner he turned and saw the flicker of bright flame casting shapes up a stone tower. That was the gatehouse he had to avoid. He cut through a series of narrow alleys bordered by workshops and storerooms, and came to the outer wall.

Va had discovered a weakness to walls, and it was this: in one direction, they presented a barrier. They could be as simple as an overturned cart in the street, reinforced with furniture and defended by a rioting mob. They could be as impressive as a city wall, sheer cliffs of finely cut stone tooled by master craftsmen. But they were only difficult one way. The other way, they were as porous as a sieve. Getting into a prison or out of a castle was easy for someone like him.

In the case of the Danilov, there was a stable butting directly onto the wall. He climbed the corral, up the sloping roof and onto the wall itself. He looked over to check he wasn't going to find himself in a river or a goose pen, then simply slid over. He hung by his fingertips for a moment, and with his toes explored the possibility of climbing down. In the end he dropped the distance, landed with his knees bent, rolled, stood and walked away. No one saw him.

For his plan to work, Va had to find Elenya. He traced around the outside of the wall until he saw the usual crowd of indigents, cripples and beggars clustered around a bonfire. He checked their faces, one by one, until he found her.

She was sitting on her own on the ground, wrapped in her cloak, staring at the flames in the heart of the fire. She radiated anger, and it compelled the rest of her wretched companions to leave her alone.

The group was centred to one side of the gatehouse, clear of the road. There were bottles being passed one to another, with the occasional fight when someone hung onto the drink for too long.

'Elenya?' he called.

She didn't turn, and he stepped out of the darkness.

'Elenya.'

This time she heard him. Her head swung round and up, and without a word she left the circle and followed him.

'What in God's name have you been rolling in?' she asked him.

'It's temporary,' he said. 'Do you have any money?'

'Yes, a few coins. There's not much to spend it on hanging around outside a church in the middle of a forest.'

'I need you to buy me some clothes.'

Her eyes narrowed. 'Something happened. You're not supposed to be here, are you?'

'No. I need you to help me, Elenya, because otherwise I can't go and find the books.'

She stopped, forcing him to stop too. 'From the start. What are you talking about?'

'I saw the patriarch. He's sending out brothers, a whole host of them, to look for the books and bring them back. But not me. He says I have to stay and pray for their success.'

'At least you'll be where I can see you.'

'That's not the point.'

'It's *my* point.'

'No – think about it,' said Va. 'The patriarch is sending only those brothers who will fight for the books. If I stay here, I could live until I'm a hundred years old.'

Even she laughed at that. 'Why, yes. Isn't that likely.'

'But if I'd been allowed to look for the books, I'd be facing all kinds of danger. Shipwreck. Disease. Wild animals. Raiders. Followers of foreign gods. Those who took the books. I could be killed in a dozen different ways.'

She stopped smiling.

Va continued. 'Don't you see? The patriarch forbids it, so I don't have letters of commendation, money for travel or food, even anything to wear. I'll have to stay: stay and be safe; stay and live a life of prayer behind this wall.'

She did see. 'You can't guarantee you'll die sometime soon, can you?'

'No. I will try and get the books back. I will try to stay alive long enough to bring them home – though I can't guarantee I'll succeed.'

'And you're much more likely to get yourself killed out here than in there.' She patted her hip. Va could hear the tinkle of coins. 'If I were to help you, which I'm not saying I will, what would you do next?'

'I'd have to leave Moskva this morning. The hospitallers will discover I'm missing when they meet for morning prayer. They'll tell the patriarch's advisers, and eventually the patriarch. I'll have a head start, but if I wait in the city, I won't make it out. They'll take me back to the Danilov and watch me night and day. This is my only chance to get away.'

'You could always renounce your vows, leave the Church, and go and look for the books as a free man. That'd save all this sneaking about. Go in there and tell them you're leaving. That's what someone with some backbone would do.'

'But I'm a monk. That's what I am.'

'Yet you're disobeying your earthly leader. You can't have it both ways. You can't choose when to obey and when not to. Even I know that. I thought you were a man of integrity, Va, but it turns out you're just like the rest of your God-bothering brothers.'

'I have to get the books back. The patriarch is wrong about me, and he'll say as much when I present him with every volume that was stolen. He'll forgive me and insist I take my greater vows there and then.'

'Do you know what's so frustrating about this?' Elenya hitched up her skirt and unlaced her purse from her belt. Va hurriedly looked away. 'We always take the most compli-cated, convoluted route to do everything. It could have been easy. You were in love with me, but I was horrified. I was too good for you, the great lady from the great family, and you were worse than nothing, a foreigner, a soldier-assassin, a murderer who was going to be strung up by his neck as soon as his luck ran out.' She threw the money at him and turned away, disgusted at herself.

Va caught the leather purse, aimed at his head. 'I wish that was still true. I'm still that man.'

'But you don't love me any more!' she screamed into the night. Close by, a big dog barked repeatedly and gruffly.

'Quiet. You'll wake the dead. It comes down to this: you've a better chance of seeing me die sooner if you help me now. Your shame will be over, and you can go back to your family and do whatever it is that noble ladies do. You can still marry.'

She looked over her shoulder at him and wiped away her tears. 'Damaged goods. No one will believe you've never touched me. I'm trapped by my feelings. You're trapped by your vows. And I can't stop feeling the way I do about you.'

'I won't forsake my vows.'

'Then we're both damned by our own hands,' she said. 'My heart's already broken, so I suppose it can't get any worse.'

He held up the purse. 'I can't take this. It has to be yours.'

'And the clothes on your back?'

'You'll own those too.'

'Do you know how stupid that sounds?' She reached out and snatched the purse away. Untying the strings, she tipped the meagre pile into her hand and sorted through them. She passed him two copper coins embossed with the double eagle. 'You need to get rid of that stink. Find a bath-house. I'll buy you your clothes.'

'Thank you.'

'I wish I could hate you.'

'I wish you could too.'

She refilled her purse. 'We'll have to be quick. Let's go.'

A city like Moskva never slept. There was always somewhere to do business, to eat, to sleep, to buy and sell. Va didn't know the specifics of which street to walk down or which door to knock on, but he could tell the mood of a place by listening and looking and smelling. The bakeries were firing up their ovens, the smiths coaxing their furnaces back from the embers into a working white heat, laundries were boiling their vats: bread and iron and soap were there to taste in the air.

Elenya bartered for unclaimed washing while Va scrubbed himself down in an ancient bathhouse. The outside of the building was blackened wood, but that was just a cover for the stone colonnades and smooth worn steps inside. Everywhere was the drip-drip of condensing steam, and rare shadows moved in and out of the mist while he plunged and scraped.

One of the attendants brought him a bundle of clothes. Some of them fitted, and none were too small. They were rough city clothes, not suitable for the rigours of the road, but he wouldn't say anything to Elenya. Most likely, it was all that she could afford. After five years of nothing but the freezing southern wind and a black habit, anything was going to be different. The boots were someone else's, still warm from their feet. He hoped she'd bought them rather than stolen them, and again he decided not to mention the matter. He washed his habit in the bath water when he'd done. He was going to take it with him, change into it as soon as he could.

He was unrecognizable to himself. Like the bathhouse, the outside was masking the true nature of what lay within. He was a monk, a man set apart from the masses to be holy, to pray and work in God's house. He'd put off one appearance and taken on another.

He used to do that long ago. Disguises helped him get close to those he'd been paid to kill. The voices of the dead said to him: 'See how it is. You haven't changed. Still Va Ironhand. Still the killer. Still the trickster. All you need is a dagger.'

He could see them all around him, pointing, accusing, showing him their ruined throats and gaping chests. He spun round and barely made it to the basin in the corner of the room. He vomited everything up, and was left dry-heaving, clutching at the wall.

'Mercy. Mercy. If I do this, if I bring back the books, will you leave me alone?'

He wiped his mouth slowly, deliberately, and when he straightened up, they had gone. A moment later, so had he.

CHAPTER 9

As far as Benzamir was concerned, a domesticated animal was one that didn't deliberately try and kill a human. He'd been around creatures that would sooner rip his head off than look at him, but he thought himself fortunate that the camel came with neither claws nor a carnivore's appetite.

It was the most disagreeable thing he'd ever had the pleasure of meeting. And now he owned one. Wahir assured him that all camels were like this one, and that it wasn't personal. Benzamir wasn't so sure: he was certain he could see evil intent in the camel's eye, just before it spat at him. Again.

He'd paid over a few of the coins the sheikh had given him to a man who seemed unnaturally delighted to make the transaction. All the camels on show looked much the same, varying only slightly in smell, temper and how much of their coat was moulting. He was led by Wahir, who seemed to know his camels well enough.

'What do I do with it?' he asked.

'If you want a saddle, you can get one.' Wahir pointed back into town. 'Have you really never ridden a camel before?'

'No. We're not a camel-riding people.'

'We'll get a saddle. You'll need to buy some water-skins, and some food for the journey. We'll need to eat.'

'Hold on. Who is this "we"?'

'You're a stranger and you need a guide. How else are you going to get to El Asnam?'

The camel sat down in the dust and started belching. Benzamir ignored it. 'I can find my own way there. I'm pretty good at that sort of thing.'

'But you're not so good around camels. You need me.' Wahir squinted up hopefully.

'And when Ibn Alam comes for me? I don't want you to get into a fight. People can get killed that way.'

'I can run quickly. Besides' – Wahir pointed to the camel, which was more or less happily chewing the cud – 'why don't I watch while you get your camel to stand?'

Benzamir was holding the rope attached to the animal's halter. He knew he oughtn't, but he gave an experimental tug. The camel growled deep in its throat, then went on chewing.

'You win. At El Asnam you turn round and go home.'

'With the camel?'

'As a gift. I can't imagine it'd be very good on a boat. Do I need to go back and buy another camel for you?'

Wahir took the rope from Benzamir and made whooshing sounds. The camel reluctantly stood on its four splay-toed feet. 'No. Only rich people have camels. Poor people walk. I explained earlier.'

The camel meekly followed Wahir. It turned as it walked and glared at Benzamir, curling its lip.

Benzamir stared back. 'None of this makes any sense. Neither does that thing.'

The temperature was rising with the sun. Men were busy in their fields, and there was a general air of industry which Benzamir felt distant from. Indolence didn't suit him, and he trotted up to walk beside the boy.

'Wahir, I've decided that you should teach me about camels.'

'What do you want to know?'

'Firstly, why do people put up with them?'

Wahir laughed. 'You're funny. Strange, but funny. My father says you have to treat your camel like you treat women. Beat them to show who is their master. Never give them a chance to stray. When they are old, get a new one.' He laughed again.

Benzamir blinked. 'You beat women? Don't they hit you back?'

Now it was Wahir's turn to look startled. 'Not that I've ever heard of. They'd be dragged out into the street and stoned. A woman doesn't raise her hand to a man.'

'Is that legal?'

'Yes. Why aren't you smiling any more?'

'I'm surprised.' He thought of his mother: anyone less likely to put up with that state of affairs he couldn't imagine. 'I'm not saying that I wouldn't fight a woman. But I'd never fight her just because she was a woman.'

'We don't fight them,' said Wahir; 'we beat them when they do something wrong.'

Benzamir tried to frame his response in such a way that would instruct the boy without showing how appalled he really was. 'I wouldn't do such a thing. My people decided long ago that it was wrong to hit women, or children, just because you could. We decided that it was not weak to choose a different way. Men and women should share both the responsibility of power and the duty of work.'

'How do you ever get anything done?' Wahir stood open-mouthed.

Now Benzamir was smiling again. 'If you knew anything of our history, you'd realize just how much we've managed to accomplish. I could tell you stories that'd make your hair turn white.' He slapped Wahir on the back. 'Stop gawping and point out the saddle I should buy.'

He ended up with Bedouin-style tack, where he'd have to crook his leg round the oversized horn on the front of the saddle. They were shown other examples with tassels and fringes: as Benzamir fingered the closely woven braids,

Wahir told him that flapping things scared camels, and that he really shouldn't go for ornamentation until he'd learned to ride.

He concluded the deal with an open slap of the palm. His bag of roughly made gold coins wasn't getting obviously lighter.

By now it was hot. Wahir suggested they rest at a coffee house, and with the camel hobbled outside, they entered the cool dark room. It was cramped, with rough tables, low chairs, the sweet smell of smouldering tobacco and the click of wooden pieces on a painted board.

'Backgammon,' said Benzamir. 'How odd to see something so familiar.'

Wahir ordered coffee and a sheesh.

'We still have to get our provisions. The water's free but the skins aren't, and you always take more than you need. I'll do all that for you if you want. Give me a couple of coins, and I'll try and get some coppers. I'm nervous around that much money.'

Benzamir sucked the top off his coffee. 'Is it a lot?'

'More than most people see in a lifetime. Though they won't say so, everyone is very envious of you. If you hadn't come by it from the sheikh, and by beating Ibn Alam in combat, I think you would have been robbed by now.'

'This is probably going to be a really stupid question, but why is the sheikh so rich and everyone else so poor?'

The shopkeeper brought the sheesh over, lit it with a hot coal and took an exploratory puff on the pipe. Water bubbled and smoke curled. He nodded and passed the tube to Benzamir.

'Thank you,' he said. He sucked in slowly, not knowing quite what to expect as he'd never done this before. His mouth filled with a sweet apple-scented aroma, soft and smooth. He grinned with relief and handed the pipe to Wahir, who was much less circumspect at his pull.

'The sheikh owns everything important. He owns the ocean-going ship which brings goods from the west. He owns the land, he owns the roads, he owns the harbour, he owns the well. On top of that, he taxes everything that comes by camel train. He takes a little more when we buy and when we sell. He takes a portion of a farmer's harvest and a shepherd's flock, a weaver's cloth and a smith's nails. My father says: *A little of everything soon adds up to a very great deal.*'

'What do you get in return?'

'We live in peace. For the most part.'

'Is that such a bad deal? People who are at war all the time – well, they're pretty miserable.'

Wahir looked sour. 'I think things should be better.'

'Of course you do. You're young. If you didn't want to change the world, there'd be something wrong with you. I haven't seen anyone starving. I haven't seen anyone dressed in rags. That has to count for something.'

'I suppose.' Wahir handed the sheesh pipe back to Benzamir. 'Everything was different long ago. There were cities that went all the way up to Heaven. People had these dream wheels that could make anything they wanted. Even the poorest orphan lived like the sheikh does – better even.'

Benzamir sucked on the pipe and watched the water bubble through the scratched glass. 'That's not really true. For every person who had everything there were a hundred – a thousand with less than you have. That's what my stories say.'

'But that was in the time of the Users. The Users took everything and kept it for themselves. That's why the world turned.'

'Wahir, how old are you?'

'Twelve. I'm just short for my age. I'll start to grow soon, and I'll be a man, tall and strong.' His chin jutted for a moment, and Benzamir recognized something of himself.

'Of course you will.' He ordered two more coffees and waited for them to be served. 'What else do they say about these Users?'

'That they thought themselves gods. That they could do anything. Allah struck them down and they were utterly destroyed. His mighty fist crushed them, and the echoes of it were heard all across the world.' Wahir was reciting now, with closed eyes, remembering what the storytellers said around their fires while camped under the stars. 'The land trembled, the seas rose, the wind was a terrible wall of sand that scoured their towns down to the rock on which they were built. Then they were gone, and nothing remained of them or their idolatry. Benzamir? Master?'

Benzamir shook his head suddenly. 'Sorry. Very vivid, Wahir. You've got a talent. Drink your coffee. We need to get the rest of our supplies.'

Wahir listed all the things he thought Benzamir would need. 'Anything else?'

'What else could a man need? That's a lot of pots and pans you're landing me with.'

'That's not much. It's only a few days, after all. Though you've got your own possessions too.'

'No. I've a fine kaftan from the sheikh and a spare jellaba. These sandals.' Benzamir smiled and puffed the pipe.

'But you have a knife, for eating. A razor for shaving. Oil for your hair. Soap for washing. Blankets for sleeping.'

'Not . . . exactly.'

'A bag for food?'

'I . . . no. I've got what I stand up in, and these two heavy bags of money.'

Wahir started to recoil. 'What are you? How did you beat Ibn Alam? Where did you come from?' His voice was rising, and Benzamir hurried to silence him.

'I'm just a traveller who finds himself on these shores.' He spoke quietly and quickly. 'I have nothing but my wits to keep me alive; those and a little luck. Or if you prefer, Allah smiled on me by sending such a rash fool as the sheikh's son to meet me. But if you shout about this all over town, the chances of me getting out of here alive are small to none. And you won't get your camel.' The best lies were those that so closely resembled the truth as to be indistinguishable.

The boy sat back down, eyed Benzamir suspiciously and drank his coffee. 'There's more to you than that,' he said.

'There is. You're the only one in the whole of El Alam who knows it.' Benzamir opened his purse and dug out three heavy coins. 'Go and buy me what I need. I'll meet you outside the mosque as morning prayers are called.'

Wahir nodded and slid the coins across the table into his lap. He looked at them, at the great wealth they held. He got up to leave, and Benzamir held him lightly by the wrist as he passed.

'I'll be very disappointed if you let me down, Wahir.'

'I won't.'

The light from outside flashed as he stepped out into the street. Benzamir settled back in his chair and noticed an ageing man on his own, staring at a backgammon board. He finished his coffee, picked up his pipe and walked over.

'*Salam alaykum, Abu,*' he said. 'I might not be a worthy opponent, but I know how to play.'

The man looked up and indicated with a nod of his head that Benzamir should sit. 'We don't get many strangers around here.'

'That's good, because they don't get much stranger than me.'

'I'll be white.' The old man smiled, showing two rows of yellowed, stumpy teeth.

It was just something else that set Benzamir apart from the inhabitants of El Alam. He had perfect teeth; perfect in every way.

Having fallen asleep to the sound of the streets, which seemed to come alive at night, he was woken by the muezzin's reedy cant from the mosque's minaret. The fact that he had slept at all was surprising; that he could allow mere exhaustion to come between him and novelty. It was hot, dry, dusty, altogether different to what he was used to. Perhaps that was what was tiring: the simple otherness of his situation.

Still, Ibn Alam hadn't attempted to cut Benzamir's throat during the hours of darkness, a darkness that was itself amazing; a night sky lit up with a thousand points of light, stars he knew the names of yet had never seen quite like that. The moon had been low and fat in the northern sky. It had looked big enough to fall on all their heads – yet it was the same moon that man had once walked on and his ancestors had looked up at. He supposed with time he could get used to it.

It was his third day, and by Bedouin custom he ought to

be out of the sheikh's palace by the time the dew dried on the ground.

Of course, his ancestors were Berbers, not Arabs, but there was little now to split the two.

He put the kaftan on over his jellaba, bundled up his spare and retrieved the two bags of money from under his pillow. He stopped for a drink of water, picked up his sandals, and that was it. He was ready to go, and it all now depended on Wahir.

The muezzin was still calling. He slipped down a narrow flight of stairs and into the courtyard. A veiled woman was drawing water at the well. It might even have been the same woman he had seen there before. She had her back to him as she strained at the full bucket.

Benzamir put on his sandals and walked carefully out to the well. He put his bundle down and picked up the slack of coiled rope. Eventually the woman noticed and gave a squeak of surprise. She let go of the rope, but Benzamir didn't. He pulled the bucket up and out, and put it on the ground next to the row of storage jars she had to fill.

'*Salam*, sister. I'm only sorry I can't do more. I must be away.'

He scooped up his belongings and hurried to the gate, leaving the woman speechless behind him.

The guard let the faithful man go out to pray. There in the square, kicking his heels against the central plinth, was

Wahir. The camel – his camel – was fully loaded and ready to go. All the kneeling creature needed was a passenger.

'Good to see you again, Wahir.'

The camel hissed its annoyance. Still, with Wahir walking in front, it would carry him to the next port. From there he could go and see the world. Even as he was straddling the saddle and tucking his leg around the pommel, he started to smile.

'Isn't this amazing?' he said.

'It's a camel. What's so good about that?' Wahir made the whooshing sound, and Benzamir grabbed a tight hold of the pommel.

He stayed on, just.

CHAPTER 10

He soon settled into the strange swaying motion, though it took more time to get used to the sight of Wahir walking ahead of him, leading the camel on a long rein. Wahir was his employee, an archaic concept that he understood but wasn't comfortable with. More importantly, Wahir felt that he was Benzamir's servant, and that would really not do, as it implied that through mere chance of birth or wealth the boy was somehow less important, less worthy, than the man. Respect was always earned, not bought and sold, and certainly not demanded as a right. Benzamir's people had moved on from such things a long time ago.

Still, he had a job to do, and part of that job was to blend in. These were his people: he looked like them, he dressed like them, and after some effort he talked like them. All that remained was to behave like them, but learning etiquette was acutely difficult, something he couldn't observe from outside society. He'd make mistakes for certain, and had to hope that he'd learn fast enough before he accumulated enough catastrophic errors to be caught out.

There'd be time to foment social discord later, if he was still alive. Right now he was a what-used-to-be-north-but-now-was-south African nomad, and he had to be one down to the very pores of his skin.

He made Wahir lead them round in a wide circle. By heading north towards the mountains, then skirting the fields that surrounded El Alam and going back to the coast, he hoped to throw off immediate pursuit. With a little luck, the sheikh's son would be so busy searching the dusty Atlas foothills that he could get clean away. He had no wish for a confrontation that could only end badly. Possibly for both of them.

It didn't take long for Wahir to leave everywhere he'd ever known behind. For all the boy's talk, his lingering looks behind him told Benzamir that his guide was in uncharted territory. To Wahir, El Asnam was somewhere over there, to the west. Between the two towns was an indeterminate distance marked out by an inconstant road. Nor was there any assurance that when they got there, there'd be a boat to take Benzamir anywhere.

Benzamir rather liked this part of his duties. He had the opportunity to go anywhere and do anything. The world was his.

'Wahir?'

'Yes, master?'

'And you can stop that right now. When either you or the

camel gets tired, stop. There's no great skill in pretending you're stronger than you are.'

'Aren't you worried about Ibn Alam?'

'Concerned. Not worried. If he finds us, I'll deal with it then.'

'Whatever you say.'

'So what have you heard about El Asnam?'

'Only what the slaves say. I'm not supposed to talk to slaves, especially ones that don't belong to my family.'

'But you do anyway.'

'They've seen places that I haven't.' It was as good a justification for breaking a rule as Benzamir had heard in a long time. 'Only some of them speak Arabic. But the older ones pick up enough to tell you what their homes were like. They don't live like us. They build houses out of wood, and it rains all the time.'

'These are the Ewer people, yes? What about their towns and cities?'

'I think they have towns, but they're not like ours. Imagine being wet all the time. I think they'd rot, and end up covered in fungus and mould.'

'Clearly not, since you've met some of them.'

'They're all taken when they're young. I don't think there are any old Ewers.'

'Perhaps,' said Benzamir, 'the slavers kill all the old Ewers while they drag Ewer children screaming from their beds.'

Wahir stopped and stared. His mouth contorted into various shapes without sound coming out.

'No one chooses to be a slave, Wahir. So be kind to all those you meet.'

The boy blushed at past memories, and turned to face the coast road again. The road was set back from the shore, on a shelf of land that sloped steeply on either side. It was only when the short, stubby grass that grew on the road itself was worn away that Benzamir could see the underlying substrate: it was dark, flat, cracked into a million palm-sized pieces.

'This road,' he called, 'does it follow the same route as one of the Users' roads?'

'The Users lived in a country far away.' Wahir was glad of having something else to talk about. 'These roads – we call them tar roads – were made by our ancestors. It's very wide, isn't it.'

'What did they use them for? What do they say now?'

'There were these travelling bazaars, dragged by many horses. You could buy anything you wanted from them. They needed roads like this because of all the wheels under the bazaars. They went from place to place, and there were gifts and slave auctions and games and processions. Like the festivals we have now, but much, much bigger.'

Benzamir nodded. 'We have festivals too. My people, we celebrate our Founding Day, and each tribe has its saints.

There's a party, and games for young and old. We tell the old stories of the saints late into the night, and there's no work that day. We sing together and play instruments. They're good days.'

For the first time since he'd arrived, he felt a sudden wrench of homesickness – not for some imagined ancestral homeland, because that was in the distant past – but for his real home where his friends and his family were. He was separated from them by more than distance now: it was the proximity of his enemies and the fact that he was alone that made his abrupt longing feel like a physical blow.

Everything was too familiar and yet too alien. These were his people, his cousins, yet they neither knew him nor knew of him. This was his country, but the stories hadn't painted the least part of the picture. He took a deep breath. The desire to pack up and go would pass. He would remain.

'Benzamir?'

'Just remembering,' he said, 'and thinking of all those nights when I'll be able to tell everyone about this camel boy I met. His name was Wahir, and he was a good and faithful friend. All the children listening will sit and wish that they could be him, walking a camel along an ancient road, the sun beating down on their heads and the sound of the sea in their ears.'

'Will you? Will you really?'

'Consider it done.'

'It's good to be in stories.' Wahir turned and smiled up at Benzamir. 'I've never been in a story before.'

'The story starts before you're born. That way, it doesn't end when you die.'

It was dusk, and there was no sign that they were on the right road. Benzamir wasn't concerned, though he could see that Wahir was starting to doubt what he'd been told. What if El Asnam lay to the east of El Alam, not the west?

'The day after tomorrow, Wahir. It's there.'

Wahir stood at the water's edge, looking along the length of the bay for anything: a hut, a boat, drying nets. It was human nature to build next to the sea, to catch fish from it and use it as a trade route. The absence of people made him shiver.

'And what if it isn't?'

'There'll always be another port with another name somewhere along this coast, even if we end up in Misr El Mahrosa itself. And there are always places to buy food and replenish water, and just perhaps get proper directions from someone who isn't twelve years old.' Benzamir laughed as Wahir's face fell. 'Leave the navigation to me just as I leave the camel to you.'

They collected driftwood and built a fire on the beach, which Wahir lit using a steel and flint. Benzamir got down low to watch him work the stone against the metal, the cascade of sparks that turned the dried cotton-fluff into glowing embers, the cautious blowing and flapping of jellaba hems that finally ignited the kindling with a hiss and a crack.

'You did that well,' he said, without adding he'd never seen it done that way before.

From the saddlebags came cheese, fruit, dried fish and bread, and they rolled out thick cloth mats to sit on. As the sun set in the east, they moved closer to the fire and shared what they had. Wahir had the tendency to offer Benzamir the first of everything, the best parts of what they had.

'There are lots of things that my people do that yours don't,' said Benzamir, 'but when we sit down for a meal, we're equals. I'm not more important than you just because I paid for this – and in all honesty, the sheikh did – and you're not less important because you walk in front of the camel. I tried to get you a mount, but you refused. That's up to you. For now, we eat.' To make the point, he took the only orange and put it in front of Wahir.

'Your people should have been crushed by their neighbours a thousand years ago.' Wahir didn't return the orange.

'We were. Then we discovered that our neighbours had weaknesses all of their own.'

Wahir reached around and pulled two pottery bottles out of the saddlebags. 'I bought these. I didn't know how good a Muslim you were.'

Benzamir took one of the bottles and eased out the cork stopper. He sniffed. 'Beer?'

'The sheikh drinks it sometimes, so it gets made. I know whose house to go to to get it.'

'I'm a very bad Muslim,' said Benzamir and drank deeply. 'Are you considered too young to drink?'

'I am a man.'

'Not where I come from.' He held out his hand for the other bottle. 'Still, one day, Wahir.'

'I suppose so,' said the boy sulkily.

Benzamir raised his finger to his lips. 'Horse bridle,' he whispered.

'Ibn Alam?'

'Honest travellers would have stopped for the night by now.'

'What do we do?'

'Get out of the firelight. Go down to the sea and wait for me to call you. Go!'

Wahir scurried away, the sand spurting up under his heels and leaving momentary white ghosts in the failing light. Benzamir stood and stepped away from the flames, letting his eyes adjust to the darkness.

After a while he saw movement across the old tar road. Two men, betrayed by their body heat and glinting knives and the rustle of cloth, bent double, running awkwardly to the seaward side of the rise.

'I see you, Hassan Ibn Alam,' he called. 'Coming like a thief in the night to rob me of my life.'

The men stopped, crouched down and hissed at each other like cats.

'Said? Have you got yourself involved in this folly too?'

There was more heated whispering, and finally one of them stood up. 'Benzamir Mahmood, I did what I could to persuade him not to come after you. He says you have shamed him and you must die.'

'What's more shameful? To learn once in the light, or to repeat your mistake in the dark? Be wise, Ibn Alam.'

The second man screamed his frustration. He rose up in front of Said and unsheathed his sword. It wasn't the sword of his ancestors.

'You'll pay for what you've done to me.'

'This time I have the option of putting you backwards on a *camel* and sending you home.'

'We're ready for you this time. You won't defeat both of us.' Ibn Alam got the corner of Said's kaftan and pulled him ahead.

'Said's heart isn't in this. I'd much prefer that you sit down with me and the boy and eat. I did what I did to earn your father's favour, not to slight you. Come, sit by the fire. I will apologize, and your honour will be repaired.'

'My honour will be repaired when I parade your head on a spear.' Ibn Alam came down the slope to the beach. Said tried to hold him back, and was brushed roughly away.

'You can't hurt me,' said Benzamir calmly. 'I won't allow

it. I have too many important things to do to let you kill me.' He could see Ibn Alam's face clearly now, ruddy in the reflected firelight. It was hard and dark with fury.

Ibn Alam lunged with his sword. The point flickered near Benzamir's throat and turned away at the last moment. He stepped back on the ball of his foot, spun, and tried to slice him in two at waist level. The sword twisted itself in his grasp and his hand flew open. The weapon skittered across the sand and Ibn Alam held his wrist.

'What is this?' he gasped.

Benzamir shrugged. 'I could explain, but you wouldn't understand. Just go, before you do yourself any more damage.'

Ibn Alam's response was to pull out his knife and throw himself at the impassive Benzamir. The knife blade seemed to be heading straight for Benzamir's chest, but at the last minute he turned aside, and the Arab crashed to the ground. Quickly he was up again, stabbing and stabbing yet never connecting.

Said dragged him away, both arms around him, his own sword quite forgotten. 'He is a djinn! Run!'

'I don't run. I never run! Let me go.'

'Flee, I say. While you still have your skin.'

Ibn Alam broke free for one last deranged assault when he realized that Benzamir was walking away.

'Stand and fight, witch.' In his madness, he grabbed the

stumbling Said's head and put the knife to his throat. 'Face me, evil one, son of Shaitan.'

Benzamir saw what was happening. 'You have to put your knife down, Ibn Alam. You're angry with *me*, remember? Not him.'

'Then bare your heart to me so I can skewer it. Only then will I spare this dog.'

'Master,' gasped Said, and the knife pressed harder against his windpipe.

Wahir had come from where he had been told to stand, back to the fire. He'd taken a burning branch from it and was advancing on them.

'Wahir! No.'

'But Said is a good man.'

'I know. Let me deal with this.' Benzamir straightened his right arm and pointed with his index finger at Ibn Alam. 'Release Said. Wahir is right. He's a good man, and you're not.'

'I will kill him first, then the boy, then you.'

'No. You won't. I can't allow this.' Benzamir raised the thumb on his outstretched hand. 'Put him down before something terrible happens.'

'Who are you to tell me anything? I am Ibn Alam. I own this dog's soul.' He started to pull the knife across and back. Benzamir pressed his thumb down and there was thunder. For the briefest of moments, almost too fast to see, Ibn

Alam was illuminated in blue light. Then he exploded with a bang that was ripped out of the air. His legs and pelvis, burned black, were thrown to the white sand, the arm holding the knife whipped past Wahir, the other in the opposite direction and into the night. Of the rest of him there was nothing left but smoke and ruin.

Said fell on his face, convinced he was dead. It was only Wahir's screams that made him look up.

Benzamir crouched down and rolled him over to extinguish the flames flickering away on the back of his kaftan. Said tried to crawl away, digging himself into the beach.

'Is the cut deep, Said?'

'It is not deep enough! Allah have mercy!'

'Said? Look . . . Wahir, be quiet for a moment. If you want to carry on making that awful noise, you can, but later. Please.'

Wahir was miraculously silent, and Benzamir grabbed hold of Said and wrestled him to his feet.

'Don't,' said the man, stumbling backwards.

'Don't what? I saved you. I want you alive. I'm not going to change my mind.'

'What did you do to him? What sorcery is this?'

Benzamir put his hands to his head. 'I really didn't want this to happen. Both of you couldn't live. I had to make a choice.' He kicked at the sand in frustration. 'If it makes you feel any better, yes, I'm a sorcerer and I used my magic finger of death to annihilate Ibn Alam. That is not the truth, and I would like to explain it all to you one day, but it'll have to do for the moment. Are you all right?'

Said put his hand to his neck. It came away bloody, but he could still breathe. 'Yes. I think so.'

'We'll wash it out and bandage it up. Turn round.' Said tremblingly and obediently complied. Benzamir batted the back of his kaftan. 'A bit charred, but he was closer than I'd have liked. Sorry.'

'What manner of creature are you?'

'I'm just a man. Maybe not quite like you, but not so different either. Come and sit by the fire. I've got some beer, if that will help.'

Said walked slowly towards the fire, looking over his shoulder in case he lost sight of this devil in human form.

'Wahir, please. You too. I have a proposition for the pair of you.' Benzamir looked at the destruction he had wrought, breathed in the stink of charcoaled flesh and bone and hair. 'Shit,' he said in a language only he understood.

CHAPTER 11

The first that Solomon saw of An Rinn was a boy up a tree. There was nothing to do but allow him to stare and stare, and eventually scramble down and disappear. Solomon walked on along the ridge of the hill, then headed down towards the sea, towards the torn spire of wood smoke that rose, source unseen, from the cliffs. Clouds that continually threatened rain hung over his head, and everything seeped damp. His boots, used to plains dust and desert sand, were dark with dew and brown with mud.

There were no black tops – tar roads, they called them in the civilized north – to follow, and Solomon had the feeling that he'd come about as far as he could away from anything and everything. The Outer Ocean beckoned, and beyond that the fallen cities of the Users, full of bones and magic.

He passed the tree the boy had climbed, and stopped for a drink from his stone bottle. There was a trickle of water left, and up until four moons ago he would have finished it and thrown the bottle away, either to smash into shards or to be picked up gratefully. Solomon used to be that rich.

Out here, on the edge of the world, he stoppered the bottle and hid it away in his worn leather backpack. Then he shouldered its weight once more and walked into town.

He called it a town, but it didn't seem much more than a few crude houses, rough stone for walls and turf for roofs. There was a rutted track which led down between the buildings to the sea; it didn't stop, just went on from land to water. There were boats, little ones, bobbing up and down in the swell, and the paraphernalia of fishing draped over frames hammered into the soft, sandy soil.

He nodded to himself as he looked around. There was one structure that seemed more permanent: it looked like a church, judging from its isolated position up the slope. It was low, like all the other buildings, but it had a stone tower on one side, and a cluster of standing stones about its base. Grave markers of some sort. It had to be the church.

He walked on and saw figures in the shadows of the doorways, heads rise up from behind walls and duck down again. Then someone had the courage to come out to meet him. He wore a thick cloth skirt and top made of greasy wool. He carried a spear with a hooked metal end; carried it in front of him as if he might have to use it. There were noises behind him too, and as he slowly turned round, first the menfolk and then the women and children all emerged to see him.

When the last one had arrived, and Solomon stood in a wide, respectfully silent circle, he cleared his throat and announced: 'I am Solomon Akisi, and I bring you greetings in the name of His Magnificence, the emperor of Kenya.'

The man with the fish-spear looked around at the rest of his tribe and stumbled forward: he had been pushed by someone from behind.

He spoke. Solomon nodded, not understanding a word. He knew a good deal of World, but there were always differences in the way it was pronounced. He tried again. He tapped his chest and spoke slowly. 'My name is Solomon Akisi. I am a Masai, from the Kenyan empire.'

The native was a good head shorter than Solomon, but what he lacked in height he made up for in breadth. He was an ox of a man, chosen for his brawn, not his brain.

'Solomon,' said the man, just as slowly.

'Yes,' said Solomon. Trust his luck: he had fallen in with people no better than savages. 'Do you have a name?'

'Rory macShiel,' replied the man.

Then there was a commotion from the back of the crowd and a short – but they all were to Solomon – red-faced woman stepped out, her grey hair awry, wiping her hands on her already filthy apron. She turned on the rest of the townspeople, haranguing them at length, pointing and shouting and stamping her feet.

At first he thought it was some odd local custom, but then it became apparent that she was genuinely cross. It did serve one purpose, though. After a few uncomfortable minutes he realized he could understand her; imperfectly for certain – some of what she said had no meaning at all, but the sense of it was clear, and she used mostly World words. There was enough to work with after all.

She was saying: 'A man comes to us, and all we can do is stand and gawp and point and say to each other "Oooh, doesn't he look different to us – isn't he tall, isn't he black?" and none of you have the second thought to offer the poor soul so much as a cup of water and a how-do-you-do. The priest's away and you turn into a clutch of clucking chicks looking for a wing to hide under. Ashamed of yourselves yet? You ought to be at this fuss and hullabaloo. Where's our manners? That's what I want to know. Have we lost them under some rock? Should we go and search for them and come back and greet our visitor properly when we've found them?'

She paused to draw breath, and macShiel managed to interrupt her. 'Have a heart, Rose naMoira. What are we supposed to think?'

'Think? That's good coming from you, Rory macShiel. You no more think than you please your wife.' The woman held her thumb and index finger slightly apart and waved the minuscule gap in macShiel's face.

A boy, the same boy who had climbed the tree, laughed out loud, earning him a cuff around the ear.

'That's enough, Rose naMoira macArthur. You hold your tongue.'

Solomon realized that the focus of attention had somehow slipped off him. This had not been his intention at all.

'So where are my grandchildren?' demanded Rose naMoira. 'You take a daughter of mine and there's no issue. A macArthur's belly is fertile.'

'I'm warning you, woman,' said macShiel. For a moment he looked ready to gut the woman from waist to neck, until another woman, younger, taller, darker-haired, pushed her way through. She glanced up at Solomon, then stood between the arguing pair, arms outstretched, fingers splayed to keep them apart.

'Go home, Mother, and you too, husband. What sort of welcome is this? Apologies, sir.' She made a strange movement, almost a bow, but her knees bent and she held the sides of her dress for a moment. Then she wheeled macShiel round and marched him back through the crowd. Those who didn't stand aside fast enough caught his shoulder in their sides.

'Enough of him,' said Rose naMoira. 'What's your business here, Solomon? A good Bible name, Solomon, though I've never heard of Akiz.'

'Akisi,' said Solomon. He drew himself up to his full height. 'I would make my home here, if I am allowed, for a while at least. I can help you, if you would only help me.'

'There'll be no worshipping of idols or strangely named devils, will there?'

'I believe I follow the same God that you do.' Solomon pointed to the church high up on the hill.

The sudden panic at possibly having a pagan in their midst receded. The men slowly returned to their nets and pulled their children with them. The women had looms to attend to, and vegetables to weed, and babies to feed.

Solomon was left in the middle of the village, all but ignored. Rose naMoira was still standing next to him.

'Pah! Ignorant peasants, the lot of them. You'd better come home with me, Solomon. And mind, there'll be no funny business.'

It took him a moment to comprehend her, then another to take offence, holding up his hands in horror. 'No, no. I would not. Good lady, you must understand that you are fortunate to have me in your house. I will repay you many times over.'

'Really? Can you work a loom? Handle a boat? Gut fish and smoke them? Can you husband cattle or shear sheep? Work wood or metals?' At each shake of his head she grew more insistent. 'What do you do in this world?'

'I am a natural philosopher, good lady.'

'A what? Will that feed you and clothe you and keep you warm at night? Will it protect you from thieves and make you well when you fall sick?'

'I believe so.'

It was the woman's turn to shake her head. She led them to a square timber-framed hut, the gaps between the wood filled in with a rubble and mortar mix. 'This I'll have to see. Where you come from, are there many like you?'

'You mean philosophers, or black men?'

'I imagine you're all black, even the women. But what is it you do?'

Solomon ducked down very low to enter through the doorway. It was dark and smoky inside. The light from the single window shone directly onto the handloom that was next to it. All else was shadow. It was a hovel, nothing more. How he had fallen.

'Let me show you something. You must keep this to yourself for the moment. There will be time later for wonder.' Solomon let his eyes adjust to the gloom, then set his pack down on the only table in the room. He undid the straps and smiled, knowing that only his smile would be visible. 'Do you have a lamp?' he asked.

Rose fetched a lamp that smelled of fish oil, and lit it with a hot coal from the smouldering peat fire. When she put it next to Solomon, he could scarcely tell the difference.

He opened his pack and began to pull out the tools of his trade: an odd flat-bottomed jar, a cork stopper with a hole bored through it, thin copper wires scavenged from some rubble field, a small rod of white metal. Lastly he drew out a square of folded cloth and carefully opened it out until it all but covered his lap.

'Do you have any vinegar, or acid fruit?'

The woman frowned at all the strange objects and strange speech. 'I've some apple cider. It's on the verge of turning, and I was going to use it for pickling.'

'Bring it to me.'

She brought him the glazed clay bottle and a horn beaker. She poured some out for him as if he were going to drink it. He sniffed at its contents. The odour was sharp and unpleasant.

'There are ways of concentrating the essence of the acid to produce a more powerful effect. This should do for now,' he said.

He filled the jar with the cider, and stoppered it with the cork, making sure to wedge one of the copper wires against the rim. He slid the metal rod down inside the jar through the hole, and wound the other wire around it.

'What are you doing?'

'It is easier to show you than to explain.' He looked up briefly and smiled again. 'Look on the might of the Kenyan empire.'

Rose only looked doubtful. Solomon touched the wires to opposite ends of the draped cloth.

The cloth began to glow until it was bright enough to cast shadows against the soot-stained ceiling. The woman stared with astonishment.

She stretched out her hand and touched the weave of the material. Her rough fingers caught the nap, and as she pulled away, she teased out white silk threads that made their own light. 'How can this be?'

'The jar is what we call an electropile. It is a little engine, which makes the cloth shine. My people, we grow the plant that makes the cloth. Does this answer your question?'

'No. What's an engine? Is it sorcery?'

'No incantations, no spirits. Just liquid, metal and plant fibres.'

'I don't know about this. Father Padroig will have to be told.' Rose looked around at the inside of her hut, then wet her fingers and snuffed out her own lamp. 'Can you hang the cloth on the wall? Does it matter if the cloth is torn, or pierced?'

'Yes, yes and yes. It is all the material I have, so we must treat it with the utmost care. But it is strong, and there – I can drape it over that roof beam. Move the table closer and I can place the electropile on it.'

She watched as he undid the wires, and the cloth turned dark, like a cloud passing in front of the full moon. 'Will it last for ever?'

'Nothing ever lasts for ever,' said Solomon. 'The electropile will need fresh vinegar regularly, new conductors occasionally, and eventually the cloth will rot and fall apart. It will last a while, good lady.'

He moved the jar onto the uneven stone-flag floor and carried the table to its new position. He climbed up on it, though with his height he had little need to do so, and folded the cloth over the dark balk of timber. He adjusted it so that it hung just free of the tabletop, and climbed down again.

'What else do you have in that bag of yours?' Rose asked.

Solomon put a hand over the backpack and tapped his temple with a long dark finger. 'What is in that bag is of little importance compared to what I hold in here.' He reconnected the electropile, and again soft white light exposed corners that had not seen illumination since the roof went on. 'I am hungry,' he said.

'Lord have mercy, if He doesn't strike me down for being a fool and a sluggard. Sit, Solomon. Bread, fish stew. You'll have your fill.'

'Thank you.' He sat at the table. 'You have welcomed me, and I am grateful.'

She came over from the fire with a wooden bowl full of steaming stew. 'No more talk now. There's eating to be done.'

After he had eaten three bowls of fish stew, she took him on a tour of An Rinn, and ended it by taking him up the hill to the church, where they sat on the graveyard wall.

'It is very green,' observed Solomon. 'You are blessed with good rains.'

'It rains all the time,' said Rose.

'Interesting. So the stream is always full and never dries up. It is not so in my country. And the wind.' He turned his face to it, smelling the salt carried on the air. 'It never stops, does it?'

'I suppose not. Sometimes there are storms that last for days on end. There's no fishing, and folk have to make do with what they have in stock.'

'And what about those things that you cannot make for yourself? Where do you get those from?'

'From the market in An Cobh.'

'And how far away is that?'

'Two days on foot. More with a cart; less by sea, but the tides are difficult and the wind unfavourable. Why do you ask so many questions, Solomon?'

'Because,' he said, 'I need to know about you and how you live your life if I am going to help you. Things will begin to change here. For the better, always for the better. If you could, Rose, what would you change first?'

'You talk strange,' she said, 'not just funny, but strange, like you've been touched by some madness. Can you bring back my husband? No. So I'm still a widow, no matter what you do. I should be at my loom now instead of wasting time up here. If I'm to have enough goods to trade before winter comes, I'll need to make more cloth. We need pots and pans and needles and hooks and knives and linen, and if there's anything left over, spices and herbs and wax and tar and a hundred other things.' She got awkwardly down off the wall. 'Can you help me with any of that? I thought not.'

She stalked off, back to her house, and left Solomon on the hillside, pondering. After a while he walked over to a stand of tall trees and began to pick up sticks. He would beg some wool for thread to bind up the wood, perhaps even make some fish-bone glue. Some off-cuts of linen for little sails. They didn't have to be big; they just had to work well enough to persuade someone to apply themselves to a new task.

Then he'd show them just what he could do.

CHAPTER 12

ory macShiel was down on the shore, sitting on an upturned hull, caulking it with wool waste. Solomon watched the man drive in the knotted lines of twisted fibre with a bronze-edged tool, packing the joints between the planks to make them watertight. He used the caulker in hard, fast stabs, working off pent-up aggression. He didn't look like a man who should be disturbed.

'Sir?' said Solomon.

macShiel carried on working the length of caulk until the last of it disappeared into the hull. Then he looked up. 'What is it?' he said sharply. He reached into a bag and twisted up more wool.

'I have a gift for you,' said Solomon, and held up his creation for macShiel to see.

'I've no time for toys, stranger. I appreciate your peace-making, but there's no strife between us. Just between me and my wife's mother, the witch.' He drummed his heels on the wooden boards for a moment, listening to the hollow sound it made, then went on with his work.

'I'll leave it here,' said Solomon. macShiel waved without

looking, and Solomon carefully planted the main shaft into the sand. He made certain he got it as vertical as he could manage, then gave the wheel a little turn to start it moving.

It squeaked into life, and Solomon walked slowly away, back up the beach. He'd got as far as the first line of tussocky grass when a voice called him back.

'Solomon Akisi. Wait.'

macShiel was on his hands and knees, examining the rapidly turning wheel. He put out a hand to stop it, then let go again, watching how the wind caught in the four little triangular sails mounted on short masts, and especially how the sails turned by themselves as they spun round.

Solomon walked back. macShiel stopped the wheel again and examined the rigging on each sail, pushing it this way and that.

'What do you call this?' he asked. 'This here – the wood that holds the sail taut.'

'That is a jib. The line that holds it to the left or the right is simply a jib line. You can let it in or out, depending on the wind. This is only a model.'

'I know that, man. But look.' macShiel turned the wheel so that one sail pointed into the wind, hanging uselessly. 'The sail is crabbing. I turn it, and suddenly the wind catches it and there's force there. It's as if . . .' He looked up, open-mouthed. 'I'd heard rumours that this could be done, but I could never work out how.'

'My own people, the mighty people of the Kenyan empire, use this for their own ships. You are using square sails, yes?'

'Yes.'

'You cannot turn into the wind with them?'

'No.'

'You can with this.' Solomon bent down and began to draw in the wet sand. 'The wind comes from the north, say. But you want to sail north, to your fishing grounds. Currently you would have to stay at home and mend your nets, or be forced to row all the way. With a jib, and some changes to your hull, you can go north, fish and come back with a boat-load. You cannot sail directly into the wind, but by going close to it, you can tack this way and that, always close but never broaching.'

macShiel sat on his haunches, looking from the spinning wheel to the diagram on the beach and back again. He stroked his beard. 'What changes to the hull?'

'A deeper keel. There is a device called a freeboard which is suitable for small boats like yours.'

'Show me.'

Solomon drew on the sand again.

'I see,' said macShiel, and lapsed into deep thought.

Solomon was prepared to wait: he knew that with each turn of the wheel powered by its four swinging sails, what he desired moved inexorably closer.

Finally macShiel stood up and dusted the back of his kilt free of sand. 'What do you want in return?'

Solomon smiled broadly. 'Ah, we understand each other. Neither of us are of this land. You came from over the water, just like I did, though not so far. But we will not fit in, no matter how long the dirt stays under our fingernails or the salt sits in our hair.'

'That might be true, but it doesn't tell me what you want.'

'I want those.' He pointed to his crude model. 'I am not a craftsman. I want, say, four of them. Twice the size and solid, with good bearings. Each one will need a shield to cover the leeside of the machine, so that the wind will not slow the wheel down, only speed it up.'

'Four, you say? I don't know about that. The first one will be the most difficult. After that, maybe, maybe not. I'll build you one. There's a lot of wood, and maybe some iron that'll be needed. Not an easy task at all.'

'Your wife's mother has no right to call you an idiot, Rory macShiel. Two then. Build me one now. Then take one of your boats. Put a freeboard on it, and a mast with a jib. I can tell you if the construction is right. Then after you have sailed it to An Cobh and back in a day, you can build me another.'

macShiel flexed his great muscles, as if readying himself for the task. He spat in the palm of his hand, then offered it to Solomon. He saw him hesitate. 'You have to shake on it. Otherwise it's not binding.'

Solomon didn't want to appear too eager. Just the right

amount of reluctance was needed. He put on a forced smile and took macShiel's spittle-smeared hand in his.

'Done.'

Solomon called it an aeoleopile. Everyone else called it macShiel's device, and every day the residents of An Rinn would stand for a few moments on the hillside overlooking the boatyard, just to check its progress. They acknowledged the idea as Solomon's, but the making of it was both the wonder and the folly. It took shape slowly on the stretch of beach he used to make and repair boats. macShiel laid the pieces out, searched his seasoned wood and steamed straight lengths into curves, which he pinned together with oak nails.

Solomon fretted over the size of the thing. It was clear that macShiel had embraced the idea of the self-turning wheel, but not what it was for. Solomon wanted it to spin steadily and strongly, but macShiel built on a scale like himself, solid and unyielding. It would be a miracle if it turned at all.

It grew and grew. There was a frame, with little wooden rollers, to lift the wheel up into the wind. The axle hung down, which is just how Solomon wanted it, and he was able to pass on the measurements taken from a quern stone. The town's boys were a specific problem. They would throw stones at the machine, and laugh as they were chased away.

'Are we ready, Rory?' said Solomon.

'I think we are.' macShiel was sitting on the wheel,

rigging up the final sail. 'I can feel it wanting to turn beneath me. There's raw power there like a charging horse or a strong current.'

'Like a lion,' said Solomon.

'A what? What are they?'

'Like a cat, but bigger; bigger than a man. They have huge claws and great teeth, and they can bring a cow down with one bite.'

macShiel chuckled. 'Nothing like that exists in this world, man.'

Solomon bristled. 'I have seen them with my own eyes.'

'Of course you have. Now then, are you sure that brake is on?'

A lever, a massive friction brake, was lashed to the side of the wheel, and Solomon shook it. 'It is on.'

'Good – being up here when this moves is a sure way to lose a leg.' He finished the rigging and pulled the sail up. The wind caught it as it rose and it snapped out tight. The mechanism creaked. 'Do you feel that? Do you feel it?'

'I feel it.'

macShiel jumped free and brought up his knife. 'Now we'll see. Hold the brake.'

Solomon reached up and held the brake against the wheel. macShiel cut the rope tying it on. 'Let her go.'

At first nothing happened – for long enough to draw jeers and hoots from the crowd on the hill. They had not been invited and the event was unannounced, but the towns-people knew that the device was nearing completion.

Then the lull in the wind was over, and a gust caught the sails. The wheel started to turn, slowly at first, and gradually picked up speed. Soon it was flying round, sweeping the air with a deep swoosh every time a sail shot by.

It silenced the people of An Rinn, but had the opposite effect on macShiel, who turned to them and whooped and called and danced and lifted his kilt at them, shouting his defiance and triumph. They came closer, grudgingly. One of them was Rose naMoira.

'That's all very well, Rory macShiel, but what's it for?'

Solomon pushed the brake against the wheel, and it slowed to a stop. macShiel tied the device off and looked to the Kenyan for help.

This was Solomon's moment. If he failed to convince them of his greatness now, he would leave them to their ignorance and find somewhere else, more worthy of his talent. He unwrapped a heavy stone from its cloth cover. 'Do you recognize this, Rose?'

'Is that not my quern? Solomon, have you taken my quern?'

'Yes, Rose. This is your quern.' He hefted it and carried it to the axle. The end of it had been shaped to fit the square hole in the top stone. He had a small pile of sea-worn boulders to raise the bottom stone into place directly under it. He let the top stone drop slightly, and it fell into place.

'What's he doing with my quern? How am I supposed to make flour if he's taken my quern? And is that my barley, Solomon?'

'It is your barley too. Free the wheel, Rory.'

macShiel slipped the knot, and the wheel started to turn again. Except this time it turned the top stone of Rose naMoira's quern against the bottom stone with a rhythmic rasp.

Solomon poured a handful of grain into the hole at the centre of the top stone. The stone turned, and fine dust started to cloud out of the rim before blowing away in the wind.

There was a collective inrushing of breath, even from macShiel, who should have guessed long ago the purpose of the wheel. Solomon realized he had many more surprises in store for him.

Rose went to look at her quern stone, which up to that point had only ever been turned by hand. She took the pouch of grain from Solomon and copied what he'd done. More flour dribbled out.

'It could do this all day, couldn't it?' she said.

'All night too, if you needed it.'

Her eyes narrowed. 'If this was a spindle, I could spin thread on it.'

'If it was an auger, I could drill holes with it,' said macShiel.

'And a hundred other uses,' said Solomon, addressing them all. 'This is my gift to you all. Use it as you can. Rory macShiel knows how to make more if you need more – he has promised me his next one – but I have other dreams for you to make and use.'

'Next time,' said Rose, 'you should make it up in the town. There's not much point to it being down here.'

'Of course, dear lady. We must dismantle the device and carry it back with us.' Solomon leaned on the brake, and he could hear the collective sigh as the wheel hissed to a halt.

He had them in the palm of his hand, and it was all he could do to stop himself laughing.

He led the procession up the beach and down the main street. There would have to be a new building to house the device, but for the moment they could erect it at the far end of the street. It would be there when they stepped out in the morning, and again as they closed their doors for the night.

'Why you, Rose?' some woman was asking. 'My barley needs grinding too.'

'Because no one else would take him in except me. It's only proper that I have first rights. Besides, Rory macShiel's family.'

'You have nothing good to say about him, Rose naMoira macArthur.'

'Perhaps I've changed my mind, Shelagh.'

macShiel was fastening the oak nails on top of the frame again, and it was clear that he was listening to the exchange. He looked at Solomon, who nodded silently back.

'It's a good work, Solomon Akisi, a good work all round.'

'It is that. But this is only the beginning for you, my friend. You will soon be working on your boat, and then another aeoleopile. While you are doing that, you must think about what you want next. Is it true that your wife walks to the spring every morning and every evening for water? In my country, only the poor do that.'

'But we are poor, and blessed for it. There's fish in the sea, and we have meat and bread. We have clothes on our backs and faith in God above that tomorrow will bring no evil things.' macShiel hammered in the last nail and waited. So did everyone else.

'God said, "Be fruitful and multiply. Fill the Earth and subdue it." It is our duty to Him not to lose a child to sickness, to make our toil less burdensome, to break the spirit of this world into service for the next.' Solomon didn't need a platform to stand on. They all had to look up at him, except macShiel, and even he hung on the Kenyan's every word. 'When I came here, across the land and the sea, what was my impression? Of a land that was empty, untamed, unloved. Seas of rubble, not one stone on another. We should not go back to the ways of the proud and wicked Users, who brought destruction on their own heads, but neither should we grub around in the mud like base creatures. Are we not loved by God? Does He not send us good things, like wind and rain and sun in its season?

Does He not provide meat and milk? Who are we then, to despise what we are given? Are we that ungrateful that we squander what is freely provided? Are we such sinners that we show disrespect to God's magnificent creation?'

'No, Solomon, we're not. But these new things you promise us: we've never needed them before. Why should we suddenly need them now?'

'Are you children, or are you men? Will you not take responsibility for providing for your families? Who here will still have their wife grind their grain by hand? Will you, Rory macShiel, make the daughter of Rose naMoira turn the quern when there is an alternative? Will you force her to fill her jars at the spring when there is a cistern in the centre of town? Will you have a happy wife, or one who narrows her eyes at you and is too tired for contentment?'

macShiel was beaten, and he knew it. It had been a day unlike any other. 'I just don't know what Father Padroig's going to say when he sees this from the top of the hill.'

'He will thank God for sending me to you. But what is it that you want? Do you want me to leave you?'

'No, no. Of course not, man. We want you to stay. Don't we?'

Solomon watched as their faces told the truth of it. They loved him and feared him.

'Very well. I will stay.'

PART 2

CHAPTER 13

Solomon was looking out over the bay from his room in the church tower. He liked to be high up, to see everything in a single sweep, to watch the patterns of nature and consider their causes.

The boy Brendan called down from the roof. 'Master Solomon, I can see Rory macShiel's boat coming round the point.'

He checked for himself and saw the triangular lateen sail emerge past the black rocks on the headland and tack for the harbour.

'What did I tell you, boy? An Cobh and back in just one day.' Solomon climbed the ladder to the belfry, with its single bell, and then out onto the windswept roof. He leaned his elbows on the waist-high parapet to steady his telescope.

Brendan macFinn stopped pulling on the rope that wound through a pulley system and down over the edge. 'Master Solomon? Can I look?'

Without taking his eye from the eyepiece, Solomon

answered: 'When you have finished your chores. Would you rather carry everything by hand? Have I not saved you work?'

'If you lived on the ground like other folk, there'd be no need for all this hauling.'

Solomon did look up, slowly and deliberately. 'Do you tire of your duties so quickly?'

'No, Master Solomon.'

'Should I look for another apprentice?'

'No, Master Solomon.'

He checked that the boy looked sufficiently contrite, then returned to the telescope. macShiel sailed the new design of boat well, using the sail to its best advantage. But even with the optics, Solomon could see little evidence of the trade goods he had asked for. Where was the copper to line the cistern? The iron tools he had wanted?

'Something is wrong,' he said, and slid the collapsible tube together. 'macShiel has a face like a dark sky.'

'We say like thunder.' Brendan caught sight of the basket peeking over the parapet, and he swung what the African called the winch round so he could deposit the load on the stone roof.

'My saying is better.' Solomon started to climb back down. 'Carry on, boy.'

He tried to think what might have happened. The weather was good, the winds favourable. They had loaded his boat with cloth and leather of good quality. Those had gone, so he'd made land. Perhaps there was a caravan on its way then. macShiel had been able to buy so much that it would have to be sent on later.

He had all but convinced himself that he was right by the time he left the church tower and started off down the hill. There was much to do, and a caravan of the right riches would make his plans go easier. Progress wouldn't have to crawl along. While the aeoleopile was already housed and being used by a grateful townspeople, the pipework for the cistern was slow in appearing. It appeared that macShiel was the only real craftsman in the entire population. The others knew skills of one sort or another, but nothing that was of any real use. Even macShiel refused to teach another man, or take on a boy. He was saving his knowledge for his own non-existent sons.

Curse him.

There was another crowd around macShiel as he beached the boat and furled the sail. Solomon was fed up with these spontaneous crowds, as if they had nothing better to do than get the latest gossip. They were why his pipes were so long in the making.

At least they parted for him as he swept up, the hem of his robe picking up wet sand from the beach.

'Did you get there? An Cobh?'

macShiel threw a rope from the bow and waited for someone to tie it off before he jumped into the shallows.

'Aye, I made it all right.' He stopped to break off one of the arrow shafts embedded in his hull. 'I nearly didn't make it back.'

He waded onto the shore and thrust the broken arrow at Solomon.

'What is this? No, it is an arrow, I know that. What is the meaning of this?' the Kenyan asked.

'It means that as I sailed towards An Cobh, I could see black smoke rising into the sky. Most of the buildings are wooden: fires happen – I was worried for them but not for me. As I came into the harbour, a half-dozen men on the quay demanded that I surrender my boat in the name of the High King of Aeire. I was still a good distance away, and I'm glad they didn't wait until I was alongside. There weren't any other boats around, and that surprised me until I saw the tops of their masts all sticking out of the water.'

'Which High King did they say they served?' asked someone.

'Like I was going to hang around and find out! They weren't taking my boat, and as soon as they saw that I could turn round in a trice, they started calling out to me to stop. One of them had a bow and, God save me, he was good. I had to throw the cargo overboard or he would've done for me.'

'Husband? What's going on?'

'I'm all right, Eithne.' He took the woman in his arms,

and she saw the state of his boat over his shoulder. She pushed him back and started checking him for wounds.

'Not a scratch on me, wife. Leave me be.'

Solomon threw the arrow shaft down. It stuck, feathers up, in the sand. 'Will someone explain what is going on? Who is this High King? Why is An Cobh burning?'

'Who are we to explain the doings of the King of Coirc? He's annoyed his neighbour, and they've laid siege to An Cobh. The city still stands, for the harbour is outside the main walls, but they must be losing because they'd never give the place up without a fight.' macShiel swung his wife round by her hands. He pretended to be hard, but it was clear that he was glad to be home.

'Will they come here? Are you not subjects of the king?'

'That's not how it works, Solomon. The Kenyan emperor might command huge armies with – what did you call them: elephants?' macShiel's mocking tone burned Solomon's pride yet again. 'It must have got serious for the two kings even to have drawn their swords. It's a shame for An Cobh, but look at us. We don't count in the schemes of great men, and we're glad of it.'

'I cannot believe you take this so lightly.'

'If Father Padroig were here,' said macShiel, 'he'd say, "There's more than enough evil in one day to be worrying about tomorrow." Now, if you'll excuse me, I'm going home. With my wife,' he added pointedly.

He strode away up the path to the town, and the crowd began to disperse. Some of them started off up the path themselves, while others formed small knots and pointed at macShiel's boat.

'Don't you mind him, Solomon,' said Rose. 'It's bad enough with the sea trying to kill you without some fool with a bow trying to spit you like a pigeon. If he's angry enough, I might even get a grandchild out of this.'

'Can you see what this means?' said Solomon. 'All those things you cannot make yourselves I will never be able to have. An Cobh is in flames!'

Rose naMoira linked her arm through Solomon's and pulled him away. 'Calm yourself, man. There are more markets than An Cobh, though that is the closest and the one we've always sold and bought at. There's one at Loch Garman that I know about, south and west along the coast.'

'Will not your king punish you for trading with another?'

'Mercy, Solomon, why would he do that? If he can't keep his own house in order, why shouldn't we trade elsewhere?' Rose stopped him and turned him round. 'If that's how your emperor carries on, then I'm glad he's over the water from us. We're just simple folk and all we want is to be left alone to fish and weave. If anyone tried to take our crops, well . . .'

'You could not stop them, could you?'

'I suppose not, but we'd appeal to the king and he'd be honour-bound to help us.'

'What if it was the king?'

'You know, you're giving me a headache. Kings don't behave like that. That's not what they're for. They're supposed to protect the likes of us, not rob us blind.' She kneaded her temples with her knuckles. 'Do you understand now?'

'No, not really.' Solomon skulked off to the shore line and threw some pebbles into the slowly rising sea. 'If this is the case, why is the High King laying siege to An Cobh? What has the King of Coirc done to deserve such a thing?'

'Am I the king's adviser that I would know?' With that, she left him trying to bounce spinning stones across the wave-tops.

He had no copper for his cistern, and his design for a water-powered drop forge would have to wait. He did, however, have another plan. He threw the last of his stones and watched as it hopped once, twice, three times, then sank. He went back to the church tower.

'Brendan macFinn? Where are you, boy?'

'Here, master.' Solomon could hear scrabbling above him as he entered. The sudden sounds of industry could not fool him.

'I have an errand of the utmost importance.' He climbed the stairs up to his room. When he got there, he found Brendan standing exactly in the middle of the room, his hands behind his back, and looking nowhere in particular.

Solomon's gaze travelled slowly around. His copper still, taken from the poteen makers, hissed and bubbled gently. His writing set and book were tidily on the table. His light-cloth shone brightly enough, held on the wall in a wooden frame.

'What have you been up to, boy?' His voice was a low growl.

'Nothing, master,' said Brendan, too quickly.

'Whatever it is will have to wait. You need to take a message for me to the High King, who is currently at the gates of An Cobh.'

The boy blinked in surprise. 'But Master Solomon, I don't know the way.'

'Then you will have to find it. You are the only one I can trust with such an important task.'

'Master, I've never left An Rinn. This place is all I know.'

Solomon brushed his excuses aside. 'Then it is about time your horizons were broadened. Can you read?'

'No, master.'

'Good, for this message is for the High King only.' He sat at the table and started to trim his quill. 'Can the High King read?'

'I don't even know who the High King is. We heard last autumn that it was a man called Cormac, but the year before that it was someone different. Perhaps they take it in turns.'

Solomon dipped his quill in his inkpot – Father Padroig's inkpot – and opened his book. He turned to the back and started to write, carefully and with the occasional crossing out and furrowed brow. 'You will need, boy, food for the journey. The weather is fair but the night is cold, so take a blanket with you. I will seal this letter, and no man but the High King himself is to open it. If you are stopped by the High King's men, you are to tell them that the emperor of Kenya sends his greetings to the High King of Aeire. His name is like coin in the hand, boy, so choose to spend it wisely.'

He took a knife and cut the page free, then held it up to the light. Satisfied that it was dry, he folded the sheet up so that no writing was exposed. Brendan was still standing there, hopping from one foot to the other, in a state of high agitation.

'Master Solomon, please.'

'In my country, apprentices who refuse to do their master's bidding are beaten with sticks. Then they still have to do their duty. If you want to wait here while I get a stick, I will be glad to act as a master should.' Solomon held out the letter. 'Who do you give this to?'

Brendan's shoulders sagged in defeat. 'The High King.'

'Where will you find him?'

'An Cobh.'

'No, outside An Cobh. He is laying siege to it. I expect

that he will send men and horses back with you to find me, so you must guide them here. Do you understand what you must do?'

The boy took the letter and turned it over in his hands. 'Is it west or east of here?'

'East. Towards the setting sun. If you follow the coastal path, you will get there some time tomorrow. And yes, you must leave now. No going down to the town to say goodbye to your mother.'

'But . . .'

Solomon got up and stood in front of the boy. He was huge compared to him, far taller than any adult had a right to be. He held the boy's shoulders and shook him firmly. 'Are you not yet a man? How many summers have you seen?'

'Thirteen in all.'

'Then in my country you would be a man, with a man's privileges and a man's responsibilities. Why do they keep you as a child? Should I look for you playing with the babies, wiping their bottoms and rocking them to sleep? No? Then be a man, Brendan macFinn, a man your father can be proud of. Take what you need for the journey and be about your master's business.'

Brendan took a blanket and slowly descended the stairs. Solomon went up to the roof and watched as the boy eventually left and started off over the hill, weighed down by his provisions. He stayed for a while to make sure that the boy didn't double back, then went down to check on the still.

The smell from it was acrid, briefly burning the lining of his nose. It was a good, strong acid he was distilling, just right for his electropile. He walked around the room, checking by hand the things he had checked by sight earlier. He knew the boy had been meddling with something, or at least ought to have been. Curiosity was the best trait a natural philosopher's apprentice could have.

He had a trunk. It used to contain the priest's vestments, but he had emptied it out and moved it up into the tower. He opened it up and decided that the contents had been moved around. Brendan had been nosing inside, and Solomon thought it a most excellent moment. Even as the boy tramped the hills towards An Cobh, he would be thinking about the marvels he had seen. When he came back, he would beg Solomon to explain them to him. One at a time, and never enough, Solomon would.

He took out the heavy cloth-wrapped shapes and laid them out on the table: a set of three glass prisms that would not just bend light but shatter it into a rainbow. He dug deeper to find an oilcloth. He opened it out to reveal a brass machine that fitted into the palm of his hand, and another cloth that held a handful of steel discs, pierced in the centre and serrated around the circumference.

Further down was a big, solid object, wrapped in some animal skin that Solomon failed to recognize. This was his prize. He heaved it out and laid it on the table next to the prisms and the machine.

Reverently he unfolded the furry skin and ran his hand over the cold metal cover of a book.

CHAPTER 14

When they came, Solomon was outside the graveyard, making a crude model of his water-lifting gear from sticks and seed pods. So absorbed was he in ensuring that his makeshift axle turned freely that he failed to hear the sound of hooves until the riders were picking their way down the steep hillside towards him.

He looked up, startled, and saw six horsemen in a single file. Each of them carried a round shield on his back and a spear tied off on his saddlecloth. The leader, a man with shaved cheeks and chin but a prodigious moustache, held Brendan macFinn in front of him.

Solomon rose to greet the High King's men, and dusted his hands off against his legs. He assumed a formal pose and waited, a fixed smile on his face.

Then he realized that the moustached man had his hand over the boy's mouth. He dithered for a moment, unsure of what to do next.

Brendan bit down on the man's hand, and in the brief

moment when he could, he shouted: 'Master! These aren't from the High—'

The man grabbed the boy's shirt and heaved him off the horse. The other horsemen urged their mounts into a gallop. Brendan rolled to a stop and staggered to his feet. Solomon was still rooted to the spot.

'Master, run!'

Finally Solomon moved. He vaulted the graveyard wall and sprinted for the tower, his heart hammering hard inside his chest. He shouldered the door open, then slammed it back shut, fumbling for the single bolt. He shot it home and stumbled backwards. He was safe for a moment.

There were footsteps, and the latch rattled.

'Open up, Solomon Akisi.'

'Who are you? What do you want?'

'We want a word with you. The King of Coirc doesn't like it when his friends try to stab him in the back.'

The King of Coirc? Solomon swallowed hard. The fool boy must have given the message to the wrong man.

'I will not let you in,' he stammered. 'There has been a mistake, I am certain.'

'Oh yes, for sure. A mistake in assuming that the good people of An Cobh couldn't see off some pretender to the High King's office. Now, herald of the Kenyan emperor, are you going to open this door and talk to us face to face?'

Solomon saw everything in a moment. How the boy had

wandered through the remains of the battle at the gates of An Cobh, wondering where everybody was, when some vassal of the King of Coirc spotted him and asked him his business.

Of course, the letter had been taken straight to the king; warriors despatched to find out who in the land would offer his services to the defeated High King. How would they kill him in this country? Beheaded? Hanged? Drowned? Trampled? There were so many ways to die.

'Right, boys,' said the man, 'get him out.'

There was a brief pause, a grunt, then the tip of an axe blade thudded into view.

Solomon turned and ran up the stairs to his room. He went straight to his trunk and felt for the brass machine. There was a key on a chain dangling from it, and he managed to slot it home at the third attempt, his fingers shaking.

'Turn the key, turn the key,' he muttered to himself, even as the sound of splintering wood echoed up the stairs.

He got the metal discs out, scattered them on the floor in front of him and picked one up. He pushed it home on the retaining pin and pressed the whole length of the device hard against the stone floor. Metal slid against metal, and he leaned harder. The spring inside squeezed tight and the locking mechanism clicked.

He raised his arm and sighted down it just as the top of a shield raised itself above the stairs.

'If you move, I will kill you,' he said.

The man laughed. 'He sounds like he's soiling his breeches. Come on.' He moved further up the steps, and one of his companions edged upward behind him.

'I warn you both. Get away from me.' Solomon held the device with both hands to steady his wayward aim.

'Look,' said the first man, 'he doesn't even have a knife.' He lowered his shield and swung his axe in a practised circle.

Solomon pulled the trigger and the steel disc whirled around, shot forward and buried itself in the man's forehead, just above his brows. He stood for a moment, amazed and confused by what had just happened. The axe slipped from his fingers at the same time as the blood welled up out of the cut and down his face. He fell forward with an almighty crash.

Solomon concentrated on reloading: putting the key in and turning it, grabbing another disc, slotting it home, compressing the spring. As he looked up again, he stared at a spear point.

The remaining men stood around him, so close he could smell their sweat.

'Drop whatever that thing is,' snarled the moustached man. When Solomon didn't instantly obey, he stepped forward and put his booted foot on the African's wrist. 'I'll break both it and you if I have to.'

Solomon forced his fingers apart. The mechanism tripped and slammed the spinning disc against the floor. It ricocheted against the stone flags with a flash of sparks and buried itself in the chair. Such was the impact that the chair rocked backwards on its rear legs and, after an agonizing wait, fell over.

'Do you give in now?' said the leader.

'I yield,' gasped Solomon, aware that the bones in his fingers were starting to snap.

'Kill him, Eoin, and have done with it.'

'Trust me, I want to. But we've got our orders.'

'Look what he's done to Daibhi. Kill him now. We'll all back you up.'

'There's to be no talk of killing, Mici. He'll stay alive long enough to give his account to the king, and pay his blood debt too. On your feet.' The man called Eoin poked Solomon with his spear.

Solomon got up, nursing his hand.

'He's a giant. That's not natural,' said one of the men.

'I assure you all of my tribe are this tall. Some even taller,' said Solomon. He looked around at his captors. Mici wanted to run him through. The others would not stop him, either. Fortunately Eoin was in charge of the band of barbarian warriors, and they seemed to defer to him completely.

Unfortunately he had just killed one of their number, and that was going to count against him.

'On my honour, I will not seek to escape,' he started, but Eoin pushed him back and back until he hit the wall.

'Damn right you're not going to escape. Mici, go and round the horses up before the locals decide to stew them. Colm, find something to tie this butcher up with. In fact, Mici,' he shouted, 'get two men from the village and tell them to dig a grave. We'll need to send Daibhi off to his maker here. Manus, see if you can find the priest.'

As his men scattered, Eoin picked up the brass disc thrower.

'Careful,' said Solomon.

'It's you who should have been more careful with this thing.' He gathered up the discs and turned them over in his hand. 'Did you make this?'

'Not myself. My people did.'

'These Kenyans of yours. Where do they live?'

'Far over the water, where the sun is straight up at midday, and there is no summer or winter.'

'So we've established you come from la-la land and that no one's coming to rescue you. Kilian, watch my back. I'm going through his stuff.'

Solomon had to watch as Eoin ran his rough and ignorant fingers over his quill and ink, his notebook, then suddenly noticed the light-cloth hanging from the wall.

'Mary, Mother of God. What's that?' He pawed at it, and kicked the electropile. One of the wires lost contact with the cloth, and the light faded away.

'Please do not break that,' said Solomon, and involuntarily

stepped forward. Kilian raised the spear, forcing him back. 'It is of some value. Your king will not thank you if you damage it.'

Eoin looked sour, but desisted. He turned his attention to the trunk. 'Anything in here that's going to kill me?'

'No, I assure you.'

He kicked the box. 'Funnily enough, I don't trust you.' He moved some of the objects around with his spear haft, then put it to one side. 'What's this?'

He pulled the pelt-covered book out and dumped it on the floor. He rubbed his hand through the fur and slowly pulled it free. The book inside slid out onto the stone. He repeated: 'What is this?'

'It is a very valuable book, full of the most amazing secrets.'

'No, you idiot. This.' He waved the pelt at Solomon. 'This is good. Which animal did it come from?'

'I do not know. It came with the book.'

Eoin manhandled the book onto the table and heaved open the cover. 'It's like it's made of iron. Who'd do a thing like that?'

'The ancients would,' said Solomon, 'for their most precious knowledge.'

'A Users' book? Cursed thing.' Eoin turned the first page and stared at the spider-like writing. 'Can you read any of this?'

'Some. The more I study it, the more I learn.'

Eoin touched the next page and brought his finger quickly to his mouth. 'It cut me.'

'You must be careful,' urged Solomon.

'So you keep on saying. First your boy bites me, then you kill Daibhi, then your book has a go. It's not safe to be around you, black man.' He sucked his injured digit. 'This is what we're going to do. We're going to truss you up tighter than a chicken, then we're going to load all this nonsense on the horse we now happen to have spare, and then we'll let the king decide what to do with you.'

'I am grateful.'

'The Devil take your gratitude.' Eoin threw the book back into the trunk, causing Solomon to wince. 'If it were up to me, you'd be swinging from a set of gallows. But old Ardhal might have other plans for you, and I'm not going to gainsay my kinsman.'

'I understand,' said Solomon.

'And stay clear of Mici for a while. He and Daibhi drank together, got drunk together and, for all I know, woke up sober together. Don't go angering him.'

Soon enough there was one of the crowds that Solomon hated, gathered at the churchyard gates.

When the king's men led him out, wrists tied behind his back, a great murmur rose from the townsfolk.

'Where are you taking him? What's he done?' asked Rose loudly.

Eoin walked him up the path to the gates, a strong hand on Solomon's arm. 'Besides the fact he killed one of my men? He turned against the rightful king by promising to help another. There's a reckoning to be had for that.'

'Oh, Solomon, you didn't, did you? See now, I explained all this to you, and you wouldn't listen. *Don't meddle in the affairs of kings*, I said, and now look what you've done.'

'Hush, woman, and stand aside,' said Eoin. 'Manus, any luck on the priest?'

'He's not been seen hereabouts for over a month.'

'So where is he? Woman?'

Rose crossed her arms. 'It's *hush* one moment, it's *woman* the next. Which is it to be?'

'Just answer the question, good lady.'

'Father Padroig went last saint's day on a pilgrimage, to the Holy Shrine of Our Lady of Kilkenny.'

'And he's not got back yet? Shouldn't you be worried about him? Have none of you looked for him?' Eoin looked from face to face, and one by one, each turned away. 'Or has this stranger dazzled you so much, even moving into the church and turning it into his own house, that you haven't missed him?'

For once Rose naMoira was silent.

'So who's in charge here? Apart from the priest?'

Again, as before, a reluctant Rory macShiel was pressed forward until he was at the front.

'Are you macShiel? The boy Brendan said you and Akisi had a falling out.'

'He nearly got me killed at An Cobh. I didn't take kindly to that.'

'Is the boy all right?' asked Eoin.

'He could fall on his head from now until midwinter and not suffer. Thank you for treating him right.'

'He's only a boy,' said Eoin, 'though he should choose his master better in future. You need to send someone to Kilkenny, make sure that the father's still there. Can I trust you to do that?'

'I'll go myself,' said Rory.

'Good man. We still need to bury Daibhi in holy ground, so if you can find someone to lend a hand and say a few words . . .'

As he watched shovels appear and the green turf turned back, Solomon felt a mix of emotions. Foolish, for having done such a foolish thing: how was he to know that the siege of An Cobh would fail so quickly? He was used to stories where sieges lasted for months, years even. Foolish too not to choose the winner and to send a half-wit boy to do a man's job.

There was hope, however. He was aware of his worth, very aware that King Ardhal of Coirc could not collect the blood debt if his neck was stretched. He was worth so much more alive than dead. Worth enough, surely, to buy his freedom, a position in the king's household, even the king's ear.

He had been wasting his time in An Rinn. It had been a useful place to stop, to gather his thoughts, to learn the dialect and customs of the land. But it was time to move on. It was, as everyone kept on telling him, and proudly so, an insignificant town best left to its fish and its wool.

While the king's men laid the body of their fellow in the ground, Solomon stood with the horses, wondered if he could ever find one large enough to ride, and was glad that he would be out of the place before they learned what had really happened to their priest on the road back from Kilkenny abbey.

CHAPTER 15

Benzamir took the first step out of his door and entered a world of noise and colour and scent.

The calls of the merchants wove in and out of each other; the cries of men outraged at the latest price; the guttural shouts of the camel and donkey drivers goading their beasts through the narrow streets; the hammer of brass and copper and tin and silver and iron; the rasp of cut wood; the chip of stone; the last bleat of a goat as its throat was cut to the incantation of ancient words. The flash of saffron and carmine and azure and crimson and olive and pomegranate, on clothes and on walls and over archways and covering shutters. The glance of dark eyes beneath a veil.

It was the smells that fascinated him most: he could identify each one, pick up its signature over the others if he screwed his eyes up and concentrated hard. There, bread; there, cinnamon and pepper. Again, as he let himself drift with the mass of people pushing at him from all directions – sharp sweat, stinking fish, burning charcoal, over-ripe melon, the damp alluvium of the Nile, the dry wind from the desert.

It was amazing, and his senses sang at the banquet delivered to him quite without payment. Misr El Mahrosa, the city on the Nile from the dawn of civilization to the present day, and it still stood, vigorous, dazzling, rich. He stepped briefly out of the way of a cart pulled by two chained Ewer slaves, and continued his wandering, his sandals treading the hot, dusty paths trod by generations of people. Once or twice he looked up at the slits of bright sky between the buildings, attempting to orientate himself using the towering and elegant minarets as landmarks.

Said and Wahir found the streets terrifying, too crowded and alien for them ever to be comfortable with. They would emerge later, after the dawn rush had dwindled to a manageable trickle of traffic.

Not Benzamir. He revelled in the contact, in the sheer press of the bodies against him. He dived in like it was clear, cool water, and only came out reluctantly. He was so proud of them all, every one – every indigent beggar, every shoeless urchin, everyone who clung to life on the back of this great beast of a city – that he thought his heart would burst.

As the purposeful yet chaotic movement of the streets drove him on, it washed him up in a metalworkers' quarter. Smoke and sometimes flames poured out from open doors. Sparks flew and anvils rang with industry.

'*Salam*,' said a worker, plunging a red-hot piece of work

into a bucket by the door. The water hissed and spat, then merely bubbled.

'Let me see,' said Benzamir, and the man lifted the tongs he was using clear of the bucket.

The object clasped in the tongs was a knife blade, as long as Benzamir's hand, a beautiful blue steel, forged and not cast. The edges would need to be ground, and a haft attached to the spike protruding backwards from the guard, but already it was a fine piece of work.

'Do you have others like this, finished?'

'My master's inside. He'd be pleased to meet you.' The man ushered Benzamir into the dark heat of the forge.

'*Salam alaykum*,' he shouted over the hammering. There was a boy, no more than Wahir's age, heaving at the leather bellows, pumping the coals to an incandescent white. The smith, stripped to the waist and gleaming with sweat, brought out another knife blade from the heart of the fire and placed it on his anvil. He worked it hard, beating life into it with his hammer before the cherry-red glow faded. He held it close to his face and nodded with satisfaction.

Benzamir could tell he was in the presence of greatness, a man who didn't mind what others thought of his work because he held himself to the highest standards.

The smith handed the blade over to his servant to be cooled in the bucket outside, and took notice of his customer.

'*Salam*. Come and drink with me. We'll talk, and you can tell me the news.'

There was a back room, separated from the forge by a simple heavy curtain; once through, Benzamir could see that the room faced a courtyard full of light and shadows.

'Selah,' said the man. 'If I had any other name, I've forgotten it by now. Selah the Ironmaster at your service.'

'Benzamir Mahmood at yours.'

'Not from round here? Up the coast?' Selah plumped up some cushions with his huge hands and indicated that Benzamir should sit.

'Most recently from El Alam, my ancestral homelands.' It felt strange for him to say that. He'd never used those words before in his life, and he suddenly felt rootless and sad.

'But you're a traveller. A merchant, buying and selling, not getting home as often as you ought.' Selah sat opposite and clapped his hands. A door behind a tapestry opened and a woman came through carrying a tray of coffee and sweets.

'Almost. A soldier looking for his people's enemies.'

'Let's look at you. Yes, you could handle a sword. You have the eye.'

'I was admiring your fine knives. You don't see craft like that often.'

'Now you're flattering me. I do what I can with these poor hands, and it provides well enough.' He touched the woman on the arm, indicating ownership, but the way his touch lingered showed much more.

She poured the coffee in two steaming streams and set Benzamir's cup before him first.

'Thank you,' he said to her.

'If I was rich,' said Selah, 'I'd have more than one wife. But I'm not, so I have to put up with what I have.'

The woman moved Selah's cup across the low table to him and he smiled lovingly at her; his gaze followed her as she left.

Benzamir had the man's measure. 'Master Selah, you make fine knives, but the finest knife needs the finest metal.'

'That it does, my soldier friend. Which is why you'll find me down at the diggers' market, picking up only the best finds. I have a reputation for paying well, and the diggers bring me only their choicest pieces.'

Benzamir had heard that word before, but had failed to discover its full meaning. To him, a digger was one who dug, but it was clear that digger was a profession, and an important one.

'Tell me,' he said, 'does anyone here in Misr El Mahrosa take iron and make steel from it? Do you?'

'Now you're asking. Steel is to iron what teak is to cedar. Both useful, yes, but in these parts both steel and teak are as rare as hen's teeth. I'm told that the Kenyans can make steel' – he snapped his fingers – 'like that. But for me, in this little forge? It's hard. I've done it once or twice, to prove to doubters that I can. Mostly brass and iron does. Steel is a rich man's metal.'

'I've two compatriots who'd be delighted to wear your knives at their belts. So would I, Selah. We can settle a price later, but what about these diggers? Where do they find their treasure?' Benzamir lifted his coffee cup and breathed deeply. 'Very good. You honour me with your best.'

'From the hills of Yamin, brought up by camel train by the Kenyans. It's a vice, but an agreeable one.' Selah raised his cup and saluted his guest. 'You've heard of El Iskandariya, of course.'

'Yes. It used to be on the coast, south of here.'

'You sound so certain. In a time that was and was not,' said Selah, 'there was black land, rich and well-watered, between here and the end of the estuary. There were cities on the plains, huge and populous. Many farms, lots of children. But the Users hated us, and they tortured the seas to make them rise up in torment and swallow these cities whole, and Iskandariya was lost beneath the waves.' He shrugged. 'So the stories go. But there are tar roads that disappear out to sea, and the fishermen sometimes drag up things. Diggers go and dive there, and believe they are diving on the ruins of Iskandariya. Other than that, the diggers dig where they can. Some organize expeditions and visit the rubble fields of the far south, where the Ewers now live. Rich pickings, if they make it back.'

'That's fascinating. You're interested in metals, of course. But what else do they dig up?'

'All sorts of treasures. Some things are just junk – interesting curios, nothing more – but there's gold and silver and gemstones. More likely than not plucked from in amongst the bones of the ancients, the robbers. And sometimes' – Selah leaned forward and lowered his voice, sharing a confidence – 'there's something special. Maps. Books. On thin sheets of cloth, not written by any human hand.'

Benzamir took a rose-water jelly and bit it in two. 'I've seen one, or at least a copy of one. A set of maps owned by an imam, clearly taken from a pre-Turn book.'

'If you're interested, I could arrange an introduction for you. I've had word that there's a market tomorrow at the pyramids. Meet me here an hour before dawn, though I'd advise you to bring your men. Honest traders like myself are in the minority.'

'Great riches bring great wickedness,' said Benzamir, watching how the light played through the pink sweet in his hand. 'I'll come, and yes, I'll bring my companions. Thanks for the warning.'

They concluded a price for the knives, and Benzamir left Selah on his doorstep. He slowly worked his way back to his lodgings, and heard his name shouted down from a window as he approached.

'Master Benzamir! We were beginning to think that the city had swallowed you whole.'

Benzamir took a step back and squinted upwards. 'It's not as scary as you think, Said. And stop calling me your master. You're your own man, my friend.'

'I don't call you master for your benefit. I call you master for mine. The grander and more important you appear, the more status I have.'

'Is that how it works? So am I a step up from Ibn Alam?'

'Immeasurably greater, master.' Said turned from the window. 'Wahir, you lazy boy. The master is at the door, and all you do is sit and eat dates. Go and pour some water, fetch a towel.'

'Said, I can wash my own feet,' Benzamir laughed.

'Quiet, master. Someone will hear you.'

He sounded genuinely concerned, and Benzamir stopped joking. He shouldered open the heavy door that led to the shared courtyard, then up the steps to his rented rooms.

He *salamed* two of his neighbours before beating off the attentions of Wahir and finally sagging down on a divan.

'Where did you go? What did you see?' asked Wahir, who still hovered with the bowl in his hands and the towel around his waist.

'I found a man called Selah the Ironmaster, who makes fine

weapons out of scavenged steel. He's also invited us on a little adventure tomorrow morning. Before dawn, if you please.' Benzamir held out his hands for the bowl and set it between his feet. Taking the towel, he said to Wahir: 'If you're desperate to do something, you could find me some beer.'

'But I want to hear about this adventure,' Wahir said, hands on hips.

'Then you'd better hurry, insolent boy,' said Said.

'Enough. But he's right, of course. No stories without beer. My people hold very dear to that.'

Wahir went at a run, and Said sent a scowl after him. 'You're too easy on the boy. At his age, he needs discipline, and to show respect to his elders.'

'He does, in his own way. I like his enthusiasm, and I don't want to squash him. I know it seems like bare-faced cheek a lot of the time, but if it doesn't bother me, it shouldn't bother you.'

'What would have happened,' said Said, 'if you'd talked to your father like that? He would have beaten you with a stick. My father did to me, and it didn't do me any harm.'

'What your or Wahir's father do with their sticks is no concern of mine. I've not got a stick, and even if I had, I wouldn't use it on a child.'

'He's almost a man.'

'Then I would have to give him a stick too, and we'd make a fair fight of it.'

'You're very strange, master.'

'Not as strange as I am thirsty. Said, what do you know about the diggers?'

Said snorted. 'Apart from the fact that they're all pirates and thieves? That they'd sell you, your mother and your grandmother as slaves as soon as spit at you? Nothing, really, beyond that we should have nothing to do with the dirty grave-robbers.'

'Ah,' said Benzamir, 'that's a shame.'

'Why do you say that?'

'Because tomorrow, while it's still dark, we're all off to the pyramids to see the diggers' market. Selah asked if I wanted to go, and I said yes.'

'We're all going to have our throats cut – except you, of course – and left for the vultures. And the pyramids? Don't you know that the reason why the diggers go there for their infernal market is because no one else dares to. At night. What were you thinking?'

'I need to look for something – something my enemies might be using for trade. It'll look like a User artefact, but new and clean and working. It'll be the sort of thing that these diggers won't be able to resist. They'll try and sell it to me, and I'll try and find out where they got it from.'

'Master,' said Said, 'when you talk of such things, I get very confused. Mainly because I have no idea what you're saying. You talk around yourself like you're processing

177

around a sacred stone, circling what you want to say but dare not.'

Wahir came crashing back through the door. His reed basket clinked promisingly. 'What did I miss?'

'Master Benzamir tells us that we're off to get butchered like sheep at the hands of diggers tomorrow.'

'That doesn't sound so good,' said Wahir, and pulled out three bottles of beer. He handed one to Benzamir, one to Said, and unstoppered the one he was left holding. 'What?'

Benzamir put his feet up on the divan. 'I was about to say you're still too young, but considering what I'm about to tell you, I imagine you'll need a stiff drink. Listen then. You'll think me mad, but everything I say will be as true as I can make it.' He drank some of the beer, washing the dust of Misr away, loosening his tongue. 'Very well, then. There was a time that was, and was not.'

CHAPTER 16

It took Benzamir several goes to work out the best way to start. Each time he saw blank incomprehension on the faces of his friends, and he frowned with the effort.

'I'll try again. My ancestors lived where you did, in and around the hills of El Alam. They moved from the mountains to the coast and back. They traded their sheep and their goats, they raced camels, they lived in tents. They were Bedouin. In those days the rains were poor, the desert hot and harsh. But they were sons and daughters of the land, and for all their poverty they were a proud people. They had friends too; one friend especially, a powerful king who would give them magic. They made a special fire out of the sunlight. They sucked dew from the sand. Under the king's guidance my people grew in both wisdom and wealth. It was a good time.

'So when the king was attacked by his enemies, the Bedouin of El Alam rose up to fight with him. They stood shoulder to shoulder and said they would live and die as brothers. The king had many ships, and there was room enough for all my ancestors and their families. They sailed away to far distant shores, and there they gave battle. When they fought, they won. They discovered both a courage they had once doubted and a destiny they had never dreamed of claiming.

'They carry on the fight to this day. There have been seven centuries of war and I've fought with them. It's a terrible, glorious sight. You've both seen the power I can call on. Imagine a whole battlefield like that, and more. A mountain, razed. A river, boiled dry. Fields turned to glass. Wherever we find our enemies, we confront them and show them no mercy. They don't understand mercy, don't know what the word is. They're a plague, a disease that we can't yet cure. They eat and grow, and that's all they do. We have to kill them, every last one, and when we're finished with them . . . ?' He hung his head. 'More often than not, we've destroyed everything else too.'

'But – but,' said Said, 'if you are here, then your enemies must be amongst us. If that's so, then who will survive such a battle? If you can destroy a mountain, how much easier is a city?'

'Don't be afraid, Said. Misr will live for another thousand years. The enemies – the Others – are not here. Those I'm trying to find are people like me. They fought with us once, but now they've turned against the king, his people, and mine. They're counted as rebels, traitors, and worse.'

180

'That's hardly a comfort, master. If you need our help' –
Said jabbed himself in the chest and pointed at pale, trembling Wahir – 'then things must be very bad.'

'Said, Wahir, I know this is hard for you. I don't expect
you to fight them. I don't expect to fight them either, but I
do have to find them and take them back to answer to the
king. I need help finding them, preferably without them
knowing that I'm looking for them. One man on his own
asking difficult, unusual questions raises suspicions that
three companions won't.'

'I'm not afraid,' said Wahir, jutting his chin out. 'I'm not
afraid of the Others or the traitors.'

'No, it's right to be afraid of the Others. But the traitors –
I'm angry with them. They should know better.'

'It's an incredible story,' said Said, 'but at least I can understand it, not like your talk of before. Your starships and your
floating tray of knives. I really didn't get that at all. Nonsense.'

'Orbital weapons platform,' murmured Benzamir. 'I'm
sorry this has taken so long. Trying to find the right words is
difficult when you don't share the same history as my people.'

'Are you really a magician?' asked Wahir.

Benzamir thought about the answer for a while, stroking
his long nose with a finger. Finally he said, 'Yes. And so are
the traitors. That's why I don't want you to fight them. I don't
want either of you to come to any harm. Promise me that
you'll leave them to me when the time comes. Said? Wahir?'

He made them both say solemn vows that he hoped were binding, or at the very least that he could remind them of at the appropriate moment.

'Master, why don't you just use your magic to find them?' asked Said.

'Because,' said Benzamir, 'most of the ways I could try would let them know I was here, and looking for them. They'd be next to impossible to find after that. They might want to turn the tables on me, make me the hunted one. There are a lot more of them than there are of me.'

'You're more powerful than they are, master, surely.'

'Kind of you to say so, Wahir. Perhaps I am.' Benzamir finished his beer and discovered that there was sediment at the bottom of the bottle that didn't taste at all good. 'Gah. Another bottle, quick.'

Wahir hurriedly handed him another.

When he'd cleared his throat repeatedly, he continued. 'This isn't about who's stronger, or more cunning, or who's got the biggest army backing them up. This is about what's right and wrong. I have right on my side, but what's the use of that if I don't find those I'm looking for and deliver them to face the king's justice? Every day that passes allows them to believe they've got away with it. It makes them bolder.'

'That won't happen, will it?' said Wahir. 'You'll teach them the lesson they deserve.'

'That's what I'm here to do. Anything left unsaid, Said?'

'One thing, master. Where in the world do you live? I'm sure that we would have heard of a race of powerful magicians.'

Benzamir worried at his bottom lip with his teeth. 'How long have you known me?'

'Since the year end. Five moons?'

'Because I'm sure I've explained this a dozen times, and I'm so sorry you still don't understand. Very well: a race of magicians. You've heard of some, Said, and you, Wahir. You've told me stories about them, both of you.'

He waited, and suddenly Wahir gave a low moan of panic. 'Users. But you can't be one.' From kneeling on the floor at Benzamir's feet, he started to back away. 'They're all dead.'

'I'm not a User,' said Benzamir quickly, 'My people's power now surpasses even the Users'. We're the secret in their history that no one knows.'

'What are you?' breathed Said. 'Are you an angel or a devil?'

'I'm a man. A man who likes beer. My people – they're like me. We live and love and fight and die, just like you do. Except we've spent seven hundred years building on what the Users knew, and you've spent seven hundred years forgetting. That's the only difference between us. Cut me, and I bleed.'

'How can I cut you?' said Said. 'No weapon can even touch you.'

Benzamir shot out his hand, grabbed Said's wrist and pulled the bigger man close. 'You're my friend, Said, and I do this because I love you, not because I want you to love me.' He pulled Said's dagger from his belt and passed it along his own exposed forearm. A line of blood bloomed from the lengthening wound and started dripping on Said's writhing fingers.

'Enough!' shouted Said. He used his strength to push Benzamir back onto the divan and stared at his bloodied hand. 'Don't do any more. Don't mutilate yourself, master. Friend. You are a man. You are Benzamir Mahmood.'

'Wahir? See?'

Said helped the boy up and dragged him over to Benzamir. 'He's a man after all, Wahir. One of us.'

'You're not a User?'

'No, Wahir, I promise. I'm not a User. The Users have long gone, and they won't be back.' The wound was starting to hurt. He hadn't meant to cut so deeply, but Said's knife was blunt at the tip, and he'd had to press harder than he'd wanted to. 'A User wouldn't be standing here, asking for a bandage while he bled all over the floor.'

Wahir laughed, an explosive sound that was more nerves than mirth. 'I suppose not.'

'Then get me a bandage.'

Wahir used a towel temporarily wrapped around Benzamir's arm to staunch the flow, then went out to find an apothecary. Said sat down on the divan too, his fist knuckling his chin.

'What is it, Said?'

'What is it again that we're looking for at the diggers' market?'

'Something that looks like nothing you have ever seen before. Ignore what you recognize, but look interested if someone offers you some bizarre piece of twisted metal that they themselves don't understand. I don't doubt that most of what the diggers deal in is either mundane or faked. But the better ones will know when they've got real treasure, even if they have no idea what to make of it.'

'And why would your king's enemies want these?'

The towel was turning red, but Benzamir knew that underneath, his skin was already starting to knit together. 'You've got it the wrong way round. The traitors will be giving away their magic, offering it to show their good intentions, using it as currency and influence. What I need to discover is where it is these artefacts come from. Can you do that for me? Can you be discreet while doing it?'

'This trail you hope to find: it might lead all the way to your enemies' door.' Said moved his fist to slap it in the palm of his hand. 'I see now. So that's how we'll find these dogs and send them back to beg for mercy. They can't hide for ever – not from you, and not from me.'

'Thank you, Said. Thank you.'

CHAPTER 17

In the hour before dawn, very little moved on the streets of Misr except for thieves, whores, their victims and their clients.

The muezzins were still asleep, and only the bakers toiled at their ovens. No one noticed the three figures slipping from a door, each wearing his heaviest cloak and carrying an oil light suspended from a stick.

'How will you find this Selah again?' asked Wahir. 'I've seen the way you explore, and it's a wonder you ever make it back to us each day.'

'It's a knack: how I find my way around is a little incidental magic that hurts no one. We'll find him, unless he's already gone because we've spent too long here talking.'

'It's cold and I'm tired. And I'm too young to die.'

'Oh hush. It's this way.'

They were accosted only twice – once by a shadow-clad man who stumbled out of his hiding place and thought better of it after Said had shown him his sword, and again by a shaven-headed Ewer woman, trying to buy her freedom. Said was all for whipping her back to her owner, but she was already missing an ear.

Selah had a much more impressive retinue than Benzamir: the street outside his forge was full of men talking in low voices and testing the edges of their weapons.

'*Salam,*' said Selah, 'to you and your' – he hesitated as he guessed Wahir's age – 'men.'

Benzamir could feel the delight in Wahir without looking. '*Salam*, Selah the Ironmaster. Are we expecting more trouble than usual?'

'No, this is normal. I'm not a soldier like you are, so I have to hire my protection. Besides, more men to pull the cart. Are you ready?'

Selah gave the order to light the tar-soaked torches, and then led the way through the narrow streets at the head of the procession. The solid wooden wheels of the cart creaked and clattered as it was pulled along, and the flickering orange flames made their path shift and change every step they walked.

'Have you ever seen the pyramids before?' asked Selah.

'Not close up. I've heard that they're very impressive.'

'Once they were like staircases to the stars, each edge sharp and straight, not like now. Heaps of broken-backed stones that crumble to the touch. But what heaps, my friend! They are enormous, and each one made by hands like ours. It hardly seems possible that all that work was done just to provide somewhere to bury a man.'

'They were kings,' offered Benzamir by way of an excuse.

'All the same, what madness possessed them? I can only imagine the size of their vanity, each one trying to out-build the king before. No, a scrape in the earth, a shrouded body, a few prayers, a pile of stones. Good enough for any man, I say.'

'And I'd find it hard to disagree.'

The passage of a large group of armed men moving purposefully through the streets of Misr had scared everybody else away. The cart bounced along noisily into a suddenly wide road.

'The east gate. Across the Nile is Al Jizah. This shouldn't take too long.'

There was a ramp up to the gate, and a group of city guards to be bribed to let them through. They knew Selah well enough not to overcharge him, and the gate was pushed open with only a few minutes' haggling.

'A little baksheesh,' he said, patting the money bag at his belt. 'The real money is elsewhere.' He made sure that all his men got through, and Benzamir checked that Said and Wahir were still in amongst the crowd.

There was another ramp leading from the gate, heading down towards the river, and from the tide marks on the stonework, the walls of the city just about held back the annual flood waters. For now, the black ribbon of the Nile glittered in the moonlight, and the flare of fires down by the river indicated the presence of ferrymen who would carry them across.

The worn mounds of the pyramids were dark and brooding, five millennia old and showing their age.

Selah had hired barges, and they all lent a hand to manhandle the cart off the floating landing stage and onto the floor of the boat.

'I thought you said no more ships.' Said lit his face by bringing his lantern close.

'It's only a very little one. There's no chance of you being seasick.' Benzamir thought he could detect a greenish cast to his friend's skin. 'Is there?'

'The river's wide, and my stomach's lurching like a camel's hump. We'll have to see.'

The bargees were casting off, their thick ropes thudding onto the decks and following them on. One of them noticed Wahir trailing his hand in the water and unleashed a barrage of abuse in the local cant.

'What? What?' he said indignantly, as those who understood laughed, and passed word on to those who didn't.

'You've never seen a crocodile, have you?' said Benzamir.

'No, what's that?'

'Big, with teeth. They live in the river and eat boys for breakfast.'

Wahir jerked his hand out and counted his fingers.

The current carried them downstream, and the rudder man used his tiller to bring the barge safely across. Benzamir heard the scrape of sand under the flat hull, felt the bump as the boat grounded.

The western sky was starting to lighten, and Selah was silhouetted against salmon-pink cloud. 'It's time, my friend. Let's see what these filthy diggers have brought us today.'

The ground on either side of the road was wildly uneven, and with the sun so low behind them, the shadows exaggerated every pit and rise. Even the rich Nile sediment couldn't cover the suggestions of walls and cellars, and further away from the river, where the trees thinned and scrubby plants and low bushes held fast amongst the ruins, it was obvious what they were walking through. Wahir ran through the loose stones and tough grasses, leaping from high point to high point, turning round every once in a while just to take in the strange scene.

'There aren't any rubble fields like this anywhere near El Alam. Imagine the treasure that could be under our feet.'

'Come down from there, boy. What treasure there might have been was taken long, long ago, and digging isn't for us.' Said pointed at the road. 'You'll fall down a hole or break your neck. You come here and walk with the rest of us.'

'He's excited, that's all,' said Benzamir. 'His world is suddenly huge.'

'I'd rather he didn't see it from a stretcher.' Said made certain that Wahir was making his way towards them, then took in the vast expanse of chaotic ground. He shivered. 'There are dead people here. These were their homes and they still live here.'

Benzamir looked back at the rose-coloured walls of Misr. 'The city stretched out as far as here, taking in all the east bank, all the west, up and down the river as far as the sea. They called it El Quhira, the Victorious. Can you imagine that many people?'

'No. Especially now that they're all ghosts. The dead outnumber the living, and it frightens me.'

'I can see why the diggers chose this place,' said Benzamir. 'No one in their right minds would come to their market unless they had to.'

'Yes, well,' said Said pointedly.

'For a big man, you scare easily.'

'And you take things too lightly. You've power in your fingertips, but there's going to be a time when it's of no use to you. There's worse than Ibn Alam in this world.'

'I know. Look, Wahir. We're almost there.'

As they walked, the pyramids had grown from shadows in the distance to vast, looming entities: two huge structures and a smaller third one. There were other remains too: walls and ramps; tiny pyramids now no more than weathered bumps; and a headless lion lying in the dirt.

At the foot of the Khufu pyramid there was an array of widely spaced tents flapping in the hot wind from the Sahara. Each tent had its own retinue of draught animals and wagons, with a perimeter of armed guards eyeing each other up.

They weren't the first buyers, either. There were horses ridden by merchants and slave cages pulled by oxen parked up at the outskirts of the camp, and the colour of the locals' clothes contrasted with the black of the diggers, who moved through the tents like crows.

Selah made sure that his men were clear on their orders, then came over to Benzamir. 'Well, my friend, are you ready to do business?' He rubbed his hands together in anticipation.

'If we can. Hopefully they'll have something we want.'

'These diggers have a fearful reputation, but be confident around them. They can smell fear and will rob the sight out of your eyes if you give them a chance. I'll arrange some introductions for you, but regretfully I can't do more. My dealings should be done by midday, if you want to travel back with us.'

'You've done more than enough, and we're grateful.' Benzamir looked at his sceptical companions. 'They don't look very grateful, but trust me, they are.'

Selah stepped back with a bow into the midst of his

bodyguards, who took up a less than discreet distance from him. 'As Allah wills it.'

He walked away, and the men around him fell into step.

'You see,' said Said. 'That is how to meet diggers. With numbers. Master, we are just three. And one of us is a mere boy!'

Wahir was about to spring to his own defence when Benzamir silenced him with a raised hand.

'Look around you. Who will people remember in a day's time? Selah, or us?' He pointed to a flamboyant merchant in purple and green, walking on the hot ground shadowed by a canopy carried over his head by slaves. 'That man there, or us? We're nothing. I prefer it that way.'

Without waiting, he strode off towards the first tent.

The guards were Ewers, their pale faces shiny with grease and sweat under the weight of their iron helmets. They carried spears decorated with little metal trinkets dug from the ground, which glittered and tinkled in the early light.

'Is your master receiving guests?'

The men crossing their spear heads over the entrance looked at them with blank incomprehension.

'They do not use our language, master,' whispered Said.

'Really? What do they use then? I know lots.'

'I don't know. Try them all.'

So Benzamir tried ancient versions of several long-dead

European languages, and had most success with English. There were sufficient words the guards recognized for him to make himself understood. The spears uncrossed and all three of them went into the soft white light of the tent.

It was spartan inside. A rug had been unrolled across the floor, and three folding chairs arranged more or less at random in the middle. The back of the tent was open, leading out towards the display of goods on offer. A man with his back to them was talking to another hidden figure. He was alerted to his visitors' presence by Benzamir's affected coughing.

'Buyers,' he said. He lifted his eye patch to give his cloudy pupil a better look. Wahir curled his lip and took a step back. 'Child not for eating?'

'No,' said Benzamir. He was struggling; there just weren't enough words to go on. He hoped that he'd mistranslated the digger; surely he wasn't a cannibal? 'Buyers, yes.'

'What have you? Chinks?' The man scratched his stubble and lurched forward. One of his legs was false. Possibly both.

'Chinks? Coin, yes.' He tapped his purse so that it made a noise.

'Boy?'

'No, not boy. Definitely not boy.'

The digger looked disappointed, then consoled himself with the thought of legitimately minted money. 'What buy you? Metal like friend Selah? Much iron, much copper, some lead, small tin.'

Benzamir chanced his arm. 'User tech. Anything that works.'

The digger's whole body language changed in an instant, from hard but fair trader to furtive runner of contraband.

'No User machines for me. Shah run clean business.'

'Of course you do. You leave all that sort of stuff behind for your rivals to find, Prince Digger. What do you have?'

'Shah won't trust stranger, though friend Selah says good of him. Shah asks stranger to leave.' He barked out an order, and a giant pale-eyed Ewer stepped through the rear entrance.

'We're leaving,' said Benzamir, and hurried Said and Wahir out into the sunlight.

'I didn't understand any of that,' said Said, 'but even I can tell it didn't go well.'

'It was fine up to the point where I told him what I was looking for. I may as well have asked for his head on a stick. I'm not well enough known here.'

'Perhaps they think you're a Kenyan spy,' said Wahir.

'What does a Kenyan spy look like? No, that was a silly question. What I'm saying is, this could take a very long time and be utterly futile.'

'Don't be down-hearted.' Said pointed to all the other

tents spread out at the base of the pyramid. 'There are others we can try. They might not be as suspicious as that one-eyed, one-legged digger.'

'We'll work our way down the line. Wahir? Special job for you. I want you to listen in on other people's conversations, see what the locals are saying. If you hear anything interesting, let me know. And if you can track down some food, that'd be useful.' Benzamir put his hand on the boy's head. 'You can do that, yes?'

'Yes, master.' Wahir looked less than certain, but determined to do his duty. He strode off purposefully, searching for an opportunity to eavesdrop.

'I just hope no one tries to eat him.'

'Why do you say that?' Said's hand went to the hilt of his sword. 'Why would anyone want to do that?'

'Doesn't matter. I'm sure that wasn't what he meant. Come on, we've got our work cut out.'

They were rebuffed more often than not. Only twice did the diggers show him anything of use. One had an old chemically powered projectile weapon, beautifully preserved but useless: no firing pin, and the owner had no idea what a firing pin might do or look like. The other had a cache of holograms – fragile plates of plastic that showed pictures of a white-skinned family dressed in a succession of outlandish clothes: they were eating at a table; they were standing in front of what could only be their house; they were sitting in a long white box, laughing.

Benzamir's fingers felt all around the pictures and found what he presumed would be the play button. The power had long since evaporated away, and the images stayed frozen in time.

'Amazing, but not what we're after,' he said, and reached up to push Said's mouth closed.

Back out in the sun and the wind, Wahir came running up. 'Master! I've found a man selling food. And I'm told that you need someone called an agent, and that Alessandra is who you want to talk to.'

They talked as they walked.

'What does this agent do, Wahir?'

'I was talking to a man by the horses. He said that his master always used an agent and that unless you knew exactly what you were looking for, you were going to be drugged, robbed and buried in the sand.'

'I'm sure he did,' said Benzamir, 'but what does the agent do?'

'They match buyers and sellers, for a proportion of the sale. And you hire them if you're after something unusual. That's what we're doing, isn't it?'

'Yes, it is. Good work, Wahir. This Alessandra . . . it's a woman's name.'

'I think she's a Ewer. Free, so the man said. Her skin is a

bit like yours, a little lighter, but not that southern white-ness that makes them look like they're dead. She's waiting for you where they're serving the food.'

'Now I'm seriously impressed,' said Benzamir. 'Lead on.'

Wahir crowned his achievement by introducing Benzamir to the woman in a thoroughly self-important manner, putting himself as her equal, and portraying his master in such glowing terms that she might have been fooled into thinking Benzamir was a king in his own land.

Alessandra wasn't deluded by Wahir's fine words. She didn't stand up for them; barely acknowledged them with her dark eyes from under her patterned headscarf. She raised a foot and pushed back a chair. Benzamir took this as permission to sit with her.

He undid his purse and handed a fistful of coppers to Said. 'Get yourselves something. Mistress?'

'I'm fine,' she said.

'Will you be all right, master?' asked Said, weighing the money in his hand.

'I'm sure my virtue will be perfectly safe, Said. I'll call if I need you.' Benzamir sat in the proffered chair and looked out at the pyramids, framed between two tent poles.

'You came with Selah. Him, I trust. Who are you?'

'Benzamir Michael Mahmood.'

'Which tells me nothing about what you are or where

you're from. Your boy does you credit, though. I'm to believe you're a powerful man from a faraway land who's come looking for traces of the Users.'

'More or less the gist of it.' Benzamir tried to guess her age and her experience. 'You're highly recommended.'

'Of course I am. I know all these scoundrels, and what they've got stashed away in their strong boxes. No matter how much they protest, they'll always part with it for a price.' She twisted her lips into a rare smile. 'What is it that you're looking for – and failing to find, I might add.'

Benzamir played with his fingers. 'How are you on professional confidences?'

Alessandra was taken aback. 'Are you doubting my integrity?' Her muscles tensed, readying her to get up and go.

'I'm sorry,' apologized Benzamir. 'That isn't what I wanted to say at all.' He waited for her to ease back into her chair before continuing. 'If I told you that I wanted User knowledge – maps, books, machines – would you tell someone else who asked about me what I was looking for?'

'No.'

'Good.' He slid his purse across the table, and was silent while she checked its contents.

'You are joking.' She looked up at him and tossed the bag back contemptuously.

He sighed. 'That's a pity. Sorry to have wasted your time.'

He gave a little bow with his head and put his hands on the arms of his chair. 'Pleasure to have met you, mistress.'

'Oh, sit down, Mahmood. It's not like business is so good that I can't trade a few hints with you.' She raised her hand and snapped her fingers. 'Coffee.'

Benzamir was distracted by a distant figure. 'That's Wahir. What's he doing up there?' He was starting to climb the Khufu pyramid.

Alessandra reached under her clothing and gave him her telescope, an oiled brass tube with hand-ground lenses at either end. He admired it briefly, before putting it to his eye.

'I suppose he was going to do it sooner or later. It's just too tempting.'

'He'll climb halfway up, get scared and come back down. I've done it once, and it's surprisingly steep.'

'But you went all the way to the top, didn't you?' Benzamir closed the telescope and handed it back.

'Of course. Where are you really from?'

'East of here, along the coast. My people lived in the mountains there.' Benzamir reached forward for his purse, and Alessandra trapped his hand on top of it.

'Live, or lived? In which case, where do they live now?'

'I'm hiding things from you, for which I apologize. The people I'm looking for would like to find me as much as I'd like to find them.'

'I don't have to talk to you.' She took the tray of coffee from the boy, put it on the table and waited for the answer.

'We live on our ships, and we sail the oceans. We're a people without a land, but we've been away so long, all land looks strange.'

Alessandra snorted at his reply. 'I've never heard of you, and I make it my business to have heard of everything. You know the emperor of Kenya lays claim to User machines?'

'That'll explain why no one will admit to having any.'

'There was something earlier this year. Two, three moons ago maybe. A book. It was in circulation, passing from hand to hand because no one knew quite what to make of it, or what to do with it.' She poured the coffee into two cups, took hers and cradled it in her hands.

'What sort of book?'

'A metal book. Full of writing no one could read; full of pictures.' She swallowed coffee, looked around for eavesdroppers and lowered her voice. 'Some of the pictures moved. Just a little, as if they were trapped in the page and couldn't get out. And each page was a thin sheet of something that no one had seen before. Couldn't cut it, couldn't burn it. Very strong. Because no one could do anything with it or make anything out of it, it had a curiosity value. Who bought it last?' She tried to remember.

'Who sold it first?'

'I don't know. It just appeared. The digger I saw with it

said he'd bought it from a Kenyan, so where he'd got it from I've no idea. You tend not to ask too many questions of the emperor's subjects.'

'Sorry – just a moment . . .' said Benzamir. Wahir was coming down the side of the pyramid much too quickly. He used Alessandra's telescope and trained the lenses on him. Wahir looked scared half to death. 'We're going to have to go. Said!'

In a moment Said was at his side. 'Master?'

'Apologies, Mistress Alessandra. Your telescope.' He handed it back and started running towards the pyramid.

CHAPTER 18

Benzamir managed to get to Wahir before he fell. They slid a way down the side of the pyramid, finally jarring to a halt against a block of stone.

'Slow down. You'll kill yourself.'

Wahir took a deep breath. 'Chariots,' he said.

'I know.'

'To the north.'

'Wahir, I know.' Benzamir made certain that the boy wasn't going to slip down any further and climbed up a little way. In the distance he saw a dust cloud, rising to the sky and obscuring everything behind it. But in the foreground, following the line of the flood plain, was a horde of chariots, their horses already at the trot.

'There must be a couple of hundred of them,' he said. 'Isn't that an amazing sight?'

'What are we going to do?' gasped Wahir.

'Apart from look at them?'

'Master! It's an army. Look where they're heading.'

'You spoil all my fun,' said Benzamir. If he concentrated, he could hear them: hooves pounding, wheels clattering, traces jingling. They were coming straight towards them at a speed that didn't inspire confidence. They weren't advancing. They were attacking. 'Right. Let's get off this pyramid for a start.'

He grabbed Wahir's arm and headed down. He spotted Said standing next to Alessandra, who was using her telescope to decide for herself whether to panic or not. Once she'd seen enough, she headed straight for the stand of horses, shouting as she went. Said was left to wait.

'Master, it's the Ethiopians.'

'Is that good or bad?'

'How should I know? Trust our luck to get caught up in a war.'

Benzamir and Wahir jumped the last stretch and landed in a heap at Said's feet. By the time he'd helped them up, the camp was in uproar. The black-clad diggers were frantically trying to save what they could, using the men who hadn't deserted at the first cry. There was a bloody riot beginning at one of the slavers' compounds, and the local traders from Misr had vanished back towards the river.

'The ferry?' suggested Wahir.

'It won't do any good. The Ethiopian commander's sent a small force down the far bank to cut off any escape. We're going to have to head the other way.'

'Into the desert? That's madness,' said Said. The approaching chariots were rumbling like distant thunder.

'I'm not going to see if I can face down an entire army, not even for you two. Come on.' Benzamir headed for the smallest of the three pyramids and called back. 'Seriously, hurry. Whatever it is they're after, I don't want to have to either fight or answer awkward questions.'

They ran, and Benzamir aimed them directly at the approaching charioteers.

'What are we doing?'

'Broken ground to the north. Chariots are going to have to go to the river first. They'll turn before they get to us.'

'How do you know all this?' panted Said. 'You've never been here before.'

'The advantages of satellite photography, my friend. Head for that hill. There's a ruin on top – we can hide there.' Benzamir pushed Said onwards and took Wahir's hand. 'This isn't the time for dawdling.'

The valley they headed into was dry, but full of tough, thorny bushes that had to be avoided. The dust cloud was now almost above them, and the noise was incredible. There were individual cries of men and horses above the relentless rumble of wheels.

'Up,' urged Benzamir. 'You can rest when you're dead.'

Wahir was too exhausted even to complain. Eventually they made it to a low stone wall on the crest of the hill. Said threw himself over the top, and Benzamir tipped Wahir after him.

A horse whinnied close by, and they all ducked down.

'Can't you use your magic to make us invisible?' Said rolled onto his back and started to pick the thorns out of his legs.

'Yes, I could, but it'd take too long to explain why I can't right now. Keeping out of sight is much easier.' Benzamir risked a look. The whole of the Nile valley in front of him was swarming with chariots chasing individuals on foot and forcing them to surrender. When they stood and fought, they were cut down without hesitation, trampled by the horses or run through by spears.

Some of the diggers were getting away, but only by leaving all their merchandise behind. Those who had stayed to pack up were encircled and rounded up. The ferrymen had deserted their fares: nor could they land on the Misr side. They were stuck midstream, and useless to anyone.

Benzamir sat down behind the wall and pressed his back to the crumbling stone. 'I can safely say the Ethiopians knew precisely what they were doing. They weren't after the men as such, more the goods. If it hadn't been for Wahir, we'd have been caught.'

Wahir hauled air in and out of his lungs and took the compliment as his due.

'What do we do now, master?'

'We wait, Said. We wait here until nightfall, when I can get us back into the city. We've water, and we can find some shade. Though if that horse doesn't shut up, it's going to attract all sorts of unwelcome attention.'

The horse down below their ruined temple was neighing and grunting. Now that the chariots had mostly slowed their thunderous charge, it was all too obvious.

'It could be hurt, master,' said Said.

'In which case I'll have to go and put an end to it. Great.' Benzamir put his hand out. 'Borrow your sword?'

Said slid it out of its scabbard and Benzamir secreted it under the folds of his kaftan. 'Don't be seen, master.'

'I'll do my best.' He lay across the top of the wall, rolled off, and was gone.

Benzamir longed for his adaptive armour; anyone he came upon would have had to fall over him before spotting him. The paradox was that it was too obviously different to wear.

Instead he kept low, using what cover he could. The air was still stirred up by the passage of the chariots, everything surrounded in an ochre haze. The Ethiopians had nearly finished with the diggers, and he wondered how Selah had got on.

The horse noises were intermittent, but they came from the same place every time. Benzamir presumed Said was right about the animal being injured: he couldn't heal it so it would be a kindness to put it out of its misery. He slunk lower into the valley until he could spot the chestnut head tossing this way and that behind a stand of thorns.

He managed to get upwind of the beast and took a good look at it. It seemed at first sight to be unharmed, but its reins were caught in the sharp branches of a bush. He crept closer, and the horse turned to see him, breaking out in a fresh wave of sweat. It shook its head violently from side to side, trying to free itself, and only managed to scratch its muzzle in the struggle. It made even more noise, and Benzamir had to dance past flying hooves and nipping teeth to get hold of the reins.

'Quiet, you stupid animal,' he said firmly, 'or I'll silence you myself.' He cut the reins with his eating knife, and the ungrateful horse bolted away out towards the Ethiopians, over a body lying in the dirt.

He recognized the pattern on the headscarf. Alessandra was more or less out in the open, and he'd be dangerously exposed if he even tried to see if she was dead or alive. There was no question of him trying to reach her; it was a matter of waiting for the right moment.

Then it was too late. A chariot wheeled by, and the spearman patted the driver on the back and pointed. The soldier jumped off, the metal plates of his armour glittering, and started towards both Alessandra and Benzamir.

Benzamir froze, and watched breathlessly as the soldier tapped the body with the haft of his spear. He smiled and called back to the chariot as he saw the shape move. Then he took a step back and poked her with more force.

Alessandra stirred and looked up. The Ethiopian saw that she was not only a woman, but a Ewer. He urged her to get up, but it was clear that she had no idea which way was up, let alone how much trouble she was in.

'This is going to end badly, no matter what I do,' muttered Benzamir. He rose from his hiding place, sword in hand, and said in his best Amharic: 'Put her down. You don't know where she's been.'

His intention was clear, even if his words were obscure. The soldier immediately took a defensive stance and shouted for help. Benzamir came at him at a run. The spear was levelled at his belly, and at the last moment he slid under the iron point, his feet connecting with the Ethiopian's shins.

He curved his body round his sword blade, tumbled out of the fall and swung hard and fast. Metal met wood, and the spear shaft splintered and shivered out of the man's hands.

The soldier hesitated before lunging at Benzamir with both hands outstretched. He spun aside, moved his body behind and kicked out again. Sprawled in the dust, the Ethiopian never saw the double-handed clubbing blow descending on the back of his helmet.

Benzamir jumped up, and the chariot driver turned his long knife in a nervous circle. Then he turned and ran for the horses, Benzamir dogging his footsteps. He caught him, lifted him and threw him. The knife spiralled away. The Ethiopian aimed a fist at Benzamir's face. He didn't even bother to dodge it, just crowded forward and jabbed his forearm hard across the man's windpipe.

Exhilarated, Benzamir retrieved Said's sword and ran back to Alessandra. She was holding the side of her head and there was blood slipping between her fingers.

'What . . . ?' she said, slurring.

'You can thank me later,' said Benzamir. 'Right now we have the entire Ethiopian army breathing down our necks.' He dragged her upright and threw her over his shoulder. 'Hang on.'

He was halfway up the hill again when he heard Said shout, 'Master! Archers!'

'Like this couldn't get any worse.' There was a rattling in the rocks to his right, and another behind him. He glanced round, and there were more arrows already in flight. He was invulnerable, but he couldn't extend his protection to Alessandra. He let her fall to the ground and straightened his arm.

The arid scrub exploded once, twice, three times. He followed up the initial barrage with a series of detonations that forced the bowmen to run for their lives.

Said scrambled down to meet them. 'Your power is awesome, master. The infidels are routed.'

'And in a moment they'll be back with reinforcements. In the meantime half of Egypt will be talking about this. Have your sword back.' Benzamir scooped up the woman and hurried back to the ruins.

Wahir was busy watching the plain. 'They have infantry, master, with swords and shields. They're massing in the valley.'

'You know,' said Benzamir, 'this is precisely what I didn't want to happen. And I'm ashamed that part of me is wishing that I'd left her to the soldiers.' He explored the wound on her head, and she moaned and gasped as his fingers probed.

'Will she live, master?'

'She'd better, after all the trouble she's caused. I can't feel any bones moving around. Alessandra? Can you hear me?'

'What? Who's that? Who are you?'

'Benzamir Mahmood. Your horse threw you.'

She sat up, and dry heaved.

'You've got concussion, but we can't stay here. There are soldiers coming up the hill, and while I'd like to fight them all single-handed, I'm averse to bloody slaughter.'

Said looked shocked. 'Do we surrender? We don't have anyone to ransom us. We'll end up as slaves.'

At the mention of slaves, Alessandra started to thrash around. 'No. No. Not again. I won't.'

'Hush. No friends of mine will ever be slaves. We just have to wait for a short while, and help will be here.'

'Master,' said Wahir, 'the Ethiopians have split their force into two. They're going to attack from two sides.'

'We won't be here when they arrive. Just don't panic.' Benzamir pulled Wahir down out of sight and patted the dust next to him. 'Said, sit here. We need to keep close together. I'm doing this on minimal guidance and it's not as accurate as it could be.'

A concussion that made the ground jump; a geyser of dust and rock; a shriek from Wahir and Alessandra; a bass bellow from Said. Even Benzamir flinched, and he knew it was coming.

Half buried in the stony soil was a fat silver tube, streaked with soot and strange coloured patterns.

'Sorry. That was closer than I would have liked,' apologized Benzamir. He spat out a mouthful of debris and dangled his legs over the edge of the crater.

The cylinder opened up like a flower and the contents fell out. Wahir looked over the rim in astonishment. 'How did you do that?'

'Magic. Here, hold this.' He passed up what looked like a metal skullcap and unrolled a length of thick black cloth on the broken ground. He did something to it, and it suddenly went rigid like a slab of stone. Then he hooked on four spheres the size of grapefruit, one to each corner.

'Master?'

'No time to talk. Sit on that, and don't take up too much

room. It wasn't designed for four. Said, get Alessandra over here.'

Said was reluctant to even touch the Ewer woman. Benzamir had to growl at him to make him put his hands under her shoulders and drag her.

'Just sit next to Wahir. I'll do the rest.' He helped her down into the hollow and propped her up against Said's back. 'Wahir? The cap.'

'What's going to happen?'

'This. Hold on tight.' Benzamir clapped the skullcap down on his head, looked distracted for a moment, then the cloth rose into the air.

Everyone shrieked, even Alessandra, which Benzamir took to be a good sign.

'Abracadabra,' he said, and showed all his teeth in a wicked smile. The front of the craft dipped down, and they started to move forward, over the crater, over the low wall, down the slope into the valley.

He took a moment to destroy the evidence: the discarded cylinder vanished in two fearsome explosions, transforming it into unrecognizable scraps of shrapnel.

Someone shouted behind them, but there was no storm of arrows or javelins. Benzamir liked to think that the soldiers were so stunned to see a genuine flying carpet that all they could do was stand and stare.

CHAPTER 19

The strange, stiff rug with its mostly gasping and quivering passengers dipped in and out of the landscape. Benzamir thought that his wonderful sleek carpet steered like a cow; later he'd have to take it for a spin all on his own, no encumbrances.

Wahir was the first to relax and enjoy the ride. He soon stopped clinging to the edge of the carpet with one hand and Said's arm with the other and knelt up, spreading his arms out wide.

He laughed. 'Look, master. I'm flying!'

'Yes,' said Benzamir, 'yes, you are. Can you feel it? The way your stomach gets left behind when we crest a hill?'

'I can feel nothing else,' mumbled Said, who still had his eyes screwed shut.

'You're the first people in nearly a thousand years to feel that sensation. You're moving faster than anyone of your generation, your father's or your grandfather's before them.' He got into a crouch, then stood, balanced on the balls of his feet. 'Isn't this just fantastic, Wahir?'

'Yes, master. This will be a story that will live for ever.'

'There's no greater praise, though I'm afraid we're going to have to stop before Said is ruinously sick.' He looked thoughtful, faraway, and the carpet coasted to a halt.

Before it came to rest on the stony ground, Benzamir hopped off and ran alongside. He turned and looked back.

'Are they following us, master?'

'Even if they wanted to, they couldn't. We've done a day's march in a matter of minutes.' He bent down and helped Said to his feet. Said stepped off the rug, fell to his knees and kissed the ground.

'Boats, barges and now this sorcery. Will my torment never end?'

'My heart bleeds, Said.' Benzamir put Alessandra's arm around his shoulder and his arm around her waist, and led her in a stumbling walk to the top of the hill they'd landed on. 'How are you feeling?' he asked her.

'Like I've been trampled,' she said.

'You might well have been. Anything else broken or injured? Sorry, but I've been throwing you around like a sack of flour in the market.'

'No, just my head.' She felt the matted blood in her hair and tried picking some of it out. It hurt – her face screwed up in pain, and she desisted. 'How did we get here?'

'We flew on my magic carpet.' It sounded so good that Benzamir said it again. 'A magic flying carpet.' He grinned and chuckled to himself.

'I thought I was dreaming. Then I thought I was dying. When I realized that I was doing neither, I was terrified. What are you?'

Wahir wandered up, the desert soil crunching under his sandals. 'He is Benzamir Mahmood, the mightiest magician in the land.'

'Which land?'

'Any land,' said Wahir proudly. 'He is the greatest to have ever lived.'

'Thank you,' said Benzamir. 'I know how it works, but embarrassing me doesn't do either of us any good.'

'Oh,' said Wahir.

'Besides, I'm much more interested in why Alessandra was following us.'

'She was?' Wahir sat down quickly and gazed intently at the Ewer woman. 'Why would she do that? Will we have to kill her?'

'I don't know. I hadn't really thought about killing her, as I'd only just saved her. It'd seem rather a waste. What do you think, Alessandra?'

She looked at Wahir, then at Benzamir, then down the hill to where Said was kneeling, his forehead touching the ground, hoping that the world would stop spinning. Then she looked further out, to the empty desert, the bright blue sky and the fierce, burning sun.

'Can I talk my way out of this?'

'Quite likely. I'm always willing to trade knowledge.'

'The book I told you about, the one sold by a Kenyan . . . It was stolen from the emperor himself. The word went out that he wanted it back, but by then it had disappeared into the back streets of Misr. Now there's a stack of Kenyan gold to the man – or woman – who can find it.'

'And you thought that I was after the book and the reward. So where do the Ethiopians come in?'

'When you headed off in a different direction to everyone else, I didn't know what to think. I chased after you, but that stupid horse dumped me on my head. And thank you for rescuing me.'

'You're welcome.'

'The Ethiopians give tribute to the empire. I can only assume the emperor has run out of patience and that they're here with orders to find the book. The obvious place to start looking for it is at the diggers' market.'

Benzamir leaned forward and started drawing in the dust with his fingertip. 'What's tribute?'

'You'd know if your people ever had to pay it. Rather than having your country invaded, your population enslaved, your cities sacked, you pay. You pay and pay and pay, and maybe they'll leave you alone. To be fair, the emperor used to protect us from the Caliphate; they raided us from the sea all the time and made our lives a misery, but they suddenly stopped five years ago. All we do now is pay and get nothing in return.'

'We have other words for it,' said Benzamir, 'but I understand now. This book that the emperor is so desperate to get – had you ever seen anything like it before?'

'No,' said Alessandra, 'never. I brokered one of the deals, but it couldn't be over fast enough for me. User machines are just things, but this was alive in a way that scared me. It was sold, I took my fee, and the buyer sold it on the next day for a fat profit. That was the last I saw of it, though I heard of it moving through the diggers and booksellers, back and forth, selling each time for ever-increasing amounts of money. A king's ransom by the end. Then it went quiet.' She turned slightly and took another look at Benzamir. 'Are you really a magician?'

'Really? No. Does anyone believe me when I deny it? No. It's easier to answer yes.' He looked at Wahir's expectant face, then took off the metal skullcap, which was becoming uncomfortably warm. He rolled it around in his hands and continued almost at a whisper. 'If I wanted to, I could destroy the emperor, reduce his palace to dust and scatter his armies to the four winds. But it's always been easier to destroy than to build.'

'You could do all that?' asked Wahir.

'Yes.' Benzamir got up and walked away, and stared out into the eastern desert, towards the invisible mountains he might have called home.

Hesitantly Alessandra joined him. 'You don't look like that kind of man.'

'Thank you.'

'Are you boasting?'

'No,' said Benzamir. 'We need to find some shade, or we're all going to fry to a crisp, godlike powers or not. We need to clean your head up too. Come on, let's get back to the carpet.'

As he stalked away back to where Wahir was waiting, Alessandra called after him. 'I've made you angry. I'm sorry.'

'No,' he said without turning, 'not angry. Sad. Every time someone finds out who I am and what I can do, they stop being my friend and start being my follower. I just didn't expect that.'

They found shade in the shadow of a cliff wall after a short flight over the desert, past the point where the surface was merely stony and into the endless sand sea. There was a spring that trickled water down the rock and collected in a cool, dark chasm before it vanished in the blinding heat of the day.

Benzamir summoned another bright cylinder, but this time he pointed up into the sky to show where it came from. They followed where his finger led, and high up in the deep blue zenith a line of light was being drawn. Where the light faded, a tail of smoke appeared before being blown ragged by the wind. Then even the light went out.

The object plummeted to the ground a decent distance away, smacking into the ground in a high-thrown shower of sand. Benzamir went out to collect its contents.

After he'd brought back a single slim case, he said to Alessandra: 'You'll need to come out into the light where I can see what I'm doing.'

'What are you going to do to me?' she asked.

'Stop you from dying. For today at least.'

She sat on a ledge of sandstone and looked fearfully at the case Benzamir opened. 'What is that symbol? The red diamond?'

'Traditional to my people. It means medicine.' He was building a machine out of separate parts, twisting and pushing them until they clicked. 'Tilt your head over away from me.'

She complied, trembling. He pressed the machine to her neck and she felt a sharp scratch.

Firstly, 'Ah! What was that?' Then, 'I feel strange.' Finally, 'I . . . Benzamir?'

Alessandra leaned back, and her eyelids fluttered closed.

Benzamir put the gas gun back on the lid of the case, picked up a pair of long-handled scissors and started cutting the hair away from her wound. He worked quickly, cleaning the blood off in thin red rivers that stained the surrounding stone and applying a thin square of wet material straight from a sealed can. Then he reloaded the gas gun and shot her again in the neck. He moved her back into the shade and left her to sleep off the anaesthetic.

'Master?' asked Said. 'What are you going to do with her now?'

'I don't know. What did you have in mind?' Benzamir filled his water skin from the spring and upturned it over his head.

'She knows of your powers. What's to stop her from talking?'

'Nothing, I suppose. Gratitude?'

'Everyone has their price, master,' said Said. 'She used to be a slave. She knows that money will keep her free.'

Benzamir was silent in thought. When he looked up again, he asked, 'Where's Wahir?'

'Exploring. The king who sent you wants you to find your enemies. Already some of the Ethiopian soldiers have seen your flying carpet, and your – you know . . .' He pointed his finger, except that when Said did it, nothing blew up. 'There have been two of your wondrous deliveries from the Heavens. Now you've healed this Ewer woman with your magic, and master, it's dangerous.'

Benzamir put his hands to his face and slid them slowly down to his chin. 'I know. It's all very different to what I imagined. I thought I'd wander around, pick up clues, find the traitors and take them back. It's a lot more complicated than that, Said.'

'It's like ripples, master.'

'Ripples?'

'Yes, a stone in a pool. The movement spreads outwards until all the surface is disturbed.'

After a while Benzamir said: 'You know, you can be quite wise at times.'

'Thank you, master. You have two choices. Stop making waves, or—'

'Go faster, so that the waves will always be behind me.'

'Yes.'

'We need to find Wahir before he breaks his neck. I'll take the carpet and have a look. Will you stay here with Alessandra?'

'I'd rather not, master.' Said looked away.

'She's unconscious. She can't try and seduce you.' Benzamir punched him on the arm. 'It's all right to like her. She is very pretty.'

Said folded his arms and narrowed his eyes. 'She's an infidel woman.'

'And plenty of those never found their way into a harem, did they?' Benzamir started for the carpet, still basking in the sun.

'She could still ruin everything for you.'

'Not if we run fast enough.' Benzamir dug out the skullcap and slipped it on. The carpet rose into the air, turned lazily and met him halfway. He stepped on and sat cross-legged, just like he'd seen in the picture books. He ought to have a turban; instead, he wound his headscarf around his face until only a slit remained for his eyes.

The front of the carpet dipped as if bowing, then steadily accelerated until Benzamir's kaftan was snapping and cracking behind him. Loose sand billowed up in his wake, two perfect spirals that arced upwards and fell back with balletic grace.

He turned, hard and tight. To his left, the desert. To his right, the sky. Straight ahead, the horizon running in a line up to down. Then he came back, gaining height, rising up the rocks like an eagle in an updraught.

Wahir was on top of the plateau, poking around inside a ruin, a black arched back with ribbing extending down into the dust.

'Master, what is this? It looks like some great beast.'

'It's difficult to tell.' Benzamir uncrossed his legs and found the ground. He patted one of the ribs, still upright but carved and worn by sand and time. He walked underneath it, and along the spine, picking his way over the half-buried debris until he was outside again. Diggers had been here before them. Only the ribs remained. 'It's an aeroplane,' he said.

'A what?'

'A flying machine. These struts are some sort of

composite, carbon tubes and resin. It used to have a skin, and wings, though they seem to have fallen off. There were seats, rows of them, all the way down. People travelled from city to city in them.'

'Is it a User machine?' Wahir got down on his hands and knees and scraped away some dirt near Benzamir's feet. 'Will there be anything working still?'

Benzamir got down beside Wahir, though he didn't attempt to dig. 'Listen. Seeing things like this, and your reaction to them. It worries me.'

'Why, master?' Wahir sifted dust and wind-worn grit through his fingers.

'Because it doesn't inspire you. You don't look on this and wonder how you could make it for yourself. You just wonder at the power and foolishness of the Users, see what there is to scavenge and walk away, shaking your head.' He saw Wahir's reaction and quickly added: 'It's not just you. It's everyone. Anything the Users left behind is impossible for you to recreate. So no one tries. Someone should be trying.'

'Master, I know your ways are different to ours—'

'It's like Selah. He finds it easier to get his steel from the diggers, and in a generation there'll be not a single man who remembers how to make it for himself. It'll be lost. Not for ever, but lost all the same.'

Wahir stopped scooping and sieving. 'What's wrong, master?'

Benzamir unwrapped his headscarf and let the end dangle in the dirt. He gave a sad little smile. 'You see, Wahir, this is what temptation is like. You know the story of Eden, the apple, what it represents? The traitors: they fell. They gave in, for all the best motives, for all the wrong reasons. Me? I can feel it too. The push, the voice telling me that it's right to eat.'

'When you talk like this, I don't understand. Is it because I'm too young?'

'No. It's because I'm always trying to hide the truth from you.' Benzamir sighed and slapped the carbon fibre support with his hand. It shivered for a moment. 'I'm trying to save you from this, from all the works of the Users. And suddenly I don't know if it's the right thing to do any more.'

He got up abruptly, and the flying carpet glided over towards them.

'I trust you,' said Wahir, 'whatever it is you have to decide.'

'Thank you,' said Benzamir, kicking up dust with his sandals. 'I hope I won't let you down.'

'Master, where are we going now?'

'Something that Said and me were talking about – how the faster we go, the less chance there is of getting caught. So: the Kenyan emperor wants his User book back. I'm rather interested in having a look at it myself. Let's go and find it before he does.'

CHAPTER 20

The first that Va and Elenya saw of An Rinn was a boy up a tree. The boy disappeared down behind the leeside of the hill and was lost to sight.

'We can expect a welcome, if not news.' Va strode out with renewed vigour, leaving Elenya in his wake.

'This Kenyan – this rumour of a Kenyan – has led us halfway across the world, and six months later we're in Aeire, the arse-end of nowhere. But it's all the same to you, isn't it?'

Va declined to reply.

She shouted: 'You're a bigger gossipmonger than the whores at court!'

'We're closer now than we've ever been,' he called back.

A stone skittered past him, kicked by Elenya. It fell into the roadside ditch. He stopped and waited for her, his black habit flapping and snapping in the wind as she adjusted her small pack.

He, of course, had nothing. Poverty was one of his vows.

'God has led us here,' he said when she had caught up.

'You've led us here, and don't pretend otherwise.'

When they crested the hill, they could see the rough huts and natural harbour that made up An Rinn. The wind blew in their faces, and they caught hints of wood smoke and cured fish, seaweed and soil. On the flank of the hill towards the headland was a stone church – a single nave with a tower, as was the style in these lands.

'Look,' said Va. 'There, at the end of those houses.'

Four sails processed round above the turfed roofs.

Va picked up the hem of his habit and started to run down the dirt track. The machine slowly revealed itself between walls and trees and the folds in the ground until it was laid bare before him. He stood at the foot of one of its huge supporting beams and looked up at it, amazed and appalled in equal measure.

Under the machine was a woman with a sack of grain, feeding it a handful at a time into the ever-turning millstone. She had her back to him, until the boy they had seen climb down from the tree slipped out from behind a building and gestured to her.

She frowned at him, said something in her barbarian language that sounded like a scold, but the boy just waved more frantically. Eventually, with a long-suffering shrug of her shoulders, she glanced behind her.

She stopped. She put the sack down. She stood and wiped floury hands on her dress.

Va finally noticed that he was being stared at, but all he could think about was the soft swoosh of the sails and the low clatter of the wheel as it turned over his head.

'What manner of abomination is this?' he muttered. 'This has to be the Kenyan's doing.' He shook himself violently to break the spell, and the woman jumped back with a shriek.

She shouted at him; tried to shoo him away as if he was a chicken.

'Who built this?' he raved. 'How can you bear to have it here?'

Neither could understand the other. Va was demanding answers, the woman was barking questions, and soon they were surrounded by the villagers, who had no idea what to make of any of it.

'Out of the way, get out of the way, will you? Nice going, your holiness.' Elenya pushed into the circle. She looked up at the windmill and patted one of the uprights. 'This is new.'

'The Kenyan, I swear it.'

'I'll ask.' She pulled back her hood and cleared her throat. Her beauty commanded silence. 'I bring greetings from Mother Russia,' she said in their language.

The woman who had been having the pointless argument with Va sniffed. 'Who's she? And who are you? And who, in the Good God's name, is this rough thing? If he's supposed

228

to be a monk, he's like none I've ever seen before. What sort of cross is that? What's he saying? Is he mad, or drunk?' She leaned closer to smell his breath, forcing Va to step back against the crowd.

He was pushed from behind to the accompaniment of jeering and hooting.

'I apologize for Brother Va's rude and abrupt manner.' Elenya kicked him to get him to stand still, but she succeeded only in making him dance away from the blow. 'Yes, he is mad, though he's harmless enough. Mother Russia is a land far to the south and west, across the sea and beyond the Franks.'

The locals looked at one another: naFraince marked the edge of their knowledge.

'We're looking for a man – a man who stole something from the brother. This device tells us that he's been here.'

'You mean Solomon Akisi,' said the woman.

Va was listening carefully. Now his enemy had a name.

'Is he a Kenyan?' asked Elenya.

'Sent from the mighty Kenyan empire, as he was fond of saying. Gave us greeting in the name of his king – emperor – whatever he called him.'

'Good woman, we need to speak to him.'

'He's not here,' she snapped. 'The King of Coirc has him, and good riddance, I say.'

'Why, what did he do?'

'Filled our heads with dreams and foolishness, that's what he did, him and his natural philosophy. I said no good would come of it, and I was right. These simpletons were too easily deceived, but—'

'Rose naMoira, it was you who took him in!' said an outraged voice.

'That was common courtesy, macFinn, and I won't have you saying otherwise.' Rose singled out a man in the front row and jabbed him in the chest. 'You're never one for sharing in the good times, but as soon as something goes wrong, you're hanging around your neighbours' thresholds complaining and bellyaching until they give you what you want just to make you go away.'

macFinn snorted like a pig. 'How dare you, you harpy, you morrigan! I keep a well-stocked house and don't you forget it.'

'Silence! In Patrick's name, silence!'

The crowd parted, and a man in a skirt stalked forward.

'Rory, you're back.'

'Well now, Mici, so I am.' The man's face was pinched and white. He stopped, looked at Va and Elenya, and almost turned away. Then he looked back. 'Who are these people?'

'They've come for Akisi,' said Rose.

'Don't mention that name in my presence again. I won't have it, you hear?' He bowed his head and rubbed at his beard. His hand came away as a clenched fist. 'I went to Kilkenny, asked the abbot there if they'd seen Father Padroig. They had too. He spent a week with the brothers at the abbey, and then they sent him on his way, back to us. I asked in the villages on the Kilkenny road if they remembered seeing a white-haired priest pass through, and they all did.'

macFinn interrupted. 'Where is he then, macShiel?'

'He's dead, man! He's dead. I found his body in the ditch, half eaten by crows, less than a day's walk from here.' Rory macShiel's voice caught in his throat and he crouched down, letting fat tears fall into the dirt.

A dark-haired woman squeezed through. She touched macShiel on the arm, and he clung to her as if she was life itself.

'It was Akisi, damn him to hell!'

Elenya pulled Va to one side and whispered to him in Rus: 'We've arrived at a very bad time. The Kenyan seems to have killed this village's priest some time in the past. Now he's with the local king, in some place called Coirc.'

'We'll have to find out where this Coirc is,' said Va. No one was paying them any attention. 'So he's a murderer as well as a thief.'

'We don't know that. We don't even know if it was him who took the books from you.'

Va growled in frustration. 'We're so close. I can smell it on the wind.'

'That's just shit and fish guts.' Elenya examined the mill as the crowd gyred away along the main street, macShiel at its centre. A few of the men glanced back at her before being pulled away. A boy hung back, the same boy who'd spotted them earlier. 'Young man, come here a moment. What's your name?'

'Brendan macFinn, if it please you, mistress.'

'We're both very sorry for the loss of your priest, Brendan. We'd very much like to help in any way we can.'

Brendan macFinn alternated between looking at the ground and staring into Elenya's eyes. 'Yes, mistress. I don't know. I could ask my father.'

'In a minute, perhaps. Who's the man who went to look for the priest?'

'Rory macShiel. He builds boats, and he built this too. He and Master Akisi worked together.'

'Master Akisi?' Elenya arched an eyebrow, but smiled as well.

Young macFinn clutched at his heart as if he could feel it melting. 'I was apprenticed to him for a while. He had secrets, mistress. All sorts of secrets. He could make and bend light, design machines, and he had this book, a big silver book. I sneaked a peek inside once. The pictures moved!'

'Thank you, Brendan.'

'But then it all went wrong. There was a battle at An

Cobh, and Master Akisi chose the wrong side, and I got captured, and the king's men came for him, and he killed one of them, and they took him away.' He gasped for breath. 'And now I've found out he killed Father Padroig, and I don't know what to think any more.'

'It'll be all right.' She held him at arm's length, a hand on each shoulder.

Brendan macFinn couldn't quite believe that such a beautiful creature was actually touching him, speaking kindly to him. 'Yes, mistress.'

'Now off you go. Thank you.'

The boy reeled away as if stunned, and Elenya turned to a sour-faced Va.

'You do the child no favours,' he said.

'Just because you're immune to my charm doesn't mean I haven't still got it. Akisi has a book – the boy says he saw one volume. One, mind; not all twelve.'

'He'll know where the others are.'

'If he's still alive. He could have been executed by now. He killed a king's man when they came to claim him.'

Va bit at his hand. 'I pray it isn't so.'

'Do you think your prayers are going to be more use than these people's? They've lost their priest to this man, and they'll be calling down bloody vengeance on his head.' Elenya shook her head. 'Why should God listen to you and not to them?'

'Because if he's dead, the trail goes cold and I can't get all the books back, and it's God's will that I do.' Va slammed the palm of his hand hard against the wood of the mill, causing the whole structure to sing. 'Anything else is just wrong.'

'So what will you do?'

'Wait until these savages have come to their senses. Where's bread? Where's salt? It's not like this in Mother Russia.' Va stormed down to the harbour and sat down heavily on a creel.

The little fishing boats bobbed in time with the waves, and his eye was inevitably drawn to one in particular that had something strange hanging from the mast. The last time he'd seen something similar, it had been on a Caliphate warship.

He'd burned them all, and everyone on board.

At the back of his mind the whispering accusations began, and grew as the tide came in until it filled his head with noise.

He had no hair to tear out. Instead he threw himself down on the stony beach and battered the cobbles with his fists.

'Va? Va, you have to stop. The man macShiel is here.'

He looked up from his supine position, panting. The tide had crept in and he was wet with sea and sand. macShiel asked Elenya a question, but indicated Va.

234

'He wants to know what you were doing. A reply that doesn't make him question your sanity any more than he does already would be welcome.'

'Penance. Tell him my sins are many and great.'

She repeated the answer, and the kilted man seemed satisfied.

'Ask him about that boat.' Va pointed. 'Is that the Kenyan's doing?'

macShiel nodded. 'It's how they build them in his land. I have to admit, it is better: faster, more manoeuvrable. You can do things in it you can't with a square sail.'

'Tell it to naFraince. The leaky bucket we came here on wasn't fit for a river.'

macShiel laughed, then remembered the dead priest. 'He stole something from you.'

'A book, one of a set. We know he has it – the boy's seen it. It belongs to the patriarch of All Russia, and it's my holy duty to take it back.'

'Good luck then. The word I hear is that King Ardhal has paid the blood-price to the family of the man he killed here. If he now works for the king, you might have trouble.'

'Did he really kill your priest?'

macShiel sucked air and blew out his cheeks. 'Who else? Adding up the days, Father Padroig and Akisi' – he turned and spat – 'were on the road together. One of them didn't arrive.'

Elenya interrupted herself. 'All this talk is thirsty work.' She gazed out to sea and said nothing more.

'These are bad times, mistress, and we forget ourselves. We lose our manners as well as our self-respect. I can't even raise men to get the father's body.'

'What did he say?' said Va, and when Elenya finally told him, he got up. 'I'll go with him. I'll have seen worse, smelled worse, done worse.'

'That's true enough, Va,' she murmured. She relayed his offer.

macShiel was genuinely moved that a stranger would help where his kinsmen would not. 'Come and eat with me, and we'll do what needs to be done later.'

They followed him through the village, past the curious, fearful and sometimes lustful stares. None of them said anything though, because it was all too different and no one was certain of anything any more.

CHAPTER 24

They stayed hidden behind a twisted hedge of thorns while the army passed by. Va lay on his stomach, perfectly still, the hood over his head arranged in such a way that he could see out with one eye. Elenya sat at his feet, facing out into the field and away from the road. Her grey cloak and hunched shoulders made her look like a boundary stone, unmoved for years.

Peering through the slit between brown soil and black wood, Va had watched the horses go by, the infantry go by, and finally the cattle-drawn carts laden with supplies. It had taken half the morning, and now there were the followers that tagged along behind every army. Wives, whores, thieves, cooks, musicians; some of them all those roles in one.

The last pair of feet disappeared from view, and Va turned onto his back. 'It's only a small army. A thousand fighting men, a hundred horse.'

'But none of them landless peasants being led to their slaughter by some crazed mercenary sick with love.'

Va swallowed hard. 'No, I suppose not. But it looks like High King Cormac is going back for another try.'

Elenya stood up and stretched. 'Who isn't the real High King at all, just some upstart from Mumhan.' She slung her bag over her shoulder and started for the gap in the hedge. 'This isn't going to be easy, you know,' she said.

'It still has to be done.'

'You can't just march in and demand the book back.'

'macShiel said this Ardhal is an honourable man. Honourable men don't like the idea of owning stolen property. So, yes, that's exactly what I'm going to do.'

'Except you'll need me to translate for you, or did you think he spoke Rus? I could tell him that you're some odious tree-worshipper from the far south holding me hostage, and that I'm throwing myself on his mercy if only he'd free me from your cruel ownership. And you wouldn't be able to tell until they fetched the rope to hang you.'

'You wouldn't do that.' He frowned at her slight. 'I do know some World.'

'Va, when you commanded your vast armies, how did you manage to tell them what you wanted them to do?'

'I had people.'

'It's a good job you still do. Now it looks like An Cobh is going to be under siege again, you'll have to work out a way of getting in and out without being killed by either side as a spy.'

Va knocked a stone out of his sandals. 'God will provide.'

'Whenever you say that, I know you're going to do something stupid and trust to luck.' Elenya searched her bag for the hard yellow cheese macShiel's wife had given her. 'The problem is, it always works, doesn't it?'

She twisted the lump of cheese this way and that until it broke into two unequal portions. She kept the smaller and gave Va the larger.

They trailed the army until noon, when they stopped at the top of the hill overlooking An Cobh. The soldiers marched on and started to arrange themselves in the valley below, slowly working their way round to cut the promontory off from the land. The horsemen darted this way and that, issuing orders and rounding up the livestock that hadn't been withdrawn inside An Cobh's stone walls.

'This is a rubbish siege,' said Elenya. 'They can still get supplies in by boat. They'll give up in a week and go home.'

'If they had any boats. Didn't macShiel say Cormac burned them all last time?'

'True. But they can always make more.'

'They don't seem too worried.' Va stood as tall as he could, his hand shading his eyes. 'Ah. They've got a couple of galleys coming into the bay.'

'So it's not so rubbish.' Elenya watched the valley as the soldiers put up tents and built fires at intervals around the walls. 'This rabble seems quite organized. Bit of a setback for you.'

'Something will turn up.'

The gates of An Cobh were closed. The walls were crowded with figures, going this way and that, all too far away to tell what they were doing. Wood smoke started to obscure the scene further.

'All this for just one book,' said Elenya.

'I know. But you said the thieves were led by a black man.'

'I said a man in black. I couldn't tell the colour of his skin.'

Va looked at the way the sentries were arrayed. 'I should be able to slip through the picket during the night. The walls are climbable. I might need some rope.'

'And what about me? How do you propose to get me in?'

Va tutted. 'That's up to you.'

'You won't leave me behind.' She put her hand lightly on his arm.

He flinched and put his own hand to cover where she had touched him, as if burned. 'I need to check on the defences on the far side of town.'

'Then we'll walk together.'

They were halfway round the horseshoe curve of the surrounding hills when fresh black smoke rose in two pillars behind An Cobh. Va tried to make out what had happened, but the rock on which the town sat hid the shore from view.

'They must be firing the port.'

'Who, Cormac or the king?'

'I can't tell. It doesn't make sense, either way. Cormac will want to take the town; the King of Coirc will want to keep it. There's no sense in burning it all to the ground.'

Then one of the boats hove into view. Its rigging was alight, along with most of the foredeck. It was abandoned, and it heeled over to starboard without check. The crew were tiny white splashes in the choppy sea.

Pushed by the wind, the hull turned towards the shore, the flames whipping up along the deck in great roiling tongues. The mast tilted, wobbled and fell hissing into the water.

'What happened to that?' said Va. He took a faltering step back, then steadied himself. It reminded him too much of the other fire, the other boats.

He started down the hill. He had to conquer his fear.

'Va! Va! Stop.' Elenya jumped at him, took him around the waist with both her arms and dragged him down onto the scrubby emerald grass.

He tried to push her away without touching her, and twisted his body so that she was forced to let go. By the time he looked up again, the sky was cut with a dozen smoky lines, arcing out from the town walls and aiming high over the encamping army.

The first trail stopped with a sharp cracking sound and a puff of white smoke. Instantly all the other trails bar one did the same, the noise blending into barrages of noise that echoed down the valley.

The High King's men turned from the stricken boat to look upwards.

The first few to be hit simply couldn't believe it. They grasped the sharp metal flights suddenly protruding from their bodies and tried to pull them free. The ground bristled with spikes, and finally one man raised his shield in time as his comrade next to him sank to the ground, his open mouth neatly skewered.

Va tried to get up, and again Elenya pulled him down. Another section of the wall had loosed burning fingers of smoke that reached up and out. The horsemen in the line of fire wheeled about, uncertain what was happening to them, undecided which direction to run. Those who dithered were cut down by the hard rain.

A new tactic: more smoke and fire, this time aimed directly at the reeling foot soldiers. The streaks hit the soft earth at a shallow angle. Some buried themselves, others skidded across the sheep-cropped grass. All paused for breath, then vanished in a flash of light, a snap of thunder. Anyone close by fell down as if dead.

'Think about the book,' said Elenya in Va's ear. 'Think of what I'd have to tell the patriarch – that you threw your life away.'

'But they're dying,' he groaned.

'And you can't save them. Lie still.'

The High King's tent seemed out of range of the King of Coirc's devilry. He had to watch his army being massacred before him, yet remain untouched himself. Each section of the wall threw high spikes, followed it with the low-aimed explosions, and those left alive ran from the field screaming and crying.

The King of Coirc had one last trick. A single stripe of sooty smoke burst from a tower, wrote a dark line across the strange-smelling sky and petered out. Then it flashed into life again, falling beyond Cormac's camp and destroying a blackthorn tree. The would-be High King got the message. He leaped on his horse and fled back over the hill. His abandoned kinsmen kicked over the fluttering banner and rode to the top of the hill. There they stopped and waited for the remnants of the army to straggle their way back to them.

'Can I get up now?' said Va.

'It's over,' said Elenya. 'Yes.'

He got up and brushed himself down, his heavy cross bouncing on his black-clad chest. His hands were trembling.

'Va?'

'He's opened the book.'

'How do you know?'

'Because,' he said, pointing towards An Cobh, 'that's what's in the books. The Users put all their secrets in them –

243

the same secrets that destroyed them and Reversed the world. I need to get those books back now, before it all happens again.' He watched the gates of the town swing open and the king's men walk slowly out of the shadow of the gatehouse.

'They look as shocked as anyone else.'

'So they should. They've been set on the road to Hell by their king and this damned Kenyan thief.' He strode off down the hill.

'Va, you can't.'

'I can and I will. God is on my side.' He clutched his cross in both hands. 'He is my shield and my sword.'

He walked on. Not all of Cormac's men had been killed outright. The injured called out to him in their strange foreign tongue, holding out their hands and pleading with him. Va walked on, even though it was agony for him to do so.

He was back outside the city of Novy Rostov, his bright plates of armour red with blood, his sword arm numb with effort, his helmet battered and jammed on his head, his calf cut and bleeding, his left shoulder a mass of pain and bone fragments. Every step he took, he trod on someone, something: a pool of dashed brains, a coil of intestines, a shattered torso, sightless eyes, unidentifiable human mulch that had once been a daughter or a son.

The dead were lucky. It was the still living who were

cursed. They moaned. They cried. They sobbed. The sound of ten thousand voices in agony cut his soul in two.

At the gates of Novy Rostov, where the bodies gathered in drifts like snow, the last Caliphate soldier had raised the stained and ragged crescent standard of his people. He swayed as if drunk, only his spear keeping him upright. And finally Va reached him, wading through the corpses of both their armies.

There was no ceremony, no honour. Va raised his sword, put the broken point of it against the soldier's throat, and the man just stumbled onto it, glad finally to be free of the torment of seeing and hearing.

He fell, and with him, Va's sword. He'd not touched it, or another, again. His moment of victory had been shown for the catastrophe it was. He had raised an army, trained it, organized it, led it. It had been his tactics that had crushed the Caliphate's encircling troops, liberated Novy Rostov and broken the power of the caliph for a decade to come. All for what? Love. He'd been the last man standing, and he'd known in that moment that nothing could possibly be worth that carnage.

That was why, walking through the wounded, battle-torn and bleeding, he could ignore everything. Elenya was right: he couldn't save these men, but he could prevent a greater calamity by reclaiming the stolen books.

Someone caught his robe and he heard the word for

'father'. He was calling for a priest: not a true priest of the Orthodox Church, the one true Church that had preserved God's message inviolate and unchanging for ever. These people's priests were full of strange doctrines and heretical practices that made his heart burn with indignation.

Two days ago he'd buried one as best he could. He couldn't bring himself not to call the man Christian.

'Father.'

Va looked down. The man was burned, hand and face. His left foot had gone. His eyes gazed up wetly from amongst the blackened ruin.

'I'm not a priest,' said Va.

The man didn't understand Rus. But Elenya was there, kneeling beside him, whispering into his ear. He moved his head slightly to see her, this angel who had appeared and provided the gift of tongues.

'It doesn't matter,' he said in Elenya's voice, 'you're a man of God. Pray for me.'

'I have God's greater work to do. I have to go.'

He held on tighter to the hem of Va's habit. 'I'm frightened,' he said.

Shamed, Va sank to ground, furiously wiping tears away with his coarse sleeves. He put his hand on the man's forehead. 'There's no reason to be afraid. We're soldiers. We go here and there as we're ordered. You were obedient to your earthly lord because you're obedient to your heavenly lord.

Men betray you because they're weak or foolish or arrogant and uncaring. God won't let you down. Trust Him.'

Elenya spoke unfamiliar, hesitant words, then said to Va: 'He's dead. He's gone.'

'No,' he gasped. He saw that it was true and tore at his habit. He leaped up, spun round and found the next man still living. He crossed himself, kissed the cross and started to pray for the man's soul.

He was tapped on the shoulder. When it happened a second time, Va spat out: 'What?'

A boy from An Cobh stood behind him. He was offering some strips of clean linen as bandages and a skin of water. He was ash-white and looked as if he was about to cry. Va recognized himself in that lost face.

'Give them to me,' he said, and gestured. The boy took fright at his foreignness, and it took comforting words from Elenya for him to relinquish his death-grip on the water.

The man on the ground had an iron barb in his thigh, another in his side. His skin was grey and felt clammy to the touch. When Va looked, he realized there was a vast pool of blood soaking into the ground underneath him.

He worked quickly, applying a tourniquet high up on the man's leg, almost at the groin, and tightened it with one of the spikes that had dug into the turf nearby.

'This man will die if we can't get that arrow out and the hole sewn shut. Tell him,' said Va to Elenya.

The boy looked from the monk to the woman, and ran off back into town.

'I think he's going to die anyway,' she said. 'But why did you change your mind?'

Va absent-mindedly smeared blood on his forehead. 'I hate myself. I hate the compromises I make all the time. Life breeds sin, and I'm dirty with it.'

'There, there. Just sometimes you forget yourself and do what's right.'

Va sat back on his haunches. Up on the hill, a pitiful few had gathered together. In the valley, at the edges, robbers were at work, killing the wounded and stealing from the dead. Closer to the town, the King of Coirc's men were moving across the fields, spreading out.

They were as appalled by the manner of their victory as Cormac's men. Guiltily they picked up those they could save and carried them inside the stone walls.

CHAPTER 22

No one questioned him or challenged his right to enter the town at the end of the day. He'd worked tirelessly, dressing wounds so that they might not turn to stinking rot in a few days, easing the last moments of those who were never going to see another sun rise.

He had preferred pulling arrows and sewing cuts and mopping blood to the prayers and the sanctification of souls. The men weren't Rus, knew nothing of Orthodoxy, acknowledged someone other than the patriarch as their spiritual leader. Their own heretical priests had helped them far more than he could, because even as he crossed their foreheads with cold, shining water, he felt as if he was betraying his vows.

Va and Elenya walked behind the last of the carts laden with dead together with the people of An Cobh, as if they'd earned their place amongst them. Something made Va look up and back as they passed under the gatehouse. Staring down on them were two men, one with grey hair and a heavy gold chain, the other in a rich purple cloak: the King of Coirc and the Kenyan, Solomon Akisi.

The king failed to notice the incandescent rage directed at him, but Akisi caught a sudden chill and shivered. He whispered in the king's ear and gave a surreptitious gesture, pointing out Va in the crowd below them.

As the townspeople left the procession to return to their own houses, their number thinned. Finally it was just the cart, the driver and a man with a prodigious moustache whose hands were as bloody as Va's.

He addressed Va directly. Va looked blank and glanced at Elenya.

'He's inviting us to share his plank with him.'

'His what? Is this some sort of insult, or a barbarian greeting?'

'Plank. No. Board? Table.' Elenya checked her translation with the man. 'Yes, he wants us to come and eat with him. He says it would honour his building. Household. Family. Sorry, it's been a long day. To be honest, I don't think I care what you say, I'm saying yes.'

'I don't see us overwhelmed with offers. These people have no idea of hospitality.' Va sized up the native. 'Tell him we'll go with him.'

'My name is Eoin macDonnabhan,' said the man, 'and my house is yours on this sad day.'

He led them through the shadowed, narrow streets that were reminiscent of Moskva at its poorest. At some points they had to turn sideways to squeeze though the gaps between the walls. It was as if An Cobh had been grown, rather than built. macDonnabhan pointed out the important local landmarks – a stone tower, a marketplace cross, a long open hall with vaulted arches – and as Elenya patiently translated for Va, he started to address his remarks to her instead.

Va was party to less and less of the conversation, and eventually was left out altogether. When they arrived at a house close to the eastern wall and went in, he was momentarily surprised and left out on the doorstep.

Inside there was space and light and warmth, the calling of voices and the barking of dogs. Outside, he was quite alone. Then Elenya leaned back and asked him: 'Are you coming in?'

'Yes. What were you talking about all that time?'

'I'll have to tell you later. Va, do you trust me?'

'I . . . suppose so. What are you doing?'

'Trying to help you, though I don't know why.' She jerked her head. 'In, and try not to frown at everything.'

Va stepped over the threshold. Someone reached behind him to shut out the night, and a hand at his back ushered him into the room. macDonnabhan clapped his hands twice, and talking from all, young and old, trickled to an expectant hush.

A dog as tall as the youngest child pushed its way through the forest of legs and sniffed tentatively at Va's hand with its thin muzzle. Its nose was wet, and it spent a while exploring the interesting smells he'd collected since he'd last washed.

'They're waiting for you to introduce yourself,' said Elenya.

'Oh. Va. Brother Va. I'm sure His Holiness Father Yeremai, patriarch of Moscow and of all Russia, the patriarch of the Orthodox Church, would send his greetings.'

Elenya told them her name too: 'Knyazhna Elenya Lukeva Christyakova.' She explained what Knyazhna meant.

The Aeireanns drew breath as one. macDonnabhan scuffed his feet on the stone floor and looked at the filth he was covered in.

'These aren't my best clothes, Princess,' he said.

'That's all right,' she said with a sigh. 'I'm not at all princessy.'

He motioned to Va that he should follow him. 'Brother, we need to clean ourselves up before we sit at the table. You travel in exalted company.'

Va could see that macDonnabhan didn't doubt Elenya's title. They didn't need to see her dressed all in gold, servants and handmaidens trailing behind her, passing down the central aisle of Novy Rostov's cathedral. They could tell just from how beautiful she was.

A tub of hot water waited for them in a back room, together with bars of yellow soap and linen towels. macDonnabhan mimed what to do with them, and Va fought back a scowl. He said in Rus, his face determinedly neutral: 'We have baths a hundred times more grand than this where I come from. I come from the centre of Christian civilization, not some bog at the end of the world.'

They stripped and washed. One of macDonnabhan's men – family by the look of him – brought in new clothes. Va dunked his habit in the washing water and started to scrub.

macDonnabhan shook his head. 'Women's work,' he said.

Va brought his sodden habit out and wrung it. The muscles on his arms stood out like cords. 'My work,' he said in World. 'My cloth. I have God's orders.'

'Holy orders?'

'Yes.'

'I understand.' macDonnabhan said something to the man who'd brought his clothes, who ran off. 'Wait, please,' he told Va.

He dressed in a linen shirt and trousers, put boots on his feet and took out a small tin of ointment. He waxed his moustache until it was stiff. Va plunged his habit in again, beat it on the side of the tub and twisted the water out again. He was about to put it on, when macDonnabhan's man burst through the door again, carrying a coarse brown bundle.

'Holy orders,' said macDonnabhan, presenting Va with the cloth.

Va put down his dripping habit and shook out his

present. It was a monk's habit: the wrong colour, and it was going to drown him. These apostate Aeireann brothers were built on a different scale to him. macDonnabhan was trying so hard, he was making it difficult for Va to keep the strict vows he had made.

'Dry, yes?' said Va, pointing to his own black habit.

'Yes.'

Va put on the habit, gathered up the mass of loose material around his waist and tied it off with the cord. He picked up his cross, kissed it and put it back around his neck. Wearing brown was wrong. It wasn't Orthodox. But it would have to do.

Back in the main room, Elenya was surrounded by the women and children, the men standing back and talking amongst themselves. When Va and macDonnabhan appeared, the women went off to fetch the food while the children took their chance to crowd closer to a real princess and touch her long dark hair.

The men moved tables and benches; beaten metal plates and worn metal knives appeared out of chests; jugs banged down and horn cups clattered. macDonnabhan took his place at the head of the table and made sure that Va sat to his right, Elenya to his left.

'It suits you,' said Elenya to Va.

'Only until mine is dry. Have you learned anything useful?' Va tightened the cord again.

'All these people are one family; a clan, they call them. macDonnabhan is the clan name, and Eoin macDonnabhan is the head of the clan. He used to be in favour with King Ardhal, but since the Kenyan came he's lost status.'

'Will he help us?'

'I believe so, but it might depend on the Rus capacity for drink being greater than the Aeireann.'

'What could they possibly brew here that's stronger than vodka?'

'Something called uisge, apparently. Ah, here comes the food.'

Honoured guests got the best portions and the strongest drink. There was bread, potatoes, mutton and beef, and ale so dark and bitter that it was difficult to swallow without pulling a face.

Eoin macDonnabhan started off brightly enough, then fell more maudlin as the evening wore on. He drank more and ate less. He started to speak about the king, and his clansmen shushed him; about Solomon Akisi, and they talked louder to drown him out. The woman of the house, who was Eoin's sister and not his wife, attempted to persuade him to retire to bed, but he called for uisge so insistently that eventually a stone bottle was brought in.

He drained his cup of ale and poured in some of the

golden liquid from the bottle. He stood unsteadily, raised his drink and toasted: 'The King of Coirc, may he rot in hell.'

No one replied, so he drank alone.

Va took the bottle and dribbled a thin stream into his own cup. He sniffed at it, and his eyes watered. He got to his feet. 'Tsar Ardhal.' He flicked his wrist, swallowed and paused a moment while the room slipped in and out of focus.

Elenya reached for the bottle, charged her cup, stood and drank defiantly. Still none of the macDonnabhan. clan would join in. So she picked up the bottle, tipped yet more uisge into Eoin and Va's cups before filling her own. The three stood there, separated by language and culture but united by common purpose.

'Who'll drink with me?' said Eoin. 'Who'll drink with me but the princess and the foreign brother? Will my own family desert me? Will they stand by and watch as their king takes us all on the road to perdition?'

'Eoin, it's the drink talking,' said his sister. 'Apologies, Princess, Brother.'

'It is not! It's loosened my tongue, is all. Did you see what happened out there today? Did you see? That wasn't a fair fight. It wasn't a fight at all. It was bloody slaughter and that's the beginning and end of it.'

'We were defending our homes.'

'Our quarrel was with Cormac, not his men, and we spitted them like rabbits over the fire.' He picked up his knife and slammed it down in the remnants of the leg of mutton. 'We didn't give them a chance. We didn't warn them. We just butchered them, even as they ran. Even as they ran, I tell you.'

His last comment hit home, and the men stopped calling for him to sit down and reluctantly began to nod.

'You see the truth of it, do you? Since when have the men of Coirc stabbed anyone, even their enemies, in the back? We're men, I say, not murderers.'

'Suppose you speak right, Eoin macDonnabhan,' said his sister's husband. 'What would you have us do? You don't have the king's ear any more. He listens to no one except Solomon Akisi.'

'Then we need a new king,' said Eoin into the silence.

'He's going to get himself killed,' said Va in Rus.

'Then do something,' said Elenya.

'Speak for me.' Va cleared his throat. 'There is another way. Rather than a new king, would you not prefer your old king back?'

'We would,' said the brother-in-law, 'but he's been bewitched by the Kenyan.'

'I came here to find a book—' said Va, and Eoin interrupted.

'The metal book? It's a User thing. I said it was cursed.'

Va snarled. 'He stole it. He killed my brothers. He burned my monastery. That book is the patriarch's, and I'm taking it back to Moskva with me.'

His sudden change of demeanour startled the macDonnabhans. One or two of them clutched at their knives.

'I want the book. But if you want me to take Akisi too, you're going to have to help me.' He looked around the room. 'The book is cursed. There's spilled blood on every page and worse: if you start to live like the Users, you'll die like the Users. Do you want the sea to swallow you up? Do you want your houses in ruins? Do you want your good name to be used as a profanity, just like the Users'?'

'You're going to have to slow down, Va,' said Elenya. 'You're going too fast.'

'I've said all I need to say. If they've got any balls, they'll bundle Akisi into a sack and deliver him to me.'

'It's their king they're going against. It's not their balls they're worried about; it's their necks.'

Eoin raised his cup. 'I'll give him all the help he wants. I swear it to be true.' He drank.

'You won't remember in the morning, Eoin. You'll wake with a thick head and a sorry heart, and the only thing you'll be swearing to is that you said nothing of the sort.'

'Shut up, Deirdre. I've had enough, understand? Of your nagging and the king's madness. We'll do it tonight, then, if you don't think I've the stomach for it tomorrow.' He swayed against his chair. 'Bring me my sword.'

One of Eoin's cousins went to fetch it, and he was pulled back by another. They started to fight, great ruddy fists windmilling. Pulled apart, they fought those who restrained them, the dogs barked wildly and the room descended into chaos and uproar. Why the plates looked so battered was explained by Deirdre macDonnabhan throwing one at her brother. He ducked in time and launched the dregs of his drink at her face.

Va grabbed the bottle of valuable uisge and retreated to the bathhouse door. Elenya dodged a meaty beef joint and vaulted an upturned bench to join him. Two silver streaks of dog dashed past on their way to the bone, and they began to fight too.

'Barbarians. I told you.'

'They love fighting. You should be pleased.'

'They love fighting each other.' Va kicked the door open and slipped inside. 'Fat lot of use they turned out to be.'

Elenya put her back against the door, and the sounds of cracking wood and crunching knuckles dulled. There was another door that led outside, and they sat on the back step together.

'Another day wasted,' said Va. 'Another day with the books out in the world, turning men's minds from the things of God to the works of the Devil.'

'You're as miserable as they are. *Woe is me, I can't do a thing,*' she mocked. 'When did you ever need man's help, Va Angemaite, when you have God on your side?'

There was a half-moon blinking in and out of the clouds. Va looked up and chewed at his lip. 'I've lacked faith. How stupid of me. How could I possibly doubt? My cause is right, isn't it? So who can stand against me? Not this Ardhal, King of Coirc, not the clan macDonnabhan, and certainly not the thief Akisi. Wait here.'

He went back into the bathhouse and quickly changed the brown robe for his own damp black one.

'We don't wait for the Aeireanns. We do it now.'

CHAPTER 23

Important men never lived in the lowest part of town. It was a truth that Va had seen again and again. They somehow believed that altitude gave them status, and they sought out the tallest tower or the highest peak to better look down at the mortals below. In turn, the little people had to shield their eyes and crane their necks to catch sight of their masters. It was political architecture, designed to preserve and reinforce power.

It made it absurdly easy to remove the ruling class of a city. Va had done it before, creeping from one well-appointed house to another, slipping in from a balcony designed for show or a wide tower window, leaving behind him a grisly trail of misery and confusion.

To find the king and his new adviser, Va had looked up, up, until he found the stone tower overlooking the foul-smelling workshops turned over to alchemical practices. Such was their confidence that they had no enemies within the walls, there were no guards.

Va and Elenya passed silently through the deserted sheds,

stopping to inspect the barrels of white salt, yellow powder, black dust, and the half-finished tubes waiting for their packing of metal arrows. The door of ill-fitting planks allowed Va to squint out at the base of the tower.

'There's a light in the top window. That's where he'll be.'

'Alone?'

'Probably.'

'And if he's not?'

'I'll have to improvise.'

'I won't stop them from killing you.'

'You already have.' Va slid a coil of rope over his head and one shoulder.

'A moment of weakness. No one should have to die like that.' Elenya looked through the door herself. 'It doesn't look easy.'

'I've climbed worse.' He rubbed his fingers in the dust and kicked off his sandals.

'Who would have thought that your former profession would come in so handy?' she said wistfully. 'You've renounced violence, but not sneaking in through windows.'

'King Ardhal won't let me have the book now. His mind's been corrupted.' He slipped the latch and eased the door open a fraction. 'All I can do now is take it.'

'And Akisi too.'

Va pulled the door back shut. 'What?'

'You're going to have to either kill him or kidnap him. You can't leave him here, even if you do get him to tell you where the other books are.' She blinked in the darkness. 'You don't think he's going to stop making these weapons for the king just because you've stolen his book back, do you?'

'I . . .'

'You did. Don't be such an idiot, Va. You're obsessed with the books when it's not the books you have to be worried about. It's what's in them that's important, and that's now in Akisi's head. Do you know what else he can build? I don't, but I wouldn't want to be around when he does. Finish him while you have the opportunity.'

Gnawing at his fist, Va pulled a variety of faces. 'I won't commit an act of violence on him.'

'It would have been so easy before, wouldn't it?' said Elenya. 'A knife at his throat, dig it in, twist it round. And when he broke, gabbled out all he knew, drive it home, up into the brain. Or side to side, making his throat gape and suck air as he bleeds.'

His hand was shaking. 'I won't. I can't.'

'You do what you have to do. I won't tell the patriarch.'

'But I will.' He took a series of deep breaths, trying to steady himself.

'What are you going to do then?' she hissed.

'I don't know.' He opened the door again and slipped out

across the courtyard, ducking through the shadows made by half-formed arrow launchers.

Elenya tried to call him back, but he was already at the base of the tower, exploring the gaps in the stonework with his fingertips. The blocks were hard black basalt: the joints hadn't weathered much, and there were finger spaces only where they'd been poorly fitted together.

Va would have chosen the door rather than the wall, but he planted two fingers in the wall and wedged them in tight. He leaned back and took two steps up. He was off the ground, and somewhere above him was another handhold he could use, no matter how small.

He spent as much time searching for a grip as he did actually ascending. He was forced to move into the shadow just by the way he had to climb, and after a while he shut his eyes and let his hands see for him. He was a black spider with pale legs, and it would only have taken someone to glance up for him to be discovered.

But the wizard's tower filled the residents of An Cobh with dread, even the watchmen who were supposed to guard the town's walls. No one was looking.

His face a mask of pain, Va reached the high window. He stole a peek.

Akisi had his back to him. He was sitting at the table, writing in a book with a quill. He was definitely alone.

Va knew his muscles were starting to lock tight. Another

moment and he'd not be able to do anything. He raised one foot onto the window ledge, then worked his shoulders into the space. Akisi carried on his scratchy writing.

He took a moment to recover, then unfolded himself onto the floor. He stretched silently, and he could see the glint of silvery metal over the Kenyan's shoulder. He remembered the fire, the blood, the cold, the rain, the earth. He remembered the Systema.

From where he stood it was just two steps to the back of Akisi's chair, and still he didn't turn round. Va put his right arm across the Kenyan's throat and squeezed it tighter with his left. He lifted slightly, then pulled backwards to increase the effect.

Akisi's long-fingered hands came up and tried to dislodge Va's strangle-hold. He scratched and shuffled for the next few heartbeats, but he was unable to make a sound. Va knew that he'd found the pressure points when Akisi's arms flopped down, and his whole body went limp.

He could let him die simply by simply standing there and maintaining his hold. He felt the acid rise up in his throat again even as the voices started whispering to him.

'Oh God, oh God.' He let go abruptly, instinctively catching the chair as it rocked backwards. Akisi lay on the floor, very still. Va looked at what he'd done – what he'd almost done. He checked Akisi's breathing and pulse, and decided to turn a moment of sin to virtue.

He had to work quickly. He hog-tied him hand and foot with his rope and gagged him with a strip cut from the hem of his purple cloak. He scanned the desk.

The writing book went into the fire without a second thought. There were some loose papers with it. Some were diagrams, and these joined the flames. One was a map, strange and roughly drawn. He folded it up and tucked in his habit.

The cold metal cover of the User book chilled his hands as he picked it up. This was what he'd come for. The first of twelve. He looked for something to put it in, and found himself staring at the glowing square of cloth hung on the wall. The sight of it, the unnaturalness of it, offended him so much that he snatched at it, ripping it down. The light left the weave immediately, and he was left clutching a bundle of black material eminently suitable for book carrying. He hastily folded the book into the cloth and used more of Akisi's cloak to tie it closed.

But the room was full of the ghastly works of the Users. The cloth was the least of it. The whole place smelled strange, metallic to the tongue. It had to go. He was suddenly at one with the holy Wreckers: it all had to burn.

Va threw the rest of the cloak into the fire. It hung half in, half out, and the burning wood had already been supplemented by dry paper. Then he was distracted by Akisi coming round and struggling with his bonds.

'This is justice, thief,' Va said in Rus. 'I've got the book and I've got you.' He picked up the heavy table and jammed it against the wall underneath the window, then tied the free end of the rope to one of the table legs.

As he started to drag Akisi across the floor towards the window, the man squeaked and moaned behind his gag. He tried to twist and turn, but the rope held him excruciatingly tight, so that he was powerless to resist his progress up onto the table and head-first out of the window.

Va stepped up onto the table behind him, belayed the rope around his shoulder and waist, and pushed with his foot. Akisi tumbled out of sight, and the rope snapped taut with a creak.

Let him fall. An accident. He wouldn't mean to break the Kenyan on the courtyard below. He could let the rope slide out of his fingers and it would be over. That particular book would be closed for ever.

Eleven more volumes, he told himself. Eleven more. He mustn't kill Akisi. He swallowed the bile down.

When he could trust himself again, the fire had spread from the hearth to the rug. He forced his hands open a fraction, and the rope started to pay out. He was almost at the end of it when it went limp. Akisi had reached the ground.

He snatched the black bundle of cloth up from the floor, where it was starting to scorch, and slipped his forearm through the bindings. The room was filling with smoke, some of which had to be filtering down the tower. Perhaps firing the room hadn't been such a good idea after all. He had been too zealous.

Back onto the table, turn, loop the rope once and step in, bringing the loop up across his back. Step out onto the ledge, and fly.

The rope hissed against his callused palms. He didn't need it to stop him, just to slow him down. The ground rushed up and he pressed his knees together, bent his legs and waited for the hard earth to slap the soles of his feet.

Va rolled with the blow and sprang up. Above him, thick white smoke was billowing out of both the window and the chimney, and the flicker of wild flames lit it in bright orange and red.

Elenya ran out to him. 'What the hell have you done?'

'God's work,' he said, cutting through the rope that still snaked upwards to the tower window.

'If the fire spreads to those sheds, what do you think will happen?'

'I . . . don't know.'

'Stupid, stupid man. You'd never have won Novy Rostov like this. You'd never have lived long enough to pick up a sword in the first place.' She kicked Akisi. 'Pick him up and get us out of here. I came along to watch you die, not get myself killed.'

'The harbour,' said Va.

'We have to get there first. You going to carry him all the way?'

'Yes. Here,' he said, pressing the book on her. 'Don't drop it.'

He sliced the rope that joined Akisi's hands to his feet, then attempted to throw him over his shoulder. Akisi struggled wildly, jerking like a beached fish, and Va couldn't hold him.

Elenya slapped the Kenyan's face hard. 'He won't kill you, but I will. Be still.'

'I wouldn't let you kill him.'

'Then you'd end up fighting me.' The first piece of roof collapsed, sending out a shower of sparks into the night sky. 'Can we run away now?' she said.

They dodged through the courtyard and began to hear voices raised in panic, from both inside and outside the tower. A gate burst inwards, and it was only luck that enabled them to hide behind the still-swinging door. A group of men stopped, looked, dithered, then ran towards the tower. Slates were sliding down, shattering, as the roof timbers gave way. With the men fully occupied dodging the bombardment, Va and Elenya ran out of the compound and into the darkened streets of An Cobh.

'Do you know which way we're going?' said Elenya. The book was awkwardly heavy, but not as heavy as Akisi.

'The sea is this way. I can smell it.'

They turned a corner and came face to face with a group

269

of people wrapped in shawls and cloaks, woken by the noise. An elderly man thought nothing of giving chase, his nakedness exposed by the blanket he held around his thin waist flapping in the wind.

The cry went up, and soon they had a stretched-out trail of followers dogging them through the streets. Only if they threw their burdens away were they going to escape.

Then, in front of them, the clan macDonnabhan blocked their way. Va turned and saw that their pursuers had formed a knot at the last junction. Elenya put the book under one arm and reached for her knife.

'You call this a plan? Half the town is looking for you.' said Eoin macDonnabhan. He cleared his throat and called, 'Everything is under control. We have them now.'

'Will you take them to the king?' someone shouted back.

'They'll get what they deserve, for sure.' In a lower voice, so that only his clansmen, Va and Elenya could hear, he added, 'A sound hiding for getting caught. Now drop Akisi and look beaten.'

Va hesitated, and macDonnabhan stepped forward, brandishing a sword as tall as he was. Elenya held out her knife and levelled it at macDonnabhan's heart.

'For God's sake, Princess, do you not recognize friends when you see them? I swore you help, and though it feels like a ceilidh is going on in my head, a macDonnabhan keeps his word.'

She poked Va in the ribs. 'Put Akisi down. Now.'

'But—'

'No buts. It's now or never.'

He slid him to the ground. Akisi's eyes showed relief and gratitude, though only for a moment. Clearly expecting to be cut free, he squealed and kicked as two macDonnabhans picked him up as he was and rushed him away. Eoin macDonnabhan held up his hand to acknowledge the crowd and pushed Va and Elenya after Akisi's retreating feet.

'Go. Hurry. Did you not steal any horses? Horses would be better than a boat.'

'We didn't steal any horses,' said Elenya.

'And I thought the sons of Aeire were mad fools.' He hurried them along. 'We have to get you out of the town, then out of the king's land.'

'What about you?'

'It'll mean exile for us, which won't be easy, but the clan macDonnabhan has favours owing in Ciarra.' They reached the small port. Amongst the sunken masts of waterlogged boats there was a rowing boat, oars stowed across the seats.

Va, stumbling on beside Elenya, asked her: 'What are they doing?'

'They're giving us a chance. I suggest we take it.'

Solomon Akisi was dumped in the bottom of the boat. It rocked alarmingly, and water sloshed in the bilge. Va clasped Eoin macDonnabhan to him like a brother, surprising himself more than the Aeireann. Then he stepped onto the seat and started fitting the oars in the rowlocks.

'Goodbye, Princess,' said macDonnabhan. 'The world is wide and we may yet meet again. Perhaps then you'll be able to give your heart to a man who'll cherish it, rather than reject it.' He looked askance at Va, who in his unintelligible tongue was already urging a clansman to untie the mooring rope.

Elenya held his steadying hand as she climbed into the bow. 'Find comfort elsewhere, Eoin macDonnabhan. I'd make a poor wife for any man.'

'You judge yourself harshly, Princess Elenya. May the road rise up to meet you, and the wind be always at your back.'

Va hauled on the oars, and they inched away from the dock. With his next stroke they moved further out. A wave caught the bow, making the boat bob up and down.

'What was macDonnabhan saying?' grunted Va. He pulled again, and slowly they headed out to sea. Lights moved through An Cobh: the tower was a ruddy beacon of flickering light, and smaller fires of torches and lanterns dashed about like bugs.

'He was wishing us Godspeed.' Elenya tapped the book on her lap. 'And I was wishing him the same.'

CHAPTER 24

'When you said I could watch you die, I didn't believe you.' Elenya was kneeling up, letting the salt spray from the white wave-tops soak her to her bones. The darkness around them was soft, the high cloud turning the moon-glow into a rainbow-touched pearl. 'You always seemed so indestructible. Not a man, a force of nature. You could do whatever you wanted and the world had to bend to your will.'

'You were mistaken.' Va pulled at the oars rhythmically, each stroke as strong as the last even though he grunted with pain. The sea water was opening the wounds on his hands. He fixed his attention on the Kenyan, who was huddled in the stern, the struggle long since frozen out of him.

'Do you remember the first time we met?'

'I remember the last time.'

'Why didn't you want me?'

'Because I'd moved Heaven and Earth to win you, and all I was left with was Hell.'

'I was in my wedding dress.'

273

'And I was red, head to foot, with other men's blood. The only white you could see were my eyes.'

'I was yours, Va. Totally, completely yours. Who could have imagined a love that would turn a murderer into a saviour, a gutter-born orphan into a king, a mercenary into the greatest general for a thousand years? At that moment you had everything.'

'And you think me mad for dropping my sword and walking away? It was madness that drove me there. A cold dose of sanity was what I needed.' He looked over his shoulder. 'Are you looking out for rocks or do I have to do that too?'

'We'll miss them.'

'And you can see underwater, can you? There are too many breaking waves.' He turned the boat further out to sea and gave the black headland a wide berth. An Cobh and its sparking fires finally dropped out of sight.

'Shall I untie Akisi?'

'No. You can ungag him if you want.'

She stood up and fearlessly stepped over Va to the stern. She tried to loosen the knot at the back of Akisi's head, but it had shrunk with the cold and the water until it had welded itself together. She took out her knife, and momentarily enjoyed the abject fear that drained the Kenyan's face of blood. The blade slipped between his cheek and the gag, and she cut, not particularly caring how she did it.

He spat out the remnants of the cloth. 'Are you mad? Setting out to sea in this? Who are you? What do you want?'

'Isn't it obvious?' she said. 'Of course we're mad. But we've got the book, and you. Why don't you tell us who you think we are?'

'Are you with Cormac? If you are, I can do a deal with him. I can do much more for him than I ever did for Ardhal. He took me by force. He made me work for him.' Akisi looked from Elenya to Va, and back again. 'I'm telling you the truth.'

'What's he saying?' asked Va.

'He's trying to save his own skin. He thinks Cormac sent us.'

'Tell him who we really are. It's a long time since I've seen a man piss himself with terror.' He glanced up at Elenya. 'Just because I have to try and love my enemies doesn't mean I've succeeded yet.'

'What language is that?' said Akisi. He pushed himself with his bound legs so that he was more or less sitting upright.

'Rus,' said Elenya. 'Va is from the monastery of Saint Samuil, Arkady. Recognize the name?'

'Va? No.'

'The name of the monastery, stupid. It's the one you burned down to get to the books.'

'I got this book from the emperor himself, not some monastery. Where was it?'

275

Elenya sat on the stern. 'Va, he's denying all knowledge of Saint Samuil. What do you want me to do?'

'Hold on tight.' Va shipped the oars and stared at Akisi, then took in their position. They'd rounded the headland, and there seemed to be a beach in the next bay. They were sheltered from the worst of the easterly wind, and the waves were pushing them towards the shore.

Finally Va got to his feet and braced himself against the gunwales. Then he started to rock the boat. Slowly at first, then more and more violently, so that water started splashing over the sides and swamping the boat.

'Enough!' shrieked Akisi. 'Enough. I stole the book. I stole it and I'm sorry. I didn't think the emperor could reach this far.'

Elenya held up her hand, and Va stopped. 'You stole the book from your emperor? Not from the monastery?'

'I've never heard of the place. I don't know where it is. I don't know what you want from me. I just want to get out of this boat before it sinks.'

'We're not going to sink, are we, Va?'

Va sat back down and started bailing with cupped hands. 'Did he admit it?'

'After a fashion,' said Elenya. 'He says he stole the book from his emperor, not from you. Which means that the emperor of Kenya stole the books, killed your brothers and burned everything to the ground.'

'What do you know about this man?' Va gave up bailing and picked up the oars again. The pre-dawn light gathered strength and showed the broad mouth of a river in the bay. He began to row the heavy, waterlogged boat towards land.

'The emperor of Kenya is the most powerful ruler in the world. His influence stretches as far south as the Maghreb, where it meets the Caliphate, and thanks to you, maybe further. If he wants your books, you might just have to let him keep them.'

'Never. I have to take them back to the patriarch, every last one.'

'I've seen maps. He rules over a vast area of land far to the north. It's much bigger than the tsar's kingdom; it'd take months just to get from one side to the other. Imagine the armies he'd command. And he has spies everywhere.'

'I still have to go.'

'And you know the way?'

Va thought of the map caught in the folds of his habit, its edges scratching his skin. 'If it's that big, it won't be too hard to find.'

Akisi asked Elenya: 'What did he say? Will he kill me or let me go?'

'We're not talking about you. We're talking about the books you and your emperor thieved. Va seems to think that the patriarch should have them all back, starting with yours.'

'But His Imperial Highness would never permit it.'

'I don't expect he permitted you to swipe one from under his nose either, which is why we find both you and it at the edge of the Outer Ocean.' Elenya watched the shore grow closer. 'If we sink, you drown.'

'Don't you think I know that? Untie me.'

'You see, *he* probably would. I wouldn't. I was outside the monastery the day you attacked it. I saw what happened. I've seen worse, but that was on a battlefield. These were men of prayer, and you showed no mercy.'

'I have no knowledge of this,' said Akisi. 'I wasn't there; I know nothing about what went on. You can't hold me responsible.'

'What about what you did to Cormac's army? Can I hold you responsible for that?'

'Ardhal made me do it. I was his prisoner.'

'You can be ours just as willingly.' The water swirled around Elenya's ankles. 'Va, can't you make this leaking tub go any faster?'

Normally so pale, Va had gone red in the face with the effort. 'Could you do better?'

'I wouldn't have filled it with water in the first place, so probably, yes. Akisi says he was Ardhal's prisoner, although he doesn't seem very grateful to be freed.'

'I know the look of a man when he's in a position of power, and when we came in through the gate, he had that look. He's got a snake's tongue, Elenya. Don't believe a word he says.'

'He's a man, isn't he? That's enough never to trust him.'

Va struggled with the oars one last time, and the sea was finally level with the gunwales. It slopped over the sides with a sucking sound, and the hull dropped away under them.

Akisi shrieked again, certain he was about to die.

The bottom of the boat rested gently on the shingle underneath and tipped slightly to one side. Elenya looked around and sighed. 'That appears to be that.' She stood up, stepped overboard and waded the rest of the way to the shore.

Without her weight, the wood tried to rise in the sea. Va unhitched the oars and wedged the blades under his seat. He got out too, and the hull lifted clear of the bottom. He felt in the water for the painter, and having found it drifting backwards and forwards like a frond of seaweed, he put it over his shoulder and started dragging.

When the rowing boat became grounded, Va cut Akisi's leg bonds and made him walk. He then pulled the boat clear of the sea and tipped the water out onto the stony beach. The book flopped out, a heavy, wet lump.

Akisi instinctively stepped towards it, and Va growled deep in his throat. 'It's not yours, thief.' He let the boat fall back and picked up the jet black bundle.

'Any idea where we are?' Elenya searched the sky for clues.

'Between An Cobh and An Rinn.' He walked further up the beach and onto the edge of the scrubby marshland, cut by a hundred riverlets. He got out the map he'd taken from the tower and shook it so that it opened.

'What's that?' asked Elenya.

'Something I took from Akisi.' He passed it over.

She held it up to the first light of the sun. 'I've seen better drawings made by children. I'm assuming this bit here is Aeire. This is the other landmass we skirted crossing from Frankland. That's supposed to be an island too, yes?'

'Is this to scale?' Va turned his head to make better sense of the lines. 'Ask him.'

Elenya waved the map at Akisi, who sat and shivered in the poor shelter provided by the boat. 'Where did you copy the map from?'

'The book. Not this one. Another one.'

'Another one. How many did you steal?'

He hung his head. 'Two.'

'What did you do with it?'

'Sold it.' His head came up again. 'I had to eat, didn't I?'

'You really are a little shit, aren't you?' Elenya turned the map upside down. 'He took it from another of the books. And before you ask, he sold it for food.'

'Where?' Va was suddenly agitated.

'I don't know yet. If you want, I can go and hold his head under the water until he tells me. Or not, and he drowns.'

'No, don't.' He took the parchment from her. 'Have you

seen a pre-Reversal map before? They look wrong, so this might be of limited use.'

'This is the Inner ocean. The emperor's lands are to the north, so that'd be at the bottom of the map. And look, he's marked a route from down here on the coast, up this squiggly line to this bay here.'

Va turned the map the right way up again. 'The Caliphate is here, to the south and west. Mother Russia is south of there again, off the map. This is his escape map. Find the point furthest from his emperor, and go there.'

Elenya bent down and wrung the water from her skirts. 'It's day. We ought to think about getting away from here. Ardhal will be out, looking for his man.'

'We need to leave this island, get this book back to the patriarch and find the one Akisi sold. Then we must retrieve the ten remaining ones from the emperor of Kenya, wherever he is.'

'That should be straightforward enough,' said Elenya, her voice tightening. 'After all, getting the first one was a piece of piss!'

Va bared his teeth and growled like a wolf. 'You can go home if you want. I will not rest. Now get Akisi on his feet. We've a walk ahead of us.'

She cupped her hands around her mouth. 'You, Kenyan. Up.' Then to Va: 'Where are we going?'

'To see a man about a boat. A man called Rory macShiel.'

*

They took the boat across the mouth of the river and started the climb up the valley. Solomon Akisi followed reluctantly, alternately pushed and pulled when his speed dropped below what the two Rus thought acceptable.

Halfway up, during one of his frequent rests, he spotted a group of horsemen on the wrong side of the estuary. He opened his mouth to call out, and felt something sharp prick his neck.

'Crouch down, Akisi. And if you make a sound, I'll stick you like a pig and leave you to bleed.' Elenya put her other hand on his shoulder and showed him the way to the ground.

The horsemen wheeled around aimlessly, then one of them spotted the abandoned rowing boat on the far shore.

'I should have set it adrift,' said Va. 'Fortunately the river's too wide for them to cross.'

'The nearest bridge could be just upstream.'

'It doesn't mean that they'll come back here. They might take the road, or follow the river.'

'What would you do?'

'Split up and cover as much ground as possible.'

'Which is what they're going to do. They're not stupid.' She watched the men ride off inland with renewed urgency. When they were far enough away, she pulled her knife away from the African's throat. 'Careful how you go, Akisi. The cliffs are high, and you might trip.'

They gained the top of the hill and started along the edge where the land met the sky. The sea boomed below, and the wind whipped up the sheer rock face.

'Cold?' asked Elenya of Akisi.

'Miserably so. Cold, hungry, tired. I need to rest again.'

'We don't have the time. If you want to stay warm, walk faster.'

'Why are you doing this to me? Him,' said Akisi, jabbing his tied hands at Va, 'him I can understand. He's a fanatic. Nothing else is in his head. But you – you're not like him at all and I don't see why you're helping him. You could have a much better life than this, I'm certain.'

'You understand nothing at all,' she said, 'because you've never felt what I feel about him. He is my sun, and I revolve around him whether I choose to or not. I might hate myself for it, to be used in such a way by someone who swears never to return my love. I help him because I can't help myself.'

'You're mad.'

'You pointed that out to me earlier. But I won't take your pity. Where he goes, I follow. And for the moment so do you.'

She pushed him on again, to where Va was waiting.

'We're here,' said Va.

Akisi stopped sharply. 'It's An Rinn. Why did you bring me back here?'

Va scanned the church, the collection of houses, the windmill. 'I can't see any of Ardhal's men below.'

'I won't go,' said Akisi. He dug his heels in.

Elenya spun the knife in her hand. 'If you're worried that they'll find out you killed their priest; they already know.' She kicked him in the gut, then threw him down the slope.

A boy sitting in a tree spotted them coming. They saw him climb down and race along the road and through the village as fast as his legs would carry him. As he passed, people came out of their houses, and after looking at each other, they shielded their eyes and looked up the steep slope to the east.

CHAPTER 25

ory macShiel had a harpoon, and looked as if he wanted to use it. He only hesitated because of the presence of Va and Elenya.

'You dare come back here, Solomon Akisi? After all that you've done?'

Akisi looked surprised, shocked even, at the reaction of macShiel and the half-dozen other men behind him.

'My friends, I can explain everything.'

Incensed, macShiel made to stab the Kenyan, and was dragged back at the very last moment by Brendan macFinn's father. The point of the spear brushed Akisi's chest, forcing him back against Va.

'Let go of me, macFinn – you hate him just as much as I do,' macShiel managed between the flurry of arms and legs. 'What did you do, Akisi, put your fingers around his neck and squeeze the life out of him? Then bashed his brains out with a rock while he was helpless?'

Va jerked Akisi upright, and Elenya stood in front, ready for when macShiel struggled harder and broke free.

'Who else but a stranger would kill a priest? No one on this holy island would even think about such a heinous act.' He jabbed his finger at Akisi in lieu of his harpoon, which he'd lost in the melee. 'I accuse him of murder. All the time he was here, he knew what he'd done. He even took over the church. He planned it all from the start, damn his cold heart.'

'You can't have him, Rory.' Elenya stepped aside, and for the first time macShiel realized that Akisi's hands were already tied. 'He has to come with us.'

'What is this? What else has this murderer done?' The hands that held him fell away, and he stepped forward.

'We told you we were looking for books stolen from a monastery. We found one.' She asked Va to bring out the book from under its cover.

Brendan macFinn, at the back of the crowd, jumped up and down. 'That's it. That's what I found in Master Solomon's trunk. See?'

'He knows where the others are. He might be able to help us get them back. We need him alive. For the moment.' Elenya patted macShiel's arm. 'Sorry, Rory, but this is important. Va thinks that the world will end if we don't take them all back to the patriarch.'

macShiel's shoulders slumped, the fight suddenly gone out of him. 'Will it?'

'I don't know,' she said. 'Willing to risk it?'

'But what about Father Padi?'

'Akisi stole two volumes of the book from the emperor of Kenya. I imagine he'll get what's coming to him. He's also complicit in the murder of forty monks, so we could always take him back to the tsar when we're finished with him.' She linked arms with macShiel and walked him away, leaving Va holding Akisi by the scruff of the neck.

Va had understood little of the exchange between macShiel and Elenya, but he knew this for certain: if the people of An Rinn wanted to hang Akisi, there was little he could do to stop it.

But it must not happen. He needed to know what he'd done with the second book. He pulled the cover over the one he had managed to retrieve and wondered what had happened to the wolf fur that had previously wrapped it.

Rose naMoira barged her way through. Akisi appealed to her, and she deliberately turned her head away, shunning him with tight-lipped disappointment. She spoke directly to Va; Elenya was still talking to macShiel. He was on his own.

'I don't understand you. Little words and slower, please,' he asked.

'You must go from An Rinn. Now.'

'We will. But why?'

Rose struggled with the problem of reducing her speech down to the level of a child. 'We are cursed.'

'Cursed?' Va wasn't sure he'd heard right.

'This man, his book, that woman, you. All cursed. Bad things happen here now. You go, and God smiles on us again.' She stamped her feet and strode through the crowd of villagers.

Then macFinn stepped forward. 'What will you do with him?'

'Only he can say what he has done with the book. He will tell us and we will get it.'

'He'll lie and cheat all the time.'

'I know lying and cheating,' said Va. 'Listen, King Ardhal is Akisi's friend. We stole Akisi. Ardhal will want him.'

macFinn snorted. 'After what he's done? A priest killer?'

'No. Please hear me. You know of High King Cormac? His army is gone. Gone, dead.' He didn't know the word for scattered, but he tried the next best thing. 'Broken, like glass. This man and this book did it for Ardhal. Ardhal loves Akisi. They are as brothers.'

He clasped his hands together tightly to show the bond between the king and the Kenyan. macFinn grew acutely uncomfortable.

'We can't openly defy our king. But we can't let him escape his punishment either. What do we do?'

'Give him to me. I will be his—' Va's words finally failed him. He carried on Russian, hoping that macFinn would get the sense of it. 'I'll be his tormentor, his constant reminder that he's a thief and a murderer and a liar and the cheat. That he values the User book more than he values life. I'll be on his back from the moment he wakes to the moment he collapses from exhaustion. And when he gets up again, I'll be there, picking up where I left off. He will grow to be the sorriest man you have ever seen. As God is my witness, he will pay.'

macFinn backed away from the sudden outburst of passionate, unintelligible words. He looked behind him for support, but the people were determined to keep their distance from this wild foreigner.

'macFinn!' shouted a woman. 'Come away, man. The brother is touched, either by God or the Devil.'

'Damn your heathen tongue, can't you understand one word of honest Rus? I'm trying to stop a disaster worse than the Reversal, and for the want of a translator, the whole world goes to hell. Elenya? Tell these people I'm trying to save them.'

'What do you think I'm trying to do? There are complications.' She was with macShiel, and the woman Rose, and macShiel's shy wife. Looking at them, Va realized she was Rose's daughter.

'What could be more important than saving the world?'

'You'd be surprised.'

He gave up with macFinn, and pushed Akisi every step of the way over to where the others stood. 'Why is there a problem?'

'Mainly because they don't see why it is their problem. We brought it with us; we can just go and take it away again.'

'That's what we're trying to do. Don't they understand?'

'Va, you've got to calm down. Shouting at people in Rus just makes them think you're demented,' said Elenya. 'I'm not used to thinking in nearly three different languages at once and I'm getting a headache. To put it simply: we need macShiel and his boat to take the three of us and the book to the mainland. However, macShiel wants to hang Akisi for killing the priest and doesn't see why he should go anywhere with him.'

'But Ardhal won't want Akisi to die because he's too useful,' said Va.

'I've explained that. They're torn. On one hand they won't let him go because they want him to face justice. But if he stays, Ardhal will let him live. So they do nothing but quarrel with us and each other, and those horsemen we saw will soon be here and it'll be too late to make any sort of decision.' She sucked air in between her clenched teeth. 'If you're going to do something, I'd do it now.'

Akisi fidgeted nervously between them. 'I'm not stupid,' he said. 'I can tell what's going on. I don't want to go with you, and I like the idea of a rope around my neck even less. Just turn me over to Ardhal and I'll take my chances with him.'

Elenya clattered him around the head with her hand. 'You shut up. You're coming with us, whether you or they like it or not. There'll be no going back to making killing machines for Ardhal or anyone, and my knife will be sticking out of your eye-socket the second I see one of Ardhal's men coming down that road. Do you understand me?'

'You wouldn't dare.' He squared his shoulders and smiled for the first time in a day.

'Va, you have to make them give you a boat and Akisi. How you do it is up to you, but time is running out.'

Va turned away, beads of sweat springing up on his forehead. He could do it: grab macShiel by the neck, hold him in such a way that if he moved, he'd die. He could force him to his boat, compel the others to push it into the waves. They'd be away. Easier still to put a knife to Eithne's breast, threaten to kill her instead.

'No!' he screamed. He knelt on the cold, wet ground, clasped his cross so tightly that the edges cut his hands and squeezed out fat drops of bright blood. He choked on a prayer, and it turned into a sob.

He blinked back the tears of shame and rage, and staggered to his feet. At last everyone was quiet, watching him with a mixture of fear and pity. A baby was crying in the distance, inside one of the houses, and there was the persistent creaking and squeaking of the millwheel, turned round by the wind in its sails.

'Listen,' he said softly, and beckoned with his bloodied hands; 'listen to my story.' He sat down on a moss-covered rock and waited as the people of An Rinn crept cautiously closer. Elenya moved behind him, the better to translate, and dragged Akisi with her. 'Once there was a land where the summers were not scorching and the winters not harsh. In that land there was a king, who was a good man and loved by his people. No one went hungry, and everyone had a home.

'Then there was a calamity. There came men from the far south and formed a mighty army. But there was worse. They commanded a dragon, who used to fly about over the good king's land, burning the houses, destroying the crops and eating the cattle. The people were terrified, and they petitioned the king to save them.

'But the king was old and tired, and his sons were not yet ready to fight, let alone fight a dragon. He sent word out to all his friends, but while sympathy and good wishes were returned, no help came. The king despaired, and his peaceful kingdom was doomed to lie in ruins.'

A little girl squeezed her way to the front and, thinking that this was a normal storytelling, sat at Va's feet. She looked up at him, waiting for him to continue.

'I . . .'

'Go on,' hissed Elenya.

'Then, just as the king's hall itself was attacked by the

dragon, a magician came striding in. He bowed low to the
king and introduced himself. He had heard that there was
trouble: he would send the dragon back to its fiery home,
and perhaps then he would chase the southmen all the way
to their ice-caves. The king was frightened, but he had only
to listen to the thunderous wing-beats of the dragon above
his roof to be convinced. He gave his permission, and he
waited inside with his sons while the magician went out to
do battle.

'Everything went silent. Eventually the magician came
back in, his cloak smouldering, to tell the king that it was as
he had wished. The dragon had gone. The southmen were
driven away. In return, he wanted nothing but to live and
work and study in the king's land.

'But the southmen were furious. They looked for their
own magician, and they came back with seven. The lakes
boiled, the trees burned, the very air caught fire. The good
king's magician was not strong enough to defeat the seven,
so he sent for his three brothers. They left the king's hall,
and everything went silent.

'Eventually they came back in to tell the king that it was
as he had wished. The seven southern magicians had been
defeated, and the southmen driven back to their ice-caves.
They wanted nothing in return but to live and work and
study in the king's land.

'But the southmen were incandescent with rage. They

summoned a demon from the lowest pit of Hell, and seventy appeared. They sent them swarming over the country, destroying everything that was good about the land. The rocks that made the mountains cracked, the sea rose up, the wind blew so hard that every building save the king's hall was knocked flat. The good king's magician and the magician's three brothers were not strong enough to defeat the seventy, so they called on thirty angels. They left the king's hall, and everything went silent.

'At last they came back in to tell the king that it was as he had wished. The seventy demons had been consigned back to Hell, and the southmen buried alive in ice. But there was no longer a kingdom to protect. The beautiful country where the summers were warm and the winters mild was no more. And the old king wept, for he knew that he should have fought the dragon himself.'

Va stopped, and so did Elenya. They waited.

'I won't let you go, Rory macShiel; not on the strength of a story.'

'Let go, woman. The monk might be mad but he tells it truly. We have to fight our own dragons. Leave me be, Eithne.'

macShiel finally broke through, pulling his wife behind him. 'I've no wish to see my land, or anyone's, put to ruin. I'll take you wherever you want to go,' he said.

'Not so fast, macShiel. My boat isn't as fancy as yours, but it'll do the job just the same.' macFinn squared up to the other man, tucking his thumbs into the waistband of his breeches.

'Who put you in charge, Mici Finn?' shouted a voice. 'I'll take them, and I won't get lost.'

'Who said that? Was that you, macDooley?'

Seizing the opportunity, Va took macShiel's arm and pulled him close. 'Where's the boat?'

'Down in the harbour. We'll leave these hot-heads arguing over their precious honour and get on with the job, yes?'

Va barely understood, but a glance at Elenya confirmed what he'd hoped.

'We need to run,' she said. 'Look.'

On the crest of the hill, two silhouettes of horse and rider.

Akisi thought to delay them by breaking away, his mouth half formed into a shout. macShiel spun round and struck his jaw with one of his work-hardened fists. The Kenyan went down, and Va scooped him up.

'Go.' Elenya took the book from him, and Va threw the length of Akisi's body around his shoulders.

The tide was out, and macShiel's boat was beached with three others.

'Get him in, then yourselves.' macShiel shouldered the bow like a bull and heaved it into the water, his feet gouging holes in the shingle. He kept pushing until he was up to his waist.

Va waded in after him and tumbled the groaning Akisi into the bottom of the boat. He grabbed hold of the side and pulled himself in afterwards. He put his hand down. The book was jammed into it, then Elenya's hand.

He stiffened, then shut his eyes and hauled her in.

macShiel turned the boat out to sea with a mighty heave and scrambled aboard.

'Get the sail up,' he ordered. 'Pull that rope there.'

'What?'

'For God's sake, man, this one.' He waved it in Va's face.

The horsemen were in the town and heading for the harbour. Va started to pull on the rope, hand over hand. Wet canvas crawled up the mast, fluttered in the wind, then snapped taut as macShiel loosened the jib line. Then he jammed a piece of wood shaped like a fish's fin through the floor of the boat, and all the aimless rocking and splashing suddenly transformed into a surge of movement.

They were fast enough to leave a white wake behind them, which the greedy waves soon obscured.

CHAPTER 26

The little boat made steady progress all through the day, heading westwards towards the rising sun. When that climbed higher in the northern sky, macShiel made certain that it was on his right shoulder. Crouched in the stern, tiller in one hand, jib line in the other, he eyed the thin line of dark land in front of them.

'Aeire's behind us. We have to go north around that, then follow the coast.'

'Whose land is it?' asked Elenya.

'We call the land Sasana, and it's a wild, lawless place. Best avoided.'

Akisi, jaw still aching where macShiel had hit him, said: 'They are more barbarous than either of you. They spend their time in filth and fighting.'

Elenya stared him down. 'No one asked you.'

He fell silent and looked away, rubbing his chin with a wet hand. Salt water was supposed to be good for bruises.

macShiel swung the tiller, and the boat turned to the north-west.

The hull bucked as the wind gusted round to a different quarter. The sail canvas wriggled like a worm, and macShiel slackened the jib rope. Elenya pulled hard on its opposite number and the jib came swinging around. The three of them in the stern ducked. The sail snapped taut again, and Elenya passed the end of the rope to macShiel, who tied off the one he was holding before accepting the new one.

Va sat in the bow with the book, straining his eyes through the bursts of spray from the prow at a smudge on the southern horizon.

'What's that?' he said, pointing sternwards.

Everyone turned, and Elenya stood, one foot braced on the gunwale. She shielded her eyes from the glare and squinted.

'Looks like another boat.'

'It wasn't there a little while ago.'

macShiel gave the tiller to Elenya and had a closer look himself. 'Bigger boat than this.'

'Did he say it was a bigger boat?' asked Va, craning his neck. 'How can he tell?'

'Don't be an idiot, Va.' Elenya kept the boat steady with difficulty. 'Sit down.'

But Va tucked the book in the angle of the bow, and in two short steps he was halfway up the mast with his legs wrapped around the wood.

macShiel balked. 'Get down, man. You'll have us over.'

'I can see two masts,' he reported.

'Down!' macShiel reached up to take hold of Va's habit, and the boat started to lean. He threw himself across the boat to steady it. Akisi squeaked in fear.

Finally Va dropped down.

'Never do that again,' warned macShiel. 'Brother or not, you won't be welcome aboard my boat.'

Oblivious to the threat, Va said: 'It's not Ardhal. It's not even an Aeireann ship.'

'And you're the expert, Va?' Elenya kicked Akisi away from her.

'I thought only macShiel had this three-sided sail. That one has too.'

Elenya told macShiel, and he chewed his lip. 'Northerners. Could be slavers.'

Even Akisi roused himself from his petulance to see. 'Is there a flag?'

'Whatever flag it shows, it's not going to be good news for us.'

Elenya put her hand on macShiel's. 'Rory, can we get away?'

'I don't know.' He gave one last look around and took the tiller back. 'Jib's coming round.' He turned the boat to the south-west, then pointed to the bailing bucket at Va's feet. 'Wet the sail. Catches the wind better.'

While Va scooped up sea-water from over the side, Elenya

asked Akisi: 'Worried it might be the emperor coming to get you?'

'Yes.'

'He'll have you soon enough. I'd be more worried that it was a caliphate boat.'

At mention of the Caliphate, Va went cold inside. 'They mustn't catch us. I have to finish my mission.'

'I don't care about your mission,' said Elenya, 'and if the Caliphate capture you, well, the best you could hope for is a quick death. At worst – well, I'm told there are ways of keeping a man alive through even the worst torture imaginable.'

'And we both know what would happen to you.'

They stared at each other long enough to make both macShiel and Akisi uncomfortable. Finally Elenya said: 'Whoever it is, I don't think we want to meet them.'

'Why is the monk scared of the Caliphate?' Akisi snorted with mock laughter. 'It strikes me that something as mundane as an army should hold no fear for him.'

'It didn't when he broke the siege of Novy Rostov, destroyed the Caliphate's dreams of a greater empire and slaughtered their soldiers to the last man. But he now believes he's got more important things to do than be a plaything of the caliph.'

macShiel looked at Va with new eyes. 'He did that? On his own?'

'He started with nothing. He raised the peasant army. He trained them. He led them. He watched them kill and be killed. He won.'

'I know what you're doing, Elenya,' said Va. He launched the bucket of water at the sail and went back for a second fill. 'Don't. You mustn't boast of things that were a sin.'

'You saved Novy Rostov. You saved me.'

'I lost two armies: my own and the Caliphate's. I emptied the countryside and filled the tombs. That's nothing to be proud of. Just stop. Please.'

Elenya pulled at the strand of hair that had caught in her mouth and turned away. Va wet the sail again and took stock of the other boat.

'macShiel. The boat: it follows, yes?'

macShiel checked for himself. 'Yes. I don't know whether we can make it to land in time. Our problems won't end there either.'

'Better than caliph,' said Va emphatically.

'You're probably right. I much prefer being the master of my own destiny,' said macShiel, 'and that ship is moving faster than we are. Right about now is where we ought to throw things overboard to lighten the load.'

They looked at each other. Aside from themselves, there was nothing to get rid of.

'You need me,' reminded Akisi. 'I know what's happened to the other book. I can even take you to Great Nairobi.'

'If it was up to me,' said macShiel, 'you'd be fish food. It's the monk and Elenya you need to convince. Are you worth the risk of getting captured by their mortal enemies?'

'Yes.'

Elenya told Va: 'The choice is this: throw Akisi over the side and give ourselves a better chance.'

'Or?'

'Or not. Can we find the second book without him?'

'Of course we can. We found this one. It'll make it difficult, but not impossible.' Va put his hand down on the book. 'But I won't allow it.'

'Even with the Caliphate breathing down our neck? Look.' Elenya waved her hand with a flourish. The triangular sails of the other boat were much larger than they had been.

Va pointed ahead. He could make out hills and valleys among the shadowed land. 'We might make it.'

'Va,' added Elenya, 'what happens if it is the Caliphate? What will Akisi do then, but sell his skills to them. You want to see their army with An Cobh's weaponry? Better for everyone if he goes.'

'I can't be party to this,' hissed Va. 'I won't have his blood on my hands.'

'Then I'll do it. You're right: I've no particular wish to end up in a harem and raped repeatedly. I didn't when they were outside the walls of my city and I haven't changed my mind.' Elenya slipped her knife out. 'Me or the fish, Akisi.

You have a choice, which is more than you gave the priest you killed or Cormac's men.'

Akisi backed away as best he could. 'For God's sake, woman. I can't swim!'

Va struggled to the stern and stood between the two.

'Will everybody just shut up and sit down!' shouted macShiel. 'You want whoever it is to pull us out of the sea like drowning rats? Then keep on jumping around like madmen. Even if I kicked you all out, we wouldn't stand a chance. That ship is going twice our speed, or hasn't a little thing like the plain truth broken into your argument?'

They all sat, subdued.

'What do we do?' asked Elenya.

'Furl the sail. Wait and see what happens.' macShiel undid the jib rope and let the sail flutter aimlessly.

'I know what I'm going to do,' said Va, and ducked under the jib. He reached for the book and shook it out of its cloth wrapping. He put it on the gunwale and heaved it over the side.

'No!' Akisi lunged for him, his fingers brushing the metal cover and somehow pinning it to the outside of the hull. The book's weight slid it down until it was underwater. A wave came up, slapped Akisi full in the face, and as he gasped, the book slipped away.

'If I could bear the sight of you following it, then you would,' said Va.

Akisi clawed at the expanding circle of wavelets. The book glinted once, then vanished.

'How could you? It's lost. The knowledge. The wisdom. Gone.' His face contorted, his voice cracked.

'Nothing is lost for ever,' said Elenya, 'and we have more immediate problems.'

The larger boat was coming up fast, its prow lost in breaking waves. The crew climbed spider-like up the rigging and started to stow the taut, wind-filled sails they had unfurled for the chase.

As it came alongside, it dwarfed macShiel's little fishing boat. A rope fell to the deck, and they looked up. A row of grinning dark faces peered down at them.

macShiel tied the rope off, and they bumped against the vessel's hull. Va swayed. 'It's the Caliphate.'

'It might not be,' said Elenya. She called up in her best Turkic, 'Is this one of the caliph's ships?'

The answer came not in Turkic, but in something else. Then two of the sailors were elbowed aside and a man wearing a black turban leaned out. 'Who's this that greets us in the name of our enemy?'

'Me,' shouted Elenya. 'The caliph is our enemy too. We thought you were his men.'

'May Allah pluck out my living entrails and feed them to the vultures if that was true. I spit on the caliph and his sons.'

'You know Turkic though.'

'So do you. Come up. We can discuss terms.' The turbaned captain ordered his men to throw down a net, and Elenya climbed the side of the ship, followed by Akisi.

Va and macShiel looked at each other. 'You first,' said Va.

'My boat. You first.'

Va stared at the sea. He might make it to shore, but probably not. It was still a very long way, and once there, he'd have to contend with the incurably violent Sasans. Could it be that this boatload of foreign devil-worshippers was being used by God to His ineffable ends? He had to trust the Almighty's plans, not second-guess Him – or worse, assume he knew better.

God was God. If Va believed anything, it was that he was a servant, and servants did not question their master's orders. He climbed up the net. Rough brown hands helped him over to the deck.

macShiel followed Va. 'What type of ship is this, and who are its crew?'

'I think they are Mahgrebi,' said Va. 'Slavers.'

'I'll not be taken,' said macShiel. 'I'd rather die first.' He backed to the gunwale and looked at the drop.

Va laid hold of him. 'Do nothing. Keep quiet. Trust God.'

Elenya broke off her Turkic discussions. 'Listen to him, Rory. There's a way through this that might mean we stay

305

free, but you need to keep your nerve. If you don't want to trust Va's invisible friend, trust me instead.'

She carried on talking to the captain in the one language they had in common, the language of their shared enemy. Akisi gnawed at his knuckles. Va kept a tight grip on macShiel's arm and, for his part, muttered his way through a prayer of deliverance.

The sailors stood around them in a loose semicircle, hands on their short swords and clubs, which dangled from sashes around their waists. Their interest and intent was clear. They only held back because their captain hadn't given the order to subdue the captives.

Then the captain and Elenya slid their palms together. A deal was done, and the order finally given.

Va and macShiel stiffened as the sailors rushed them, but only Akisi went down under a barrage of blows. He was dragged, heels scraping along the deck, to one of the hatches.

'What? What have you done, you witch? You've tricked me. You can't treat one of the emperor's subjects like this. I appeal to the emperor himself for justice!'

He was pushed into the hold, and the sailors swarmed after him.

'You can stop hanging onto each other like frightened girls,' said Elenya. 'I've made a devil's pact, but it's bought us some time.'

'What did you say? And what's happened to Akisi?' asked Va.

'I told Captain Haida that we were agents of His Imperial Majesty, the Kenyan emperor, escorting a prisoner back to Great Nairobi to be tried by the emperor himself.'

'And he believed you?'

'No. But neither can he take the risk of not believing me. If he's wrong, he'll lose his ship, his liberty and probably his life. What he's going to do is dump us at the nearest friendly port in the Maghreb and let the local Kenyan ambassador sort it out. We're not slaves, and if we play this right, we can get passage all the way to Kenya.'

'And what of me?' asked macShiel. 'Do I go with you?'

'You still have your boat. Go back to your wife while you still have a chance. Every moment you stand here takes you further away.'

'They're setting me free?' He was already half over the gunwale.

'In the name of God, get on with it, before they change their mind.' She reached forward to push him away, and he caught her arm.

'I should say something.'

'Goodbye, Rory.' She pulled away, and his fingers slid from hers.

They watched him cast off, and soon he became a dark spot on a darker ocean.

Va folded his arms in satisfaction. 'God blesses us even in our darkest moment.'

'Oh, shut up. Where do you think I learned Turkic?'

Va shrugged.

'Novy Rostov was under siege for two years. My father thought it politic that I learned: better to survive as some Turkman's wife than as a common slave-whore. Everything I ever do is a compromise, an expedience against something worse. One day I'll do something just for me, and surprise everybody. Now,' Elenya told him, 'act like you're in the pay of the Kenyans, or they'll guess the truth. If they do, I might get to see you die sooner than you'd like.'

CHAPTER 27

Benzamir had never thought of himself as a thief before, but since only thieves skulked around in shadows made in the dead of night, he had to accept that that was what he was.

He craned his neck out around the corner. At one end of the street was Said, revealed by the slightest glimmer from a shaded lantern. At the other was Wahir, perched like a gargoyle in the join between an ornate ceremonial arch and the roof of a bathhouse. A white strip of cloth waved.

'All clear,' whispered Benzamir, and he and Alessandra slid with their backs against the wall down to the doorway. The gaps around the frame were dark, and the occupants long asleep.

A tight-fitting wooden trapdoor was set into the side of the building, right down at the level of the dusty street. Benzamir crouched down and pushed it. It rattled, but didn't move. Alessandra squatted beside him and tugged her black headscarf away from her mouth and nose.

'Locked?'

'Not for long.' Benzamir reached into his leather satchel and came out with a thick metal tube. He pressed the open end of the tube to the corner of the trapdoor and drew slowly around three sides of it. Part way along the third side, the door swung open under its own weight.

Alessandra darted out her hand to stop it from making a noise. Benzamir pushed her arm away, and the door slapped against the cellar stonework.

'Hot,' he said. 'Molten hot. Give it a moment to cool.'

He checked Said and Wahir again, then slid through the opening. When he was sure of his footing, he helped Alessandra inside.

The ice store was cool and damp, the sound of dripping water playing softly. It was completely dark.

'I'm scared to move,' said Alessandra.

Benzamir could see: the dark-blue blocks of ice wrapped in sheets of hessian, the pink ceiling above him, the turquoise of the shelving and the dull red rectangle of the entrance, spotted with white where he'd cut through the retaining bolts with his laser. Alessandra was a mix of oranges and reds, except for her mouth and nose, which flared brightly as she breathed.

'Don't worry. The floor's perfectly level.'

He spotted an ice hook, which he used to wedge the trap-door closed again, then looked in his bag for a couple of light-bees. They fluttered out, causing Alessandra to gasp, and after circling the room, they stationed themselves a little way behind and above Benzamir's head.

She shielded her eyes as the glow from the bees grew from a pinprick of light to a radiance that amazed her.

When Benzamir turned to look at something new, the bees moved.

'You have two faeries following you.'

Since they were always behind him, his instinctive glance just made the lights flit this way, then that.

'I suppose it must look like that.' He grinned, checked his bearings and walked the short distance to a damp, crumbling wall. 'This one?'

She nodded. 'Al Ahiz's house. Do you want me to start moving the ice out of the way?'

'No point. It's not going to be there in a minute. Now, are you sure?'

'Al Ahiz has a cellar just like this one. He won't use it to keep books in, because it'll be as damp as this one.'

'I really hope you're right, otherwise we're about to consign two moons' worth of sneaking around and spying to oblivion.' Benzamir fetched out a smooth metal sphere the size of his fist, black and yellow pictograms painted on the surface: a grinning skull, a double circle lying on its side, repeated in a line all the way round. 'When I say stand back, I do mean it.'

He put the ball on one of the shelves at waist height, shifting one of the ice blocks slightly so that it didn't roll out. When he was satisfied, he tapped it once and strode away, counting his paces.

'Three, four, five,' he said as he moved past Alessandra. He took her by the shoulders and moved her back another two steps. 'Six, seven. I get nervous using those things. One slip and, well – the results aren't pretty.'

The ball seemed to expand. Suddenly, violently, without a sound, it became a great bubble of cold fire that turned red, green, blue, like a diamond in the sunlight. Then it vanished with a distinct pop.

Cloth-covered ice slid to the floor with soft concussions. Shelves, suddenly robbed of support at one end, creaked and groaned. The wall itself, cut through with a perfectly circular tunnel, sagged, and loose masonry grated against rotten mortar. Even the floor had been scooped out and smoothed to glass.

'Ready?' asked Benzamir.

'What did you do?'

'The wall was in the way, so I moved it.'

'Where?'

'About three astronomical units away. Things move fast in o-space.'

'You talk such nonsense.'

'So everybody keeps on telling me.' He took a cautious step forward, followed by the light-bees. 'Careful. It's slippery.'

They slithered across the glassy floor into the cellar

belonging to the house next door. There were shelves similar to the ones recently vanished on the other side of the wall. They were empty except for cobwebs. It looked like Al Ahiz hadn't been down the crumbling stone steps for years.

Benzamir leaned his head against Alessandra's. 'He didn't hide it down here then.'

'Is this the time to ask if you have a spell for finding secret rooms?'

'Spell, no. Knack, hopefully. The Ethiopian commander can't see infra-red.' He started up the stairs and felt the trap-door with his fingertips. 'It'll open.'

The light-bees winked out, and Benzamir pushed slowly against the wood. A rug had been thrown over it, and he had to negotiate his way from underneath it. After telling his bees to shine softly, he called Alessandra up.

'You saw it. Are any of these it?'

The only gaps in the shelves were for a barred window and a thick door. The rest was floor-to-ceiling books.

'You're joking,' she breathed. Her palms became moist at the thought of so much wealth.

'Actually I am,' said Benzamir, ignorant of her avaricious lust. 'The Ethiopians would have gone through this room with a fine-toothed comb. How big is this User book?'

Alessandra took a moment to shame herself into answering. She held out her hands to the width of her body. 'It's heavy too. It doesn't just look like it's made of metal; it really is.'

'He'll have it close to him. There's no point in paying a fortune for something and not looking at it, surely?'

She ran her fingers along the uneven spines of the books. 'You don't know book collectors. Just knowing that no one else in the world has one is enough. You don't read books; you possess them.'

'In which case we might have to wake Al Ahiz up and induce him to tell us where he's put it.'

'Can we just stick to simple stealing?'

'You're right.' He plucked one of his light-bees out of the air and dropped it in Alessandra's palm. 'Start moving some of these around. There could be a hidey-hole. I'm going upstairs.'

'Be careful.' She held the bee up, and it fluttered about, getting its bearings.

Benzamir tiptoed to the door, listened carefully and tried the latch. It was only then that he noticed the ingenious lock. 'Amazing,' he said, testing the strength of the iron rods that slotted into the door frame. 'If I wasn't on this side of the door, and I couldn't just slice through the hinges with a laser, I'd be completely baffled.'

He gripped the lock mechanism in both hands and heaved it through a quarter turn. The bolts slid out of the frame with a well-oiled click. He tried the latch again, and the door swung open.

The light behind him faded to nothing. He was in a

corridor that was dark to normal vision, but not to his; the cool night air made blue streamers where it seeped in around the high window, and the door that led to the courtyard was outlined in azure. A couple of cats prowled in from another room, disturbed by the noise. At least, Benzamir hoped they were cats. It was difficult to tell just from the heat bloom, though they moved with a casual feline assurance.

He knelt down, let them sniff him and butt their sleek heads against his hand. He scratched each one between the ears, then shooed them gently away. He glanced through to where they had come from: a kitchen, with the embers of the evening's fire still warm in the hearth. Time to try upstairs.

Al Ahiz lived alone. His neighbours had joked, even as they watched a detachment of Ethiopian soldiers turn the collector's house upside down, that he had no need for the company of people: his many books were his many wives. And Benzamir, standing in the crowd with Wahir, Said and Alessandra, had watched as Al Ahiz simultaneously protested his innocence in the affair of the metal User book and urged great caution over the way rough warrior fingers abused his fragile pages.

Benzamir reached the landing and stopped to listen. Loud snores emanated from one room. The two others were locked, but not for long. They contained nothing but books. The Ethiopians had been in the house from dawn till mid-afternoon. Clearly, what they were looking for wasn't in plain sight, its metal spine turned outwards on one of the shelves groaning with age and knowledge.

Benzamir thought it a crime that any book be held a prisoner. Al Ahiz was guilty of a far greater offence than handling the emperor of Kenya's property: those books, sitting unopened, useless, rotting, represented an information abyss, a word hell. He shuddered, closed the doors again and sneaked into Al Ahiz's bedroom.

He lay on his bed, shrouded by net, like a great white whale caught by a fisherman. Yet more books were mixed in with his few personal items. The light-bee selectively lit up some of the titles, written by long dead hands in long forgotten languages. Benzamir wondered if Al Ahiz even knew what he had.

Resisting the urge to chant from the Necronomicon and translate the mystic symbols of Voynich, he checked the walls, floor and ceiling in infra-red for any telltale signs of hidden doors and secret voids.

Al Ahiz turned over, grunted, and continued sleeping. His snoring diminished to a soft suspiration.

Benzamir was at a loss. The Ethiopians had had hours to search, and had turned up nothing. Without a doubt they would have questioned the collector closely, and might have resorted to a little rough handling when the book didn't turn up. Either soft, blubbery Al Ahiz was as hard as nails, or he genuinely didn't have the book.

Where hadn't the soldiers looked? More importantly,

where wouldn't they look? If there were no hiding places built into the house, where would someone hide something of immense value?

He stalked around the room again, increasingly frustrated. All it would need was for the nightwatch, or a stray Ethiopian patrol, to come across Said, or for Al Ahiz to answer the call of nature, and the game would be up. He was putting them all in danger.

On Al Ahiz's table was a pile of outsized books, enormous tomes meant for show and public reading: a Qur'an, a Capital, and a Bible, sitting together. One at a time he carried them out of the bedroom and put them on the floor.

He pulled the bedroom door to and brightened his light-bee.

The Qur'an was an exquisite work of illumination and calligraphy, compared with the prosaic Cyrillic of the Capital. Both books were post-Turn, painstakingly copied by hand by scholar or holy man. The Bible had a heavy tooled leather and wood cover, a gilded cross supported by an ox, an eagle, a lion and a man. The clasp that held it shut was fastened by a little brass lock.

'This is the one,' said Benzamir, and faithfully carried the other two books back into the bedroom. Al Ahiz was now on his vast stomach, snorting into his pillow.

Benzamir heaved the Bible up; it was a heavy, cumbersome thing, to be processed and venerated, not carried under one arm or slipped into a bag. He staggered downstairs with it and backed into the first library, where Alessandra was still scooping books off the shelves and tapping behind on the woodwork.

'What's that?' she asked.

'I think it's what everyone in this city is looking for.' He laid it down on the floor and inspected the lock. 'I could pick it, but I don't have a bent piece of wire of the right gauge.'

He pressed the mouth of his laser against it and gave it the most perfunctory of pulses. Shiny metal slithered into the cracks between the stone flags, leaving a thin smoke trail of burned dust as it flowed.

'Ready?' he said, and flicked the remains of the clasp away. 'Normally, I wouldn't dream of wrecking such a beautiful piece of work, but I have a feeling someone's beaten me to it.'

He opened the cover, and Alessandra crowded close. Her fingers turned the pages over one by one: title page, a list of the books of the Bible, Genesis Chapter One. 'What language is this?'

'Greek. It's post-Turn, but it's an ancient translation. A shame, really . . .' He leaned forward, gathered enough of the unopened pages to take in half of Numbers, and drew them back.

Al Ahiz had cut out the centre of the Bible, leaving a rectangular space big enough for the User book. Everything from Balaam's donkey to the Damascus Road had been excised.

318

Alessandra lifted the User book free. 'This is it. How did you ever find it?'

'Luck and intuition. Maybe even magic.' Benzamir closed the Bible and left it on the floor for Al Ahiz to find in the morning.

'And really?'

'The Ethiopians are Copts. They'd never have imagined for one moment that a man would have cut up the Scriptures, let alone one as rich in history as this. It must have broken Al Ahiz's heart to do it: his loss, our gain.'

Alessandra put the book on the rug that had covered the trapdoor and wrapped it up carefully. 'Can we go now?'

'Do you think we've left Wahir and Said outside long enough yet? Shouldn't we leave it a little longer, so that their relief at our reappearance is all the greater?'

'That'd be a terrible thing to do. Wizard or no, get down those steps.' Alessandra handed Benzamir the book. 'And you can get rid of this damn glowing insect. It's just too strange.'

Her light-bee sailed across and joined his, and immediately she stumbled over the Bible.

'Don't reject something just because it seems strange. It's comfort that will kill you in the end.' Benzamir clutched the book to his chest and carefully descended into the cellar. Alessandra picked herself up and followed the fading light.

CHAPTER 28

They were back in Benzamir's old lodgings. The four of them crowded round, kneeling, staring at the still-wrapped book lying on the floor. Benzamir had ordered more light, and when the lamps had proved insufficient, stationed his light-bees over the rug.

'Master, what are you waiting for?' Wahir reached forward, and Said slapped the boy's arm and shook his head in reproof.

'I don't know,' said Benzamir, and sat back on his heels. 'I never open presents straight away. I always try and guess what's in them first, and see if I'm right afterwards.'

'But you know what's in it,' sighed Alessandra.

'No. No, I don't. I know what it's supposed to be. I'm hoping it might well be something greater.'

'The traitor's magic?'

'Thank you, Said.'

Alessandra had had enough. 'For heaven's sake.' She peeled back one of the folds of heavy cloth and let it fall back in a cloud of sparkling dust. Despite herself, she grew hesitant.

'Do it.'

She complied. The ceiling shimmered with reflected light.

'Shiny,' said Wahir, and dared to place a greasy fingertip on the cover.

Benzamir frowned. 'This isn't right.'

'What do you mean?' Alessandra breathed on the cover, watched the way her breath condensed on it, then evaporated away. 'This is the User book.'

He jabbed his finger down. 'But this is a User book.'

'I just said that.'

'I wasn't expecting an actual User book.' Benzamir pressed his palms together so that his nails turned white. 'It's not what I thought it would be.'

'Will someone tell me what's going on?'

'The master doesn't have to explain himself to you,' said Said.

Alessandra took offence and narrowed her eyes at him.

Benzamir opened the cover and traced his fingers over the map-and-leaves symbol cut into the surface of the first page. There was writing beneath it.

'Can you read what it says?' asked Said.

'Maybe. This language is as dead as a dead thing, but it gave rise to World. Anyway, there's more to reading than just the words. There has to be context and meaning and understanding.' He looked up, his face illuminated. 'This is a genuine antique. Pre-Turn. This isn't something from the traitors, dressed up to be User tech: this is the real thing.'

'Are you disappointed, master?'

Benzamir slowly smiled. 'How could I be disappointed with something as magnificent as this? Look.' He drew his fingers across the first page, bowing it up, bringing it down onto the cover. There were more words, arranged in columns, in the same precise, inhuman hand. He slid pages by until he reached one that showed a picture of some coloured balls.

There was something odd about the picture. It seemed to be set behind the book, like a tiny model. Wahir tried to dip his finger into it, and only hit hard metal.

'Where is it?'

'Watch. I think I know what this does now. Just watch the picture.' Benzamir brought the light-bees down so that the page shone.

The balls started to turn, then fly apart, disappearing under the edge of the frame. At their first movement, everyone but Benzamir rocked backwards. Gradually they edged forwards again. One ball of each colour was left behind. Each of these was broken down in turn, and then those parts turned into a pastel line of various lengths.

Suddenly the balls were back, and the whole sequence started again.

They watched, entranced, but when it became clear that nothing else was going to happen, they grew restless.

Their impatience eventually penetrated Benzamir's rapt attention. He opened another page at random and let it charge up enough to play its video clip through.

'But what does it do?' asked Said. 'Why is the emperor turning the city upside down to find this?'

'Apart from the fact that this is simply amazing? This is all the secrets of the Users in one handy volume, complete with moving pictures. Except' – and he turned the book over, opened the back cover and leafed a few pages in – 'except this is just quantum physics. It's not genetics, or cosmology, or chemistry. Or geology, ecology, or any other -ology you care to mention. There's more out there than this.'

Alessandra worried at her lip. 'There may have been another one.'

'What happened to that?'

'It went with the original seller. Apparently; it was only a rumour.' She threw her hands up. 'I don't know! Why are we doing this?'

'The master has enemies,' said Said, as if he himself understood fully.

'Magicians,' said Wahir, 'wicked magicians who would steal our souls and seal them in little bottles.'

'Enough,' murmured Benzamir. He turned back to an earlier page and watched as a Bose-Einstein condensate falteringly flowered in its depths. He tapped the picture with his knuckle, but it didn't cure the jerky rendering. 'I had hoped that this was something the traitors were putting about. But it's not; this was made here, seven hundred years ago, when the Users were at their height. I can understand why the Kenyan emperor wants this book. What I can't understand is how he came to lose it in the first place.'

'Stolen,' said Alessandra.

'That's the story, but there's more to it; more than a man trying to reclaim his property. You don't use an army for that.' He stared at the book and ran his fingers down both sides of the cold metal cover. 'I wonder what it might be.'

He lapsed into silence for so long, the others thought he might have fallen asleep. Even the light-bees dimmed to faint burning coals.

Wahir touched his shoulder. 'Master?'

Without changing expression, Benzamir said: 'Can you understand what this means? Any of it?' He nodded at the book.

'No, master.'

'No. No one could. Not, I bet, even the emperor's finest minds. Not for another five hundred years.' He looked around. 'No one in this whole wide world knows what a Riemann cut is or how to use one. Or understand that Phase theory is a subset of Unity physics. Or how to create zero-point energy using the Casimir effect without bringing the universe to a crashing halt.'

Wahir suddenly realized what he was missing. 'Except you, master. You understand the User secrets, don't you?'

'Yes.' He grabbed Wahir by the shoulders and play-wrestled him to the ground, laughing. 'But I'm not the only one, am I? Not now. Either the emperor is a compulsive collector like Al Ahiz, or he's doing a favour for someone. I want to know who that is.'

'Master?'

Benzamir sprang to his feet. 'If His Imperial Highness wants this book so badly, I think we should give it to him. In person. I think we should see what he does with it afterwards.'

'I'm not sure, master,' said Said. 'Why won't he accuse us of stealing the book ourselves, and have us clapped in irons?'

'We know he wants the book. We know that north, south, east and west, he's looking for any clue of its whereabouts. And we have it. We're bringing it to him as a gift.'

'It's as the master says, Abu Said,' said Wahir. 'The emperor would lose face if he took the book from us and threw us in prison. He'll give us gold, lots of gold, and jewels, and' – his imagination failed him – 'all sorts of presents.'

Said pursed his lips as he thought of a response, but Wahir carried on.

'We'll have to pretend to be someone else. Who will we be? Merchants, or pilgrims, or wise men?'

'We're all wise, men and women.' Benzamir smiled. He

gathered together the tiny bundle of his belongings and walked round the room, extinguishing the lamps one by one. 'But none of those.'

'Then what will we be?'

'Ambassadors. Emissaries from a faraway land, come to pay our respects and present our credentials from our king.'

'I take it you don't need me to point out,' said Alessandra, 'that we don't have any letters of introduction, and only you come from a faraway land. The rest of us won't pass as exotic enough.'

'We'll forge some at the earliest opportunity. And it's not strictly true that I don't have credentials.' Benzamir pushed the sleeve on his left arm as far up as it would go. 'There.'

'What? It's too dark to see, Benzamir.'

'Oh, hang on.' He concentrated, and the tattoo on his bicep began to glow: a double star, yellow and red, a stylized tree in green, an out-thrust palm in blue. 'Bio-luminescence. All my people have one when we come of age.'

Alessandra was quiet. 'You use your magic so casually,' she said eventually. 'But it scares me.'

Wahir leaned close in and traced the outlines of the shapes with his finger. 'What do they mean?'

'The two stars are for Mizar, which is in the southern sky. That's where I was born. The tree is my tribe, my clan. The hand is my profession – an explorer, a scout, a soldier.'

'You were never born on a star,' said Wahir.

Benzamir smiled in the night. 'I was born on a ship at the moment that Mizar was rising over the horizon. I suppose where the ship was isn't really important. These three signs have hidden messages in them that only other magicians can read, so that we can know all about each other when we meet.' He rolled his sleeve back down, and the tattoo was covered over.

'And what about your enemies? What do they have?'

'They have different symbols. But one of them is of my tribe. We should be working together, because that's what the tribe does, not fighting each other.' Benzamir finally stood by the last lit lamp. He picked it up and held it in front of him. 'He's chosen his path, and I've chosen mine. We'll see who wins when we meet.'

'There can't be any doubt, master.'

'Hush, Wahir. There's always doubt. Just because I believe I'm right doesn't mean I'm going to come out on top.'

'But you have us, master,' said Said. 'We won't stand idly by when the time comes.'

'And I've told you that you have to. Only a fool interferes with a wizards' duel.' Benzamir lapsed into silence again, then reached up to pluck the faint red lights out of the air around his head. 'We must be away before morning. I want to be able to present ourselves at the emperor's door before a messenger from Misr arrives with a tall tale about a ruined Bible and missing wall.'

'We're going to Great Nairobi?' Alessandra blinked in the half-light. 'Now?'

'Only if you want to. I've dragged Said and Wahir away from their homes. I can hardly ask the same of you.'

'I no longer remember where my home was. Sometimes I dream of a green hill, thick with trees, and goats grazing underneath them. There's a red tiled house, and a man and a woman. I never see their faces.' Alessandra bit her lip until she was certain not to cry. 'I can't go back. I don't know the way.'

'And Misr?'

'Between you and the Ethiopians, you've destroyed the market for years to come. The diggers won't be at the pyramids until an understanding is reached with the Kenyans. I don't belong here either. It seems you've ruined my life, Benzamir.'

'Then perhaps,' he said, 'you should come along with me. I can find you another.'

PART 3

CHAPTER 29

Despite their need for haste – imperative now that the news of the theft of the book from Al Ahiz's house was out and travelling like a ripple from Misr – they only used the flying carpet at night. Benzamir wanted their journey along the Nile valley and beyond to be as uneventful as possible, and there were compensations: it was much cooler, which became more important the further north they travelled.

Only Said was sorry that they hadn't attempted the trip by camel.

The closer they came to Great Nairobi, the more towns and villages and farms they encountered. So much so that in recent days Benzamir had been forced to fly higher, simply to avoid detection. It exhausted the carpet, and they had had to walk while it sucked in fierce equatorial sunlight.

It was just before dawn – swift and surprising at those latitudes – and the seat of empire itself was finally visible in the distance, full of sparkling light. Below were lanterns and hearth-fires of the sprawl that fed the city.

'See?' said Benzamir. 'Tomorrow, we'll see what we can do about getting in and gaining an audience with the emperor. Tonight we'll sleep in real beds. Right now, I need to land this thing.'

The wind tugging at their clothes lessened its grip, and Benzamir leaned out, looking for somewhere suitable. They circled a field of maize and dropped down into the middle of it. Unripe stalks bent and snapped, and they were down.

Only the strange and unfamiliar sounds of tropical Africa were heard; no voices raised in surprise or anger.

'Right, everybody off.'

Said fell off backwards and lay amongst the corn stalks, groaning. 'Another day of this and I swear I'd die.'

'It was either half a moon of this or spend till the next equinox coming up the Nile by boat. And we know how much you love boats.' Benzamir tried to stand, only to discover that his legs had gone to sleep. He had to use his hands to manoeuvre his feet from under his body and stretch them out in front of him. 'You know, in our picture books, all the magicians sit cross-legged for journeys of vast distances. It's only when you try it yourself that you realize just how impossible that is.'

Wahir, younger and still filled with wonder, leaped up as the sun broached the horizon, pouring heat and light across first the treetops and then the red soil. Said, still lying on his back like a sheep offering its throat for slaughter, grunted: 'Get down, boy. You're taller than the plants.'

He ducked down again and laid his hand on the rug-covered book. 'Can I give this to the emperor when the time comes? Please?'

Benzamir, pins and needles burning in his muscles, shuffled around on his hands and knees to detach the spheres from the corners of the carpet. 'Of course, Wahir. If you think you can carry it without dropping it.'

'As long as the emperor doesn't think I'm a gift too. I remember you saying, back in the desert, about being able to destroy the empire,' Alessandra started, 'but did you see it last night? The city is huge, far bigger than Misr. Full of soldiers and spies. I'm afraid even you couldn't stop His Highness from doing whatever he wanted with any of us.'

'No, Alessandra. No. I won't let anyone take you away from me. Trust me.' Benzamir surprised himself at his vehemence.

'Oh.'

He shooed her off the carpet, turned it from rigid sheet to flexible fabric, and rolled it up. 'First things first: we have to find our way out of this field.'

The gates of the citadel of Great Nairobi were monumental, both in size and grandeur. Covered in brass plates, they reflected the orange sun like a furnace. Those entering had to shade their eyes and hide their faces, unconsciously bowing to the edifice.

They had walked all the way, from rural farms along ever more crowded roads. Trees and crops had given way to daub houses, then to stone. Shops and markets, windmills and forges, cloth drying on lines outside dyers, wood-smoke and steam and sweat.

'This is industry,' said Benzamir approvingly. The road they were walking along was paved, with a camber to carry away the seasonal rains into deep ditches on either side. The ditch was bridged by stone flags, used by handcarts and people alike, and there was a purposeful clamour all around them.

Neither were they the only foreigners. Black Africans made up the majority, of different peoples and of none. White-robed penitents mixed with locals traders in their oranges and reds, wild-haired herders with bejewelled merchants. There were Arabs too, and mountain folk from the west like the imam in El Alam. Ewers, some paler than Alessandra, walked free without chains or collars.

Above all the sprawling city was the citadel, the beating heart of the Kenyan empire, high on a hill. It didn't crouch, squat and brooding, but soared upwards, vast ramparts of smooth stone above which peeked towers and roofs.

The emperor was behind those walls, controlling every-thing, sending out his spies. He had learned the pinnacle of statecraft: knowledge was power. Perhaps that was why he wanted the book that Wahir had tired of carrying and was now clutched by Said in his huge hands. Perhaps not.

To find out, they first had to pass the brazen doors. On either side of them were painted signs, repeating the same information in every conceivable language. Benzamir, master of the spoken word, searched for something he could read.

'I'm having problems here,' he said. 'Said, can you read?'

Said, slack-mouthed and staring up at the citadel, shook himself. 'I have to confess I never had to learn. In the madrasah we learned our letters and the Qur'an, but not the written word.'

'Wahir?'

The boy was facing the other way, looking out over the Nairobi sprawl that went on and on until it merged with the sky.

'Sorry, master.'

'Can you read?'

'If my teachers hadn't beaten me with sticks, I might have. Is it important?'

People drifted between the signs until they found the one they could understand. There were no huge crowds, but most of those who stopped to read the signs seemed to come deliberately to read, and not to enter the citadel. Benzamir watched them: after they'd finished, they turned round and went back down the hill.

'I'm rather assuming it *is* important. Otherwise why

would they be there? Alessandra? Save the ignorant men from disaster.'

At last she seemed to have conquered her fear. 'How would you manage without me?' she said, and scanned the boards until she spotted one in the hand common to Misr.

'If you read it out loud, I'll be able to understand all the others,' said Benzamir. 'You'll never have heard of the Rosetta Stone, but it's the same principle.'

'Please don't explain. I'll get a headache.' Alessandra cleared her throat and read: '*By order of His Imperial Majesty Kaisari Yohane Muzorewa and his lawful heirs and successors, no one may enter the imperial palace except with the express permission of His Imperial Majesty or his ministers. Anyone found within the palace without lawful authority will forfeit their lives. Subjects of His Imperial Majesty wishing to petition His Imperial Majesty on matters of law or state must obtain the permission of His Imperial Majesty or his ministers prior to the petition being presented.*' She coughed again. 'This is all a bit of a mouthful, isn't it?'

'Does it say anything else?'

'Hang on. *Written by order of His Excellency Yusri Hakeem Misriyyun, representative of the City of Misr El Mahrosa.* And some numbers: *two thousand, nine hundred and seventy-eight.* I don't know what that means. They seem to be slightly different on all the others.'

'It's just the year,' said Benzamir. 'Right. The plan is this: we get some letters of introduction made up, written in my native language and Arabic. Then we find out how to get an invitation to an audience with His Imperial Majesty. We can present him with the book, and then . . .'

'And then what, master?' asked Said. 'How do we ask him what he wants the book for without losing our heads?'

'The emperor won't tell us,' said Alessandra. 'He'll just thank us for the book, pay us off and push us out of the door.'

'He won't have to tell us. I've bugged the book.'

'How will insects help?'

'Magic. These are special insects that no one can see but will tell me where the book is, what's being said and even give me a picture of who's holding it.'

'Will your enemies be able to see these magic beetles?' asked Wahir. 'Is it like your tattoo?'

'It's a risk I have to take. I don't think they'll be watching for them, but even if they do detect the bugs, they won't know for certain where they came from or who set them.'

Said nodded. 'It's a good plan then. We'll need the best parchment, or vellum, and coloured inks.' He looked through the purse and brought out the last of the sheikh's money. 'If this doesn't work, we're going to starve to death.'

'To be honest,' said Benzamir, 'this is the bit that scares me most. Actually writing, using a pen or a brush, isn't something I'm too familiar with. We have machines to write for us.'

Alessandra linked arms with him and started marching him down the hill to the riotous city below. 'Then you'll have to practise first, Benzamir. I'm not going hungry again.'

They rented a room in a house close by the citadel, with a wide window that let in lots of light. While Alessandra and Wahir went out to find inks and paint, paper and ribbon, Benzamir practised his Swahili on the landlady, and Said moved the single large table over to where it would be of most use.

Then they waited. It was becoming hot, and both men grew increasingly uncomfortable. They sat on the table, as close to the window as they could get without falling out, watching the street below slowly empty as the sun reached its zenith. All the time, the spires of the citadel winked and beckoned in the haze.

'Look! A procession,' said Said, and almost fell off the window ledge. 'Merciful Allah! Is that an elephant?'

Benzamir craned his neck round the shutters and saw it was true. An elephant, dressed in heavy cloth sewn with thousands of metal plates, lumbered by. On its back was a small covered howdah carrying a driver and two archers. A handful of children had escaped their parents to watch from the street, and though they waved and called up, the soldiers imperiously ignored them.

Behind the elephant came a troop of spearmen, wearily trudging the dusty road, heads down; behind them, an ox cart pulled by a team of huge-horned cows, white with sweat and panting hard. Their load was an Arab driver, an ostrich-plumed Kenyan officer and three more people.

One was a prisoner. He had his hands chained together and around part of the cart to prevent his escape. He looked beaten, his dusty face pale next to his guard's gleaming skin. The other two were of less certain position: they shared a ride with a captive man, yet they were free to grip the sides of the rolling cart on their own. One was a man, a Ewer most likely, with a hint of white-blond hair on his pink head and dressed all in black. The man's clothing didn't seem the most appropriate for the climate, and Benzamir wondered how far he was from home.

The woman . . . Benzamir felt his hands tighten around the windowsill and the breath catch in his throat. At that moment she happened to look up and saw them gawking down at her. She returned their curious stares with cool disregard.

Then they were past, heading up the hill towards the citadel.

'Said?' said Benzamir. 'What story goes untold here?'

'I'll be back soon.' Said slid off the table, and was gone. He reappeared trotting alongside the cart, asking questions of the driver. The officer shouted at him and tried to shoo him away, but Said was persistent. Only when he'd scavenged his answers did he stop, hands on his knees, gasping for breath. He trudged back.

'You're not going to believe this, master,' he panted, and

stopped to drink the water proffered by Benzamir. 'The black man in chains is a thief. Guess what he stole?'

'The emperor's books? Did they get the other one back?'

'No. The driver said that both had been lost, and the emperor was furious. The thief is going to be tried. And hanged. Or stoned. Or something like that.'

Benzamir refilled Said's pottery mug. 'Did the driver say when the trial was going to start?'

'He said tomorrow. He said that the emperor himself was going to sit in judgement. The thief isn't a common man, but one of the emperor's underministers. I don't know what that means, but it sounds important.'

'What it means is that we're running out of time.' Benzamir tutted.

Wahir burst in, and Alessandra followed a moment later, carrying an armful of soft cotton bags.

'Master! You'll never guess what we saw!'

'You mean, the man who stole the emperor's books being taken to the citadel in chains?'

Deflated, Wahir sulked. 'How did you know? It could have been anything. Having a magician as a master isn't fun.'

Benzamir pointed down to the street. 'They came by here, and Said went to find out. Did you learn anything about the others who were with him?'

'The Ewer man and woman? No. The man in the black coat is very scary though. Up close, he's a mess of scars. He looks like a monster. The woman just watched me. Like there was nothing there, no feelings.' Wahir leaned out of the window, looking at the dust cloud drifting along towards the brass gates. 'Very pretty, in a sad way.'

'Let's get this table cleaned up and make a start,' said Benzamir, brushing the wood with his hand and inspecting the dirt clinging to his fingertips. 'We have to see the emperor. Today, if possible.'

'Why?' asked Said.

'I don't know why. It's suddenly become important.' Benzamir took the first few bags from Alessandra and examined their contents. 'When the sun goes down, we're just going to have to present ourselves at the citadel and see how far we get.'

'Master, what's wrong?'

They could all tell that something had changed, but couldn't tell what. Neither could Benzamir. He was at a loss to know how to explain himself.

'There comes a moment in every story when a small action, inconsequential on its own, turns out to be the tipping point. I think— no, I feel that if we have an audience with the emperor the day after tomorrow, it'll be a day too late. I just hope that we don't have to trust to my skill, and that the book will be enough to get us in.'

CHAPTER 30

After a few doodles and incomprehensible lines of script, Benzamir declared himself ready.

'Right,' he said. He cracked his fingers and flexed his wrists, and sat on the stool. 'Make me some red. Red's always impressive.'

Wahir tapped some of the red dye into a soapstone bowl and dripped the acid onto it until a thick, bubbling paste formed. He pushed the bowl across the table.

Benzamir picked up his brush and inspected the fine end. He sucked on the antelope hair to make it finer still, and dipped it in the ink. He looked up and saw that everyone was holding their breath.

'This could take a while,' he said. 'I'd rather you didn't all turn blue and fall over.'

'Sorry,' said Said, and held the corner of the vellum down.

Benzamir started to construct an illuminated capital, a letter clutched at by some great worm-like creature with many arms. He used green and brown, and fine brass dust to simulate gold leaf. 'It doesn't have to be perfect,' he said, mostly to himself. 'It just has to be good enough.'

Wahir mixed up a large pot of thick black paint, and while the illumination dried, Benzamir pricked out lines using a needle. When he was ready, he started to write: '*To His Imperial Majesty Emperor Yohane Muzorewa, greetings. I commend to you His Excellency Benzamir Michael Mahmood, my loyal servant, and his illustrious retinue, on this the first meeting of our two proud and noble peoples. I pledge peace between us, and authorize my servants to act on my behalf as they humbly present to you a gift, a token of the friendship that might exist between us. Yours in good faith—*' And he stopped. 'I need something that sounds impressive. But not ridiculous.'

'Who's your king? Can't you put his name down?' said Said.

'How can I break the news to you that the king has been dead for hundreds of years but lives on as an uploaded machine intelligence? Oh. I just did.'

'Why not use your father's name,' said Alessandra.

'That's a very good suggestion. It'd make the old man proud, but won't that make me a prince?'

'Is that such a bad thing?' She shrugged.

Benzamir dipped his brush in the ink one last time and wrote: '*King Benyounes Zamir Mahmood.*'

He pushed his stool back and examined the page critically. 'Good enough, or start again?'

They moved closer, pressing against him, looking at it from his point of view.

'I have no idea what all that scribbling means,' said Said, 'but it's a miracle.'

'He's right,' said Alessandra. 'It's beautiful. You've done very well.'

'Wahir?'

'It's a very impressive document, master. Only weren't you supposed to do it in Arabic too?'

With a sigh, Benzamir dropped back down on the stool, took up his brush and started writing underneath.

They added a few frills: some extra titles for Benzamir's father, which included King of the People over the Sea; a copy of the fictitious Great Seal, embossed with the blunt end of a steel needle; an extra brilliant illumination of impossible creatures and magical ships.

Then it was finished. They left it to dry on the table and lay on their beds, prickly with heat. Only Wahir lounged by the window, accepting the gift of a slight breeze.

'It's very quiet outside.'

'It'll pick up again soon. No one wants to work at the moment.'

'Slaves have to,' said Alessandra. 'Slaves work and masters sleep.'

'But listen,' said Benzamir. 'Remember how noisy it was before? This is not an economy run on slave labour.'

'So who does the work?' asked Said. He lifted his head off his mattress briefly, before letting it fall back down. 'Who collects the night soil? Who drags the stone? Who guts the fish?'

'Slave economies are appallingly inefficient – never mind their innate cruelty. There's no incentive for the slave owners to do anything different, and there's every incentive for the slaves to do as little as possible, or rise up and kill their owners. Slavery is bad for the empire, which is why I'm assuming the emperor has either banned it or at least discourages it.'

'What do your people do, Benzamir?' Alessandra got up and poured a cup of water from the pitcher. She drank half of it, then dribbled the rest of it over her face until it ran down her neck and darkened her clothes.

Distracted, Benzamir caught Said looking at her, then at him. He purposefully stared at the wooden boards of the ceiling. 'My people? We don't have money, as such. We work on a system of credit called a Gift economy. Those who gift the most to their tribe, and to all the – ah, people – some of whom aren't strictly people – have the highest status.'

They all fell silent for a while, then Alessandra said: 'So who does empty the chamber pots?'

'We use magic. If we wanted – if I wanted – I wouldn't have to lift a finger from cradle to grave. Everything would be done for me. But my status would be lower than that of a worm.'

'How much status do you have?'

'I've lost a lot, along with the whole tribe. Having a traitor in your midst, someone you've shared everything with since you were young, is taken very seriously. I have to take my share of the blame, and assume my part of the responsibility in righting the wrong.'

'What a strange life you lead, Benzamir.' Alessandra refilled the cup and gave it to him. 'I can't imagine a country where these things happen. But I think I might like to see it.'

'I . . .' Benzamir hesitated as he sat up and took the water from her. He drank to buy himself some time. 'I never imagined I would eat dates, or play backgammon in the place it was invented, or see the pyramids. How can my imagination compete with this? You have such a beautiful, complicated place to live. Exploring it would take ten – a hundred lifetimes. Why would you ever want to leave?'

She was about to say something else when Wahir inter-rupted and the moment was lost.

'Master, what is it that your enemies want with us? What could we possibly give them that they don't already have?'

'I don't know if I hoped you'd ask, or that you wouldn't. And I don't know if this is the time to answer, either.' Benzamir gnawed at his finger. 'You're right: you can give them nothing. But look at what they would give you in return.'

'What, master?'

'Everything.' He was appalled and excited at the thought. 'Absolutely everything.'

A little while before sunset they set off back up the hill. The citadel grew larger until it was all they saw: the massive walls, the formidable doors, the spear-carriers on the ramparts. In comparison, they were inconsequential. From easy talk, they lapsed into nervous silence until Said said: 'You should have a chariot, like the Ethiopians, or a string of camels, the more the better. We will be laughed at and turned away.'

'More likely killed and thrown to the dogs,' said Wahir. 'How could we have expected anything else?'

Benzamir beat some of the dust out of his kaftan with the flat of his hand. 'I know what they expect: banners, heralds, musicians, a parade of wealth and a big splash of noise and colour. All they're getting is us, a raggedy band of travellers. But' – and he grasped the big man by the shoulders – 'appearances are deceptive. If they only knew who they were meeting. The mighty warrior Said Mohammed, protector of the noble line of Alam.'

He spun round to take Wahir under his arms and lift him up. 'Then there's Wahir the Fox, trusted son, cunning spy.'

'Master, put me down. The scroll is becoming creased.'

'Good,' said Benzamir, and he creased it some more until, laughing, Wahir struggled free.

'And what about me?' said Alessandra shyly. 'Or you, for that matter?'

He bowed before her. 'You're Alessandra the Free, learned and wise, fearless and true. And me? I am Benzamir Michael Mahmood, Prince of the People over the Sea. Who would dare turn us away?'

'No one, master. We are kings in our own land!'

'Wahir, we're kings wherever we go. It isn't that you wear a crown or have a hundred servants or a thousand soldiers. It's here' – Benzamir touched his head and then his heart – 'and here. We might be dirty, smelly, tired, hungry, thirsty, scared. But we're still kings.'

'And are these supposed to be words to live by?' Alessandra tried to straighten out the corners of the page of vellum Wahir was clutching.

'Believe them. At least for the next five minutes, that's all I ask.' The line of the gate was marked by a thick iron bar set into the ground, pierced with huge holes ready to receive massive bolts. Above them loomed the arch, and inside, steel-helmeted guards lurking in the cool shadow. 'I have to believe it for the next five minutes as well.'

Benzamir stepped over the line and announced: 'I bring greetings from the People over the Sea to the emperor of the mighty Kenyan empire.'

The guards, fine-faced Africans from the north, roused themselves and their broad-bladed spears. They looked over the visitors and called their captain.

'What? What is it?' he asked wearily in heavily accented World.

'I am Prince Mahmood, and I'm seeking an audience with the emperor.'

'Can't you read?' said the captain, pointing to the forest of signs outside the gate.

'Of course we can. We're not barbarians. Wahir?'

Wahir presented the rolled-up vellum with as much aplomb as he could muster. The captain unrolled it and pretended to read it while plainly not understanding a word.

'If you haven't got a letter of invitation from the right minister, you can't come in.' He handed the document back without re-rolling it, and folded his arms.

'Master? Is he after baksheesh?' Said wondered. 'We only have a couple of coins left.'

'He's just doing his job. Unwrap the book, but don't let them get hold of it.' Benzamir turned back to the captain. 'My king has sent a priceless gift to the emperor, one I understand he'd like very much. But if you don't want it, we'll be on our way. I'm sure we can use it ourselves.'

Said unveiled the corner of the User book and held it up for a moment, then shrugged theatrically.

'Stop!' blurted the captain, then recovered. 'I mean, wait. I'll fetch someone.'

He barked at one of the guards, who dropped his spear and lozenge-shaped shield and ran through the inner gates to the space beyond.

'See?' said Benzamir. 'Some things have value beyond money.'

'Perhaps you should let us look after your gift,' said the captain. His fingers stroked the sweat off his palms.

'Perhaps it'd be a mistake to take something by force that we're ready to give freely. The king of the People over the Sea is a powerful man and would take great offence at such an action.' Benzamir took a step forward as if to show that he had not only the king's authority, but his own as well.

The captain of the guard looked down at Benzamir looking up at him. 'Your balls are as brass as these gates, emissary. You know that that book was stolen from the emperor, and that we even have the traitor-thief in the cells as we speak. I could take it from you now and you'd never be able to stop me.'

'And I can piss higher up the wall than you, even though you're taller. Trust me, it wouldn't be you who'd take the book. One of your men perhaps, if they had the stomach for a fight, but not you. You'd be flat on your back the moment you gave the order.' Benzamir tried a smile on for size.

'Sorry, but this is important. The fate of the world hangs in the balance.'

They were interrupted by a flurry of red and gold cloth.

'You may stand aside, Captain,' puffed the grey-haired man. '*I'll* be dealing with this.'

The captain was in no mood to back down, but Benzamir saw that there was no further need for posturing. The book was safe for the moment. He stepped back and let the man come between them.

'You may go to your post, Captain.'

With a grunt of annoyance, the captain turned away and stamped into the guardroom. As he disappeared, he flashed Benzamir the devil's horns with his fingers. The guards drew back and muttered to themselves as the grey-haired man beckoned the visitors forward.

Once again, Wahir offered the scroll, and the man took it. He read the Arabic script and bowed to Benzamir. 'My lord. I am Joshua Mwendwa, and I am one of His Imperial Majesty's underministers of state. I welcome you and your party to Great Nairobi, and may I express what a pleasure it is to meet new friends of the empire, wherever they might be found?'

'You may. I am Prince Benzamir Mahmood, and I bring a gift from my father the king as a token of his esteem.'

Underminister Mwendwa pressed his hands together in an attempt to stop them lunging forward and grabbing the book from Said's arms. 'Yes, your gift. A very fortunate choice. The emperor has an almost complete set of these books, and yours will be a valuable addition to the set.'

'So I understand. The king of the Peoples over the Sea is very wise.' Benzamir dug his toe into the ground and twisted it around. 'May we arrange a time to present ourselves and our credentials to His Imperial Majesty?'

'I am certain he will wish to see you at his earliest convenience.' Mwendwa nodded to the guards, who began to close the outer gates. 'But first he would insist you enjoy the hospitality of the imperial palace. A bath? Clean clothes? I can tell you've come a very long way indeed.'

They were going to be trapped, both them and the book. Benzamir decided to put a brave face on it. 'Further than you might anticipate, Underminister. We will accept your kind offer.'

Mwendwa presumed to take Benzamir's arm and usher him forward to the inner gate. Benzamir strode forward confidently, arm-in-arm with the underminister, leaving the others to trail hesitantly behind. The guards opened the inner gates, just as the outer ones banged echoing shut.

CHAPTER 34

The antechamber to the throne room was more than large enough to intimidate. Even Benzamir felt cowed by the high ceiling and the distance between the walls. The doors were tall and narrow, and made him feel like a little child.

'Master,' whispered Wahir. He'd found speaking at normal volume caused a booming echo that deeply disturbed him. 'Why are they making us wait so long?'

'I don't know. There could be a whole host of reasons, the least of which is that the emperor isn't ready yet.'

'Doesn't he want the book?'

'I'm sure he does. It's just that we're strangers here and don't know how things work.'

Wahir hefted the metal book in his arms into a more comfortable position. 'What do we do?'

'We stand around, twiddling our thumbs.'

As he finished speaking, the throne-room doors swung open, and Underminister Mwendwa backed through, bowing.

'Please listen,' he said, straightening, 'you are not to approach the throne unless invited. You are not to touch the emperor on any account. Do not turn your back to the emperor. You are to address him as Your Imperial Majesty or Your Imperial Highness. You must answer his questions fully and candidly, and not ask questions of your own. Do you understand?'

'Yes, that's fine.' Benzamir adjusted the unfamiliar blue shift he'd been given to wear and inspected his companions. 'Ready? No spitting on the carpet, Said.'

'I don't spit on carpets,' Said objected, then tutted. 'Very funny.'

'Right, best foot forward, and try and look suitably awed.'

It wasn't difficult. If the anteroom had been tall, the throne room reached almost to the sky. Benzamir's eyes were drawn irresistibly upwards to the oil lamps strung between the tapering pillars and into the darkness beyond, then down the length of the room to the dais and the golden throne surrounded by a sea of red banners that draped gracefully around it.

'Awed yet?' giggled Alessandra. Her fingers dug into the scroll and left shadowed dents.

'I've seen some incredible sights in my time, but this is right up there with the destruction of the Eta Eridane. Courage.' Benzamir started the long slow walk towards the throne, and the others hurried to catch up.

Halfway down, a functionary in a simple white robe stopped them with an upraised hand.

'Who is it that desires an audience with His Imperial Majesty?'

Benzamir's throat was dry. 'Benzamir Michael Mahmood and his companions, emissaries of the People over the Sea.'

The man bowed to the throne and announced them in a clear, ringing voice. The tiny figure sitting on the throne lifted his ebony-handled fly whisk, and they had permission to proceed.

When they eventually reached him, they discovered that His Imperial Majesty the Kaisari Yohane Muzorewa was a great bull of a man, but still dwarfed by the size of the chair in which he sat. Sweating in his robes despite the coolness of the room and the efforts of a man with a swinging fan, the emperor of the Kenyan empire looked strangely uncomfortable.

The white-robed functionary took the scroll from Alessandra's unresisting hands and presented it to the emperor with downcast eyes. He backed away down the steps, stood to one side and waited as the scroll was unrolled and studied.

The emperor kept glowering over the top of the page as he read, glancing from one to another, trying to work out who they actually were. Benzamir stayed guardedly neutral and tried not to let his eyes wander too much.

'Prince Mahmood,' said the emperor, laying the scroll to one side, 'I wish to learn more of your People over the Sea.'

'As you wish, Your Imperial Highness,' said Benzamir. 'We are travellers from the far northern sea. We pride ourselves on our shipbuilding and our navigation. We learned of your power and fame from merchants who were beginning to bring us tales of Great Nairobi. My father the king insisted that I and my companions set out at once to find you, and to offer you this book as a token of our esteem.'

'Did he indeed?' said the emperor. The gold crown on his head glittered.

Benzamir pulled Wahir forward and they gave the book to the functionary, who carried it up to the throne. The emperor hesitated as he started to unwrap the rug from it.

'Prince Mahmood, how did this book come to your father?'

'It was brought to our lands by a merchant. When we heard that it might have been acquired, shall we say, under dubious circumstances, it made my father all the more determined to deliver it to you.'

The emperor narrowed his eyes and pulled the last of the rug away. The gleaming book sat heavy in his hands – hands that were now crawling with microscopic bugs.

'You are right, People from over the Sea, that this book was lost to me and I despaired of its restoration. You do me honour in returning it without fear or favour, and I welcome you into friendship with the Kenyan empire.' He hesitated again, almost turning his head to one side, then the other, without wishing to be seen to do either. 'It is my wish that I repay this great compliment your father has bestowed on me. I would have us draw up a treaty between your people and mine, and ambassadors exchanged. While these articles are drafted, you will be my guests. I will arrange matters and, in due course, speak with you again.'

Benzamir felt a tingling of anticipation, but said nothing about it. 'Your Imperial Majesty is both gracious and hospitable. We will wait on your pleasure.' In Arabic, he added, 'Bow and leave, but remember not to turn round.'

They retreated all the way down the throne room and eventually reached the far end. The tall doors opened for them, seemingly without human intervention, and they ended up back in the antechamber. The doors swung shut with a solid bang.

'It went well?' asked the underminister. 'I thought it did.'

'Yes, it went very well,' said Benzamir.

Alessandra looked worried, and he managed to communicate to her without speaking that she should stay quiet for the moment.

'I thought that you bowed to no man,' said Said.

'Ibn Alam demanded something from me that wasn't his to ask for and that I wasn't prepared to give. That's not how

Gift works.' Benzamir glanced back at the doors. 'But sometimes you have to play the game.'

Wahir followed the direction of his gaze. 'Was there something going on that . . . ?'

'Wahir. Not now.'

'But . . .'

'Really, not now.' Benzamir turned to the underminister with a forced smile. 'If you'll show us to our rooms, there are matters of state I need to discuss with my colleagues.'

'Of course, Your Highness. Please follow me.'

They back-tracked their way through the palace until they were outside, in a garden rich with green plants and scarlet flowers. Night had fallen and the sky was once more alive with stars, the air thick with perfume and insects.

'Wahir, remember this place, just by the fountain. If we get separated for any reason, this is where you come. Yes?'

'Master, was it just me, or did the emperor seem, well, scared?'

Benzamir looked up: Underminister Mwendwa was ahead, carrying a swinging lantern on a pole, and Said and Alessandra were between him and them.

'I thought that too. We can't talk about it unless we're certain we're not being overheard. So not another word.'

Wahir turned round, looking at all the high walls and towers, fixing the garden's location in his mind. 'There are figures in the dark, up on roofs.'

'There's no reason for anyone to trust us. We don't have a history, and our story is as thin as fog. The only thing going for us is that it'll take a while for them to work out who we really are and what we want.'

'By which time we'll have gone.'

'You should have stayed at school, Wahir. You learn very quickly.'

They had crossed the courtyard garden, and the under-minister waited for them at the door to a red-stained building that had many lines of lit windows up its sheer face.

'The guest accommodation,' said the underminister. 'I trust it will be acceptable.'

They were given a suite of rooms on the third floor. The cunningly designed building had a central courtyard over-looked by balconies, but none of the windows on the outer walls would open. Thick squares of blown glass knitted together in a hardwood frame let in light, but nothing else.

Servants would bring them whatever they wanted, but they could not leave without an escort.

The moment Underminister Mwendwa had left them, Alessandra blurted out: 'What the hell is going on, Benzamir?'

He put his finger to his lips and made sure that everyone saw it, then beckoned them over into a huddle. With their heads touching, he whispered: 'These walls will have ears, I guarantee it. It's quite clear we weren't believed. We're sea people, but didn't come from the sea. We look like a bunch of Arab tribesmen, except for Alessandra, and they know the book was traded in Misr. They've every reason to throw us in a cell, but they have to treat us as guests, because they can't work out why we're doing what we're doing.'

'The emperor was very ill-at-ease,' said Alessandra. 'You must have seen that.'

'I didn't notice anything,' said Said.

'There were things he said too.'

'I don't understand World.'

Benzamir hushed them. 'For now, we're People from over the Sea. We have to stay in character every moment, together or alone. Give the Kenyans no extra reason to suspect us. There is something going on, though, outside our little charade.'

'What could it be?' asked Wahir, his voice rising with excitement.

'Shout it out, why don't you? It can't be anything to do with us; we've only just got here.' He worked his jaw as if chewing. 'The trial. The book. Things are moving too fast.'

'What of your special beetles, master? When will they tell you something?'

'When I have a chance to listen to them.' Benzamir heard a note of exasperation creep into his voice. 'We're all hungry and tired. Get some food brought up, and I'll join you later. All right?'

They all straightened up. Said thought it should be Alessandra who fetched the servants, and Alessandra bristled at the suggestion. Benzamir left them arguing and found one of the simple but neat rooms in which to hide.

He lay down on the bed and closed his eyes. By concentrating, he started to see and hear things he should neither see nor hear.

The image was grainy, contorted, a fish-eye view that was built up in incomplete layers to make a discordant whole. The sound was better, alternately booming or tinny, depending on the distance of the source from the bugs.

The book was being carried down a corridor. He could hear the emperor's heavy footsteps and sense his weight rolling from side to side in the motion of the picture.

There was someone else too. Another man all in black from head to foot, so that even his feet were obscured. He was walking in front, leading the way.

Benzamir frowned in his half-sleep. At first he thought it was the man with the scars they'd seen earlier, but it wasn't. There was something wrong about the way the man moved too.

They reached a door and went through. The emperor closed it behind them and they were alone: no guards, no servants, no advisers. Just two men in an empty room.

'This is fortunate,' said the man. He spoke in Swahili, though the sound was muffled by the folds of cloth that hung over his face. 'These Sea People have succeeded where your Ethiopians have failed. Perhaps my alliance should have been with them.'

'We haven't had word from Misr yet. There hasn't been time.' The emperor was almost pleading. This wasn't a conversation between equals. 'I don't know what to make of the Sea People. We've never heard of them before, and their story is unlikely.'

'Perhaps your spies are not as all-seeing as you wish they were. Still, we are missing one book. Is there no chance of retrieving it?'

'Akisi said the monk threw it into the sea. It's lost, I tell you.'

'You shouldn't take the word of either of those madmen. Find out where it went overboard. And if this affects our plans, delays them in any way, there will be a price to pay.'

'You dare to threaten me?'

'This isn't the theatre, Musorewa. Your pomp and your palaces might frighten the natives, but your smoke-and-mirrors act doesn't scare me. I can threaten you all I like. You can't hurt me.'

The emperor turned away. The picture flickered and spun.

'Give me the book,' the man said. 'Let me see what we have to work with. Hopefully it'll be enough.'

'You've offered me nothing but toys and promises. I want to see something real. Something that I can use.'

'Over and above what you've already been shown? Do

you have so little faith in me? I thought you were better than that, a man of vision and determination. All you want is signs and wonders.'

'It's not me you have to worry about. Akisi was just a symptom of a wider disease. He thinks what all my other ministers are thinking: we're giving too much to you. Much too much. I am emperor, and it causes unrest when they hear that I defer to you.'

'Then you should look to your own back, Your Imperial Highness. Mine is quite safe. Give me the book.' Part of the shroud came forward. No hand was visible, but the book moved away from the emperor.

The image moved with it. The man became more distinct, and finally there was an image of what lay under the hood. Two glowing points of light.

Benzamir was surrounded by his friends.

'Master!'

He was sitting up, clutching at Said's arm, wide-eyed and gasping for breath.

'Master, you cried out.'

'Did I? Sorry. Shock, surprise.'

Alessandra pressed a cup of dark wine into his hands, and he took a gulp, not rightly caring what it was. After he swallowed, he steadied himself. They looked expectantly at him.

'They're here. My enemies are right here.'

CHAPTER 32

Close to midnight, Benzamir was sitting alone in the inner courtyard of the guest quarters. Head low, back hunched, he played with his fingers in his lap, picking at his nails.

He was so absorbed in his thoughts that he didn't see the grey figure come up beside him, only noticed the sudden shift in weight along the length of the bench.

He was up and in a defensive stance in an instant, right hand high and ready to strike out.

'Master? Are you all right?'

Benzamir looked up. Wahir was on the balcony parapet, leaning against the wall, watching over him.

He dropped his arms by his side. 'Why aren't you in bed?'

'A servant shouldn't sleep while his master is awake. It isn't done.'

'Wahir, get some rest. I need you alert tomorrow, not dragging your feet around like a zombie.'

'A what?'

'One of the living dead. Partial to fresh brains.'

'Right.' Wahir swung his feet off the stonework and stood. 'You need to sleep too.'

'I'll come up soon.'

He made sure Wahir disappeared behind the curtain and finally got around to apologizing.

'Sorry for jumping. I was lost in thought.'

'A rare quality for a man,' she said, 'but I don't think you should be applauded for it.'

He recognized her immediately, and found himself completely tongue-tied. He shifted from one foot to the other and back like a fool.

'My lady,' he said finally.

'You're staring again, just like you did from the window of that cheap boarding house.'

'And again, sorry. I didn't mean to.'

'Didn't you? Why did you then?'

'It was the elephant, the soldiers, the three of you in the cart. It looked like a fascinating story.' Benzamir regained his composure. The suddenness of her appearance, the abrupt closeness of her: it had disoriented him. 'That's why I sent Said down to find out all about you.'

'Did you learn anything interesting?'

'Yes. I found out that a minister of state had stolen the emperor's property and will face trial tomorrow. But I couldn't find out anything about who you were. Or the man with the scars.'

'The man with the scars,' Elenya repeated wistfully. 'Yes, I suppose he is that. He is Brother Va Angemaite of the monastery of Saint Samuil of Arkady. And I am still the Princess Elenya Lukeva Christyakova of Novy Rostov. You may, if you wish, sit.'

He sat. 'I'm Benzamir Michael Mahmood, Prince of the People over the Sea.'

'What brings you to Great Nairobi, Prince Benzamir?'

'Books, Princess. Books.'

He saw how her body stiffened for a moment, heard how her breath caught in her throat.

'You know what Solomon Akisi stole then.'

'More than know. He sold one book in Misr, on the shore of the Inner Sea. It came to my father the king, and I have brought it back as a gift for the emperor.' Benzamir was busy remembering what he should and shouldn't give away. She knew the fate of the second book; he ought not.

'You made a mistake,' Elenya said, her eyes narrowing. 'The book was not Akisi's to steal, nor the emperor's to keep. The books belong to the patriarch of Mother Russia. And Va is determined to take them all to him, one by one if necessary.'

Benzamir listened for a moment to the creak of insects and the barking of lizards. 'How did the emperor get the books in the first place? They've come a very long way from Mother Russia. As have you, Princess.'

'Va goes where the books go,' she said. 'I go where he goes. As for the emperor, how do powerful men come to own anything? They steal it. Sometimes by law, sometimes by trickery, and sometimes they just take it by force. I was there, Prince Benzamir, when the emperor's men killed all the brothers, took the books and burned the monastery of Saint Samuil to the ground. I witnessed both the bloody carnage and the fire. They were good men. They didn't deserve to die like that.' She stopped. 'What's wrong? What have I said?'

Benzamir's hand had gone to his mouth, and he hadn't blinked all the while. 'Dead? How many?'

'Forty brothers. Not one of them picked up a weapon to defend himself. I don't understand why you're so shocked. These things happen from time to time.'

'And the emperor did this? I mean, he ordered it?'

Elenya shrugged and pulled her grey cloak tighter around her. The night air was cold, and they hadn't moved for a while. 'Who else? The books are taken from Arkady, they turn up in Great Nairobi. It's not difficult to believe.'

'No, no, it's not. The emperor has the gold, the spies, the ability to reach out beyond his borders: he could do it, if he had reason enough.' Benzamir felt his palms prick with sweat. 'Did you ever see one of these books?'

'Yes, eventually. Akisi had run to a land on the edge of the Outer Ocean. He tried to make a name for himself, sell himself and the book's knowledge to the highest bidder. He murdered a village priest and massacred an army. He's not a nice man.' Elenya looked at Benzamir quizzically from under her hood. 'I saw the book he had, but that's not what you're asking. In fact, you're asking a lot of questions that I don't have to answer. I don't know you. I don't know who you are.' She stood up hurriedly and made to leave. 'If you're one of the emperor's men, then I've said enough to get us all hanged.'

Benzamir dared put out his hand to stop her. 'Wait. You're safe with me, safe from me. Please, Princess: just one last question.'

She knocked his hand aside and reached for a knife hidden in her belt. 'Why do I feel compelled to tell you everything? It's like I've suddenly gone mad.' She was breathing hard, her pale face flushed. 'I'll answer your question if you answer mine. You're not a real prince, are you? All the ones I've ever met – and I've met an awful lot – were either effete snobs or boorish pigs, and to a man they were filled with a loathsome self-importance that made me want to vomit. Then there's you. You're different.'

Benzamir got up slowly so as not to frighten her any further. 'I am not a prince, and my father was not a king. But there *are* People over the Sea, and our interest in the emperor's library has nothing to do with learning, and everything to do with whoever it is who wants those books desperately enough to kill forty men in cold blood.' He held up his hand, palm facing her, fingers splayed. 'I swear this is true, by the promises which bind me to my tribe and my vocation.'

Elenya lowered her knife, and her sleeve fell over the blade. She bit her lip, then said: 'Ask your question.'

'What is it that is so important about these books that brings you across half a world?'

'Va believes that God will destroy the world if people learn the knowledge of the Users. Their knowledge is in the books. So if we don't get the books back, everybody will die. I never believed it. I was just content to follow him, be near to him at long last. It is agony and ecstasy in the same moment, and I thought it was enough. But as I watched Akisi's devices reduce an army to tatters in a matter of minutes, I found myself thinking, What if Va's right? God cursed the Users. He'll curse us as well.' She wiped away an angry tear. 'Again, I never meant to say so much.'

Benzamir took a step closer to her. 'No one will destroy you.'

'And who's going to stop God? You?'

'Yes.'

Elenya laughed suddenly, and she ended up crying. Benzamir didn't know what to do, so he did nothing, which was a decision of sorts. She crouched down and rocked, holding her head in her hands, sobbing and choking. Lights came on at windows, and haloes of condensation were made by curious faces.

A door opened, and one of the emperor's servants stepped

into the garden. 'My lord, my lady, is there anything the matter?'

Benzamir raised his finger to his lips and used a gesture to show that although there was a great deal the matter, there was nothing that either of them could do. The man nodded and left the door ajar.

Eventually the sobs subsided and the great racking shudders that shook her ceased. She got up, whispered, 'Forgive me,' and turned away.

'My lady?'

She stopped but didn't look round.

'The trial is tomorrow. I know that you're going to be there, to help plead for the books to be taken back to Mother Russia. Your words will be wasted, and the more you beg, the greater the danger to your life. I can't explain any more. Please be anywhere but there.'

She kept on walking. The path led to the door, and she left without another word.

Benzamir let his head fall to his chest and pinched the bridge of his nose.

'Master?'

'I thought I told you to go to bed.'

'And I'd already explained that a servant doesn't sleep until his master does. It's the way things are done.'

'I'm coming up,' he said, and used the same door that Princess Elenya Christyakova had. She had gone, though he felt he should have been able to detect some trace of her passing.

Wahir made some coffee over a spirit burner, and they took it out onto the balcony to drink.

'What did the woman say, master?'

'Something that changes everything. If we're going to talk about this, we're going to have to mutter and speak quickly. I don't want to be overheard.'

'Then we won't talk about whatever it was. Talk about something else, like how beautiful she was.'

Benzamir burned his lip on the scalding coffee. 'I rather thought boys your age weren't supposed to notice things like that. It's supposed to be, yuck, girls.'

'You told her you weren't a prince. If anyone was over-hearing that, the guards would be beating down our doors.' Wahir blew the steam off his own coffee and wrapped his hands around the cup for warmth. 'Men do and say stupid things around women; things to impress and make themselves seem more important. But not you: you say things that make you less in her eyes and I don't understand that.'

'I'm not sure that I do either.'

'So why did you tell her you weren't a prince?'

'It's not news. She saw through me quicker than the emperor did. I'm just not stamped from a royal mould, I suppose. And I did it to get some information.' Even as he said it, it sounded cheap and tawdry. 'And I made her cry like I'd torn her heart out.'

'Master,' asked Wahir, 'do you find her beautiful? I suppose that most men would. Sometimes I'd see slaves brought to the sheikh's palace. They're slaves, you don't pay them that much attention. But there was one woman, and you could see the men act differently towards her. Even though they owned her, there was something that made them be nice to her.' He leaned heavily on the balustrade, eyes staring into the distance. 'There was something. I don't know what it was. Am I still too young to know?'

'Beauty comes from the inside. It seeps out of every pore and is in every line and curve. I'll tell you the story of Ali Five-camels,' said Benzamir. 'In a time that was and was not, there lived a young man called Ali. His family had a good name, and they were fairly well off. Not as rich as the sheikh, but they had lots of camels, and places to graze them. Soon enough, Ali came of age, and his father told him that it was about time he got married. There were lots of pretty girls in the village, and their fathers were all eager that Ali should choose their daughter. Truth be told, the girls were fighting over Ali too. He was a good-looking boy, with a gentle nature, but both fathers and daughters were after the mahr and other gifts he would give at the wedding.

'Ali had different ideas. All his life he had dreamed about a woman who would love him for who he was, not for what he owned. So he set off on a journey to find such a woman. He was at an oasis one day when a poor nomad family arrived with their few goats. Ali found them good company: they shared their food with him, though they had little, and their daughter fetched them water from the well, always making sure that Ali's cup was full.

'That night the nomad and Ali were talking, and the subject of his daughter came up. The nomad said that his daughter would go to the grave unwed because of her deformity, and how unfair it was. Ali was surprised, because he hadn't noticed until then that her lip was creased, and a scar ran up her face. He agreed that it was unfair – and told the nomad that if he was willing, he would marry their daughter.

'When they returned to the village, word soon got out that there were wedding preparations going on. All the village girls were desperate to see who had beaten them, but when they saw the nomad's daughter, they couldn't believe that someone they thought ugly could have won Ali's heart. They said he was marrying her out of pity, and it wouldn't be long before he divorced her. They said all this to her face at the village well, and then asked her how much mahr Ali was giving her. It wasn't a few coins, or a goat. It wasn't even a camel. Or two camels. Or three camels. It was five camels.'

'Master? Five camels for an ugly woman? This Ali is mad!'

'Shush, Wahir, and listen. The village girls thought Ali

mad too. They complained to everyone who would hear. If Ali's bride was worth five camels, how much more than that should their husbands-to-be give them? But as time went on, the girls all got married, and they found that their mahr was much less than Ali's bride's. They stopped looking down at her, and instead started looking for the reason why Ali thought her worth five camels.'

'And what did they find?'

'They found that she was beautiful.' Benzamir finished off the last of his coffee. 'Come on. I'm going to bed, and you've got no excuse left to stay up.'

'But master,' Wahir called to Benzamir's retreating back, 'was she beautiful before Ali gave five camels for her mahr or not? These stories of yours, they don't make any sense!'

CHAPTER 33

Benzamir got up before the sun and shook Said awake. It took a while.

'Tell me you're listening, or I'll pry your eyelids back.'

The big man eventually sat up, working his mouth as if he tasted something dead inside. 'What? What is it?'

'I'm going to do a bit of housekeeping. I'll be back before the trial starts, but I need you to do something for me: we need to be near the front. I don't know how these things work, so it's your job to find out and make it happen. Understand? The front, do you understand?'

'Yes, yes. Why is it still dark outside?'

'Because it's night-time. You will remember this conversation, won't you?'

Said flopped back down, making the frame of the bed creak. 'I'll remember,' he mumbled. In a moment he was asleep again. His arm slipped off the side of the mattress and dangled above the floor.

Benzamir placed it back across his chest and patted his

hand. 'This is what too much excitement does.' He picked up his sandals and tiptoed into the main room, where the remains of their last meal still sat on the low table, attracting the first morning flies.

He was trying to decide between a mango and a banana when he heard someone behind him.

'Where are you going?'

'Out,' said Benzamir. The banana then. He offered the mango to Alessandra, who made no move to either accept or decline it. 'I've given Said instructions.'

'What was last night all about?' She folded her arms. 'I watched from up here.'

'Wahir didn't mention that. But it wasn't very private, was it?' He put the mango back into the bowl and peeled the banana, eating half of it in three quick bites. 'Our book seems to be in demand: the emperor wants it, the patriarch of Mother Russia wants it. It's a shame it's not here any more. Last seen heading north, out of the city and out of range. I can't be more definite because I don't want to make the bugs broadcast, but it's going somewhere.'

'That's not what I mean. Who is she?'

'A Russian princess. The man who came with her is a monk or a priest. Or both.' He finished the banana and draped the skin across one of the dirty plates. 'I really do need to go.'

'What did you say to her to make her weep like that?'

She was standing in his way, between him and the door. He took her shoulders and gently turned her aside. 'I told her that I would save her from the wrath of God.'

Alessandra tried to say several things, none of which would come out. Benzamir decided that it was a good time to leave, so he did.

He obtained a pass – a numbered, embossed plaque of copper – from one of the functionaries and made his way through the gardens to the gatehouse. Every so often he would look up at the buildings towering above him, at the rooftop guards with their crossbows and the gunners manning rudimentary artillery. The palace was well-garrisoned, watching for enemies from both outside and in. For all their arms and their vigilance, Benzamir knew that it was too late.

They were already here.

He puzzled over the identity of the man shrouded in black. He knew all the traitors, just as they knew him. He'd been one of them once. But the man's voice was unrecognizable; Benzamir had filtered it and tweaked it, tried to match it with the patterns he knew, and had come up with nothing. Nor had he seen the man's face, swathed as it was in dark cloth until only the faint shine of enhanced eyes could break the shadow.

He showed his pass to the guards of the inner gate just as

the sun came up. Darkness one moment, light the next. The clouds in the sky turned red, then orange, then dove-grey, and it was day. The outer gates were cranked open, and the first of the morning's deliveries of meat and milk was already wheeling in.

He stood to one side to watch as a steady procession of carts passed by, then slipped out. From the hilltop, Great Nairobi lay like a giant beginning to stir.

The mills were already turning, the fires burning. Southwards, across from the bare ground of the killing field in front of the citadel walls, there were vast kilns breathing puffs of dirty steam and sparks which carried on the wind. To the north were the fine buildings of merchants and bankers, set along wide, tree-lined roads and around fountain-set squares.

Squeezed between them in the hazy valley was where Benzamir had rented his room, and where he headed now. Yesterday he had been wearing his own clothes. Today he was in a rich man's costume, and while he didn't play the part, everyone else took their cue from his finery. Those who presumed themselves his equal nodded to him; those who did not averted their eyes and got out of his way.

And Benzamir found himself scanning every face, from the first stragglers making their way home to their beds, to the workers repairing the road, to the handcart pullers trotting towards market. Everyone: the men, the women, the young, the old, black, white, high station or none.

He was looking for someone he recognized, someone who had no right to be there, anywhere on the planet. It was making him tremble with nerves, because there was no guarantee that they weren't out looking for him.

What would he do if they found each other, passing in the street? Would they invite Benzamir to retire to the nearest tea house and talk over their predicament and their terms of surrender? Or would they run – and would he give chase?

He turned down an alley and pressed his back against the cold stone of a wall. There were forty dead men in a burned-down monastery to reckon with now. It was a complication he couldn't ignore. And he still had no idea what they wanted the antique books for.

He stepped back out and tried to compose himself. The boarding house was a little further down the road, not far at all. He kept his head down all the way and slipped past the wooden door. He closed it behind him, and felt no better.

Noises from deeper inside the building told him that people were already up and preparing for their day. He walked up the stairs, waiting at the landing for two men and their satchels full of cloth samples to pass by, then entered his rented room using the worn iron key he had been given.

The inks and paints they'd used were still out on the table. They had to go – they'd been stupid not to tidy up before leaving for the citadel. The responsibility was all his though. He found the bags they came in and started to refill them.

He was almost done when there was a sharp, authoritative banging from the street-side door. He climbed up onto the table and lay down, peeking over the window ledge.

There were four men. One carried a staff tipped with a silver antelope. Benzamir had seen enough of that symbol around the palace to know what it meant. His heart skipped. He'd been watching for his own enemies when he should have been on the lookout for ruthlessly efficient Kenyan spies. They'd had him followed, they'd seen him enter the building and now knew that he and his companions had stayed there. He had, for a moment, underestimated the empire. For most people who did that, it didn't end well.

He quickly finished with the calligrapher's materials and felt under his bed for the flying carpet. If it had still been night, he might have been tempted to use it. He put everything on the thin blanket that lay rumpled on the floor and gathered up the corners.

He walked across the landing and tried the door opposite. There hadn't been an occupant yesterday, but the room was locked. He used his laser to cut the deadbolt, and blew away the smoke with a flap of his hand as he heard footsteps coming purposefully up the stairs.

It was worth the time it took to relock his own door. He was in the empty room just as there were voices outside.

He'd have to hurry. In three steps he was at the window, undoing the shutters, looking down and around. There was nothing to climb, and there was only a small grimy courtyard to jump down into.

Benzamir looked up. The eaves of the peaked roof were within reach. He tied the ends of the blanket so that he could wear it like a papoose. The emperor's men were occupied trying to persuade the landlady to open the door. It wouldn't be long before they realized that there was nothing there and widened their search.

He stood on the sill, turned round, then straightened up and fell backwards. He caught the edge of the shingled roof, and swung himself up until he was perched like a spider on the slope. The sandals gave him no grip, and he carefully slipped each one off and put them in the blanket.

The surrounding buildings were a similar height, and there was no one to overlook him. He listened carefully. The voices faded; they had gone into the room and were searching it for clues as to who the Sea People might be or where they had come from.

He waited: the door to the room below him opened. Benzamir grew very still. The boards creaked all the way across to the window. There was a pause.

Then they creaked back to the door. He allowed himself a rueful smile: here he was stuck on a roof with a mix of pens and brushes and contraband technology, while the local police stood around on the landing, arguing with each other about where he could have possibly gone. It was yet another thing he hadn't exactly planned for.

It was time to move. He crept up to the ridge without crossing it, and made his way to the next house. He glanced back. No pursuit. Three more roofs and he was at the end of the row. A narrow alleyway separated them, leading from the street to a maze of outbuildings and animal pens.

He jumped it, lightly, surely. The absence of cries, drums or whistles told him he was still undetected. It couldn't go on. Sooner or later he'd have to return to ground level, lose himself in the morning crowds.

The spies would know that when he left the citadel, he was carrying nothing but his pass. The inks he could just abandon in a rubbish tip somewhere, but the carpet had to go too, and that would be much more difficult. He wondered how he could possibly part with it now they had shared so many days' travel, then in the next breath laughed at himself for such sentimentality.

He carried on to the next alley, keeping low all the while. He looked down, saw that the coast was reasonably clear and jumped. It was a long way down, but he didn't balk. There was no magic to the landing, just a question of absorbing the impact with enough craft so that nothing broke.

He straightened himself up, dusted himself off and joined the early morning flow of people minding their own business.

He took a walk towards the distant, belching kilns and furnaces, and came back just a little lighter.

The square had the name of a long dead king, resurrected from before the time of empire to provide some gravitas to the playful gardens and hissing fountain at its centre. Bright blooms nodded in the breeze, and the broad fronds of palm trees lacing together overhead meant that the shadows were cool and welcoming.

Benzamir watched the play of the water across the surface of the pond. The fountain spray fell in a threefold arch, breaking up the mirror reflection and sending sparkling light in every direction.

A familiar figure walked towards him, resplendent in red robes, accompanied by a servant with a parasol.

'Shall we take a seat, Prince Benzamir?' asked the under-minister.

'I'd like to say this was a pleasant surprise, but I think I know you better than that. I'll have to confine myself to saying it is merely pleasant.'

Underminister Mwendwa indicated a bench surrounded by thorny bushes with brilliant orange flowers. The functionary with the parasol took up a position a little way away; not so close as to overhear, not so far as to not come when called.

'The emperor sends his greetings to the emissary of the People over the Sea.'

'The king, I'm sure, would reply in kind, Underminister. Though I'm not certain what he'd say about your following me around. Perhaps he'd thank you for keeping his representative safe in this wild and lawless city.' Certain that the irony in his voice had been understood, Benzamir fetched out a paper bag of rose-water sweets he'd bought from a street vendor. 'Care for one?'

'You're kindness itself,' said Mwendwa, and licked his fingers free of icing sugar. 'But I'll ask you plainly: why do royal sons choose to stay in shabby guest houses and visit our iron works? I can't believe you do it for enjoyment.'

'The iron works were a wonder. Everyone should go. My father will be amazed when he hears of them. Though,' added Benzamir, 'you might want a word with the forge-master about this morning's castings. Some impurities found their way into the mix. As to our lodgings? I've slept in worse.'

'I hope you understand our caution, Prince. These are strange days. There are many visitors in Great Nairobi, and not all of them wish the empire well.' Mwendwa gave Benzamir a sideways glance. 'I call you Prince because I believe you have Kenya's best interests at heart. Not because I believe you to be a prince.'

Benzamir chose his words carefully. 'I've no reason to harm either empire or emperor, though you have to take my word for that. Underminister, why haven't you arrested me yet?'

Mwendwa bent his head low. Benzamir leaned in to hear him. 'You know of the trial of Solomon Akisi which takes place today?'

'Great Nairobi talks of nothing else.'

'He was an underminister, like myself. But he defied the emperor, who is wise in all things.'

'Even if he's wrong?'

'Ah,' said Mwendwa, 'you see clearly. You brought the emperor a generous gift, but perhaps you would have done better to bring a cart-load of gold, or sacks of pearls from the sea.'

'Underminister, I can't help but be aware of the party factions of the Kenyan court; our delegation isn't the only one to have arrived recently. As far as the Sea People are concerned, the gift of the book was most appropriate.' He let that sink in, and added, 'Then there's the Russians.'

'Will they press their case?'

'Yes. They're as passionate about their stolen property as the emperor is about his.'

Mwendwa played with the fleshy part of his chin. 'That, perhaps, is to our advantage. I and my colleagues want the empire strong, because it benefits all people, not just us. Do you get my meaning?'

'A weak empire is no use to anyone,' agreed Benzamir, 'except those who would make it deliberately weak. I'm not one of those people.'

'I had thought so, and I'm glad to confirm this. We need all the friends we can get, Prince.' Mwendwa sat pensively on the edge of the seat and looked up at the towers, the mills spinning on their high posts, the greenery cascading from rooftop gardens and windowsills. 'If all this were swept away, we'd lose so much more than mere stone and tile. The Users? They were vain and stupid. Somehow they let their vices destroy them. I like to entertain the thought that the Kenyan empire is neither vain nor stupid, and that we'll escape sharing their fate.'

Benzamir listened to the water fall and the leaves rustle. He shouldn't choose sides, as he already had his own side to be on, but Mwendwa's transparent passion for his city swayed him. 'I'll do what I can. Perhaps you can do something for me.'

Mwendwa nodded, and he carried on.

'The trial. I'd like to take the opportunity to see how the empire dispenses justice.'

'You will have an honoured place.' Mwendwa stood up and beckoned his servant. 'My presence is required at the palace. Will you walk with me? I'd like to show you more of what we might lose if we fail in our enterprise.'

Benzamir fell in at the underminister's side, and together they walked back to the citadel, shimmering in the noonday heat, high on the hill.

CHAPTER 34

The throne room had changed. Filled with brightly coloured dignitaries from the emperor's lands, every single minister of state in their high-hatted finery, the polished brilliance of soldiers' shields and the plumed head-dresses of the rich and powerful: what had been empty and impressive had been transformed into a carnival.

Sunlight fractured overhead, spearing down in coloured fragments from the windows, and the full circle of the dais was illuminated by a dome of metal and glass that had been invisible during the night.

The hall was full: the ordinary people of Great Nairobi had taken the singular opportunity to see inside the citadel walls. In front of them, holding back the masses, was a line of soldiers. Then came the plutocrats and political masters of the empire occupying gilded seats in neat rows, placed at the front of the hall.

Benzamir and Said sat with them, uncomfortable and agitated. Mwendwa had moved them from the precious but lowly positions Said had managed to obtain, and ejected two high-ranking officials from the first row. The Kenyans either side of them gave sidelong glances and whispered behind their hands at the affront.

Wahir, overwhelmed by the crowds, the strange smells and the size of some of the Masai, had retreated to the side aisle. He climbed part way up a pillar to get a better look. Alessandra stood by him, mainly to make sure that he didn't get into any trouble.

'I still don't understand why we're here, master,' said Said.

'Because something is going to happen.'

'But what, apart from what's supposed to take place?'

'If I knew that,' said Benzamir, 'I wouldn't be so nervous.' It was true: his mouth was dry, and his pulse fast and thready. He felt light-headed with anticipation.

There was a buzz of anticipation. A line of soldiers marched from behind the drapery that flanked the throne and formed a barricade of shields and broad-bladed spears. Then the sombre, black-robed lawyers took their places at the front, where desks had been set out for their pens and papers.

A commotion grew from the far back of the hall, complete with boos and jeers: the prisoner was being brought in. Wahir, from his vantage point, waved at Benzamir and pointed over their heads.

An avenue of spears advanced down the length of the throne room. Jostled despite their fearsome appearance, the escort resorted to pushing the crowds back with their shields. Ripples of movement swirled through the hall as everyone tried to keep their places and their feet.

Akisi arrived at the front and shrugged off a thrown banana skin from his shoulder. He nudged it away with his shackled feet while one of the lawyers, a man with skin so black it was darker than his robes, whispered final words of encouragement and hope. The escort fanned out to surround the throne.

Then it began. A drum beat a slow, steady rhythm, and gradually the sound of chatter drained away. Those sitting stood, adjusted their dress, tried to look as fine as they could for their ruler. By the time the first of the emperor's attendants emerged from behind the curtains, all was silent but for the booming of the drum.

The emperor, dressed in full ceremonial lion-skin and many-pointed crown, glided to the throne and paused for a moment before he sat. His gaze took in the crowd of expectant but respectful subjects, from the narrow slit of light at the far end of the vaulted hall to the helmets of the soldiers lined up to protect him with their skill and their blood.

He then looked down – at the lawyers, at the prisoner himself, and then straight at Benzamir.

Benzamir shivered uncontrollably, and Said stood a little closer.

The emperor turned his head away, and an attendant darted forward to arrange the royal cloak before His Imperial Highness sat down.

With a flick of his fly-whisk, he indicated that the proceedings could start. The nobility sat with a sigh, and after a moment one of the lawyers stepped out from behind his desk. He bowed deeply to the occupant of the throne, and gave an outline of the case in his low, sonorous voice.

Benzamir was astounded by the adjectival onslaught: treacherous, perfidious, nauseating, pernicious, heinous. Akisi's accusers painted him as a man who had suckled on the teat of the empire in his cradle, then grown up to hate everything it stood for. There were no cool, impartial justice programmes to weigh the evidence and pronounce fair judgement; compassion protocols working for both defendant and victim, unmoved by poverty or privilege. The empire's court was turning into a furnace of conflict and adversarial debate. The emperor himself was presiding, and the stakes were clearly high. The lawyer dramatically shielded himself from Akisi with trembling fingers, as if frightened he might catch some criminal contagion.

'There can be no penalty less than death itself for such actions!' he demanded.

The crowd sighed and moaned. One or two cried out obscure curses on the accused's head.

He was a hard act to follow. Akisi's lawyer stood up to hissing and groaning. He began to explain why the former minister had acted so improperly.

Benzamir touched Said on the arm. 'I've just seen someone I need to talk to.'

'Can't it wait, master?'

'I wish it could. But no.'

He tried to make himself as small as possible and slipped from his seat, crossing the rest of the row to the side. The soldiers noticed his apologetic walk with interest, but everyone else had their attention fixed on the drama at the foot of the dais.

He passed Wahir and Alessandra with a troubled smile. They watched him go to the back of the seated area and crouch down next to the furthermost chair on the very last row.

'Hello again, Princess.'

She kept her eyes firmly fixed on Akisi. 'You didn't give me reason enough not to be here.'

'Which is to my shame. I should have tried harder.'

'We need to say our piece. Here is as good as anywhere, if not the best place.'

Benzamir looked across Elenya to the bullet-headed monk. His head was freshly shaved and revealed yet more scars to go with the ones on his face and hands.

'Brother,' acknowledged Benzamir, and Va nodded curtly

back. Puzzled, he asked Elenya something, and Benzamir caught a hint of their language.

Elenya answered in the same language, and he learned more.

'Who did you tell him I was?'

'Someone masquerading as a prince of his people. I told him I didn't know why you were doing it. Which is the truth.'

'Does he understand any of this?'

'No. Neither do I. What about you?'

'I don't claim to be able to speak Swahili like a native, but well enough.'

Elenya finally looked at him. 'Will you do something for me?'

He took several deep breaths. 'Whenever I make promises to beautiful princesses, it usually ends in disaster. But it doesn't normally stop me.'

She blinked slowly and seemed to have difficulty composing her thoughts. 'Tell me when's the best time to ask for the books back,' she said eventually.

'Never is the best time.'

'You promised.'

'I did, didn't I? See Wahir over there? Keep an eye on him.'

She glanced to where he was surreptitiously pointing, and Wahir grinned at them over the top of Alessandra's head.

392

'I need to go back to my place, Princess,' said Benzamir. 'Try not to think too badly of me.'

'Why would I do that? Have you done something to be ashamed of?'

Benzamir stared down at his hands. 'Oh yes. I'm as guilty of using you as everybody else is.' He looked straight at her, right into her eyes. 'All I can say in my defence is that I really do mean it for the best.'

She sat back and put her hand to her neck. Va felt the movement, saw Elenya's reaction to a stranger's advance and purposefully ignored them.

Benzamir gave a little bow and crept his way back to his seat. Akisi's lawyer was still hard at it, working the stage, using open-handed gestures and submissive body language. His voice rose to a shout, then fell to a whisper, compelling listeners to concentrate on his every word.

'He's very good,' said Benzamir, 'even though he's fighting a lost cause.'

'How can you tell?' asked Said.

'You don't steal from the emperor and get away with it on a technicality. What sort of signal would that send out?' From where they sat Benzamir could almost see behind the curtains. There was a shadow there, deeper than black, that drifted in and out of view as the curtain waved in time with the swinging fan.

An electrical tingle tickled Benzamir's brain. He turned

his head slowly, closing his eyes, feeling for the direction of the sensation. When he was certain that it came from the same place each time, he opened his eyes. Some of his bugs were still working.

There was not one, but three dark figures together, perfectly still, eyes shining softly within the folds of their hoods. He could hear the proceedings of the court, faint and distorted, the static hiss caused by the movement of air.

Benzamir ignored the words and just looked at the picture in front of him. The emperor was on his throne; in the front ranks on the other side of his personal bodyguard were all his ministers and underministers, his generals and ambassadors of his vassal states, the merchant princes and lords of industry. Everybody who could found and run an empire was in just one room.

The fringes of electronic chatter, narrowcast, encrypted, bounced off metal and stone, and ended up in Benzamir's head.

'Said, I want you to go and tell Wahir to wave at the Princess.'

'Which princess is this?'

'Just do it for me. Wahir will know what to do next. God go with you, my friend.' He gripped Said's shoulder.

'Master? What are you doing?' Said tried to find some reason around him that would account for the strange behaviour.

'Go. Now. Or we're going to stand no chance at all.'

Grumbling, Said heaved his large frame out of his chair, blocking each person's view as he went. They swore floridly at him and, oblivious to their meaning, Said carried on, nodding and smiling all the while.

One of the guards in front of Benzamir looked suspiciously at the big man's back, then glanced up to the roof. He seemed to signal something with a twitch of his brows.

Benzamir followed his gaze. Up high in the architecture, hidden by the blinding daylight, there were spotters, archers and other weaponeers, all making sure that this show-trial went entirely according to plan. Suppressing a nervous smile, he took several deep breaths and tried to clear his mind of everything. The radio noise was growing. He felt a microwave pulse briefly map his body before it moved on. He knew what it meant.

Wahir waved just as the lawyer sat down and mopped his brow. The first prosecutor had hardly got back to his feet when Elenya's clear voice rang out.

'Your most exalted Imperial Highness, please hear my petition. You say Solomon Akisi stole your property. I say it was already stolen from the monastery of Saint Samuil in far-off Arkady.'

The instant she began to speak, all eyes turned to her. Court officials reacted to the bold woman in their midst as if stung. Akisi looked around, bewildered, his chains scraping against the floor.

'Forty good men were killed by the thieves; forty men of God who offered no resistance but prayer to the swords and the fire that was brought against them. The books belong to the patriarch of Mother Russia, and I have come to take them home.'

Va and Elenya were on their feet, Va giving his words to Elenya, she translating them into World so that everyone could hear. The soldiers cutting off the seats from the rest of the hall strained to hold the sudden press of curious, eager people back.

'I appeal to your empire's justice and your empire's law. Stolen property must be returned,' she called out.

A guard captain quickly detailed men to bring the interruption to an end. Through that gap in the fence of spears, Benzamir saw his chance and slipped forward.

He heard the whirr of spinning metal. He vaulted the lawyers' desk feet first, using his hands to maintain momentum. Three bladed discs cut into the wood, following his movement but never quite anticipating it.

The guards sent to shut Elenya up started to turn back. Those still part of the fractured line tried to reach behind them as Benzamir skipped by. He was past the open-mouthed emperor, and the air hummed with missiles. A bolt took him between the shoulders, another in the leg, the stonework around him flicking up razor-sharp chips fast enough to disable anyone they hit.

Benzamir tumbled, landed on his feet and threw himself at the crimson curtains. Arms spread wide, he netted one of the figures behind it and wrestled them all to the ground.

More bolts, more discs hammered into Benzamir, who shrugged off the metal storm and pulled hard on the fixed end of the curtain. Its anchors broke and the fixing fell down, cloth rippling after it. Both captor and captives disappeared under the folds.

Inside the makeshift tent, Benzamir tore the material and reached through. He grappled with a mess of loose black cloth in an attempt to expose the person's face, and came away with not just the coarse-woven hood, but the skin as well.

For a moment he was off guard, repelled by the texture of long-dead flesh on his fingers. Then an incredible force struck his chest and he was propelled upwards and backwards, bowling over two guards who had been about to stab down with their spears at the writhing curtain.

Benzamir managed to untangle himself first, and absently reached down to help one of the guards to his feet. Disorientated, the man climbed up Benzamir's arm and pushed his helmet back round so that he could see.

The black-shrouded figure rose, a glittering, dagger-ended limb writhing from its belly. Its head, grey, lifeless, rolled away, and from the gaping neck sprang a pythons' nest of sharp metal that cut its way down through the rotting corpse shell to reveal its true form.

Something stepped out, shining metal and glowing eyes. Benzamir had been aware of the screaming and the sudden sucking rush away, chairs toppled and thrown, but he had paid them no attention. All he thought about was that this was a thing that had never been done before. He knew what unmakers could do, had seen them fight and yet had never thought about facing one down with his bare hands. Now he had to try with three.

The curtain rose in two other places, and was nimbly turned to lace by snickering blades. Silver towers of quivering legs and eye stalks raised themselves up on knife points. They stood, poised for a moment as if waiting for a final command.

The unmakers' controllers must have been looking at him, wondering if he could, in fact, stop them. When he looked back, he could feel their remote presence, weighing him, judging him, finding him and his cause wanting.

'Don't do this,' said Benzamir. 'We can still bargain together.'

His answer came swift and deadly. One unmaker darted for the throne; two went for Benzamir, blurs of light and dark that decapitated one guard and carved the other into a bloody ruin before he'd even got up.

The soldiers who had one moment been pushing forward with all their might suddenly found themselves redundant, and wondered what had caused the sudden change in their fortunes. As the crowd stampeded, they turned to see Benzamir twisting and spinning in a vortex of motion, and another spider-like thing ripping into the imperial guard even as the emperor was lifted bodily from his throne by his attendants in an attempt to save him.

Benzamir felt his personal shield stretch and shudder at every blow, and knew it couldn't take much more. Indiscriminate fire from the roof had started to include rockets, and people were dying around him simply because there was nowhere to run to. He back-flipped out of the way, caught a spindly metal limb as it flashed at his face and turned it round. The thing staggered into its partner and they both lost their footing on the marble floor.

In that moment's respite he saw:

Wahir and Alessandra, the princess and the monk, left stranded by the retreating, panicked mob.

Solomon Akisi, abandoned by his captors, shuffling slowly backwards, not quite believing his eyes.

Said coming behind the emperor with a fallen spear and pushing him aside, just as the last of his guards fell.

The two metal creatures springing back onto their legs in front of him.

Time started again. One unmaker leaped at Benzamir, trying to bring its weight down on his body. The other started to carve its way through the crowd in a crimson haze. He ducked under the pounce, rolled forward and aimed his finger at the scuttling monster that had just sliced Said's spear in two. The glass dome overhead blew apart, and before the first shards of falling debris reached the ground, a white-edged hole punched through the back of the creature. It jerked, transfixed, then fell across the throne. Vital components ran in smoking silver rivers down the dais.

'Run!' called Benzamir, taking his own good advice, throwing himself away from the dais as the first impact of thick glass marked the beginning of the cascade of crystal and broken metal struts.

Said threw what was left of his weapon aside, took hold of His Imperial Majesty Kaisari Yohane Muzorewa and jumped back. Alessandra and Wahir pulled at them desperately, at the same time trying to protect their own faces from the splinters and shards flying outwards.

Benzamir was hit from behind. He sprawled into the outer circle of broken glass, unable to ride the blow. He rolled, and kept rolling as a series of metal feet came slicing down, one after another. He stopped, waited for the last one to descend, took it in his hands, twisted it and used it as a lever to get back onto his feet.

'Get the emperor out of here! Go!'

'But master—!'

'Go, Wahir.' He ducked, jumped and spun as three knives tried to skewer him in turn.

He saw in passing the ruin the other unmaker was making of Great Nairobi's elite – those who hadn't trampled their way to the door. But then it abruptly stopped its killing spree and reversed direction, trailing streams of gore back towards the dais. The monk and the princess ran from it, towards his friends.

Benzamir thought to intercept it, but he was too busy fighting and keeping his feet on the blood-soaked floor of the throne room.

'It's me you want!' he shouted, even though he knew that his life was incidental to decapitating the Kenyan empire.

There was a side door set in the nearest corner of the throne room. Alessandra already had it open; Said and Wahir had pushed the emperor through. Elenya was there a second later, and Va slammed it shut against the unmaker's advance. It took scant moments to reduce the wood to matchsticks, and it too was gone in a crimson-tinged blur.

Benzamir was running out of time: he now had to see if he could stretch what he had left to beyond breaking point.

CHAPTER 35

The rocketeers and bolt throwers had abandoned their posts to chase after the emperor through the palace; it was just the Kenyan thief and him. In a second it would be just him.

The remaining machine skittered towards Benzamir across a field of broken chairs. He rolled and ran. He needed clear stone floor to give him grip and count against the points of the unmaker's legs. A blinding arc of knives missed him by a fraction, air singing in his ears. The machine slid, collided with the wall and immediately started for him again.

He scooped up a hide shield and slammed it into the unmaker's body, knocking it off course and off balance. It ripped the shield from his hand; blades stabbed their way through, trying to reach him.

He wasn't there. He was underneath it, hitting joints and panels with his hands and feet, putting stress and strain on the metalwork, trying to hit something vital.

It wanted him badly. The intent to kill him was only an

artefact of its programming, but it felt real enough. Feet came off the ground in a wave, one after the other trying to spear him, and again Benzamir had gone.

An undefended eye-stalk. He took it in both hands and spun his body. The stalk came off, and he kicked to push himself clear. The unmaker tumbled away and fell in a tangle of long sharp limbs.

'Akisi! The throne!' was all he had time to say before it was up and on him.

After that there was no time to think. He let his mind slip from conscious action. If there was a stab, a feint, a sweep, he was ready with an immediate counter-attack. He blocked, leaped, spun, turned, staying only and ever only just far enough ahead of it. In a trance, beyond the effort of concentration, he danced before the unmaker's onslaught.

But it would have to end soon. He was tiring, and it was forcing him back. Once he was against a wall he'd be supremely vulnerable. It would pin him against a pillar and keep at him until his own protection was overloaded. He would die there.

Akisi had reached the throne, leaving a trail of bloody footprints through the shards of broken glass. 'Now what?' he shouted.

Time was at an end: it snapped back with a rush of noise and colour. Benzamir ducked. Chips of stone pinged across his back as a claw screeched across the wall, leaving a white gouge.

'Look up,' said Benzamir.

The sky above the smashed ceiling went abruptly dark, and a cloud of lights descended through the glassless lattice-work, spiralling down towards the dais. They resolved into shiny bubbles of metal, each the size of a melon, with dents and protuberances pocking their surface.

They streamed towards Benzamir, who arched his back to avoid one last impaling thrust. Then the unmaker turned to swing wildly at the first sphere. The leg joint flashed, metal cracked and the articulated limb went sliding across the floor, still spinning.

A cluster of spheres dived between Benzamir and the machine, driving it away, carving its legs from its body in bright sparks. It stumbled, fell, turned on its back, still lashing out but unable to move. It found itself in the centre of a gyre. Its body glowed and sputtered, craters torn explosively from its shell. Then it curled up in a ball and stopped moving.

The spheres descended. They sliced off the last three legs and settled on its still form. When they rose again, the thing had been dissected, its innards laid bare.

Benzamir started to run over, realized that his knee had been forced at some point, and limped to compensate. He bent down to inspect the unmaker's guts: the power source, the liquid motors and the insulated block of electronics, preserved like flies in amber. He was after none of those.

Finally he saw it, a black resin wafer: the transponder with its minute but vital memory. He pulled it out, cables trailing around it like cobwebs. He held it up, checked the wafer was still in one piece, then buried it in the folds of his clothes.

Akisi was still standing next to the throne, blood oozing out of his feet and mingling with that of the imperial guard. Benzamir trotted up to meet him, the spheres forming an ever-moving cloud behind him.

'Solomon Akisi, the court is adjourned,' he said in Swahili. One of the spheres glided forward. 'Lift up your arms.'

Trembling, Akisi obeyed. The centre link of his chains glowed and melted, and he was able to move his hands apart. The chain joining his feet went the same way.

Benzamir looked at the man's wide-eyed stare and slack jaw, and felt something close to pity. 'I don't know if this is punishment enough. As far as I'm concerned, you're free to go.'

'Who are you?' Akisi breathed. 'Are you a User?'

'No, I'm a magician. Now, I've other, more worthy people to save.' Benzamir turned away towards the splintered remains of the door at the corner of the hall. 'Come, my pretties.'

The spheres strung out behind him like pearls, like the last echoing cry of Akisi: 'Who are you? Where are you from?'

Benzamir had other things on his mind. 'Where are they?' he asked, and the voice in his head replied:

'*They have temporarily evaded the unmaker and are by the fountain you previously marked for rendezvous. They still have the emperor with them, but I estimate that their discovery will be in a matter of moments.*'

'Guide me.'

Schematics fell into place over his vision. Arrows and distances, hints of rooms beyond and a trail of dead people carved into the fabric of the palace by the passing of the unmaker.

Finally there was an outside door, half of it hanging on one hinge, the other half embedded in some soldier's chest as he'd tried to hold the line.

Benzamir was in the gardens, getting a live feed from above. He glanced up and knew what it had to look like: there was, inexplicably, another building over the citadel, a flying building with stubby swept-back wings and a long neck like a goose. But it was his beautiful spaceship, his Ariadne, who had brought him here and loved him like a sister.

Her lasers were sufficient to contend with the rocket fire that rose from the rooftops. Puffs of smoke and flame surrounded her in a corona.

'Where is the damn thing?'

'You're hurt,' she said.

'I'll heal. Now, can you see it?'

'No. It might have re-entered the palace.'

'Might? Do an active scan. My cover is well and truly blown, anyway.' He turned a corner and came face to face with the wide end of a handheld rocket launcher. The man behind it tensed, his finger twitching on the clockwork trigger.

Benzamir's followers arrived behind him, bobbing and weaving through the air as they surfed the bend.

The soldier fired. In the time it took the gun's mechanism to release the flywheel which spun the iron which made the sparks which lit the priming charge which ignited the propellant, Benzamir had grabbed the barrel and pointed it at a first-floor window.

The unmaker burst from the window in an explosion of wood and coloured glass, knives swinging. It met the rocket head-on and was instantly swallowed by a dirty fireball. It fell straight down behind a buttress, tangled and streaming smoke.

'Good shot,' said Benzamir, and punched his stiffened fingers into the man's diaphragm. He fell open-mouthed, and the remaining imperial guard turned to him as one.

A moment before, they had been aiming their weapons inward. Wahir had been clutching at Said. Said still had the emperor in his hands. Alessandra had been shouting at the guards to get back. Elenya had a knife at the emperor's throat, and the monk Va was pleading with her to put it down.

Now everyone fell silent as the unmaker rose unsteadily from behind the wall. They looked at Benzamir and his floating spheres, then at the smouldering machine with its blood-streaked blades. The only officer left standing, a young man who had seen more that day, that hour, than in all his brief lifetime, spoke up.

'I cannot trust you. You must know that.'

'You're both brave and wise,' said Benzamir, 'but I'd rather you told your men to lower their weapons. I need my friends alive.'

'I have my orders. You, whatever you are, will not change them.' He raised his arm to execute his final order.

The unmaker started its charge, and Benzamir lashed out his hand, finger extended. There were no preliminaries. A beam of blue-white light lanced down from the ship in the sky, cracked the air and carved the thing in two. It came tumbling on in its separate halves and fell in ruin at the officer's feet.

'Sir,' said Benzamir, 'if you want to save the empire, stand down.' He sent his remotes to encircle the group. Fifteen men, some aiming at him, some at the spinning spheres, some at his friends. Despite all his toys, it was almost certain that it would end badly.

'I will not. If you have any authority over those people, you will tell them to release His Imperial Majesty at once.'

Sweat was pouring off the officer's face, and every line of his face was taut.

'Authority, no. Influence, perhaps. But I can't persuade the princess to put down her knife if she believes she'll die in the next instant. It's all up to you.'

While they thought round in circles, matters were taken out of their hands.

Va made a grab for Elenya's blade, covered it with his hand so that even if she drew it back and across, she would not cut the emperor's exposed neck. The sudden movement made one guard reflexively squeeze his trigger, and a bladed disc sang into the air.

Benzamir presumed it would come to this. It was quick, but not entirely painless. Almost before they knew it, the guards were twitching, stunned, unable to stand, speak, grip. One man stayed upright long enough to fire his magazine of bolts at Benzamir before succumbing to the fat sparks of lightning that crackled between the spheres.

And the same blue fire that brought them down enveloped the trio of emperor, princess and monk. Light danced along blade and jewellery. The emperor shuddered and shook, Va dropped, his teeth clenched and his eyes bulging. And even if she'd wanted it to, Elenya's arm wouldn't move, and in a sickening twist of recognition Benzamir realized that if he'd made his choices differently, Ibn Alam would still be alive.

The remotes spun away to defend their master from attacks from above. Benzamir ran forward, vaulted the fallen guards, landed next to the emperor. He hurriedly checked him, but he appeared unharmed.

As the emperor rolled aside, Benzamir saw that the front of Elenya's dress was stained black with spreading blood.

'Ariadne, get us up.'

Said looked out from between his fingers, then he shook Wahir, who had buried his head behind the man's shoulder.

'Master?'

'Not now, Said.'

Benzamir tore Elenya's dress and explored the wound. The cut was beneath her ribs, the material surrounding it soaked. He pressed on the wound with the flat of his hand, and her blood welled in the hollow and then seeped through his fingers.

Her skin was turning translucent. He didn't have long. He couldn't bring her back from the dead.

Alessandra, face and hands cut, eye swollen, cheek bruised, hair scorched, said: 'What can I do?'

A lift disc hovered next to him, and presented him with yet another dilemma: there was not enough room for Ariadne to land, and not enough room on the disc for them all at once.

And if he moved his hand, she'd bleed to death.

'Get on that. Drag the monk up with you. Hang on for

410

all you're worth, and when you get up there, don't touch anything.'

She nodded once, pulled Wahir up and sent him on with the flat of her hand against his backside. Together, she and Said hauled Va on, and held his inert form there as the disc rose. As it did, so again did the rockets. Ariadne flicked them out of existence, and even then Benzamir curled his body around Elenya's to protect her from falling shrapnel. At least, that was what he told himself.

The lift disc was swallowed whole by the ship, the door irising shut behind it. A moment later it was on its way back down.

People were stirring.

'Your Imperial Highness?' he said to the spasming emperor. 'My humble and inadequate apologies, but we must go.'

He lifted Elenya up and stepped onto the disc. The wind tore at him. It was never intended to go this far, this fast. The remotes scattered as he burst through them, then caught them up in his wake. The few rockets that trailed up after him were intercepted in mid-flight.

The door spun open. Mindless of the drop beneath him, he jumped to the floor. The remotes spun back to their cage, the door closed, the ship started to move.

Va lay on the deck, unconscious. The others looked at

Benzamir, and he at them. He had so much to say, but now wasn't the time.

'Excuse me,' he said. His voice had gone quiet and controlled, in contrast to the turmoil he felt inside. But they stood aside instantly, and he carried Elenya from the cargo bay and towards the ship's surgeon.

'You cannot account for every twist of fate, Benzamir,' said Ariadne. 'Not everything is your fault.'

He turned sideways through the door and laid her on the surgeon's table. Immediately arms with needles and scissors sprang out and started pricking and snipping. A scanner grazed her body, searching both for the projectile and the damage it had caused.

Benzamir stared at his hands, at the dark spots of blood on his tunic. He felt light-headed, and he sat down on the floor, his back to the coldness of the table plinth.

'Not everything, no,' he whispered.

He heard the pneumatic hiss of arterial shunts locking into place, the sucking of vacuum tubes clearing the wound.

'Ari? I . . .' He didn't know what else to say. Something was sticking in his side, and when he touched it, he found the unmaker's transponder. He held it carelessly between two fingers, watching the light slant through it and refract into rainbows.

Later he would use it to find his enemies, and wonder at the cost of such knowledge.

CHAPTER 36

The surface he was lying on was hard and cold, yet obviously not the frozen ground of a Siberian winter. His head thrummed with a low bass note unutterable by human voice.

Then Va remembered. He dragged in a gasp of breath. Something scuttled away from him, and all he could see for a moment was a great steel spider, daggers for feet, as it spun and stabbed its way through the Kenyan emperor's guards.

He saw a dull black crab-thing wave its antennae and hurry away through a hole in the distant wall.

'Am I in Hell?' The witch had killed him with sorcery, and this place was no heaven: full of shadow, evil and unnatural shapes, machines for company. He'd fallen and failed. The past five years of austere holiness hadn't been enough to counter a lifetime's worth of slaughter and sin.

He started to cry.

The voice in his head told him not to. It told him that he had to be strong, not to fear, that no one or nothing would hurt him.

Only when the voice switched to Old Russian did he pay it any attention.

'Brother. Stand up.'

It sounded like the voice of God.

'Lord?' He hurried to his feet.

'Listen to me, Va. You are not dead, and this is not the afterlife. Neither am I your god. My name is Ariadne, and I want to help you.'

Va darted his head this way and that, looking for the source of the voice. He realized that it came from above him.

'Where are you? Why can't I see you?'

'You can see me. I am the room you are in, and every other place here. The walls are my bones.'

'Show yourself. I can't tell where you are.' Va twirled around. 'Where am I?'

'This will be difficult for you, Brother Va. You are less adaptable than the others. Neither have you had time to become accustomed to acts of casual magic. One thing I cannot allow you to do is harm me. I will defend myself against you. Whatever your reaction, you must not attempt violence.'

'I couldn't hurt you. I wouldn't.'

'I wish I could believe you,' said Ariadne. 'but your first instinct is destruction. You would try and kill me simply because of who I am.'

'I'm trying to be good. With God's help, I'm trying. Why won't you come out and talk to me?'

'You hear but you don't understand. You are on a ship, a special ship that sails between the stars as easily as a boat goes from port to port. When you were in the emperor's garden and looked up, what did you see?'

'I . . . I thought I saw a bird. It must have been a big bird, as big as a whale.'

'That was me. I am the ship. This is my body, Va. I'm not human like you, but I'm still a person.'

Va looked for a door. There was an archway leading out into a corridor, but Ariadne closed it off before he could get through.

'How did you do that?' He looked for a latch, something to open it with. 'Where are you?'

'You are confined for your own safety, Va. We must reach an understanding before I can let you roam about me at will. There is a great deal of damage you could do that would endanger both me and your companions.'

Va scrabbled around, circling the room like a caged wolf, looking for the slightest opening. Ariadne's constant conversation with him did nothing to stop the rising panic. He eventually fell to his knees and wrapped his head in his arms, cackling and weeping.

'Do you remember?'

'No,' said Va. 'I want to forget.'

'This is important, Va. When you were in the garden, what happened?'

'You're a voice in my head. I won't answer you.'

'Perhaps this will help. Look up.'

Light started to penetrate between the cracks in Va's fingers. Slowly he uncurled. There was an angel, wings unfurled, bending down over him. She held out her hand and beckoned him to rise.

'Is that what you are?'

'No. I am the ship. I'm just trying to give you a focus, something you recognize as part of your world-view. I could appear as Saint Basil or the Holy Mother if you prefer.'

'I don't understand,' said Va. 'If you're not an angel, then who are you?'

'The ship, Va. The ship. I am the ship. It's who I am. Ariadne Shipsister. This angel is an avatar, an image I can choose, but what I am is a ship. You can choose to believe me or not,' she said, 'but that doesn't change what I am.'

'A person can't be a thing. That's wrong. This place is full of evil spirits, tormenting me. I am in Hell, I must be.'

Ariadne fluttered her wings noiselessly. 'You think you know where you are. For you, it's a place worse than any hell, which is why you try to explain it using the only words you understand. If you were in Hell, there would be demons and devils and souls in torment, and you would recognize it as such. No one in Hell would ever mistake their surroundings for somewhere else.'

Va knew that what the angel said was true. 'Then you are . . .' His voice failed.

'Say it.'

'No.'

'You're wrong, but say it anyway. You have to get past this point and move on to greater understanding.'

'You're Users.' Va spat the word out. He looked around again, for anything he could use as a weapon. Wrecking was God's work, and this place needed burning as badly as Akisi's tower in An Cobh.

'We are not those people you call Users. If you'll let me, I'll explain. If you attempt to damage any of my systems, I will subdue you.' The angel folded her arms. 'Which is it to be?'

'The Users were the masters of lies.'

'And we are not Users. I haven't lied to you yet. Neither do I intend to do so. It's not in my nature.'

'The Users were destroyed by God. How did you escape?'

'Va, you have to listen to me. My name is Ariadne Shipsister. I am a starship. I was not made by the culture you call Users, and Benzamir is not a User either. The Users are gone, their bones are dust; they only live on in your memory.' The angel started to lose its shape. 'I'll leave you to think on these things. When you are ready, we can talk again.'

'Wait!' Va reached out and his hand passed through the angel's robe. He stared at his hand. 'How?'

'It's a projection, beamed into your eyes. You see it as real; it's nothing but an illusion. But this is not important. Don't get distracted by the detail, Va. I need you to concentrate.' Ariadne's angel took shape again. 'Are you ready?'

Va sat back on his haunches, a haunted look on his face. 'What if I'm not?'

'Then I will keep you unconscious until we have the opportunity to leave you somewhere safe. Time has run out. As soon as he's finished helping me sew Princess Elenya's small intestine back together, Benzamir will finish the job he came to do.'

'Elenya?'

'You were there. Wahir had led you to the garden. You were surrounded by the emperor's guard, and Elenya had her knife pressed against the emperor's neck. Benzamir and the remotes came to find you. You must remember what happened next.'

Va started to tremble. Memories of a many-armed monster rising from the ground, of Mahmood killing it with a gesture, and metal balls that darted like silver fish, and soldiers falling to the ground. Of Va trying to protect the emperor by holding onto Elenya's knife, of her folding in on herself, bright blood staining her front, of a sudden explosion of light and sound that made his whole body melt. None of it made sense; everything seemed disconnected and unreal.

He opened his hand and there was a bloody cut across his palm. As he flexed it, fresh blood and fresh pain leaked out.

'Who will save me from myself?' he asked.

'So you do remember.' Ariadne sat on the floor in front of Va. 'I have no arms to comfort you, but take heart. Elenya will live, at least for today. And by a strange turn of events, it seems that Benzamir's mission and yours are the same. You want to take the User books back home? Benzamir will find them for you. You want to keep their knowledge inside their covers? So does Benzamir. You want to save the world? That's why we're here.'

'You'd help me?'

'If we can. If you like, we have been sent by your God in answer to your prayers. Who are you to tell Him how He should respond?'

'I . . .' He was at a loss for words.

'Now listen. Somewhere on this world is a ship, like me. The people with it came with the best of motives. They want to feed the hungry, heal the sick, shelter the homeless, fill your lives with such wonder and light that you will curse them that they did not come sooner. Their power is a hundred times greater than that of the Users. They want to change the way you live utterly. The people of Earth will reach up again to the stars, and claim them for their own.

'And anyone who opposes them will be killed, out of

hand. You lost forty brothers to them, for no other reason than they were in the way: that was just the start. How many did they kill today? Hundreds. If the empire falls, which it still might, there will be ten thousand more corpses and a million lives in ruin.

'And into that gap they will stride. Conquerors. Lords. Priests. They will rule over you for ever, because they cannot die of old age or disease – and don't think you, Va, could fight against them. Even the Users would have been swept aside as if they were nothing but cattle.

'This is the hard part, Va. We left here long ago, when the Users were at their height, to save humanity from annihilation. But we've spent too many centuries away from our cradle to call this our home any more. What happens here is not up to a cabal of renegades who would crush you even as they're trying to save you. We are your children, and it's not for children to tell their parents what to do. We'll stop them from taking over, and then we'll go.'

'If all this is true, then why do they need the books? Did my brothers die for nothing?'

Ariadne bowed her head and showed her dazzling crown. 'I do not know. This is a mystery to me, and something we need to learn the truth of before we leave you.' She looked up. 'Are you hungry, Va? Are you thirsty?'

'I don't feel hunger or thirst any more. They're just things that people say. I eat when there's food, drink when there's water. If there's nothing, it's the will of God that I don't eat or drink then.'

'Don't you love yourself?'

'I hate myself. Everything I ever did was wrong, and I can't change a single moment.'

Ariadne fluttered to her feet. It looked so real, Va expected to be buffeted by the wind from her wings.

'Come and do good with us. Come and eat and drink with us and tell us your story. Then we will go and get your books and send you home.'

'I lost one,' he blurted. 'I dropped it over the side of Rory macShiel's boat so that the slavers wouldn't get it. But it's still there. Someone determined enough could find it again.'

'Then perhaps we will have to be that someone, Va.' Ariadne paused and looked sideways at him. 'Who am I?'

'You're the ship, though I still don't understand how that can be.'

The angel contracted to a glowing point of light, which hovered eye height above the floor.

'Where have you gone?'

'I'm still here. I'm all around you. Follow me.'

Va got up slowly, and the door slid aside. The light drifted on, and taking his courage in both bloody hands, Va walked along behind it. Even the footsteps he took reminded him that it was all made: the floor was slick and shiny, entirely without joints or edges. It flowed seamlessly up into the walls and curved overhead to vault the ceiling.

They came to a crossroads. Ahead was a door, but the light turned left, then left again when they came to another junction.

He started to hear voices: Arabic, and another he didn't recognize at all. The light stopped in front of the door where the others were, and faded until all that was there was a small black pebble of glass.

'I don't know what I'm supposed to do now,' said Va in a whisper.

'Go in. Greet the others. Introduce yourself. Eat bread, taste salt. Drink Benzamir's favourite beer,' said Ariadne with laughter in her voice. 'Sit with the unbeliever, the woman and the child. No one is better or worse than you.'

'But what will I say? I can't speak to any of them but Elenya, can't understand what they say.'

'There's no problem, Va. I've listened to you all, spoken to you all, understood you all. There'll be no confusion. I can play Elenya's part for everyone. I'm very smart.'

The door slid open and the pebble moved aside. Across the table sat the two Maghrebi and the Ewer woman. They had food and drink in front of them, and it was this simple thing that made him walk forward: he recognized what they were eating.

The woman looked at him, chewing slowly. He watched

her swallow. The silence grew. The boy and the man glanced at each other, and Va wondered what they had been told.

The woman's lips moved, and Va heard: 'We were going to wait for you, but' – and she held up a flat bread stuffed with meat and vegetables – 'we didn't know how long you were going to be.'

When he didn't move, she poured him a drink and pushed it across the table towards him.

'You're welcome to join us.'

There was a chair. When he sat cautiously in it, it moved under him. He started, then settled again under the others' watchful eyes. He picked up the cup, sniffed its contents. It was as the angel said: beer.

And good beer at that.

CHAPTER 37

It felt like he had been away too long. Benzamir slid himself into the pilot's chair and marvelled at the way his body eased into the contours of the seat. All the places he had travelled to, on foot, on camels, by ship, by carpet. Nothing compared to this.

'Show me,' he said, and the space in front of him turned hazy. Half the flight deck disappeared and he was looking out over the world. The sun was setting to his right, and the terminator drew a line down the middle of the Pacific. He was heading into the dark.

Once, the view that would have greeted him would have been vibrant: bright baubles of cities hung together on chains of light stretching off towards the horizon, and an elegant tower reaching from the surface to the stars, spotted with luminous insects that crawled over its face.

Everything had gone: the tower had fallen, the bulbs that burned had been extinguished. The land was a vast, blank canvas for someone to write their name large across. Benzamir was determined that it wasn't going to be any of the traitors.

'Ari? Anything?'

'We haven't been scanned. There's no broadcast signal from anywhere on the planet. And there's still no sign of Persephone Shipsister. She isn't in orbit, and her drive signature is absent. I'm worried, Benzamir.'

'She turned traitor too. Perhaps she's too ashamed of what she's done.' He looked at Earth as it rushed under him.

'There is something I need to tell you. I've been meaning to for a while. I didn't know how important it would turn out to be.'

Benzamir's view grew dark, and a vector map bloomed in its place. In it, Ariadne, smaller, faster, was cutting a chord away from rho Cancri, and Persephone was ahead of her on a different path. Given time, she would have caught the larger ship up, but time was precisely what she didn't have.

It had started as nothing more than a futile chase that was bound to end in failure, but Benzamir had asked for targeting solutions anyway. The city-ship was keeping the rebels talking, and Persephone's o-space engines were quiet.

Persephone was at extreme range, almost a light-minute distant, but she thought that she wouldn't be shot at while the human factions were still in contact. The spectrograph showed a hit, but by the time the information had got back to Benzamir, she'd jumped.

There was no way of following a ship in o-space, and Ariadne had turned for home.

'Why do you keep torturing yourself with this?' said Benzamir. 'You fired at your renegade shipsister. You shouldn't have had to do that, but we made the decision together that it was for the best.'

'It was for the best,' she said. 'I flinched. I could have burned her through. I ought to have, but I didn't. The guilty would have died and the innocent lived.' She paused, not for thought but for agony. 'I have failed you.'

Benzamir sat in thought for a long time and eventually realized that her mistakes were sadly all too human.

'Peace, Ari. Peace.'

'It would have been so much better if we hadn't needed to come here in the first instance, any of us. How are we going to restore Va's lost brothers? How do we repair the damage to the Kenyan empire? What of spaceships over Great Nairobi and drop-pods? Answer me, Benzamir. What are we going to do?'

Benzamir watched the arrows on the map, the line that marked the laser's wave-front tunnelling through simulated space until it bisected the point that was the other ship, which then made tight, random manoeuvres before vanishing from the display. Persephone's o-space vector had been calculated, the line searched, and nothing found. She and her crew of rebels had moved on.

'And look what I've done,' he said. 'Personal force-field. Satellite navigation. Language modules, light-bees, o-bombs, lasers. Five contacts on board. We share the blame equally.'

'You always said that the mission parameters were too strict, that you needed to be adaptable, flexible, able to improvise.'

'You always disagreed.'

'Perhaps your way has something to commend it after all.'

Benzamir dragged a half-smile from the depths. 'Did we make all this happen then? Is all this a result of the choices we've made?'

'I could argue Fate or Destiny. I could argue accident-by-design; that we subconsciously manipulated events so that we would end up at this point. Or we can just accept that we got here by a mix of chance and skill, and that this is, while not the best of all possible outcomes, where we are. So what would you do differently?'

'Most of it. I have people looking to me. I was never a leader, Ari. Always happier just doing my own thing. I only took Said and Wahir with me because they couldn't go back. Said especially, but Wahir needed to come along or he'd talk and talk and talk, and I was afraid someone would overhear. Then Alessandra, because I wanted her on my side rather than selling information about me.'

'Does it matter what they were? They're your brothers and sister now. I've seen the way they act even when you're not there: they follow you because they want to, not because you make them.' Ariadne paused. 'You have a princess too.'

'Yes, yes I do. And the half-mad monk she travels with. Now there's a relationship I don't pretend to understand. He stopped her from harming the emperor and nearly killed her in the process.'

'Va was indeed mad when we met him. However, speaking with him has been instructive. He believes himself to be nothing but a tool of his god, to be used as he sees fit. I was able to turn this to our advantage and convince him that our appearance was fore-ordained. He no longer poses a threat to us.'

'I can sense a but coming.'

'But what if I'm right? What if I've discovered a fundamental truth: that we are pawns in his game, rather than he in ours? I need to think on these matters further.'

Benzamir could almost feel the ship's systems slow as Ariadne concentrated on the metaphysical problem. 'Well, if we've failed, then it is the most glorious failure. We've been to Earth, Ari. Where it all began for us. The seeds of your birth are there too. What we've seen, the things we've heard, the people we've met. Those who've fought by our side. But we can't honestly count this as failure because it would cheapen everything else – every kindness shown, every smile, every laugh, every bead of sweat and drop of blood. You're right: we can't take anything back, and I wouldn't want to. So let's be content with what we have without worrying about what might have been.'

'What will happen to Persephone?' she asked in a small voice, sounding more like a little child than a ship that could leap between stars.

'I don't know,' said Benzamir. 'If it comes to it, will you fight her?'

'This time I will.'

'Then we've said everything that needs to be said. Show me the world again.'

He watched the landscape slip away underneath him as Antarctic mountaintops hung onto the last vestiges of day, burning orange peaks against the shadows all around.

'Benzamir?'

He heard hesitant footsteps behind him. 'Hello, Alessandra.'

'What is this I'm looking at?'

'It's where you live. There are things like telescopes on the outside of Ariadne, and the view is brought in here by machines.'

'It's so' – her voice caught in her throat – 'beautiful.'

'And it belongs to you, to all of you.'

'We—' She stopped, and started again, noticing that he'd ditched his palace finery for a grey quilted pilot's coverall. To her, it seemed different, almost alien. 'I didn't know where you'd gone.'

Benzamir sighed, slid from his chair and walked into the middle of the display, which swallowed his legs and left his upper body troubled only by clouds. 'I just wanted a moment to see it for what it is. You can see the scars of cities from up here, the places where roads once joined them up, strange patterns made by long-dead peoples. On top of those there are new buildings, new trade routes crossed by horses and camels, new states ruled over by new leaders, even if they do take old titles and style themselves after barely remembered legends.'

Alessandra walked forward to stand close to him, marvelling at the way the map of the world passed under her, through her. A continent she had seen only in ancient maps slid by, a spine of snow and a plain of grassland. Pin-sharp rivers and puffy crowns of forests revealed their riches.

They crossed the flooded valleys of the coast and moved out into the wave-flecked ocean. Benzamir shifted uncomfortably. 'I'm sorry. I'm being a bad host. I need to go and wake the princess, and then I can explain everything to all of you. I'd rather I only had to do it once.'

He made to leave, and she noticed his limp.

'You're hurt.'

'I know. It'll fix itself eventually.'

'I don't want to fuss.' She caught his sleeve and held him still for a moment. Then she let her grip fall and said: 'You don't need me to look at your leg, do you? You have machines to do that too.'

'Both inside and out. I'm not—' And he thought about the problems he'd had telling Said and Wahir where he had come from and how he had got here. 'I'm only mostly human. I've some extra bits and pieces that help me do my job.'

She looked him up and down. 'You look normal to me. What are you saying?'

Benzamir sighed, and tried to turn her round with a hand on her elbow. She shook him off.

'Really. What are you trying to tell me? How much of you isn't a man?'

'All the magic is done by machines. Some of the machines are inside me; the controls for the rest are also inside. My eyes aren't real. I've a personal shield grown under my skin. Things like that.' He studied her for her reaction. Her face registered a creeping realization; it was a start. 'I thought you ought to know. I don't want to hide what I am any more.'

Alessandra stared, not exactly at him, but through him. 'Is this a test?'

Benzamir nodded. 'Yes, that's precisely what it is.' He sidestepped round her to the door and hesitated. He thought for a moment that she might say something, do something, even follow him. She didn't.

CHAPTER 38

Benzamir walked slowly over to the surgeon's table, where Elenya lay sleeping. He hardly dared look at her, though eventually he did.

'Alessandra is right: when Princess Elenya has regained consciousness, I should do some remedial work on you,' said Ariadne.

'We don't have time. They know we're here. They know how many of us there are and what resources we have.'

'You mean they've worked out it's just me and you. But they haven't launched against us. They've stayed stealthed.' She paused. 'I think they're frightened of us.'

'I thwarted their coup. They're more likely to be furious than frightened.' He picked up the metal tray in which lay the serrated disc the surgeon had extracted from Elenya's guts. Blood and flesh clung to its blades. 'I wish I knew what they were waiting for.'

Ariadne showed him Elenya's vital signs. They looked well within tolerances for an unmodified human; figures that had had to be dredged out of the archives. Benzamir took the cloth off Elenya's wound. It had been sealed shut with canned skin, but the bruising was working its way out as an elliptical target in yellow and black.

He put the tray down and did what he could not risk doing if Elenya had been awake. A strand of her hair had stuck to her cheek; he brushed it free with the tip of his finger.

'Such beauty, such passion,' he whispered. 'You could turn a man to good or evil with one smile.'

Her eyes opened, and he stepped hastily back.

'What were you saying?'

To his relief, he realized she couldn't understand a word of Nu. 'It doesn't matter,' he said, too quickly. 'How are you? Any pain?'

'No. None. I don't know what you did to me.' Elenya looked down and found her dress cut, torn, stained with gore, but no visible wound. 'Where did it go?'

He fetched her the disc. 'It made a mess going in, and a bit more coming out again. We think we connected everything back together again the right way. Just don't do any heavy lifting for a while.'

'We?' she asked.

'Me. Ariadne. I'm sorry about your clothes.'

She tried to sit up and winced as the bruise compressed.

'Swing your legs round.' He tentatively put his hand behind her shoulder. 'I'll help you.'

As she stood, she felt her insides settle into different positions. She looked around properly for the first time. 'Where am I?'

'You're onboard a starship called Ariadne Shipsister. We're in a low polar orbit with a period of six hours, and we're currently at apogee over what's marked on my maps as the Arctic Ocean.'

She stared at Benzamir. 'Pardon?'

'You're safe, and that's all that needs to be said at the moment. I'd like it if you ate something, because I need to check that you've got peristalsis back.' He ran his hand over his face. 'It's a good job I have a rule that there are no stories without beer.'

'Where's Va?'

'Eating,' said Ariadne in Russian, 'like a starved man.'

'He lived,' Elenya said. 'After all that death, he lived.' Her face grew pensive, then she blinked slowly. 'Who said that? Who – what – are you? Are you a ghost?'

'Though I'm supposed to be a machine with infinite patience,' said Ariadne to Benzamir, 'even I'm getting tired of that question.'

Without reference to Benzamir, Ariadne spun Elenya a new dress of deep green silk and a woollen cloak of russet, neither of which were silk or wool.

They were clothes finally fit for a princess, and when she

entered the room, she appeared embarrassed by the others' reactions to her. Once, she would have taken awe as her due. Years of living in Va's shadow had made her forget.

Said got to his feet, knowing he was in the presence of greatness. Wahir stood too, and not because someone else had.

Alessandra did not stand. She closed her eyes and wiped away the tear that rolled down her cheek. She took a deep breath and then looked up at Elenya. She smiled, even though it was anguish for her.

Va turned away in his chair, looking as if he had just seen a glimmer of what he could have once had and then rejected. His face was set like stone, unwilling to show any emotion in case he showed them all.

Benzamir didn't know what to do. He hovered, undecided. He looked at his plate and felt nothing in his stomach but a strange fluttering. Elenya sat in the empty seat next to Va, and he could see the man wince.

Into the silence she said: 'Please, sit down, sirs.'

They ended up all looking at Benzamir. He felt sick, but steeled himself and reached forward for the jug of beer and refreshed his drink. Then he took a long pull and settled the glass back down in the ring of spilled liquid that marked its place.

'I don't know what to say. We've all got here by different routes, but you're all welcome. I'm sorry. I can only apologize for involving any of you. This fight isn't yours. It's mine, my people's, my past and my future.

'My name really is Benzamir Michael Mahmood, and I was born on a city-ship that was circling another star, far away from here. My parents and my parents' parents were all born on city-ships, or on other worlds, and this beautiful place was a only a memory. It held a special place in our hearts. It was the birthplace that we had come from seven centuries earlier; that we had sworn on our lives to protect and preserve.

'It wasn't enough for some of my people. They wanted to return and show you what we'd become; what *you* could become with their help. You die of disease. We don't. You grow old. We don't. You get mud under your fingernails and splinters in your hands and you have to work or you starve. Sometimes you starve despite all your efforts. We don't.

'So we talked about it, all of us together, for years. In the end we decided that you should be left alone to make your own way. We didn't know what we might find: you could have all died, or you could be making rockets that would take you to the Moon.'

Wahir leaned forward, rapt with attention. 'Master? A rocket to the Moon?'

'It happened before. It's just an engineering problem. We just didn't know how far you'd fallen or how far you'd climbed back up, but we decided that you should guide yourselves.'

Ariadne spoke: 'What Benzamir isn't saying is that he argued for making contact. He wanted to come back – come home, as he saw it – to breathe the air and swim in the sea. He was broken-hearted when the decision went against him, but he accepted it. Unlike some others. They persuaded a ship to come here. I chased after them. I – I could have stopped them, but they got away. The fault was mine.'

Benzamir gave a tight-lipped smile and continued: 'It took a long time for everyone to decide that I could follow them. There was no guarantee that this was where they'd end up, but I knew it had to be. All I had to do was find them. But in the end I was too slow. I made a great number of mistakes. I underestimated them and what they'd try to do to take over. I never expected them to kill so many.'

His voice died. He reached for his beer and knocked the glass over. A wave of froth, buoyed up on a golden brown tide, raced across the tabletop, breaking on bowls and plates.

'Crap,' he said softly. Alessandra started to use the hem of her dress to soak up the flood, until Benzamir shook his head. 'Leave it.'

He set his glass upright and poured more beer in.

'My mission was supposed to finish with taking the rebels back to face those they've betrayed. It's clear that they won't come quietly. But neither can I just leave them and get help. While I'm away, they could do anything. They've shown themselves more than capable of wild cruelty. So I have to stop them, and stop them now.'

'What do you want us to do?' asked Alessandra.

'I don't want you to do anything. They have worse things than unmakers, and none of you can stand up to them. You will all stay here. I will do what needs to be done. Then I'll take you anywhere you want to go.'

'What if they kill you too?' she pressed.

'Then Ariadne will take you back before she goes to report to those who sent me. I won't have any of you come to harm.'

Va stirred uneasily. He looked at his scarred hands before momentarily balling them into fists. 'Where do the User books come in? Why did your people steal them from us?'

'To tell you the truth, I still don't know. Every ship holds records of everything we know. They shouldn't need your books.'

'So my brothers died for nothing?' he said. A vein on his shaved head started to pulse.

Benzamir glanced up at the ceiling, to where he always imagined Ariadne to be. He hoped she was right when she said the monk didn't present a threat to them.

'I still have a vow I need to honour. The books must be returned to the patriarch.'

'I'll get you the books,' said Benzamir. It was simple enough to say.

'Va,' said Elenya, 'when are you going to admit to yourself that you never made any sort of vow to the patriarch? You sneaked off on your own. This vow is a figment of your imagination, and why should Benzamir help you in any way?'

'Because he is an honourable man?'

Elenya suddenly smashed the flat of her hand down on the table. Plates and beakers jumped in the air. 'Damn you, Va! You told me you were going to die. It never happened. Now you have the mighty Benzamir doing your bidding, it never will.'

'I didn't promise you anything. I said I might die. I said you could watch.' Va tried to stay calm, but he screamed out: 'What I wanted was for you to leave me alone!'

She punched him straight in the nose with her fist. Said was on his feet, climbing over the table, throwing himself between them. Elenya got in two more strikes, one to Va's stomach, the other into Said's cheek. Va made no attempt to defend himself. He seemed to welcome the blows. Alessandra joined Said and together they pushed her away.

'You ungrateful bastard. You wouldn't have got on that first ship if it hadn't been for me. You would have got nowhere. Who ended up sweet-talking everyone, who paid for everything, who got us this far? I did everything, and you still don't want me.'

She tried to get to Va, who sat with blood dripping down

his chin. Finally the Arab managed to push her none too gently back into a bulkhead and pin her there. Alessandra stopped her from clawing at his eyes by grabbing her wrists.

Elenya raged for a few moments more, then seemed to fold in on herself. Said risked letting her go, and put his hand to his face. Alessandra was more reluctant to release her grip, but in the end she felt she ought.

Elenya would not meet anyone's gaze. She found her way to the door, still looking down. It slid aside and closed after she had gone.

Benzamir put his head down on the table, feeling the damp coolness in his forehead.

'Master?' asked Wahir. 'We will not desert you.'

'You promised you'd leave the magicians to me. I'm going to hold you to that.'

'I'm not a coward,' Wahir said. 'I want to fight with you.'

Said rested his knuckles on the table. 'I'll stand with you too. It's my duty, my right. I will not step back when something so – so important needs completing.'

'And me. Everything you've said just makes it more vital that you have our help.' Alessandra wiped a line of blood from her arm. 'I made you no promise, and you are not the only one on this ship.'

Benzamir got up abruptly and swept everything in front of him onto the floor. It fell, it bounced, it broke, it spilled. Into the silence he hissed: 'I will not allow it! How could I live on knowing that you were dead?' He limped to the exit. 'Ari? Call them. Call the rebels. If they answer, we can talk. If they don't, then I'll have to dig them out from whichever stone they're hiding under.'

He left, and he had never felt so wretched in his life.

CHAPTER 39

He sat brooding in the pilot's chair, waiting for something to happen and going over everything he had said.

'Where are they?'

'They don't answer.'

'Is it likely that they've got the narrowcast?'

'Yes.'

Benzamir tutted. 'What of the unmaker's transponder?'

'The information was degraded. I couldn't get anything useful off it.'

'I thought we could use it. I even took time to get it.'

'I know,' said Ariadne. 'The initial co-ordinates it gave were just wrong. I have to distrust all the tracking data stored thereafter.'

'Show me.'

'But—'

'Humour me, Ari.'

She showed him the metric co-ordinates, based on the usual Tribal conventions. She offered him the image that those co-ordinates represented. There was nothing there but black rock and white ice.

He studied the scene. 'Why the hell would they land in Antarctica?'

'I can only surmise that they didn't, and we have to search the rest of the world.' Ariadne took away the picture and carried on hunting with her pattern-recognition software for something that resembled a spaceship on the ground.

'Bring it back up again.' Benzamir sat forward, then climbed out of his seat and stood on the edge of the display. 'Zoom in.'

'You don't mind if I continue the proper work, do you?'

'No, no,' he said absently. 'Carry on.'

He stared at the holographic image for a long time, examining it from every angle. It was spring in the northern hemisphere. Ice that had formed over the winter was beginning to melt, leaving the continent as a ragged, lake-pocked desert. The only mark on his map was for New Swabia, and the area had been called that for a thousand years.

He looked and looked again, then ducked under the floating picture to study its underneath.

'Ari, take us down.' He pointed to a hill a little way from the coast, just above a broad lake still sealed with ice. 'Just there.'

'Can I remind you that you said we didn't even have time to fix your leg?'

He walked slowly back to the pilot's chair, and sat rubbing his knee as Ariadne abandoned her methodical search for his wild-goose chase. He felt gravity shift subtly as she killed her orbital speed and began to fall.

'Give me the outside view.'

'What am I going to find?' she asked. 'There is literally nothing there. No people, no buildings, no debris, nothing more complex than sea-birds, no plant life higher than moss.'

When Benzamir didn't answer, Ariadne threw herself at the Earth, and her underside glowed with white heat. A tremor rattled the ship, and another, as air was crushed and thrown aside by her passing. Then it came constantly, a quivering high-pitched squeal almost too high to register. Benzamir's view flickered with orange light.

Wahir and Said drifted onto the flight deck.

'Master, what's happening?'

'Aero-braking. Up among the stars, speed is a trivial thing. But we're moving so fast, even the air is like a wall we have to batter our way through.'

'Is that real fire?' asked Wahir. He walked forward until he was within the projection, his legs disappearing under the shelf of land. He looked around him, dipped his hand down and poked the image.

'Real fire.' Benzamir sat upright. 'If there were people down below, they would hear distant thunder and look up.

They'd see us as a streak of light pointing down towards the ground and they'd wonder. But here there's no one to see us. There never were any witnesses when it happened the first time, and there won't be now.'

'The first time?' said Said.

'I asked everywhere I went. *Have you seen anything strange in the sky? Something falling to the ground in a fireball?* But they hadn't.' He was distracted by Wahir's cavorting through the display as the boy ducked down and up again, as if he was a swimmer in a strange, luminous sea. 'It turns out we were asking in all the wrong places.'

Benzamir, despite his aches, crouched forward, as if watching Wahir but staring into the dark around him. The light-show ended, and with it the trembling of the hull. Settling in thick air, Ariadne dropped her front and took control of flying the course to their landing point.

They circled once, and it looked no different to how it had looked from orbit. Black rock, sharp and brittle, smudged with lichen where the freezing Antarctic wind didn't tear quite as fiercely. White ice, broken at the margins into misshapen slabs, polished at the centre, gleaming like a mirror in the low-angled light.

Then they landed, and Benzamir walked back through the ship to the cargo hold. Said and Wahir trailed after him, and Va met them inside.

'The ship has stopped,' he said nasally. Two wads of linen were rammed in his nostrils.

'I'm going on a little field trip.' Benzamir looked at the men. 'Looks like a boys only expedition.'

He opened a locker and threw out three thick all-in-ones before getting one for himself. He showed them how to step into them, seal them up and activate the heating circuits.

Said's was too small. Wahir's drowned him. Va's fitted best of all, and he just looked ridiculous, with his habit riding up inside and making the overall bulge in unseemly places.

'By any scale of measurement you want to use, it's really cold outside. You'll need to put up your hood, and please, don't lick anything metal.' Benzamir collected a tool like a thick, hollow pipe and stepped over to the iris in the floor. It spun open, and the heat stole from the room. He jumped down. His boots crunched against the rock, and he ducked down to clear the last of Ariadne's hull.

The others emerged, one by one, blinking in the daylight. Va nodded approvingly.

'A good place. Lakes and hills. It reminds me of Finnland.' He looked around. 'Where are the trees?'

Benzamir adjusted Wahir's suit so that he could see out. 'Give it another thousand years, Brother, and there might be soil enough. When my people were last here, it was covered in ice all the way up to the tops of those mountains.' He pointed to a distant range.

The Antarctic air was so clear that it was impossible to judge how far away or how high the peaks were. Va was clearly sceptical.

'If you want, I can show you how the world once looked. It's very instructive.' Benzamir hefted the pipe and set off down to the lake shore, scrambling over frost-shattered boulders and skidding on patches of scree.

Va kept pace, and Wahir bounded along with all the reck-lessness of youth. Said pulled his hood tighter around his face and shivered.

They gathered at the edge of the crust of ice. Benzamir stepped out on it and gave a few exploratory jumps. The surface creaked, but held.

'Right then, gentlemen. What can you see?'

For Wahir it was all too like being in madrasah again. 'Can you not just tell us, master?'

'I suppose I could. That would be novel.' He spun the pipe in his hands like a quarterstaff. 'Come with me.'

When they were in the middle of the lake, the creaking noise became so severe that Benzamir ordered them to space themselves out. In a month's time the ice would have gone, but he couldn't wait. He swung the pipe high up over his head.

'What magic does this do, master?'

'None at all. It's a bit of pipe.' He brought it down end on, and the surface crazed and cracked. Again, and he punched a ragged hole through. Water welled up thickly and seeped across the ice. He threw the pipe to Said and unsealed his suit so that he could reach his pocket. He retrieved two light-bees, then sealed himself back up. He tipped the bees in his palm into the hole he'd made. 'Look down.'

They could see two lights blossom into life, dimly at first, then brighter. They could see the patterns in the clear ice, the bubbles of air caught like flies within its structure.

'The water is incredibly clear. You should be able to see the bottom of the lake.'

The light-bees burrowed down through the column of water and started to illuminate a shape. The bees moved around it, under it. It was huge, with two inward curving spines and a fat body like a gourd.

'What,' asked Va, 'is that?'

'I hate to be proved right, especially in this case. It's Persephone Shipsister.'

Ariadne fretted: 'My shipsister. What have they done to her?'

'We're going to have to get her out of there before we can find out.'

'She is dead, Benzamir, they've killed her.'

'Ari. We don't know.'

'There's nothing coming from her. I'm trying everything but there's nothing to get hold of. Everything is offline. This can't be true.'

'Try the embryonic remote connection.'

'It must be atrophied.'

'I'm sure it will be, but try anyway.'

She was silent while she struggled to secure the ancient protocols. With Persephone as quiet as the grave, it was just possible that she could be crudely controlled by Ariadne as if she was a pre-born ship with no mind of her own.

'There is . . . something. The bandwidth is almost non-existent.'

Benzamir turned his heating circuits up another notch and stamped his feet. Wahir and Said had taken shelter in the lee of the craft, and only Va was with him, sucking chill air through his mouth and straight into his lungs. He didn't seem to be coming to any harm.

'Can you power her up?'

'I might, if you stopped talking.'

'Oh.'

The sun swung round and started its long, slow slide back towards the horizon. Finally the ground trembled.

'Good work.'

There was nothing else for a while, then suddenly the lake ice cracked, rose, splintered, and fell in cascading sheets of crystal that in turn were bounced up again. A dark shape streaming white water broached the surface, then continued to rise inexorably.

Said and Wahir peered out from behind Ariadne and

started to edge back. The circumference of the ship kept on expanding, the ice kept on breaking and sliding, until almost all the lake was on the move. The noise was incredible, a thunderous bass roar with random concussions that made the air vibrate.

The wind caught the water falling from the hull, turned it to ice and blew it in their faces. It forced them to turn away for a moment until the storm was over, and the chunks of ice had finished splashing down into the refilling lake.

Va looked behind him. 'Bigger than yours, Maghrebi.'

'And they say size doesn't matter.'

Persephone Shipsister was three times the length of Ariadne, with two drive pods and a cavernous cargo bay. She spun slowly on her axis, then drifted overhead in search of a landing site. She took a long time to pass by. Ariadne finally brought her down a couple of ship lengths distant, and at an angle. Loose rocks tumbled away, then it was quiet again except for the hiss of the wind.

'Now,' said Benzamir, 'all we have to do is get on board.'

CHAPTER 40

Getting inside was simple once they discovered that Persephone's main cargo bay doors were open. The ship had been stripped, flooded and abandoned, nothing more than a corpse weighed down with chains and thrown into the deep.

She had been such a magnificent ship. Now she was gone. But Benzamir had to make sure.

They climbed inside the cavernous hold, full of dripping and clammy chill. Their breath condensed in clouds in front of their faces and hung there until swatted away.

Benzamir deployed his light-bees, and sent them up to the ceiling before exploring every dark crevice.

'Nothing. If it wasn't nailed down, it's gone.' He summoned the bees back. 'Why would they do this to their own ship? What could they possibly gain?'

Said turned to look back at the daylight. 'How long has it lain there?'

'Months. Maybe a year, even. But they landed here, and that doesn't make sense.'

'Perhaps they had no choice?'

Benzamir crouched down and drew on the deck with a gloved finger. 'Nobody say anything, just for a moment.'

They waited for him, listening to the sound of falling water both near and distant.

'The brain,' he said. 'Ariadne, give me the schematics. Stay close,' he told them. 'You don't want to get lost.'

He led them deep into the heart of Persephone, a little bubble of light surrounded by so much darkness.

'Said, you said they had no choice as to where to land. I think that's the truth of it. Imagine you had the whole world to choose from: why here? It's a hostile environment, months of darkness, freezing winds, little in the way of natural resources and no people – the very people you wanted to meet and change. Imagine instead that you were on a ship which you could barely control, which you had to force to the ground by doing the whole finger-of-God, blazing trail through the atmosphere thing. You'd want to land where there were no natives.' He reached a door, the only one in the whole ship that was closed. He brought the light-bees closer.

The door was deeply scarred and buckled. It had been forced shut and welded so that no one might ever go in again.

Va reached forward and rested his fingertips on the metal. 'These marks. They had to fight their way in here.'

'Let's see what they've done.' Benzamir got out his little laser and began to carefully cut away the welds. When it grew too hot to hold any more, he resorted to using the length of pipe that Said still carried.

When he grew tired, Va took over, hitting the door again and again and again until the whole ship rang with the sound. Benzamir cooled the laser down in a puddle of water, and eventually it worked again.

'Enough, Brother.'

'I'm almost through,' Va said, grunting with effort.

'I know.'

Benzamir pulsed the laser once through the last remaining weld, and the door sagged. Wahir made to push it, but he was held back. 'You might damage something inside. The brain is a very delicate thing.'

He eased the door so that he could get his fingers around it, then slid it sideways. It jammed, and he used the pipe to work it open a little more, until he could squeeze through. His light-bees followed him.

It wasn't a room intended for humans: too small, too full, too strange. Benzamir's head pressed against the black fractal radiators fixed to the ceiling, and his feet barely fitted in the narrow gap between the wall and the panels that ranged from floor to roof.

He got down on his hands and knees. Some of the panel fronts were lying scattered on the floor, and when he looked inside the narrow duct, he could see disconnected brain modules discarded where they fell. He reached in and picked one up as delicately as he could.

'Ari?' He showed her what he could see through his eyes. 'This is not good.'

'I know. What's left of her might never recover.'

'We have to try, Benzamir.'

'There are other panels loose. I won't know which is memory, which is motor control, which is high function. I'm going to put them in wrong, whatever I do. And even then . . .' He pushed back against the bulkhead and let his body sag.

'My shipsister.'

Benzamir turned the module in his hand and watched the light play across the etched surfaces. 'Some of these are damaged. Scratched. Chipped.'

'You are preparing me for the fact that, at best, she still might be . . . not Persephone. But it's in your nature to try nevertheless.'

'It is, isn't it?' He carefully put the module down and shuffled back over to the door.

'Master? Can we come in yet?'

'Best that you don't. Look, I might be a while. I've got' – he looked round at all the loose panels – 'a delicate job that needs all my attention. Take one of my light-bees and go back to Ariadne.'

Wahir put his head through the gap. 'What is that?'

'It's Persephone's brain, or what's left of it. Someone's ripped pieces out of it at random. We build them, and the ships are born into them. They were never meant to be taken apart after that. Ships are special, Wahir. They're not pets, not servants, not machines. We love each other. Which sounds stupid, just said like that.'

'Not at all, master. Like a trusted camel.' Wahir reached forward and closed his fist around one of the light-bees, then tentatively set it free above his own head. His face cracked into a smile.

'You're just like me. Now go. I'll see you back in Ariadne.'

The light in the corridor receded, and Benzamir bent to his task. He couldn't work with the thick coverall gloves on, so he undid the wrist seals and placed them just outside the door.

He lay down on the floor, stretched his arm out and slid it into the first duct. He could barely see what he was doing, relying mainly on touch and faith as he started to ease the modules back into place. He was doing it with infinitely more care than those who had removed them, but he was aware that even by touching the modules he was introducing errors: dust, grease, static, the pressure of his fingertips. He was more likely to be killing the ship than curing her.

Eventually he stopped. 'Ari, I can't carry on.'

'You must.'

He rolled awkwardly onto his back, flexing his wrist and fingers. He began to cry. 'She's gone, Ari. They've destroyed her. I can't put her back together again, no matter how much I want to.'

'Why? Why would they do this?'

'Because she turned against them. I don't know when that happened: after she'd entered the Earth's system, before they landed. She repented of her crime, and they killed her for it.'

'But to murder a ship, Benzamir! Such a thing has never happened before.'

'And they will pay for this as much as they will pay for all the other lives they've snuffed out. They were my friends, Ari. How could I have misjudged them so badly? How could I have not seen this?' His voice dropped to a whisper. 'It could have been me, tearing at this door, lobotomizing this beautiful ship.'

'It could never have been you.'

'We wanted the same things.' Benzamir hit the bulkhead with his fist. It hurt; it felt good.

'You would have stood here, blocking their way. You would have died before you let them do this.'

'I want to believe that. I don't know if I can.'

'Finish your job, Benzamir. Do your best.'

He worked methodically, taking each disturbed duct in

turn, only pausing to wipe his eyes and blow his nose on his sleeve. He was on the last duct, the last couple of modules, when he heard footsteps running up the corridor. It sounded like Wahir.

'You'll have to wait.'

'But master, you must come quickly. The princess . . .'

Benzamir pushed a module home, felt it click. He gently picked up the remaining cube and turned it so it presented the correct face to the socket.

'What about the princess?' He was cold and cramped, and hadn't thought about Elenya for the entire time he'd been working on Persephone.

'She has one of your magic devices.'

'What? What does it look like?'

'Small, round. It has yellow writing around the middle.'

He took a deep breath and steadied his hand. The last module slotted home. 'I'm coming.' He started to crawl back out of the space he was in.

Wahir didn't wait for him. 'Hurry, master.'

'Stop. Don't go near her. Just tell me where she is.'

'She's in the lake.'

'*In?*' Benzamir squeezed back through the door, caught up with Wahir, ran past and kept on going, tearing down the corridors and stairs, almost always on the point of falling. 'Ari? Did you show Elenya how to work an o-space bomb?'

'No.'

'Then who did?' He was in the cargo bay. Va was at the open doors. 'What did you say to her?' he shouted.

'Nothing. I—'

'Elenya's going to kill herself.' Benzamir jumped down, scrambled over the rocks to the lake edge, skidded to a halt and was only kept standing by Said clutching at him.

She was waist-deep in water that was barely above freezing. It pulled at her cloak and wicked up her dress, turning it black. Her hair rat-tailed down over her shoulders, and in her hands she cupped the little black orb banded with yellow.

Her passage through the water was marked by slow, swirling ice-crystals that turned the lake glassy and dark.

Said reached out and entangled Wahir as he tried to wade out to her. 'No, little one. This is not for you.'

'Where's Va?' called Elenya.

'In the ship,' said Benzamir. He splashed out a little way. A broken chunk of thick ice smacked against his shins. He kicked it away and watched it bob back from under the surface. 'Why are you doing this?'

'Because it's over. I thought that he'd be different. After five years in a monastery, he's spent months on the road with me: he needed me, my talents and my money. But he hasn't changed. He still doesn't love me. I know now that he never will.'

'And this is reason enough to kill yourself? Which you won't do with that, I have to say.'

She held up the bomb, a thumb hovering uncertainly over the button. 'I know what this does. Death is certain.'

'Oh, yes. Set it off and in seconds you'll find yourself in hard vacuum somewhere above the plane of the ecliptic. If you hurry, you might even find the point of light that's this planet before the gas bubbles forming in your blood reach your brain or your heart. That's what'll kill you.' Benzamir felt the sandy lake-bed shift under him. 'Do you really mean to do this?'

'I thought I should try. It's the only thing I have any control over.' Elenya smiled. 'I said I'd do something just for myself, rather than what everybody expects me to do.'

Benzamir lost sensation in his toes; he wriggled them, driving his feet deeper into the wet sediment, then pulled himself free with two sucking noises. 'I can't stop you, you know. You could activate the bomb long before I could get close enough to disarm you. Ariadne can't stop you either, and neither can anyone else here.'

'I know.' Her lips had turned blue. She was shaking.

'Remember when we talked in the garden? I promised you that no one, not even God, would destroy you. I've kept my word as best I could.'

She nodded, a spasm of shivers running through her.

'I don't know what else to say. It's been a hell of a day. I fought the unmakers, rescued you from the emperor's guards, tried to rebuild a ship's mind with my bare hands, and I'm so exhausted I'm weepy and indecisive. Watching you dispatch yourself to oblivion would just about top things off nicely. Elenya, I've saved your life once already. I didn't do it so you could throw it away a few hours later.'

Elenya tried to talk. Her teeth were chattering too much for Benzamir to catch all that she said. '. . . ask you . . .'

'No, you didn't ask me to. You weren't conscious, and I assumed you wanted to live. I was wrong.' He bowed low. 'Apologies, Princess.'

Benzamir turned away and started to walk back to Said and Wahir. He'd lost all feeling below his knees, and he stumbled and fell. He waved away any attempt to help him. He crawled from the water like a beast and hung his head low.

'Master?'

'Yes, Wahir?'

'Should I get the holy man?'

'He's the only one who can save her, but look – he's not here. Neither is he coming, though I expect he's on his knees just like me, railing at God for having put him in such an impossible situation.'

'But . . .'

'Just don't watch when it happens. Why do you think I'm down here?'

Alessandra was walking towards them, her robes fluttering like flags in the wind. 'If you're looking for someone to blame, Benzamir, you can blame me.'

He looked up. 'What?'

'Ariadne has been teaching me how to fight with your weapons.'

'How did you make her do that?'

'Make her? I didn't make her. She suggested it,' she said, 'because neither of us will stand by and watch you die. Elenya must have overheard us. I didn't know she could speak Arabic.' She carried on walking, past them, to the lake's edge.

'If you were on Ariadne, it wouldn't have been Arabic to her.'

'That'll be it.' Alessandra gathered up her skirts to her thighs and gasped at the first touch of water. Then she ploughed out into the lake until she was no more than an arm's length away from Elenya.

'I'm going to lose them both.' Despite everything, Benzamir rolled onto his backside and held up his arms. 'Said? Wahir?'

They pulled him up, barely daring to breathe. Alessandra faced Elenya, who had been in the water so long, she could no longer move.

'How can you stand this?' asked Alessandra. 'The water is so cold.'

461

Elenya's hands still cradled the bomb, but she did nothing with it.

'If you kill yourself, you'll kill me. I don't know if you even care, but I choose life.'

Alessandra's hand stretched out slowly. She took half a step closer. 'Princess? Elenya?'

She found that she was able to reach out and pluck the bomb as if she were taking an apple from a bowl. She held it for a moment in front of her face, then threw it into the deep water.

The men on the beach stood nonplussed, then Said patted Benzamir's arm. 'I'll fetch them out.'

He too waded out towards Elenya, creating a wave, white with foam, that flowed around his legs. As he approached her, she fell backwards into the black water and vanished with barely a ripple.

'No!'

'I have her,' said Said. He plunged his hands below the surface and pulled out a limp white body, clothed in green and brown. He gathered her up and called back to the shore. 'See! I have her.'

CHAPTER 41

Va was sitting hunched on a rock at the brow of the hill. Ariadne's drive-pod loomed over his head, blocking out what light there was that came from the leaden sky. The sun had spiralled away behind them, low on the horizon. It was inexpressibly cold.

'Brother?' said Benzamir. 'What are you doing?'

'Looking for answers. Finding none. And you, Mahgrebi?'

'More or less the same.' Benzamir kicked a rock down the slope, and watched it tumble and bounce away.

'The ship, Persephone. Did you heal it?'

'No. It was a fool's errand from start to finish. She was dead; now she's mad. All she does is sing.' He sat down next to the monk. 'For some reason Ariadne takes comfort in that. She used to play among the stars, and she's reduced to this. I should never have agreed to meddle with her.'

'So why did you?'

'Because,' said Benzamir, 'I have an insatiable urge to try and fix things. Situations, ships, people. It makes so much trouble for me.'

Va stared into the distance. 'Then you should stop.'

'I know. What's to be done with the princess?'

'You seem to ask as if I had some power or authority over her. She is free to do whatever she wishes.' Va rubbed his hands together slowly, squeezing the problem between his palms to make it more malleable. 'I loved her once. No, that's not true. I thought I could possess her once. Own her body and soul. Her rejection of me was like a fire that would never go out. And now it is me who is glacially cold towards her, and she who burns every moment of every day.'

'I would' – Benzamir stared at his feet, even as he felt his cheeks colour despite the cold – 'I would fix her.'

Va looked at him suddenly, as if noticing him for the first time.

'What? What is it?' asked Benzamir with increasing urgency.

'Should I laugh or cry? Listen, Maghrebi, this is not a game that you can win. Even you are not magician enough to change the way Elenya feels about me. Sometimes I wonder if any power in Heaven or Earth can. If you took her beyond this world, as I believe you can, and showed her every wonder of creation, do you think it would make her want me less? And you more?'

'I don't know what I'm thinking,' confessed Benzamir. 'I used to. Before I met her.'

'You're not the first. Look at me.' Va swept a hand over

the scars on his head. 'Look what I've done, what I could do. I am a monster. And yet she loves only me.'

Benzamir swallowed hard. He felt almost weightless. 'It's time we went.' But he didn't move. He stared out to sea, searching fruitlessly for the line which divided the ocean from the sky.

The hum of the ship invaded Benzamir's cabin and kept him from sleep so long that he never noticed the slide into unconsciousness. One moment he was staring, dry-eyed, at the wall, the next he was awake again with a figure sitting at his feet. There was no transition, no sense of time passing, no feeling of being rested.

He could see in the dark. What light there was from the pinpoints marking the door frame was sufficient.

'Alessandra? How long have you been there?'

'I don't know,' she said. 'A while.'

Benzamir blinked. 'Ariadne should have told me. In fact, Ariadne shouldn't have let you in.'

'She said you couldn't sleep.'

'I've become unused to this room. All the places I've slept in: cots, beds, floors, hammocks slung over the decks of ships at sea. And now I have problems. I should have gone to the flight deck; there's something about that chair.'

'She said she was worried about you.'

'Ariadne is always worried about me. It's part of the

arrangement.' He rubbed his face. 'Except she's not talking to me at the moment. I suppose I could see this as a thaw in relations.'

'Why are you angry with her?'

'Because Ariadne has an armoured hull and a gigawatt laser. You don't. She has no business asking you to risk your neck in any battle plan we might come up with. I told her so, and that was pretty much that.'

'You're going to fight them, aren't you?'

Benzamir dialled the lights up enough to allow her to see him, wrapped in a sheet, face slack with fatigue, and for him to see her properly, hunched over, tense as a steel wire.

'It looks likely,' he said. He shifted so he could sit. 'I don't want to. If they won't come with me, I'll have to make them. It's what I was sent to do.'

'Are you going to die?' Her face was pinched, pale, tight-lipped.

'It depends on how willing they are to kill me.'

'That's not an answer.' Alessandra stood up and began to pace the few steps between the walls.

'It's a sort of answer,' he said hopefully.

Her face twitched with a not-quite smile. 'And you expect me to stand by and watch?'

'I had to stand by and watch you save Elenya. Do you think that was easy for me?' Benzamir tightened the sheet in front of him.

Her breath caught in her throat for a moment. Then she said: 'I could have done nothing. It would have been easy for me to do nothing.'

'I think I know you better.'

She didn't reply, just paced and paced until she threatened to wear the floor down. Benzamir watched her, going through a series of gestures that betrayed his nervousness: palm wiping, nose scratching, toe wriggling.

Eventually she stopped and sat down again. 'Even if you live, you're going to go away.'

'Alessandra, of course I'm going away. The whole point of me coming was to make sure you'd all be left alone.'

'Left alone?' she snorted. 'You've interfered with everything you touched.'

'As has been pointed out to me by our Orthodox friend.'

'You'll go away and leave us with our memories, and our dreams of something greater than ourselves. It seems cruel.'

She was quiet for a while, and Benzamir checked the time on his internal clock. He watched the seconds tick by in the corner of his vision.

'So where will you leave me, Benzamir Mahmood?'

When he didn't answer, she left him. The door slid shut behind her, but he continued to stare at the place where she'd been. He thought about lying down again, but knew it would be pointless.

He put on his pilot's coverall and went to find some peace.

It was a part of the ship he rarely visited, and he assumed that his passengers wouldn't have found it yet. But when he reached the door, it was open, and there was a pale, flickering light inside.

She had taken two candles from their place in an alcove and placed them on the stand in front of her. One was already lit, and she was reaching out with a taper to light the other when she stopped in mid-stretch. Benzamir was certain he hadn't made a noise.

'Sorry, my lady.'

Elenya completed her task, holding the wavering flame to the candle wick and waiting for it to catch.

'You appear in the most surprising places, Benzamir.' She blew the taper out and turned to face him. 'You see it as your duty to save the weak and raise up the fallen. We only have to say your name, and you come to our aid. Are you a saint or an angel?'

'Neither, Princess. Not with the thoughts that I've had.'

'But you're no mere man. I saw you fight.'

Benzamir took a candle of his own, held it to a flame and sat it in the holder. The three lights gave only the barest illumination.

'I don't do religion very well, any of them. I don't know

if that makes me deficient in some way. I sometimes believe in a god. Sometimes I think he believes in me. Today? It had mixed results.' As he stared at the candle, he remembered Ibn Alam, he remembered Persephone.

'I haven't thanked you yet,' said Elenya. 'Even in my moment of madness, you wouldn't let me go.'

'You don't have to—' he started, but she laid her finger over his lips.

'I do. I am not cured. Not yet, not perhaps for years. But my fever was broken in that frozen sea. He wouldn't rescue me, even when I was prepared to kill myself. But you were.'

She replaced her finger with her lips. The taste was warm and sweet, brief like a wave that washes up the beach then sinks through the sand.

'What is more important is that you were all there. Said and Wahir, whom I hardly know. Alessandra, who of all people has reason to get rid of me. Her decency, her humanity, overcame her jealousy. She is much better than me.'

'What am I going to do with you, Princess Elenya?'

She knelt in front of the candles, not to pray but to stare into their fire until it blotted out everything else. 'I understand Va better having met you. When he looks at me, he sees me as I was. When you look at me, you see what I could become. Neither of you see me as I am, but until today, neither did I. It's time I went home and faced myself. Will you take me back to Novy Rostov?'

'Is that what you want?' Benzamir looked down at her bowed head. Part of him wanted to reach out and touch her, and it warred with the knowledge that if he did, neither of them would ever be happy.

'Being a princess doesn't give you much freedom,' she said. 'You're always expected to behave in a certain way even if you feel like kicking and screaming; marry who you're told without any thought of love, to breed little princes to keep the blood line going. I've done none of those things for the past six years. Instead, I've sat and waited at the gates of a monastery for a man who will not have me.' She crossed herself twice, and almost a third time before she stopped herself. 'Old habits die hard,' she said, and rose from the cold floor.

They were face to face.

'I've seen many things as I've travelled, many people. I met a man, a boat builder, called Rory macShiel; I saw him with his wife, how they behaved with each other, and for the first time in a very long time I thought of someone else but Va. I thought of my parents, and my brothers and sisters. They must think I'm dead. So I think I have to go back, even if I don't stay.'

Benzamir nodded. 'As you wish, Elenya Christyakova. I have something I must do tomorrow, but then I will take you home.'

'You know where your rebels are?'

'Once we found Persephone, it all fell into place. There will be, well, a reckoning, one way or another. We shall see.'

'Have I disappointed you?' she asked quietly.

He took his time to answer, daring to stare into her eyes. Eventually he said: 'No. For all will be well.'

'You say that. Do you know that?'

'I hope that, because that's all I can do.' He bent low and blew out the candles one by one.

It was dark again, the only light leaking from far down the corridor.

'We need to go,' he said.

'I can't see.'

'Then take my hand.'

CHAPTER 42

They were all subdued. The others looked on, pensive, waiting, while Benzamir looked at the rebels' encampment on the display, marking out features with his finger and letting Ariadne label them in luminous white. Biodome. Living hab. Primary power plant. Beached skimmers resting on a dark shelf of rock. Tubes leading down into the sea, sucking up minerals and carbon to use in the replicator.

The domes were camouflaged, blending seamlessly in with their surroundings by means of chameleonware. They had only found them because Benzamir's bugs had been tracked to the precise location.

Hunting the desert inland, he found pop-up gun emplacements and mobile mines. He weighed up in his mind whether he had enough armaments to win a head-on assault. The name on his map said Skeleton Coast. It wasn't a promising start.

Benzamir stared deep into the heart of the image. 'They must know we're coming. Why won't they talk to me?'

472

'Because they want you down there. All prudence dictates that you destroy them from here and collect their charred corpses for burial later, but they know it's you now. They know how you'll behave. You won't fire first.'

They spoke in Nu, and Ariadne would not translate.

'I still have to inform them of the Council's charges.'

'Then write it down, put it in a drop-pod and ram it through their ceiling.' Her voice was sharp, brittle with almost human anger. 'They killed a ship. They don't deserve consideration.'

'And I have to work under different rules to you. I have to live within the law.'

'You can still negotiate from a position of strength. If I land, we've lost that. If I stay up here, I am a threat.'

He thought about it. 'Well, there's more than one way down, though I can't honestly say that halo is my favourite form of travel.'

'In full armour.'

'As you say, in full armour. Oh joy.'

Ariadne wiped the display and replaced it with the real-time image of north-east Africa, hanging stationary underneath.

'It scares me when you don't orbit,' Benzamir said. 'It feels like there's nothing holding us up.'

'So I flaunt my inertial drive,' she said. 'What equipment do you need?'

'Give me everything. If I don't use it, it doesn't matter. If I do, I'll need it straight away.' He turned to the people who'd travelled with him and whom he now considered friends. 'I'm going down. I need to try and persuade them to give up and come with me.'

'And when they don't?' said Alessandra.

'I suppose I'll have to make them.'

'Can't you just . . . you know . . .?' She pointed her finger.

'Yes. I could.'

'Your course is honourable, Maghrebi, but you lack faith,' said Va. 'There'll be no need to fight your rebels. God will not be thwarted, and it's His will that the books are returned.'

'I am not going naked. And yes, I lack faith. I trust in doubt to keep me alive.' Benzamir watched Va's face sour, but he was in a fragile mood. 'I woke up the bugs on the book I gave to the emperor. I expect they're all in one of the domes below, except the one you lost.'

Va narrowed his eyes and said nothing more.

'Come on then. If you're going to lend a hand, now's the time.' He led them to the cargo bay – all those who didn't think armour weakness and weapons wrong. Ariadne brightened the lights and signalled with coloured telltales where the pieces of Benzamir's battlesuit were stored.

It took a little while to put it all back together. Said helped, as did Elenya and Alessandra. Wahir played with the parts until they were needed, when he reluctantly gave them up.

'Are you seriously going to wear this?' Alessandra looked at the result of their work, a huge figure with oversized limbs. 'It's so heavy that four of us can barely lift one part of it.'

'You don't wear it, not how you think of wearing it.' Benzamir went round the back of the giant and pulled and twisted two catches. 'It carries you. Really, you didn't think my head would go up into the helmet with my feet still on the ground?'

'Master would have to be twice his height!' laughed Wahir nervously. 'But what do you do then? It looks very fierce.'

'You crouch inside the body.' He heaved, and the back split from waist to shoulders. 'Everything is controlled by movement and thought. Like a big puppet. I walk, it walks. I run, it runs. Like this.' He clambered up until he was balanced on the suit's back like an new insect inspecting its larva-casing.

He slid in his legs, then eased in the rest of him, arms first, torso, and finally his head.

The back panel closed itself. In the darkness Benzamir waited, cocooned.

Two arterial shunts stabbed into his neck, and the gaps left in the cavity started to fill with warm syrupy liquid. It seeped into his form-fitting singlesuit and clung to his skin. It rose as far as his neck and paused.

Benzamir hated this part. His blood was getting all the oxygen it needed and more through the shunts, but it still felt like drowning.

The liquid reached his chin, covered his mouth, his nose, and up until the only air left in the chamber was in his lungs.

Slowly, calmly, he breathed out. He tried to make his mind blank out, thinking only of the vast void of space between the stars. Slowly, calmly, he breathed in.

'Everyone panics their first time,' said Ariadne. 'This is not your first time. You will live. The sensation will come and go, and you will remain.' Her soothing words were repeated over and over until every last bubble of air had gone.

'Are you ready, Benzamir?'

Without speaking, he said: 'Yes. I swear it gets worse, not better.'

'Systems check good. Sensors good. Locomotion good. Weapons good. Power plant good, with a tendency to run a little hot, so watch out for that. Coms good. Halo good. You have control.'

Without seeing, he saw four concerned faces looking up at the head part of the armour. Wahir was reaching out to tap the chest with an inquisitive finger.

Benzamir thought light, and the markers on the skin of the armour – fingers, elbows, knees, shoulders, head and feet – glowed red.

Wahir yelped and hid behind Said.

'This is normal,' said Benzamir through the external speakers. 'It's so I don't tread on you by accident.' He selected his camouflage, dialling through a swatch of designs until he came to a mosaic of shades of yellow.

He moved, testing every joint, moving his head around in a complete circle and flexing his weapon pods. Spikes and stubby hollow tubes popped out of hatches and sneaked back in faster than the eye could follow.

'I'm ready,' he said. 'You'll all have to leave now. Ariadne's going to open the main doors and there's no air-lock.'

Elenya took Said's arm, which embarrassed him greatly, and Wahir's, which pleased him inordinately, and took them away. Alessandra started to edge back, not wanting to go, not wanting to say anything that would betray her.

'It has to be done this way, Alessandra. Perhaps they'll see sense, and we can finish this without a firing a shot.' Benzamir lifted up his hand and splayed his massive composite fingers. She recognized the salute from his tattoo, and tentatively returned it.

'Come back to us,' she blurted. 'Come back to me.' She turned and ran.

Benzamir was alone. After a moment he turned and

stamped his way to the back of the hold. The lights dimmed, and Ariadne vented the air into space. The high-pitched whistle diminished until he stood in hard vacuum. Then she opened the doors, peeling them apart like flower petals, so he stood on the edge of a vertiginous drop.

The whole world was spread out before him and filled all his vision, from the azure blue of the curved horizon to the sulphurous yellow of the dunes beneath his feet. The ocean sparkled blue, and the forests to the west were rich and green. Clouds collected at the foot of mountains in streamers and over plains as towers of white.

It was then he realized that he loved it, all of it, from frozen north to sun-scorched south. For all the foreboding he felt, it was worth it just to be there at that moment, worth coming the vast distance and suffering the gnawing anxiety that he had in fact chosen the wrong side. Even if he was going to die today, he would go knowing that he had had one moment of transcendent joy.

A dispenser chugged a stream of silver remotes into the bay. They joined him as a shining cloud above his head.

Then he stepped forward, and out into the abyss.

To begin with, it didn't even seem like he was falling. The remotes fell with him, hanging next to him like drops of water, but the numbers in the corner of his vision gave him the true picture: velocity, height above sea level, external

478

pressure and temperature. When he looked back, Ariadne was all but lost against the stars.

The first wisps of air began to tear at him, initially as insubstantial as gossamer, then slowly building until it was thunder. He was roaring down. The battlesuit locked itself into the foetal position, and the vibrations reached their peak with a sharp snap of sound.

He was supersonic.

The remotes trailed away behind Benzamir, but he wasn't concerned: as the air grew thicker, he would slow down faster, and they'd catch him up. The ground was huge, swallowing up all his vision. Unenhanced, he could see the patterns of sinuous dunes snaking their way across the desert, the subtle changes in colour of the land, the acid sharp lines of rock that cut through the sand sea, the pounding surf marking the edge of the ocean.

He stayed curled for another minute, then commanded his limbs to extend. It was time he went subsonic and started manoeuvring. He waited for the shuddering to damp down as he decelerated.

'Give me tactical.'

His view changed, overlaid with terrain information, targeting graticules, marker flags, laser designators, life support stats, weapons status: it was almost too much to cope with, yet he was used to the flood of data, and welcomed it.

He painted his landing site with a laser, and the halo thrusters kicked in, turning him south and east towards a spot that lay just the other side of a dune from the main dome.

All the time, the ground was rising up to meet him. The thrusters jolted his frame as they guided him in. One minute to go. He hoped Ariadne was right about the air defence.

The domes were still invisible to the naked eye, even though his display told him where they should be. The skimmers on the shoreline were the only evidence anything was there.

Thirty seconds. Twenty . . . ten. The airbags inflated around him like a huge white cocoon. His vision disappeared: only the tactical display remained, a wire-frame representation of the world outside. The numbers counted down to zero. Time was up.

His insides shifted. Accelerometers registered a palpable hit, then he was tumbling over and over. The bags deflated as he rolled, and before he'd come to a halt, he ordered them to jettison.

The bags separated and blew away from him, turning into thick pancakes of ballistic cloth as they leaked their remaining air away. He was left standing, toes splayed on a bed of soft sand.

No one came to greet him. Nor did they try and kill him. He consulted his tactical display and called his remotes to him. As they dropped from the sky, they bobbed close to the ground, then rose again. They gathered behind him, a crowd of glittering spheres in the burning sun.

'I'm down,' he said.

'I can't see any movement at all,' Ariadne told him.

'They probably think you're going to turn them to ash if they put their heads outside.' He walked to the top of the dune with difficulty, the sand shifting under the immense weight of the battlesuit. The domes were obvious now, seen side on, the patterns of rock extending upwards in a perfect semicircle. 'Hard substrate. Tunnels?'

'There are no emissions, but that doesn't mean they haven't gone down. It's an area notorious for being inhospitable to biological life.'

Benzamir slid down the lee side of the dune. Most of it seemed to slide down with him, and he flexed all his joints below his knees to shake off the sand. The rock shelf that angled down to the sea was far easier, even if it was shimmering with heat haze. The remotes followed him, and fanned out in a wide arc behind him.

The door to the main dome was facing north, and he had to trail around the circumference to get there. He felt himself scanned, acquired as a target by three pop-ups hidden in the encircling dunes. It was an automatic response, and he responded by automatically adding them to his tally of targets.

As he approached the traditional Tribal entrance of three pairs of blast-proof pressure doors, they slid open one after another, revealing a long corridor that led into the heart of the building.

Benzamir hesitated. 'They want me to go in.'

'They should come to you. You're vulnerable under the dome.'

'They were my friends, Ari. Give me five minutes with them.' He clustered his remotes and sent them on ahead, in case there was an attempt to separate him from them. Then he followed, using them to scan and spot and give him a picture of what was inside.

The link to Ariadne cut off as soon as he entered the shielded dome.

He walked on, into the open, and stopped to look around. His tactical display lit up, measuring distances, gauging threats. The remotes spun around him, memorizing the architecture and more.

Part of the space was occupied by a triple tier of identical habitats, all grown from the same matrix, their vacant balconies looking out onto a verdant parkland with engineered trees and plants. There was a lawn, and a small lake, and a maze of pathways snaking away towards the outer wall. The glaring overhead sun was filtered to a cool yellow disc that gave only diffuse shadows.

Benzamir recognized the designer in the design.

'Glad to see Peri's had time to do some gardening in between slaughtering the locals,' he said.

A battlesuit moved from among the trees, a shadow of green and brown. It left deep imprints across the grass and finally stopped by the water. It had its own set of remotes, and there was a brief flurry of target acquisition before they settled down again.

One suit pinged the other: neither of them had thought to block the signals, or the information the transponder gave out. Benzamir gave the ghost of a smile when he found out who the rebels had chosen to speak to him.

'Mahmood. We just can't seem to keep away from each other, can we?'

'You knew someone would come for you, Nilssen. I decided that it should be me, because after everything we'd gone through together – all the arguments, the campaigning, the speeches – I thought you'd listen to me. I thought you could be redeemed, and I could persuade the Council to treat you mercifully. Was I wrong?'

'What do you think? Can you see any way back for us? Or,' Nilssen said, 'is the real reason you're here that you've come to join us?'

'I've thought about it. I've thought about it often, chasing you across the face of this planet, trying to find you without giving myself away. I'm still tempted.'

'Then why not? There's no one to stop you, no one watching what you do. No one to tell you off.'

Benzamir shook his head. 'It's too late for that. You have

far too much blood on your hands. The monastery of Saint Samuil, the citadel of the Kenyan empire, even your own ship. How could you?'

'You found her then? All very unfortunate,' admitted the other man.

'Unfortunate, Nilssen? You murdered your ship!'

'She turned against us. We nearly died. We barely made it down in one piece,' he shouted, and then, as if it would explain everything, he added: 'She deleted the Great Library.'

It did. Everything finally came together.

'Is that it?' said Benzamir. 'Is that what all this has been about? Dear God. Persephone finally found her conscience: she wiped the library. She'd beaten you, destroyed the one thing you needed. You could have admitted defeat, couldn't you? Come home and faced justice. But no. You killed her instead.'

Nilssen clenched his giant fists. 'It wasn't like that.'

'Oh no, it was much worse. You made an alliance with the Kenyans: you could trade the tech, but not the knowledge of how it worked. God forbid any of you should remember anything useful!' Pop-ups rippled across Benzamir's body, his barely constrained fury leaking through the mental guards. 'So when you heard of the books, what did you do? You stole them and had all the monks killed. A shelf's worth of antiques.'

'We needed them,' said Nilssen.

'I've heard some crap excuses in my time. Remind me again why you came? I thought the grand plan was to lift everyone up, make them like us. When did you decide to do something different? Not so much the humble servant come to Earth to save it from ignorance and barbarity. More the all-powerful god whose capricious rules have to be obeyed or else. Was that what made Persephone turn on you?'

'You're such a sentimental fool. You care too much. Every good leader needs to forget compassion and look at the big picture. You're not that sort of man, are you? I don't expect you to understand. When we played together in crèche, you were always the one who did as he was told. Always the follower, little Michael.'

Past taunts burned inside Benzamir. It was all he could do to stop himself from attacking. 'You have to answer for everything you've done. If you don't surrender willingly to me now, I will take you back in chains – real chains. I know a man who can make them for me.' He took a step forward, making the ground quiver. 'It's your choice, but you haven't got long to decide.'

Nilssen laughed. 'Surrender? To you? Why would we do that? I could never take anything you say seriously, Benzamir Mahmood. We've decided that you'll stay with us for as long as we decide to keep you. Just hope you don't outlive your usefulness.' He paused. 'What did you say?'

Now Benzamir was calm, back in control. Nilssen's moment of hesitation was all it took. 'We can't carry on this conversation indefinitely. In two minutes Ariadne will launch kinetic weapons against all your structures. If you're outside, unarmed, and under my protection, she'll hold fire and you'll live. If you're not, you can take your chances with hypervelocity sabots. Either way, your dreams of world domination are over.'

'You're lying. She wouldn't dare do that to us while you're here.'

'It's all been arranged. Feel free to call her bluff.'

'No.' Nilssen looked up. 'No! How could you do this? Tell her to stop.'

'You'll have to turn your glittershields off for that. I expect that's something you don't want to do, shipkiller.'

'It was Peri. She did it! She's the one who destroyed the brain. Not me.' He tried one last time. 'Benzamir, you were the most passionate of all of us. You wanted this!'

Benzamir balled his fists and stepped forward. The ground thundered as soil and stones sprayed out. 'I didn't want this! This disaster, this travesty, this heap of shit that you've made for yourselves. This isn't what I argued for at all, and now I've taken away all your choices. Evacuate. Take no weapons. You've got just over a minute.'

Faces started to appear at the balcony windows. They could hear every word, and they were afraid.

'No one is going anywhere,' boomed a voice.

Benzamir looked up at a first-floor hab and saw Peri Renzo looking down at him. Once, he would have responded by grinning like an idiot.

'You don't have the balls carry this charade off any longer, Benzamir!' she shouted. 'You were always such a disappointment.'

'The one thing you could never comprehend, Peri: that a man might give up his own life for what he thought was right.'

'As you wish. Peter? Take him.'

CHAPTER 43

Nilssen screamed and leaped. Weapon-pods spun and spat. His remotes darted and flashed. Benzamir was not there. He had launched himself backwards, as far and as fast as he could.

The remotes exchanged fire with each other; some fell out of the sky, molten one moment, frozen twisted ruins the next. Benzamir had more; when the opening salvo had finished, they turned on Nilssen. He staggered backwards, glowing gouges like fiery claw marks criss-crossing him.

Benzamir jumped forward, kicked a huge foot out, followed it up with half-turn and hand-spike slash that skittered shrieking across the surface of Nilssen's abdomen. Still reeling, his opponent found it difficult to strike back. But blows that would have caved in a man's ribs bounced off the shielded armour. Strikes had to be precise, timed, and meant.

Nilssen's arm came over Benzamir's shoulder, a shove gone wrong. Benzamir stepped inside, slamming his back against him and then throwing him. The battlesuit flew, banged down hard in the soft ground.

'*Warning,*' said Benzamir's suit. '*Overload.*'

He unfurled his wing-like radiator array and ran at Nilssen again. He was down to half a dozen remotes, but Nilssen, who had none left, found that as fast as he used missiles and pop-up cannon, lasers would destroy the launchers themselves. Benzamir's suit was heating up, but the radiators should shed the excess. He'd taken little damage, but Nilssen's front armour was badly compromised.

Nilssen was on his feet, but his left arm, the one Benzamir had used as a lever, was hanging useless. They fought and kicked, stabbing at each other in lightning-fast moves, remotes circling and boiling off composite when they had the chance. Nilssen fell back under the onslaught, Benzamir concentrating on the weakened breastplate for his most penetrating attacks.

The moment Nilssen deployed his own radiators, the remotes changed tactics, pouring as much heat as they could into the black wings. Instead of keeping the suit cool, they were cooking it inside out.

Nilssen dropped to his knees. Benzamir swung his fist at his head, once, twice, three times. It ripped off with a shriek and bounced away.

'Go on, then. Finish it,' Nilssen grunted.

'We could have all lived,' said Benzamir. 'Instead, we all have to die.'

The ground vibrated as if it was the surface of a drum. The air shocked hard. Plastic shattered, stone broke, metal bent, anything not tied down flew.

Benzamir was jerked off his feet. He landed curled up. The sky flashed into incandescence. He waited for a bar of molten light to vaporize the hab and everything inside.

There was a second concussion, a third, as hypervelocity sabots turned domes into craters. The power flickered as the generator vanished in a mushroom cloud; the secondary kicked in.

Still he waited. The noise and the shaking died down. He could faintly hear the lightning crack of Ariadne's laser as she picked off unshielded targets. Nothing else.

Slowly it dawned on him that she'd had no intention of destroying the living hab, despite it being the plan they'd both agreed on. She loved him too much, and she'd lied to him.

He got back up. Nilssen had fallen flat on his chest: he could no longer see what was going on, and Benzamir was in no rush to tell him. The curved front of the living block was ragged, the windows gone, the structure warped by the colossal impacts so close by. The people inside would be deaf and bleeding from the overpressure transferred through the dome, which had flexed and bent, but not broken. His remotes lay inert on the ground, stirring feebly.

The triple doors were beckoning him. He reached them

unsteadily – all his sight lines were out of true – and transmitted what he hoped was still the access code.

Before he could be proved wrong, his vision blinked red. Without hesitating, Benzamir threw himself aside, turned his shoulder under his body and jumped up again. His radiators closed and opened, hissing and crackling with effort, just as the first salvo of rockets screamed by. His pop-ups took care of the second volley, but right behind the missiles were two undamaged battlesuits still streaming with pond water.

Benzamir had spent himself on defeating Nilssen. He had nothing in reserve because he hadn't thought to keep anything back.

'Ari! Can you hear me?'

The two battlesuits were on Benzamir, going for his legs, trying to bring him down.

'*Warning. Overload.*'

He blocked and dodged, while he tried to come up with an idea that might save himself.

'*Warning. Overload.*'

He was in heat shock. He couldn't think. His instincts traded blows with the battlesuits, dodged their lunging attacks, fired off the last of his guns and rockets in an attempt to reduce them to smoking debris, and still he had two enemies to fight.

This was what they wanted, what they'd planned from

the start. They had known he couldn't resist Peter Nilssen's challenge. They'd goaded him into losing his temper and he'd ended up losing everything.

'*Warning. Critical overload.*'

He had to disengage. Run. But they were hitting him as hard as he had hit Nilssen. He kept on pulling back, letting them get the advantage, taking damage, until his back was against the first set of pressure doors.

He heard a bang. A few moments later and a little closer, another.

Then he put everything into one jump. He arced through the air, hands and feet splayed. If he was wrong, they'd be on him in a moment, and there'd be no recovery. They'd just stamp on his chest until it broke.

A bubble of utter darkness bloomed inside the dome, necklaced with flickering strands of rainbow colours. It consumed the doors, swallowed up the ground in front of them. Then, with a pop of inrushing air, it burst.

A gust of hot, dry wind blew over the white-hot edges of the severed airlock. One of the battlesuits reacted faster than the other: that one survived. Its companion was speared by a violet beam of light that shone down the tunnel and crackled with energy.

Ariadne, flying so close to the ground outside that she made the sand dance, gave the pulse everything she had. She burned through the outer armour, heated the body inside until it turned to plasma, then punched out the back plate in an incandescent wave of gas. The armour ballooned outward until it abruptly transformed into a shockwave of vapour. Burned shards of carbon and metal pattered down all around the pair of leg stumps.

The laser cut through the far side of the unshielded dome and fused a sand dune into glass, then the hellish light blinked off.

One on one. Neither had any weapons left: it was down to brute force. The remaining battlesuit caught Benzamir around the waist and started to squeeze. They staggered, locked together in a drunkard's walk. They fell into the lowest floor of the habs, destroying them, spewing gouts of masonry and fragments of supporting beams.

Benzamir realized he had both arms free. He felt for his opponent's head, wrenched it off with a tortured shriek, but still it crushed him.

'Warning. Structural failure.'

In a moment of blinding clarity, he extended a hand spike and rammed it down through the neck. The iron grip around him slackened. The other man had to know what he was doing. He kept pushing, probing and hoping.

He was shoved away, tottering back, unable to turn at the waist. The other suit, blind, started to deploy an emergency camera to work out where it was, where anybody was. The hab block was beginning to collapse around them.

Benzamir edged forward. The camera, an aerial with a fish-eye lens, spotted him, and the battlesuit kicked out at him, catching him on an already damaged leg and sending him spinning over.

He didn't have the strength to rise. He could have died then, had his enemy pressed their advantage. But he hesitated, suspecting a trick, waiting to see if Benzamir would truly stay down.

Alessandra threw a fist-sized sphere behind the battlesuit. It heard the noise, turned, and was momentarily distracted by a woman in Arab dress calmly inspecting her pulse rifle to see where her finger needed to go and firing three plasma rounds into its chest.

The bomb expanded into a thing of terrible beauty. It caught the battlesuit up past its waist, with one arm held fast. With its free hand the suit frantically struck at the space-time surface, desperately trying to break out. Dark light grew around the bubble's circumference. Then it disappeared, dragging loose dust into the vacuum.

The chest fell with one whole arm and part of the other. Blood gushed out into the glassy bowl beneath and splashed almost to the rim. Alessandra glanced down at what she'd done with a look of distaste, then beckoned hidden others.

Benzamir crawled out, chunks of debris crashing on and around him. He tried to stand. Nothing would work. His field of view grew to encompass Said, Wahir and Elenya, all holding rifles. They were aiming, more or less accurately, up at the crumbling habs.

'What do you think you're doing?' he said, then looked behind him. There were several gun barrels pointing down at them. The eyes of those behind them looked both beaten and savage at the same time.

He had to get up, put his body between them. He used his arms as leverage and opened his ruined radiator wings, but everything was broken. He was losing life-support.

'Benzamir?' Alessandra's knuckles whitened around the trigger. 'What's wrong?'

He was blacking out, and with his failing thoughts he activated the exit sequence. What was once an extension of his body became a rigid cast. The view of outside dimmed, and the liquid started to drain from the chamber. Face down, it emptied as far as his ears, then stopped.

'*Mechanical malfunction. Aborting exit sequence. Emergency override.*'

The back panel blew out, spraying those around him with viscous pink slime. The neck shunts snapped off, leaving two fat tubes stuck in his arteries. Blood started to shoot from the open ends before they clamped shut.

All this time, Benzamir was suffocating. He tried to pull his head out, free his arms. He was stuck. Something had warped inside. He heaved the first spout of liquid from his lungs, but still couldn't breathe.

He heard Arabic, couldn't work out what was being said, then World, and again missed its meaning. He was drowning, choking and vomiting and it really did feel like he was going to die.

Arms looped around his shoulders and pulled. More laced under his sternum and jerked him upwards.

His lungs emptied in one huge bubbling splatter. Then again as his chest was squeezed clear.

His body moved, slid out of the confines of the suit. Grit hissed against his knees and he put his face down into a pool of something warm. He felt a comforting hand press gently on his back, and he decided that he ought to try and breathe again.

His first attempt seemed to last for ever, and when he eventually stopped, he coughed it all out again, spilling more slimy liquid uncontrollably onto the dusty ground.

'It's all right.' Alessandra held his shoulders. 'Again.'

He sucked in air. It was too sharp; it hurt going in, it hurt coming out, and it did no good while it was there.

'Again,' she insisted.

Better. The urge to sleep, just to lie down and stop everything, started to go. He coughed again, pink phlegm staining the floor.

He tried to speak, and it sounded like he was gargling with razorblades. He spat out what was in his mouth.

'I'm bleeding.'

'Sorry?'

'I'm bleeding from somewhere. This stuff should be clear.' He rolled over, and for some reason found himself in her lap, his head in the crook of her elbow.

'You've blood coming from your ears and nose, and your eyes are almost all red. Is this normal or should I worry?'

'Normal enough. Get me upright.'

Said, his gun abandoned, pulled Benzamir up. His knees buckled, and the big man caught him.

'Master?'

Benzamir could hardly see. His eyes were damaged, full of debris and barely responsive. 'Pressure damage. I'll heal. So why haven't we been cut down like vermin? What's holding them back?'

Alessandra scanned the balconies. 'All they're doing is watching us. Some of them aren't even pointing their – you know – bang-sticks at us.'

'That sounds promising.' He called out in as big a voice as he could muster. 'You can't win. You know it. Ariadne will wait for you for ever if need be. Put yourself under my protection and you won't be harmed.' Then to Alessandra: 'What are they doing now?'

'That was pitiful. I don't think they even heard you.'

A figure in black walked in front of them, picking his way nimbly over the rubble. He looked up at the hab, then down at Benzamir. He shook his head sadly.

'I told you so. And now, look at what you've done. There's been too many deaths, too much destruction. It's not the books themselves. It's the lust for what lies inside that leads people to madness. Even you, Mahgrebi.'

'You were going to march in here and just demand them back, Va? That's madness.'

'We'll see. I understand that the longer I talk, the more your rebels are likely to understand me. Very well, then. We will talk, and they will listen. Maghrebi, I never once asked for your help. Your way of doing things is not mine. You rely on your wit and your power. I have nothing but faith to call on.' He smiled, and the effect was so startling that Benzamir gasped. 'But you have friends, and that counts for a great deal. So, I ask you now, tell your friends to put their weapons down. There has to be an end to all this, and you'll not achieve it your way.'

Benzamir saw the truth of it. 'Wahir, Elenya. It's time to give up the wands of insanely powerful fireballs.'

Wahir reluctantly put the gun down on the ground. Even more reluctantly, Elenya did the same.

'We're surrendering? To them?' said Wahir. 'What if they kill us?'

'If any of them had wanted to kill us, they would have done it by now. All it would take would be one person willing to pull the trigger, but they don't seem to have anyone left who'd do that.'

They waited.

'Why don't they give up, master?' whispered Said.

'Pride. They've nowhere to go, no way of getting out of this, and their schemes are in disarray. But they had such high hopes. They wanted to do good and save you from yourselves. It turned out to be one long slide into disaster, and they still can't quite believe it.' Benzamir coughed, and it hurt.

The white-dusted face of Peri Renzo climbed over the wreckage of the ground-floor habs. She had a small gun in one hand, obviously aiming it at Benzamir's head. It took him a few moments to recognize her, a few more to realize what she held.

He heard the weapon power up.

'You've actually collected some of the natives and brought them along for the ride? How incredibly predictable of you, Benzamir. How excruciatingly noble. Even while opposing us, you do the very thing you would stop us doing.'

Va stepped between them. 'You are the leader of these people?' he asked.

She tried to aim around the monk, but he shifted his weight easily and always managed to block her view.

'Again, I ask you: are you the leader here?'

'Yes, what of it?' she growled in frustration. 'Get out of my way.'

'No. I will not.' He walked closer until Renzo was forced to point the gun at him alone.

'What is it you want from me?'

Va leaned in so that she could see his scars, see the fury that burned behind his eyes, feel the searing rage seeping from every pore of his skin. 'By the authority of His Holiness Father Yeremai, patriarch of Moscow and of all Russia, I demand that you give me back my books.'

Only then did she see him for who he really was. He knocked her weapon hand aside like he was swatting a fly, took another step and he was so close, their breath touched each other's lips.

'Now,' he said.

What was left of the colour in her face drained away.

'I should have introduced you,' said Benzamir. 'This is Brother Va of the monastery of Saint Samuil in Arkady. He's the sole survivor of your raid to steal the User books. He's come all this way to get them back. He didn't come with force of arms like I did. He just wants the books, and he'll stay here until he gets them.' He looked at each of the faces behind the rifles, twenty people he would once have called friends. 'Who's going to tell him why his brothers died? Which one of you?'

One by one, they lowered their gaze.

'I can still give you sanctuary. Take it while you still can.'

Renzo turned away, let her gun fall nerveless through her fingers, and with a sudden sigh the others followed.

'They knew from the very start what would happen,' said Benzamir.

'How do you know, master? Can you read their minds?'

'Look at all the weapons they brought with them, Said. No matter what they say, this is the evidence that cries out the loudest.'

'Benzamir?'

'Alessandra?'

'You are the best, bravest man to have ever lived.'

'Not me. That one there.' He shuffled himself forward, dragging his feet stiffly until he could slap Va's shiny head. 'You did it. The patriarch will be so very proud of you.'

Knowing that he had disobeyed his earthly father in every last matter, Va started to shake, not with cold, but with sobs. Benzamir drew him in and held him the best he could, whispering words of Old Russian in his ear like an angel, Said and Alessandra supporting them both.

'What happens now, Benzamir?' Alessandra asked.

He said nothing, but instead made some stupid, spur-of-the-moment decisions he might now actually live to regret.

CHAPTER 44

He was back where he'd started, standing on glittering white sand under the heat of a midday sun. The Inner Ocean had long ago washed the beach clean of the remains of the slave he'd dragged from the water and hadn't had time to bury.

'Do you remember, Said?'

'How could I forget? You grinning like you were touched by the sun, and Ibn Alam swinging his precious sword around.' Said reached down and scooped up a handful of dry sand, then let it trickle through his clenched fist. 'You punched me in the throat, then tied me up.'

'Yes,' said Benzamir, 'but I'm not sorry.'

'And I'm not asking you to apologize. It was the will of Allah that brought us together that day, and more fool Ibn Alam for not recognizing it.' He wiped off the last of the sand from his palms. 'And look. It's the will of Allah that we've returned, safe and sound. Not a scratch on us.'

'No one will believe your story. You haven't lost an eye or a leg, you haven't gained a single scar. Perhaps—'

'Master! You've saved us from diggers and armies and monsters and who knows what else. That we've lived is a miracle.' Said slapped Wahir across the shoulders, making the boy grunt. 'To say anything else would be ungrateful.'

'Except,' said Benzamir, 'you return as Said and Wahir, man-at-arms and camel boy, and not as the friends of Prince Benzamir Mahmood. I'd like to do something about that if I can.'

'You won't ask Ariadne to float over the sheikh's palace? Please, no. They'll stone us all.'

'It'll look really impressive.' Benzamir could see Wahir weighing up the idea.

'It would be a gift too far,' pleaded Said. 'Don't honour us in that way.'

'I had another idea. A gift that you might accept.' The lift disc slid down the beach, laden with bolts of cloth. 'We can bury these above the high-water mark, or stash them in a cave if we can find one. You can collect them later when you've got a camel or two in tow.'

Said fingered a deep blue cotton. 'This is a king's ransom.'

'Not really. It leaves me short on azo-dye components, but Ariadne assures me that we're not going to need them on the way home. You can sell these for a good price, and you're wise; you'll know what to do with the money. A business buying and selling. Mahr, even, if you met the right woman.' He bent down. 'And for you, too, Wahir. Said will share what he gets with you, but I want to make certain you benefit from this, just in case your father decides that your good fortune should be his alone. Said will look after what's due to you until you can control it yourself.'

Wahir looked serious as he considered his options. 'Camels, I think.'

'I never doubted it for a moment.'

'Though I don't think I'll be like Ali Five-camels. That story was just too strange.'

'Trust me. You'll change your mind one day. You'll want to give five camels and consider it a bargain. Love never counts the cost.'

Pulling a face, Wahir mumbled: 'I'm too young.'

'And yet the time will come around, like it or not.' Benzamir got up again. 'It's going to be nightfall in Novy Rostov at this rate.'

'Ariadne is faster than the fastest bird,' protested Said.

'She is, but Novy Rostov is west of here, so it's mid-afternoon there already.'

Said and Wahir looked sceptically at each other.

'Ask the imam. He'll tell you I'm right.' Benzamir gave up. He hugged Said, slapping him repeatedly on the back, then swept up Wahir and swung him around. Wahir laughed and howled as his heels left the ground. 'We have to go.'

Va, Elenya and Alessandra gave more circumspect farewells, and Wahir had one last word with Benzamir.

'I'll never see you again, will I?'

'If everything goes well, then no. I don't expect to come back. But if I do, we'll smoke a sheesh and talk about old times, and you can tell me all your news. I expect it to be interesting, though,' and he wagged his finger. 'Adventure is burning in your soul. Never let it go out.'

The others were carrying the heavy rolls of cloth up the beach, and Benzamir took one, put it over Wahir's shoulder, then gathered up an armful himself and added it to the pile. There was nothing more to be done.

'I'll remember you every day I'm alive,' called Benzamir, walking backwards towards Ariadne. 'Peace be on you both.'

No matter how fast he blinked, his eyes filled up with tears. He stumbled into the cargo bay and did something he hadn't done since he was a child: pressed his face into a corner of two walls and let the sadness take him.

Getting to Novy Rostov unseen was all but impossible. Ariadne couldn't change her skin colour – she was a spaceship, not a spy drone – and Benzamir didn't want to wait until nightfall to leave. He wanted his grief to be compressed into one overwhelming lump, then finished with, not strung out like a wire until he broke on it.

So they rose into the sky until they looked no more than a crow, and crossed the Inner Sea from east to west. Ariadne's drive didn't produce a vapour trail, but her passing shed a ghostly mist which spun and broke up in her wake.

Those who looked up would have seen a dark shape dart across the sky, followed a few moments later by the rumble of distant thunder that seemed to roll on for ever before fading. But as they approached the Caliphate, heavy snow clouds bunching down from Siberia shielded their approach.

They watched from the flight deck, radar punching through the cloud layer and discovering what lay beneath. The Black Sea fell away, and they slowed as they came to the Bay of Azov, dropping lower all the time.

'There,' said Elenya. 'See where that finger of water reaches up between the hills? Novy Rostov is on the south bank.'

Benzamir looked at Va. The monk's jaw was clenched tight shut, and beads of sweat glittered on his head. 'Brother?'

Va didn't move. His gaze was locked on Novy Rostov.

The radar painted a picture of the city, balanced on a ridge of land between the sea and a river. Brutal stone walls enclosed a warren of streets and alleys, and at the eastern end a second enclosure surrounding an ugly squat castle and a bright-domed cathedral. The fields around the walls were vacant, the forests further out, deserted.

'Where should I land?' asked Ariadne.

'Forgive me, but I don't want a fuss. Matters will be hard enough to explain. My family own a summer retreat upstream. There's a dock, and the house is above there, facing north,' said Elenya.

'No,' said Va. 'Not any more.'

'How do you know? You never went there.'

'I had it destroyed. There was a detachment of Caliphate cavalry billeted there. During the night my army surrounded the place and burned them, and their horses, alive. You're right. I never went there. But I ordered the action and welcomed the report. To this day I don't know if you had any servants there, or what happened to them.' He wiped his face with his hand. 'I was protecting my left flank.'

Elenya watched as Ariadne sought out any sign of the wooden dock or the comfortable dacha. There was a path from the river that led to a clearing. Nothing more.

'I've always tried to make you understand what it was like, what I actually did to break the Caliphate's siege. We took the barges they left and sent them downstream, laden with rock oil and wood. People burned themselves to death guiding the fires to the heart of the fleet, because it was the only way we could guarantee success. They gave up their lives gladly, sometimes singing as they went.'

Benzamir slipped from the pilot's chair and stood beside the monk. 'Don't do this.'

'They died because I asked them to.'

'Perhaps they died because they thought the cause was right?'

'The cause wasn't right. The Caliphate wasn't the enemy. *I* was. Because I wanted her, I gave them war.'

'Whose cause is ever right? My motives for coming here weren't pure. If I hadn't accepted the decision of my people, I would have been on Persephone Shipsister. I'd have ended up justifying the murder of your brothers for a pile of metal books.'

Va was close to vomiting. His skin was translucent, dripping sweat onto the deck.

'One decision separated me from them. Everything that followed afterwards was because I chose to stay with my people, even though I thought it was the wrong thing to do.'

'The voices,' said Va. 'They curse me.'

Benzamir spun up a map of the Inner Ocean. 'Alessandra? Tell him. Tell him about Misr.'

She looked confused for a moment, and looked at the map. 'You saved us,' she said in sudden recognition. 'You did, didn't you? The Caliphate's navy was strangling Misr's trade, always threatening a landing. The Kenyans had turned us into an armed camp. Then it suddenly stopped. You broke the Caliphate's back right here at Novy Rostov, and they lost their stomach for fighting.'

'You don't understand,' started Va, but Alessandra gasped.

'Five years later the Caliphate wasn't in any position to stop you from following Solomon Akisi wherever you wanted. It's almost as if' – and she put her hand to her mouth – 'you knew.'

Va doubled over, spewing out everything he had. Benzamir took an instinctive step back. Va retched again, almost kneeling in his own filth.

Elenya watched, her face void of expression.

'I am no prophet. I didn't know. Believe me, I didn't.' Va's voice was hoarse, rasping.

'Neither did I know that your mission and mine would coincide so completely when I submitted to the Council's authority. We make decisions based on imperfect knowledge and uncontrollable passions. We have to live with the consequences.'

'I killed them all.' Alessandra tried to give Va water, but he held her wrist. 'Every man and woman and child. I've tried living with it for six years. I thought bringing the books back would give me some comfort. I bargained with the dead. I thought we had a pact.'

Benzamir wrestled Alessandra from Va's grip, and she backed away, cradling her hand across her body and flexing her fingers.

'It's not forgiveness you want, it's redemption. It's within your reach.'

'Then why do I feel so utterly wretched?' Va howled.

'Because you don't understand what it is you've saved the world from. You saw their buildings and their weapons. You caught the blunt edge of their plan that left your brothers dead and you chasing across the face of the planet. I had to look straight into their corrupt and diseased heart. You should be happy, Brother Va. You should have peace.'

'I feel no peace.'

'Then,' said Benzamir, 'the enormity of what you have done escapes you. I can only thank you, and wish you well.'

Shiny, scuttling crabs started to clean the floor.

'How can I believe the things you say?'

'He doesn't lie,' said Elenya. 'He's been honest with everyone he's met. Listen, Va. All those people who died because you loved me, the thing you hate the most about yourself, has been taken and changed and turned into something different. Alessandra and Benzamir are right: if you hadn't beaten the Caliphate here, you'd never have got the books back. Va, look at me.'

He did so, eventually, reluctantly, sick still on his chin, on the hem of his robe.

'It wasn't for nothing. It wasn't for me. It wasn't a mistake. It had to happen. I don't pretend to understand how any of this can begin to make sense. But it makes more sense than twenty thousand peasants and soldiers going to their grave over a woman.' She smiled at the irony. 'Even if that woman was me.'

Benzamir guided Va back a step to let the crabs do their work.

Elenya continued: 'No one's trying to say their deaths are now justified. Somehow, they've . . .' She gave up, shrugged and sighed.

Va nodded miserably, and Benzamir asked Ariadne to land.

'Where, Benzamir?'

'Close to the city. There's a blizzard blowing, it's dark, and if we're quick, we won't be seen.'

Ariadne settled through the layers of low-lying cloud. The display showed a blinding swirl of snowflakes superimposed on the radar-mapped landscape.

'I'll go now.' Elenya held up her hands. 'I don't want any of you to come with me. Promise me you'll stay here, in this room.' She glared at each of them in turn, waiting for them to acquiesce.

'Good luck, Princess,' said Alessandra. 'I hope you . . . I don't know – have a long and happy life? Is that too much to ask for?'

'I don't know. Any sort of life will be welcome.'

Benzamir raised his hand. 'Princess Elenya,' he said, and there was a catch in his throat.

'Tell me again,' she said.

'All will be well.'

There was silence, punctuated only by Ariadne telling them they had landed.

'Va? Have you nothing to say to me?'

'God go with you, wherever you are. And I'm sorry.'

The corner of her mouth twitched in the memory of a smile. 'I release you, Brother Va Angemaite. I won't chase after you again.'

She strode from the flight deck, her machine-fabricated boots clicking on the floor. The door shushed and cut off the noise completely.

'I've opened the cargo bay doors,' said Ariadne. The display twisted: Elenya was standing at the doors, eyes half closed against the snow flying at her face. Then she jumped to the ground, and with her ankles swallowed by drifting snow, she ploughed towards the gates of Novy Rostov.

Benzamir realized he'd been holding his breath. He puffed, and patted Va on the back. The monk didn't move. He seemed frozen in place.

They watched as the figure on the screen broke into a run, uphill, until she was dwarfed by the city's wall.

'It's time to go, Ariadne. We're almost done.'

CHAPTER 45

There was a smear of light left on the eastern horizon as Benzamir carried two more books outside and set them on the growing pile. Two light-bees buzzed behind him.

'Thank you,' said Va. He counted them up, like he'd done every time, then squared off the books to be neat.

'Are you sure this is all right? We can't get any closer to Moskva without the tsar riding out with his knights, but it's still a long way.'

'It won't be a problem. In the morning a patrol will come down the road and they'll find me here. I'll send a message to the patriarch, and he'll send a cart.' Va rested his hand on top of the uppermost book. 'I don't know what he's going to say about the one that is missing.'

'Well,' said Benzamir, 'if he gives you any trouble, tell him he'll have me to answer to.'

'You're being irreverent. The patriarch is a righteous man. If he wants to admonish me, it's his privilege to do so and mine to accept whatever punishment he hands out.'

'I don't think any man alive could have done more. Eleven out of twelve's not bad.'

'I promised him I'd get them all.'

'It's fish food. No one will trouble it for a thousand years.'

'Ariadne said we could go back and get it.'

'It's not Ariadne who'll be diving in the dark looking for it. You have to appreciate that while it's trivial to protect something at one atmosphere from vacuum, it's a whole different engineering solution when you're trying to hold back several tonnes of water. Even if I still had the battlesuit, I don't know if I could have done it. And I'm not skinny-dipping in the Outer Ocean for anyone, not even you, Brother Va.'

Va tutted. 'And what of Solomon Akisi?'

'What of him? Worried about all the things he's read? Don't be. They'll only serve to drive him mad. He's seen the far future, and he knows he'll be long gone before any of it comes to pass. Even if the emperor pardons him, his ingenuity will constantly crash into the barrier of what is possible.' Benzamir laughed. 'You knew him: what do you say to that?'

'It sounds like justice.' Va looked around, still surprised not to see Elenya.

'How does it feel?'

'Feel?' He turned north, to where Novy Rostov lay far away. 'Does it matter what I feel? What's important is that she's free.' He turned his head and looked at the ground. Snow stuck in the ploughed furrows, leaving the ridges as iron-hard stripes. 'I failed her. I was never what she wanted me to be, except for that one brief moment when she thought me everything and before I realized I was nothing.'

'Everything that was said to have happened: did it?' Benzamir idly opened a book; Va pushed it firmly closed again.

'Yes,' he said quietly. 'That and more. Having Elenya became all-consuming. Idolatrous thoughts. Pride, envy, lust, anger. I was so deep in sin.'

Benzamir coughed. 'She does have that effect on people.'

Va looked up. 'I know. She hated the way men always looked at her. Though not you. She said as much. But you never asked her to go with you.' He frowned. 'Why not?'

Benzamir leaned forward and rested his elbow on the books to stop himself fiddling with them. 'I'll answer that if you will first.'

'I have found something infinitely better: a life spent in simple service to God, the patriarch and my fellow men.'

'Nothing about your life will ever be simple, Va. I suddenly realized I wasn't the solution to any of her problems. I saw my future in that moment.'

'God gives His wisdom to all, but only the wise take notice of it. You're an ungodly heathen, Benzamir Mahmood, but apart from that it can't be denied that you make a better Christian than most.'

'High praise indeed, Brother.'

'You became an agent of God's will, whether you knew it or not, cared or not. I feel that there's hope for the world when I think of your example. If God can use even you—'

'What is this? From high praise to faint praise?'

'I'm sorry,' said Va. 'I don't presume to know the mind of the Almighty.'

'I'll get the rest of the books.' Benzamir climbed up through the hatch, to be replaced by Alessandra.

She was still dressed as a Mahgrebi woman, but she had her own light-bees and a translator drone following her around.

She passed Va another book, and he stacked it with the others.

'A fine night,' she said. She was uncomfortable around him, he could tell, though she was trying.

'Alessandra. What is it about me?'

She jumped down. 'You do nothing in half-measures, Va.'

'Isn't that good?'

'It's frightening to normal people. Soldiers hire themselves out, march here, march there, wave their spears and go home. You stopped the Caliphate in its tracks, destroyed its armies and changed history. Monks pray and sing and look after the sick and the poor. You travelled across continents with no idea of where you were going and ended up saving the world from undying creatures with god-like powers.'

'What else should I have done?' said Va, genuinely perplexed.

'You? You're incapable of doing anything different. It was the only course of action you could possibly take. Robbers steal your books of forbidden knowledge. You, and only you, were ever going to get them back, no matter what obstacles stood in your way. And look.' She pointed to the metal books. 'You were right.'

'Anyone else in my position would have done the same. It would be their duty.'

'Anyone else in your position would have either curled up into a little ball of terror, or would still be wandering around foreign lands trying to work out which way was up. You're an extraordinary man, Va. Everything about you is just about held in balance, like you're standing on a needle. It's agony for you there, but you know it'd be much worse if you fell. If you learned to calm down a little, perhaps mere mortals like myself wouldn't be so terrified of you.'

'I'm sorry I asked.'

She laughed. 'Don't be peevish. You call Benzamir a good man. So are you. But you have to realize that failure is sometimes inevitable.'

'With God, all things are possible,' he retorted.

'And you said you didn't know the mind of God. He has to teach you humility somehow. Who better to learn it from than a woman?'

'You were eavesdropping.'

'Just like me,' said Benzamir. He handed down the last two books and picked up a tray before joining them on the ground. He breathed in the smells of Earth: damp air, frozen soil, rotting wood. 'This is it, then.'

The tray held three beakers and an ancient stone bottle.

Alessandra picked up the bottle, opened the stopper and recoiled as the vapour assaulted her nose. 'What is that?'

'It is' – Benzamir hesitated – 'not of this world. But it won't kill you.'

He held the beakers together and Alessandra poured a generous measure in each. 'Steady,' he said. 'The tsar'll find us asleep in his fields in the morning. And an inconveniently large spaceship not quite touching the ground.'

Sighing, Alessandra raised her beaker. 'To friends.'

'No, no, no,' said Va. 'You're doing it wrong. A toast is the reason to drink. It gives meaning to it, and the drink is the amen. Like this: Rory macShiel helped me, even when his own wife begged him not to. Without him, I'd never have recovered the books, and so I drink to him.' He tilted his wrist and sank all the liquor in one gulp.

Benzamir shrugged and followed suit. Alessandra sipped at hers.

'Now. Said.' Va reached for the bottle again. He topped up his beaker, and Benzamir's.

'I'll take him,' said Benzamir. 'Said Mohammed is

gracious in defeat, humble in victory, ferocious in battle and wise in the ways of peace. He is a good friend whom I will never forget. For him I wish long life, good health, a good wife and many camels.'

This time they all drank like Russians. The bottle went round again.

'Wahir?' said Va.

'Why not?' Alessandra massaged her throat to force her voice from it. 'Wahir, with his head full of stories, his endless questions and unquenchable enthusiasm. Not quite a boy, not yet a man, but he's seen and done more in his short life so far than many will ever see or do.' She drank again, and gritted her teeth as she swallowed. 'Gah.'

'Solomon Akisi.'

Benzamir reached for the bottle, missed, and tried again. 'I thought you hated him.'

'Hate is too strong a word,' said Va. 'He was courageous and determined, but he sought the wrong goals. It made him misuse his power, to lie, to cheat, to steal, to kill. But he defied his emperor and unwittingly led us all to Great Nairobi. For that reason alone I'll raise my glass to him.'

They were silent as they toasted Akisi, knowing what was coming next. There was only one more. And then they would have to part.

Benzamir coughed, took a deep breath and started.

'No,' said Va. 'This is my duty. Elenya Lukeva Christyakova, Princess of Novy Rostov, loved me for six years without hope. Despite everything, she followed me, became my voice when I couldn't talk, and my guide when I couldn't find my way. I disappointed her, ruined her life, destroyed her dreams, and she still stayed with me. I hope and pray that wherever she goes, the Holy Mother, Saint George and Saint Basil will protect her.'

After they drank for the last time, Va smashed the bottle on the ground.

'I've lost all feeling in my legs,' said Alessandra.

'Then I'll have to carry you,' said Benzamir.

'How long will it take you, to get where you're going?' Va looked up into the broken sky, dark cloud partly obscuring the bright stars of heaven.

'A week.' Benzamir followed his gaze. 'Depends on the amount of in-system travel we have to do, and what we find at the other end. City-ships sometimes have to move in a hurry. We'll round up a fleet, some people to act as guards, then come back for the rebels. But we'll resist the temptation to come and see you.'

'That's for the best, I think. I want only a quiet life.'

'You'll be patriarch before you die. You can't help but do things well.'

'I've no ambition for myself.' Va clasped Benzamir to his chest and pounded his back. 'But Godspeed to you. Finish